Praise for Jody Shields's
THE WINTER STATION

"*The Winter Station* is a novel set in Russia that to its great credit reads like a Russian novel. Set early in the twentieth century, it is a story of courage, love, resilience, and loyalty during a season of absolute terror. Jody Shields is a fearless writer, with the integrity of a worthy creator, and this novel won't be easily forgotten."
—Daniel Woodrell, author of *The Maid's Version* and *Winter's Bone*

"During a bone-chillingly cold winter in a Russian-controlled outpost city in Manchuria, people are mysteriously dropping dead, their bodies vanishing before they can be identified or examined for cause of death. The city's medical commissioner begins to investigate and realizes the city is gripped by a deadly plague."
—Mackenzie Dawson, *New York Post*

"Jody Shields has transformed the scantly recorded memories of the Manchurian plague into a rich narrative, factual in its details and vitalized by the moral complexities of prejudice, politics, honor, and responsibility."   —Erin Willis, *Lincoln Journal Star*

"Based on real events, this is the kind of fiction that fascinates with its power to evoke time and place, morality and mortality, tenderness and love."   —Sukey Howard, *BookPage*

"In *The Winter Station,* Jody Shields imagines a new season, one vibrant with intrigue, longing, and history...This book bears a distinct pulse; its beats are tender, evocative, and full of mystery."
—Affinity Konar, author of *Mischling*

"Shields writes movingly of the human cost of this forgotten epidemic. She reminds us that, to an imperceptible enemy, the lines dividing nations are only a mark on a map...A sensitive and atmospheric thriller."
—Cindy Pauldine, *Shelf Awareness*

"Like a delicate calligraphy, Jody Shields paints a starkly moving picture of our elusive humanity, as ephemeral and beautiful as snowflakes falling from a frozen sky. The images are unforgettable, and the book highly recommended."
—*Historical Novel Society*

"Jody Shields's entry into the canon of pathogen literature, *The Winter Station,* exposes the agonizing anxiety only one type of enemy can conjure. What Shields evokes in her greatest passages, as her czarist Baron battles an epidemic in turn-of-the-century Kharbin, is a fear that pours from the temples: the recognition that we can be set against a swift and terrible force majeure, the scythe of God."
—B. David Zarley, *Paste*

"If you love historical fiction, you don't want to miss *The Winter Station*...It's the perfect moody book to read on a chilly winter day."
—Elizabeth Entenman, *HelloGiggles*

"Readers will be captivated by the atmosphere and the various essay-like ruminations, which evoke Peter Høeg's *Smilla's Sense of Snow.*"
—Jen Baker, *Booklist*

ALSO BY JODY SHIELDS

The Crimson Portrait
The Fig Eater

THE
WINTER
STATION

A Novel

JODY SHIELDS

BACK BAY BOOKS
Little, Brown and Company
New York Boston London

Back Bay Books / Little, Brown and Company
Hachette Book Group
1290 Avenue of the Americas, New York, NY 10104
littlebrown.com

Originally published in hardcover by Little, Brown and Company, January 2018
First Back Bay paperback edition, December 2018

Back Bay Books is an imprint of Little, Brown and Company, a division of Hachette Book Group, Inc. The Back Bay Books name and logo are trademarks of Hachette Book Group, Inc.

The publisher is not responsible for websites (or their content) that are not owned by the publisher.

The Hachette Speakers Bureau provides a wide range of authors for speaking events. To find out more, go to hachettespeakersbureau.com or call (866) 376-6591.

ISBN 978-0-316-38534-3 (hardcover) / 978-0-316-38533-6 (paperback)
LCCN 2017946258

10 9 8 7 6 5 4 3 2 1

LSC-C

Printed in the United States of America

To Trevor King

In memory of
Crispin Tobey
Debra K. Turner

There is no brushstroke that is not a detour.

—*Shi Buhua*

TO MANCHURIA

SUNGARI RIVER

FUCHIATIEN

B

PRISTAN

C

TO MUTANCHIANG POGRANICHNAYA

KITAYSKAYA ST
DIAGONALNAYA ST
CENTRAL STATION

A

G

F

E

H

NOVY GOROD

D

TO HSINKING MUKDEN

KHARBIN

A   RUSSIAN HOSPITAL
B   CHURIN'S
C   RUSSIAN CEMETERY
D   RUSSIAN CONSULATE
E   AMERICAN AND
    JAPANESE CONSULATE
F   BRITISH CONSULATE
G   FRENCH CONSULATE
H   ST NIKOLAS CATHEDRAL

THE WINTER STATION

CHAPTER ONE

When Andreev said two bodies had been discovered outside the Kharbin train station, the Baron had an image of the dead men sprawled against snow, frozen in positions their bodies couldn't hold in life. His focus sharpened on Andreev's face, faintly pink, only the triangle of his eyes, nose, and lips visible surrounded by the rough hood of his sheepskin coat. It was noon and the sun already cast the faint blue haze of twilight that was particular to this place in September. The sun would set in less than three hours and the temperature would hover near zero.

The Baron's breath exploded into a cloud in the freezing air. "Exactly where were the bodies found?"

"Alongside the train tracks." Andreev's arm waved in the direction of Central Station just behind them. "Somewhere between the tracks and the train station."

"Who told you?"

"A contact who works for the railroad. He traveled here on the last train from Mukden to Kharbin."

Mukden was two hundred verst away, a walled city, once the ancient imperial capital of Manchuria, since eclipsed. "Is your contact reliable?"

"As death."

"When did he see the bodies?"

"A day ago."

Frozen solid and covered with snow, the bodies could have remained undetected for weeks. Or until May, when the snow melted. Or until discovered by wild dogs or wolves.

"He watched soldiers put the bodies on a cart at night. Their lanterns were covered. No witnesses but my Mukden informer."

"Strange." If Andreev's report was true, some official had given orders to the lowest-level police about the bodies. He built the scene in his imagination to block the dark chink of evidence that the investigation had happened in secret. Why hadn't he been notified? He was the city's chief medical examiner and a doctor at the Russian hospital, only two streets away from where the bodies had been found. He should have been consulted or signed a death certificate. He was self-conscious about his lack of information as Andreev watched him, measuring his response. It was necessary to keep up a façade in front of Andreev, to maintain the tinsel appearance of a link to powerful General Dmitry Khorvat, the czar's administrator. The general ran the city like a private business, with absolute authority over all Russian military and civil matters in Kharbin. The Baron owed his appointment to Khorvat and kept it only at his pleasure.

In medical school on the Universitetskaya Embankment in St. Petersburg, the Baron had learned a methodology for diagnosis: the dissector must learn to discern order. First, establish the facts of how the Russians had managed the deaths. "No bodies were brought to the hospital. Nothing reported in the newspapers *Molva* or *Russkoe Solve*." He made a dismissive gesture. "So I assume the dead were Chinese?"

"Yes." The hood of Andreev's jacket jerked up and down in confirmation.

"That explains the lack of official interest." A dead Russian would have left an investigation, a vigil, memorial candles at St. Nikolas Cathedral. Unidentified Chinese were ignored in death. Kharbin was a divided city, laid out like a game board between the Chinese and the Russians. Perhaps the Chinese authorities had retrieved the bodies? Perhaps the dead were prominent Chinese, assassinated for a political motive? "Tell me, had clothing been stripped from the bodies?"

"Were they stripped? No. He didn't say the bodies were naked." Andreev's voice revealed that he was puzzled by the question, but his answer was quick, information traded for a grain of praise from the older man, an aristocrat and son of a diplomat in the czar's service.

Why two dead men near a crowded train station? A bold gamble. A risk of witnesses. There were easier places to leave bodies, as Kharbin was surrounded by the wilderness of the Manchurian plains. "The murderers must have a good alibi." The Baron shifted his weight to keep his feet from becoming numb on the snow-covered ground.

"Or an alibi from soldiers who took the bodies."

"What's your picture of the crime, Andreev?"

"The men were tricked or forced onto the tracks. They fought the robbers who assaulted them. Later, their bodies were removed so as not to alarm other travelers and the Chinese authorities."

You would choose an answer that was crooked, the Baron thought. There was no point in a search, as the exact location of the bodies was uncertain. The corpse movers would have churned the snow, added their own tracks, obliterated evidence. Two deaths marked only with words. He felt an obligation to continue the questioning.

No one else would bother. There were no trained police or investigators in Kharbin, only soldiers and veterans who stayed after the war with Japan and were drafted into the Zamurskii District Special Border Guard Corps. They served Russia, the occupying power in Manchuria. The Russian soldiers coexisted with the Chinese and Japanese military, all waiting for an incident that would allow them to expand their presence in Kharbin. Perhaps the dead Chinese men would be that incident. "How close was your witness to the bodies?"

"He watched from the train window."

"Did he notice blood by the bodies?" The Baron's voice was neutral, but he began to wonder if Andreev himself had actually witnessed the discovery of the two corpses.

"Blood? No, it would have been too dark for him to see blood on snow. It was after three o'clock." He exhaled.

Andreev's breath wreathed around his head, and the Baron silently noted this indication of tension. In Manchuria's harsh, cold climate, the breath was a visible sign that betrayed emotion more immediately than words. "True. We lose the light early these days." He scrutinized the other man's face for a moment too long and Andreev looked away, breaking eye contact.

The Baron would never have associated with Andreev in St. Petersburg, as he was lower class, a worker. It was unlikely they would ever have met. But in Kharbin, Andreev was a fellow Russian and necessary as a servant. He located anything for a fee. The man was flexible as curved script, with barbs that extended across the city, from the furriers on Kitayskaya Street to black marketeers, suppliers for potatoes, kerosene, Krupp pistols, silk for dresses, lanolin, French wine, writing paper. Andreev bartered, bought, and occasionally stole goods. There were always shortages, as everything was imported from Moscow, St. Petersburg, south from Beijing, Shanghai, west from Vladivostok and Port Arthur on the Pacific coast.

It was rumored that Andreev was a government informer, one of the numerous double and triple agents who served Russia in Manchuria, likely paid twice over for the same information about scandal and crime.

Self-possessed, Andreev had the guarded single-mindedness of a missionary or someone who had witnessed great cruelty. He divined the compass that others used. "The desire for possessions, for ownership, is the glue holding us together here in Kharbin. Not courage or love of the family or the czar or freedom," Andreev had once explained. "Even the missionaries count the Chinese in church. The number of souls saved." His voice had been scornful. Yet he had located frankincense for St. Nikolas Cathedral to replace a lost shipment and was deeply moved when the archimandrite blessed him for his work.

The Baron patiently returned to his questioning. "And your Mukden contact. Does he have a name? Or is his identification also an impossibility?"

Andreev shook his head. "He's safely returned to Mukden." He looked over his shoulder nervously, although they were alone, bracketed by ridges of empty train tracks.

"Your mysterious contact had no other information?"

"I told you that there wasn't enough light for him to see."

"But he recognized the soldiers."

Andreev laughed. He appreciated the joke, as Russian soldiers in their huge fur hats and stiff-skirted coats were unmistakable.

His feet were numb on the uneven ground. It was useless to try to provoke Andreev into revealing more information. It was too cold. It had been a mistake to interview him outside.

"You claim there are two bodies that cannot be located or identified. And your source of information about the bodies is absent and anonymous. If you were younger, if you were a child, I would dismiss you without kindness for wasting my time."

"That's all the information I have for you, Baron." Nothing fazed Andreev. The conversation had been concluded.

"Can I offer you something in exchange for your generous information? A token of appreciation?"

"You owe me nothing, sir." Andreev grinned. "Situations change. Someday I may need a favor from you."

This question and answer of Andreev's pretended graciousness was a ritual between them. The Baron's sheepskin mittens were thick as a towel and he fumbled, pressing several rubles into the other man's outstretched hand.

He watched Andreev's bulky silhouette vanish into the blue shadow of Central Station. Although shivering with cold, he was unwilling to walk into the building, as the heat would dissolve his clarity of thought. He needed time to collect himself.

A few minutes later, he slowly walked through Central Station, suddenly aware that he stank inside the closed animal skins of his clothing. He watched two soldiers fidgeting with the guns slung across their chests and approached them cautiously, as they were probably already drunk, though it was barely past noon. The soldiers, from habit, did not pay attention until he introduced himself as a doctor. Everyone has a complaint for a medical man.

The younger soldier was disheveled, sweating in his thick coat. He managed a lopsided grin along with his name, Shklovskiy. "We've been standing here for days." He shuffled his boots. "Mother of God, my back aches."

The Baron made a sympathetic noise. "Your gun is heavy."

"We can manage." The second soldier, Rakhimanov, scowled.

"You soldiers hardly need my advice. I see all the beggars are gone from the station thanks to your good work."

"Gone for the moment. But trouble arrives with every train. No undesirables allowed here. Move along!" Rakhimanov slapped his gun.

"Difficult to push so many undesirables from the station."

Rakhimanov glanced around, clearly enjoying his ability to intimidate. "We watch everyone who walks in the door. Some pretend not to see us. Some move away too quickly. Chinese beggars. Army deserters. Smugglers. We lock up anyone we please. Anyone suspicious."

"That could be everyone here." The Baron offered a flask of vodka.

The soldiers laughed and greedily shared swallows from the flask.

"Who gives you orders?"

"Diakonov. General Khorvat's deputy." Shklovskiy volunteered more information. "We stopped five passengers last week. Four men and one woman. Russians and Chinese."

"Did you register their names?" The Baron let his eyes wander to the door, allowing his distraction to soften the question.

"No. We don't carry paper and pencils. Others do the petty work." Rakhimanov scratched under his hat and thick blond hair fell across one eye. "But I could do without the sick."

"The sick?"

"Anyone who looks weak. Has a cough. Stumbles. Or maybe they're just drunk. It's hard to tell the difference."

"What happens to them?"

"We bundle up the Chinese, and not tenderly, I can tell you." Rakhimanov leaned closer and his breath was strong with alcohol. "Men come and pick them up."

"Who picks them up? The police?"

"I don't know. They have a cart." Rakhimanov studied the rifle in his hand.

"Where are they taken?"

"No idea."

"And the dead?"

The soldiers didn't look at each other, but their hesitation betrayed shared information. Shklovskiy crossed himself. "The dead are respected, sir. But there are no corpses here at the station."

"Don't waste your sympathy," said Rakhimanov. His fingers nervously tapped the handle of his gun.

Shklovskiy poked his fellow soldier. "He's a doctor."

Rakhimanov ignored him. "Tell me something. Is it true the Chinese have no souls? Everyone in the border guard says that it is so. They do not worship God."

The Baron's expression appeared tolerant. No point in delivering piety. "I'm a medical man serving the body. How could I say whose soul is blessed to enter the kingdom of God?"

His evasion disappointed them. For Russian soldiers, the Chinese were faceless dogs, indecipherable pagans who deserved rough treatment. An early name for the first Russians who traveled in China was *luosha,* a tribe of man-eating demons.

The Baron wished the men luck. Distracted, he moved across the cavernous, dimly lit station, misjudging distances, gently colliding with travelers in bulky padded coats, the physical contact as muted as if he were walking underwater. Heat radiated from the massive white-tile stoves in the corners of the waiting room. A group of Russians stood near a wall, crossing themselves in front of an icon of Saint Nikolas, the city's patron saint. The bank of small candles below the icon, wavering at every movement, were the brightest spots in the space.

It was against protocol that the sick hadn't been taken to the hospital where he was in charge. City bureaucracy had been circumvented, but by whom? Someone had given orders to remove the two dead Chinese from outside the station. Were the bodies and the passengers detained by the soldiers linked? Was he the only official who hadn't been notified? Since this had been deliberately hidden from him, he couldn't discuss it with General Khorvat. Perhaps the general was also in the dark.

Was the search for sick passengers a screen for another purpose? It reminded him of the secret police in St. Petersburg. After threats were made against the czar, the police searched residences and businesses, supposedly for illegal church literature from Baptists and Old Believers but actually for evidence of bomb-making.

His speculation produced nothing but a clumsy half-drawn picture. He left the station and was slammed by cold air. Outside, the snow's dizzying progress was measured by its sting against his cheek.

Later, he finished a cup of tea standing by the window in his office, purely a habit, as there was no view. The double glass panes were filled with white sand as insulation from the cold and remained opaque until May, when snow first melted from one side of the immense tile roof of Central Station.

At home, he didn't share the day's events with his wife. Li Ju turned to him when he entered the room, as always, invariably looking up from her embroidery, a book, or a game of mah-jongg, ready to change the direction of her day for him. He would insist that he didn't wish to disturb her but was secretly pleased. Other women had turned their eyes to him in calculation or desire but her attention was a bouquet.

Li Ju was polishing a bowl at the table, and he stooped slightly to lift it from her hands. "Let me carry the bowl for you."

Her face tilted up to him and the water in the silver bowl reflected the curve of her cheek and for a moment the two balanced shapes filled his eyes. An older woman might have whispered an intimacy, but Li Ju simply smiled, transparent, acknowledging his admiration.

As a very young girl, Li Ju had left a missionary orphanage to work as a servant in the Baron's household. She accepted his care with a child's straightforward happiness. She lived under his roof, slept on a small mat of wadded silk and cotton for years before they became lovers and shared the *k'ang* bed. When she became an adult, his expectation was the same. Nothing changed. The habit of days. He didn't believe devotion was a debt owed to him for providing her with a home but he had become accustomed to her deference.

That night, he was jolted awake and sat up in bed. He was swept with shame. Two men had died violently and he had shaped it into a story about his own authority. His place in the world. "Mother of God," he whispered and crossed himself.

But he was haunted by another image, dark and jagged. The dead Chinese could easily have been thrown in the Sungari River and their weight would have broken the still-thin ice, the thickness of two fingers. Then he wished that this had been done, that the bodies were in the river, and he imagined this as if he were drowning, looking up at the sky through the ice one last time, his eyes already liquid.

In the morning, the Baron and his wife lit a candle for the dead at St. Nikolas Cathedral on Central Square. Their hands cupped together around the warm candle and the flesh of their fingertips glowed translucent pink. His wife was not a believer but the ritual of contemplation was familiar to her. She tipped her head back and her face was suddenly hidden in the darkness. The building was an immense shadowy height above their heads, its bulb-shaped domes, the *lukovichnye glavy,* were compact as a hive, made with countless wood shingles overlapped against the Manchurian wind. The entire structure was built without a single nail, joined together with minute wooden pegs so that no pinpoints of reflected metal disturbed its dim interior. Perhaps its peaceful assembly, the lack of violent hammering, was an offering to God.

CHAPTER TWO

When Baron von Budberg had first arrived, Kharbin had no history. It was a camp. The first child had not yet been born. There had never been a wedding or a funeral. No eye had looked at the landscape through a curtained window. No shadow had been cast by a church tower. Kharbin was established in the Manchurian wilderness in 1898 by order of the czar, a Russian city built in China, an arrogant stake of empire.

A hereditary aristocrat, a Russian diplomat's son, a doctor, the Baron traveled from St. Petersburg to Manchuria in 1904 to serve as a medic in the imperial army after the disastrous war with Japan. He worked, partially protected from heat and stinging blackflies, under a makeshift canvas tent. The pay was poor, the conditions primitive, the weather insufferable, and the silence absolute.

During his first year, the Baron learned to forget what made a city—the streets sealed with paving stones, vertical pressure of buildings, the shifting pattern of pedestrians and vehicles. He suffered a constant feeling of oppression from the flat land and the enormousness of the sky. There was an ocean overhead. Could a man's bones splinter under the pressure of this weight?

The wind was a constant harsh presence, sweeping the scent of primeval forests down from the immense northern territory, the ancestral home of the Manchu rulers. In the summer, the wind was weighted with yellow sand that filled cracks in buildings, silted up windows and the railroad tracks.

Kitayskaya Street was impassable with vehicles stuck in the snow. The droshky stopped and the Baron and Andreev began to walk, their impatience slowed to caution as they stepped carefully, struggling for balance on the frozen surface. Andreev clutched his arm. The sidewalk in front of the luxurious dress shops, the corsetiere Louvre Atelier, the German store Kunst and Albers, had been swept to a glittering eggshell-thin layer of ice. Long thin spears of ice, yellow with embedded dirt and grit, barred the windows of Churin's department store.

Something, a rough piece of ice, fell at their feet and Andreev glanced up at the windows. "See? The sand never leaves us. Frozen into the ice. Then it melts. Then it blows back at us in the summer. There's either sand or snow in the air."

"Mercifully, the snow only lasts for half the year."

"More than six months. It slows down my import business."

The Baron was amused by the seasonal nature of Andreev's smuggling. "Yesterday I became lost on Mostovaya Street. So many new buildings had been constructed in two weeks that the place was unrecognizable." He gestured at the saplings thickly wrapped in coarse fabric, barely visible above the snow. "Russian grandeur. They dream of transforming the street into the czar's garden. It's folly."

The proprietor of the Volga restaurant lifted the Baron's heavy coat from his shoulders and ushered the two men through the overheated space to a table in the back. The Baron sat down, wiped his damp face, waited until the cold air in his lungs was exchanged for the dense tobacco smoke in the restaurant. Andreev watched him silently. He looked as if he needed a shave, although it was just past noon.

"Early cold." The Baron coughed.

"Reason enough to drink until the dwarf arrives." Andreev had promised to introduce a friend of his, Chang Huai.

"A friend or a business friend?"

"Friend. He's famous in the city. And deserves the acclaim. It's cold work standing in front of Churin's department store smiling at rich women."

The warmth returned to their feet after half an hour in the restaurant. The Baron ordered *zubrovka,* vodka flavored with buffalo grass. He brought up the matter of the equipment ordered in July, two months ago, now certain to be held up by early snow in Hailar. He was expecting an examining table, optical equipment, Braun photographic apparatus, medicine, and sterilizing solutions from Berlin, everything destined for Kharbin's hospital. Andreev had been paid to secure the shipment, since railroad employees routinely plundered crates during transportation, seldom bothering to cover up evidence of their tampering.

"Which month do you believe our shipment will arrive?"

"I never predict. But I'll ask the stationmaster about the delay."

"He always has an excuse. Possibly your bribe wasn't generous enough."

Andreev corrected himself. "I will pay the stationmaster to fix the delay." He worked inside his circle of contacts to smooth transactions.

"If the train was overpacked, my crates were likely sacrificed to make room for cases of vodka."

"Drink is more precious than medicine in this place. I once knew a missionary who successfully smuggled in vodka under Methodist Church literature. No one could bear to inspect his dull crates."

How Andreev came to Kharbin was a mystery. One trader claimed he was a Russian army deserter. Another man, a Hungarian, swore Andreev was a mercenary who had sold exotic animals, Siberian tiger cubs and bears, at a market in Dairen on the Yellow Sea. His skin, weathered brown even in winter, contrasted with his eyes, the pale green of celadon. Andreev rarely spoke about the past but his hands were marked with scars. The Baron had recognized the slashes were originally bone-deep, perhaps made by an animal or a knife.

They'd known each other for years but even when eased by vodka, they rarely discussed anything personal, never shared a meal at the Baron's table, although Andreev was frequently invited. *How old are you?* the Baron once asked, and Andreev, startled, blinked as if threatened and didn't answer. The Baron wasn't certain the man was literate.

Did Andreev enjoy women? Did he have a lover? The first time the Baron had introduced Li Ju to Andreev, he'd noticed the other man's calculated gaze. Was it envy, sympathy, measured judgment? If it was criticism, perhaps it was directed at him. He couldn't interpret his reaction. Maybe Andreev sensed the Baron's loneliness, his hunger for approval, for dismissing authority.

Although he called Andreev a friend, he had no idea where he lived. Messages for him were left at a restaurant on Novotorgovaya Street near the French embassy. He fully expected that Andreev would simply disappear one day. Their friendship had its risks, and the Baron was careful not to reveal gossip or details about his patients. It was useful for Andreev—and others who might pay for this information—to know who among the Kharbin elite was in frail health or troubled by sleeplessness, pregnancy, melancholy, violence.

He scrutinized Andreev's face to see how far he dared to proceed. "Did someone give you new information about the bodies at Central Station?"

Andreev was coldly dignified. "No. Who would be interested?"

"You tell me."

"No one. Russian officials don't care about dead Chinese. The crime is too small."

"Not for the dead men's families." He'd blundered. Perhaps it had been a mistake to be so straightforward.

"You waste your time with the dead." Andreev idly pulled apart a piece of bread on his plate. "I only deal with the living. And what they need. And sometimes what can damage them. Baron, I consider myself your brother, but you'd aid a poor serf with a cold nose. That's your character."

The Baron stiffened at his words but then slapped his hands together. "Agreed. I'm a lover of strays." He no longer cared if Andreev knew that officials had withheld information from him. "I need to know where they took the bodies from the train station. I want an address and the name of the official who gave the order. That's all."

While the Baron was speaking, Andreev studied his glass without drinking, his eyes in a haze of calculation. He lazily waved for the waiter to return with the bottle.

"It's only information. Facts. It will be worth your time." The Baron slid around, imposed another angle, hoping Andreev would be receptive. "I'm interested in preventing a future crisis with the Chinese."

Andreev chewed a bit of bread. "I see why you pursue this. You want to find who in the chain plotted against you." He didn't expect an answer and checked his pocket watch. Chang Huai was over an hour late.

The dwarf finally made his way through the shadowy room, his top hat a sharp black edge moving just above the sea of white tablecloths. He was greeted affectionately by other patrons, some making a show of leaning over to pat him on the back or shoulder. A soldier playfully grabbed his queue and Chang spun around with a shout. The room fell silent and the startled soldier stepped back from the dwarf's fury.

As Chang reached their table, the waiter hurried over to install a thick cushion on his chair. The Baron had resisted the impulse to assist Chang, but he nimbly vaulted up into the chair at the table. Fully extended, his legs reached just over the edge of the seat, and his face was level with the two men's. The Baron was surprised that this made him slightly uncomfortable.

Andreev smiled. "You must know Chang Huai. The doorman at Churin's department store. One of our most recognized citizens. Everyone's eyes are always on him."

"Yes, everyone knows me. I have gold buttons on my uniform. A black hat. You're handsome, Andreev, but no one notices you wrapped in that shabby sheepskin jacket."

"Chang knows every elegant woman in the city by name."

"I open the door for the ladies with their furs. They have many pet names for me. Ninochka."

The Baron no longer noticed the man's diminutive stature, as his exuberance made him almost handsome.

The waiter, a Russian in a red vest, brought *bitki* and thick caviar sandwiches on a tray. He returned with small glasses, bottles of clear and colored vodka, Nega and Bogatyr, both distilled in Kharbin. The Baron raised his eyebrows at Chang.

"Beluga caviar. *Malossol* grade. I have an account here. For Churin's best customers." The dwarf smirked and poured *rubinovaya* vodka, slightly astringent with a brilliant orange tint from mountain ash berries. *Pertsovka,* vodka with pepper, was his choice.

Their first glasses of vodka were finished in a single swallow. The dwarf's face instantly flushed.

"You're a useful friend," Andreev said to Chang.

"I am. At times." Chang rested both elbows on the table. "I am practically king of Kharbin, ranked just below our beloved General Khorvat. I see and hear everything." He turned to the Baron. "Your wife is Chinese?"

The Baron nodded. "We've been together seven years."

"You're married?"

"We had a Buddhist ceremony. I asked the czar for permission to wed. He refused unless Li Ju converted to the Russian Orthodox Church." Then, because he was slightly drunk, he added, "She's never forgiven me, although it's not my fault. My family—my brother—doesn't know we're married." He was embarrassed, as he'd never confided this to Andreev. But because Chang had the aura of an outsider, a charmed figure, he'd spoken quickly, without hesitation.

Chang puzzled over this information until Andreev explained that Baron Rozher Alexandrovich von Budberg was a hereditary aristocrat from St. Petersburg, a diplomat's son. Aristocrats must have permission from the czar to wed outside the faith.

The Baron quickly retreated from this description. "First, by my own choice, I am a doctor, head of Kharbin's hospital. I served as a medic in the imperial army during the war with Japan. I remember when Kharbin was nothing but a group of tents on the Manchurian plain. There were no women or children."

"Flies and sand?" Chang encouraged him.

"Yes. Every single summer day, the wind blew fine sand under my collar, in my pockets, even into my socks. There was no escape, even inside the tents. The place was a wilderness. A homesick soldier once told me the flat landscape here was a prison. No matter where you looked, the view was always the same. I knew the man spoke truth." The memory of these early days always came back to him with the heavy animal scent of the pony-skin blankets he pulled over himself at night. He bit into a sandwich, the caviar familiar, thick and salty on the tongue. "Now the streets have cobblestones and they say forty-two languages are spoken here."

"You've had a curious career for an aristocrat."

Andreev silently shook his head, surprisingly protective, but the Baron answered. "In my way, I try to ease suffering. I treated Chinese and Russian laborers who'd been injured setting track across Manchuria for the Chinese Eastern Railway. They had broken bones, diphtheria, whooping cough, pneumonia and frostbite in winter. On payday, when they drank, there were wounds from swords, pistols, and bamboo canes."

Chang's arms swept out as if to embrace him. "A rare Russian. Generous to the world." He loved to talk and it was difficult to interrupt him. "There's never been a city like Kharbin. You know how the Chinese describe Kharbin? The 'pearl on the swan's neck.' Heilongjiang Province is shaped like a swan and Kharbin is a pearl on the curved Sungari River. What poetry for our beloved grimy city, home to gamblers, criminals, and exiles."

"That explains why everyone is so happy here."

Chang laughed and poured more vodka for himself. "The Chinese are here to make money and leave."

"That would be the end of Kharbin. Nothing would be left but the railroad, since the Chinese outnumber Russians one hundred to one," said Andreev.

"I have no loyalty to the Chinese. They have no charity for me. My money comes from Russians. They throw it at me." Chang finished his vodka.

"But with all your riches, where do the Russians allow you to live? Only in the Fuchiatien district with the starving workers." Andreev was drunk and scornful. "The Chinese built this city but they can't walk where they please. They can't carry a weapon, not even a harmless cane, into Novy Gorod, the Russian district."

The Baron nodded in agreement. "We're the occupiers. Our glorious officials forget we're a Russian colony on Chinese land."

Chang wagged his finger at them. "Treason."

The Russian government had established Kharbin and divided it into four districts that were side by side but not equal. Each district had its own distinctive identity and architecture. Rich Russians lived in Novy Gorod within the sound of the bells of St. Nikolas Cathedral. Pristan was a commercial district where all types of businesses flourished. The first worker barracks were built in Staryi Kharbin, Old Kharbin, also called Xiangfang, or Fragrant Mill, by the Chinese. Now soldiers billeted there. The Chinese were restricted to Fuchiatien, a shantytown on low land near the Sungari River. A Chinese settlement set within a Russian settlement in China.

The waiter hovered around them, refilling their glasses with *rubinovaya,* accompanied by his strong smell of tobacco and sweat.

The dwarf leaned closer to the two men at the table. "It has been a day of surprises. I drink with an aristocrat." His glass of vodka moved in the Baron's direction. "And this morning, I covered a sick man in the street with my coat. Sick or dead. I can't say. But no one should stare at a suffering Chinese."

"Bless you." The Baron peered at Chang but the angle of his face made it hard to read his expression. "Was the man known to you?"

"No. He'd fallen outside Churin's store. Probably sick from exhaustion. Or cold. He was a laborer in a thin cotton jacket. Which I did not touch."

Andreev shook his head, unexpectedly sympathetic. They drank to the unknown man.

"Ask me any question," Chang said. "I will tell you everything. With one exception. It is my duty to guard the image of Churin's store."

The Baron was becoming light-headed from the vodka. Remembering that he hadn't washed his hands, he stared at the glass, marred with his fingerprints, a bloom like fungus over its surface. "Tell me what you believe happened."

Chang's eyes filled with tears. "There are many unfortunates in Kharbin. Maybe the man was a sign. Russians and Chinese see a man lying on their street. There's a crowd. They talk."

"But what do they say?" Andreev was sprawled in his chair but his body was tense.

"The Chinese are warned not to trespass in the Russian quarter. But here's a Chinese on their street. Soldiers have failed to make the place safe for Russians. The Russians are worried."

"Where did they take the sick man?" The Baron couldn't calm his voice.

Chang proposed a toast and held up his glass, spilling a little. "To the sisters of Congrégation des Missionnaires de St. Xavier. To Sister Agnes."

The Baron struggled to focus on the information. Missionaries had built a hospital in Kharbin, operated by a group of nuns. "How do you know Sister Agnes, my friend?"

"I have the grandest invitations. I'm second to no guest and have skills useful for all."

"What's your history?" the Baron asked. The dwarf was young, but he couldn't have been born here.

"I came into the world between Tashinchiao and Anshan on a river ferry. Later, I was sold for a good price to a kind British gentleman who saved me from my murderous mother, who intended to drown me and avoid the shame of a cursed child. The next man who bought me wasn't a gentleman. A Chinese."

"You escaped from your master." Andreev was genuinely impressed.

Chang was quite drunk, cheeks deeply flushed. He stood up on his chair, looking down at them, holding a napkin as if about to perform a magic trick. For a moment, the Baron feared he intended to stand on the table.

"I escaped with a lady who brought me to Kharbin. I can beg for money in ten languages. I can sing in an additional two languages. I can dance and juggle. I can do a handstand on a donkey's back. I moved from entertaining in the market to Churin's door." He sat down with a jolt in the chair and giggled. "You wouldn't believe the offers that I receive. Offers of money. Travel. A seat at the head of a table. Gamblers make bets about me." He smoothed his queue, lowered his voice. "There isn't a woman or man that I cannot please. Women are curious about me. And children tell me their secrets, as I can pass for one of them. That is, if I've had a good shave. My chin must be clean or they don't trust me."

They drank to the health of innocent children. Andreev stared at Chang, the glass tipping in his thick hand on the table. Chang gently put his hand over Andreev's.

"Flesh and blood. Exactly like you, see?"

His face scarlet, Andreev jerked his hand away and a knife clattered to the floor. Chang silently kept his eyes on Andreev, and the Baron sensed some kind of exchange had been made between them.

Two musicians began to play scales on a violin and a cimbalom across the room. The Baron swayed slightly as he stood up, hand fumbling at the back of his chair. "It's late." To his surprise, Andreev remained seated, mumbling that he'd stay for the music.

The Baron moved unsteadily between the tables as he left the restaurant.

CHAPTER THREE

The first double gate to the Baron's home, the *zhalan men,* opened into a wide paved courtyard off a narrow lane. At its far end, a second elaborately pierced gate led to another courtyard bordered by servants' quarters and the kitchen. A formal entrance gate of carved brick and wood painted with auspicious characters guarded the third courtyard and the small buildings of the living quarters. In summer, oleander, pomegranate, and fig trees bloomed and a lotus floated in the cistern next to the steps. Potted chrysanthemums grew in containers in the inner courtyard, and by October, the faint scratch of their drying petals in the wind was a reminder of the temporality of life, considered the flower's purest expression.

The house was a traditional Chinese residence in Fuchiatien, the district occupied by Chinese. The innermost room in the house was the Baron's old-fashioned scholar's study, simply furnished with a plain square table, chairs of blackwood, pigskin trunks, and a felt-covered *k'ang* bed. The room was heated by small iron stoves in the corners that held burning balls of compacted coal dust and clay. A pair of carved wooden screens were set at an angle to the door. If evil spirits entered the room, they'd strike the screens and be stopped. All the furniture was aligned to face south to ensure feng shui. Even blindfolded, the Baron could have found his way through every room, as the furniture was all identically oriented. This arrangement was common in Chinese households.

The rare visitors were startled by the severity of the house, the spare furniture, the lack of bric-a-brac, the brick floor. *But there's no comfort here,* they said. This was true. How well he'd learned from the Chinese. His family would have considered the house cold, bare, suited only for the poor who could not afford furnishings.

A large painted metal box in the study contained his family's voluminous correspondence, his most precious possession. The letters dated back to the eighteenth century, when the czar had elevated the family to the aristocracy. The letters had been written in gilded rooms in Paris, Vienna, Berlin, Krakow, Copenhagen, and Helsinki, where his grandfather and father had had diplomatic postings. He'd memorized each word, stroke, ornate ink flourish, watermark, wrinkle, and fold of the letters. The distinct styles of handwriting on the envelopes were as familiar as his own hand. For years, he'd corresponded with his brother and cousins in St. Petersburg, adding their letters to the stacks of ribbon-tied envelopes and papers in the metal box. Posting a letter from Kharbin and receiving a reply was a process that spanned three or four months. Although it was not a conscious decision, he had gradually stopped writing and lost all contact with his family. In Manchuria, the family and personal history could be erased like a sentence in a diary. He was untethered. With the detachment of an observer, he realized that he'd pass the rest of his life here and would be buried in Manchuria.

The Baron thought his wife would understand him better if she knew his background, the many places he'd lived in St. Petersburg and diplomatic postings across Europe. He described the family house in St. Petersburg and their dacha, surrounded by birch trees and gardens, on the Île des Apothecaires on the Neva near St. Petersburg. His family homes were filled with things of value and valueless things: stationery with the family crest, engraved silver picture frames, mother-of-pearl caviar spoons, buttonhooks, niello bibelots, his father's gold-tipped fountain pens, a collapsible rubber washtub for bathing, gold-painted porcelain dishes. A life weighed and given value by possessions and then the renunciation of the possessions. He had stepped away from this torrent of objects, assigned everything to his brother, when he left St. Petersburg. But it seemed the objects followed him, as they were replicated in the residences of the wealthy in Kharbin.

He tried to describe the details of the family homes for Li Ju as if they were photographs or postcards. But there was a space where their languages didn't overlap. What was the Chinese word for *mantelpiece*? For *attic*? For *eaves*? He struggled to translate the nuances of Russian into equivalent words in Chinese or English.

"We'll visit St. Petersburg someday," he had half-promised Li Ju, and she smiled. But he couldn't imagine returning to Russia. Manchuria had so thoroughly transformed him that he would marvel along with her at the city's tramcars, the gilded spire atop the Admiralty building, the view from the Strelka, the life-size jeweled icons and pillars of lapis lazuli in St. Isaac's Cathedral.

Chinese calligraphy was the Baron's solace in the evening. On the narrow stage of his desk, under lamplight, a rectangle of white paper was the shape of discipline. He could barely fathom the perimeters of its difficulty, the years of practice, but this elusiveness and uncertainty was part of calligraphy's seduction. When he was lost, nervous about executing a brushstroke, he had learned to wait calmly until the character was visualized and wavered into shape, opening like a novelty flower of folded paper in water. He sometimes dreamed about written Chinese characters, angular brushstrokes, thick and thin, scattered like dark hay over a field of white paper or his wife's hair loose against a pale cushion, black as sticks. Paper was a surface with the impermanence of snow.

Unlike the majority of Chinese women, his wife, Li Ju, could read and write. She had also learned English and a little Russian at the Scottish Presbyterian orphanage, memorizing text from the standard prayer book so that her speech was fractured, curiously old-fashioned, laced with *thee*s and *thou*s. Li Ju solemnly recited passages from hymnals, gesturing at the proper places as she'd been instructed. "'My heart swells, O Lord / I am a river beside you.'" Her hand flickered in the direction of her heart. He didn't always correct her or offer an explanation of text that was unclear, but this allowed him to keep something back from her just as she hid within her own language. At times, he believed that he wasn't subtle enough for his extraordinary young wife.

Once, she had playfully given him a calligraphy lesson, blackening the tip of her finger on a cake of ink. She sat in front of a dark screen, and her upraised finger with its black spot slowly stroked Chinese characters in the air so he could follow the long lines and dots as she described each one. Finished with the lesson, he cupped her hands in his and inhaled the scent of her skin, identifying the incense she'd handled earlier that day. "I know you microscopically" was his joke, but it was an unfamiliar word to her. He couldn't properly explain it so one day he brought Li Ju to his office. She squinted into the microscope at the bright piece of transparent glass securely balanced inside, the light sharp as a cut.

Another time, she gently shaped his lips into the correct speaking position with her fingertips. His mouth could not find the Chinese pronunciation of *hs* from the Russian *ch*. He stuttered. "It is because of your mustache," she had teased. But it wasn't only his lips. His ears couldn't distinguish the tones, the emphasis on words with their complicated inflections. One syllable could have four different tones of voice and four different interpretations, simply by the way it was pronounced.

Li Ju was young, a kernel, perfect as a bud. The underside of her lip was as pale as melon, her fingernails the beige of almonds. He was convinced that nothing was finer than her skin, opaque as milk at the roots of her black hair. He was ashamed of his own skin, slack, sun-mottled with age, and his hands, huge and rough, aching at night. He was almost fifty years old and the time spent at army camps and prisons working in freezing temperatures had permanently marked him.

He knew nothing about her family. She was silent about her life before the orphanage. Did she remember a home, her mother, father, sisters or brothers? Or had she been too young for memory? Or was memory too painful? Li Ju was her original name, the sisters at the Scottish Presbyterian orphanage claimed, but the identity of the person who had delivered her was unknown. He could have requested the immense registration book be taken from the shelf at the orphanage and opened to the page where information about her was recorded. Each child was documented in case a relative or family member wished to reclaim him or her in the future. Some parents who gave up their child left a small memento for identification, an item as simple as a button, a toy, coin, a scrap of paper with a verse. But an investigation into his wife's past seemed like a betrayal. He left her history in the book at the orphanage. It was hers alone.

Li Ju owned nothing of her own as a child. The clothing, shoes, and books provided by the sisters at the orphanage passed from her possession to others. He bought the few things Li Ju requested—silver-embroidered fabric, a stone seal carved by a master, a fighting cricket in a cage.

He was always urging her to eat. *Take this,* he would say, *please taste this,* and it became a tender joke between them. *Eat more cake, noodles, lamb, ask for my attention, my eyes, my hand.* In their house, they alternated creating a place setting for each other at the table. She disliked the rich Russian food he had specially prepared, the dark heavy meats, *pashtet, kholodets,* pork in jelly, lamb with pickled and salted fruits. *It tastes thick,* she said, shaking her head. *I won't eat.*

Li Ju was cautious. Careful about taking space in a room, food from a plate, blocking light from a window, heat from a stove, becoming breathless when she spoke. Perhaps the sisters had been overly strict with the children? He encouraged her to be less deferential, more spontaneous. He did not expect complete obedience. But she craved routine, predictability. He told himself that she was just timid. Not fearful. Once, as a joke, he'd silently slid a teacup to the edge of the table when she was distracted and had looked away. She noticed the cup immediately and covered her mouth in distress. She did not cry.

"Please," he said. "It's not important that the cup has been moved. Everything is made to be moved. It cannot be stopped."

She shook her head.

He gently put his hand on her arm and she closed her eyes. "But my touch changes you too." Li Ju kept her eyes closed. But he knew her entire focus was on his hand against her skin.

Even after their years together, he studied her constantly, marveling that she stayed with him. Over time, his memories of her changing face and body were a honeycomb of multiple images.

The sisters at the orphanage had infused all the children with lessons of gratitude. Their lives depended on it. He wondered if Li Ju's gratitude, like her appearance, would continue to alter, and then she'd leave him. After all, a woman who has been rescued once may seek another man for aid or a transformation. Another rescue.

The orphanage established by missionaries was one of the few safe places for abandoned children in Kharbin. The Baron had visited to find a servant, a child to train as an apprentice, one who could learn a trade. He'd first considered rescuing a child from the street but reasoned that adopting an orphan would free a place for another child. The sisters were unable to feed every mouth. It was an endless chain.

The orphanage was poorly furnished, with only a long table, small chairs, and a wardrobe. A cage near the window held a pair of canaries. He stepped around the rolled-up sleeping mats in the largest room, his boots aggressive on the wooden floor, a brisk tattoo over the voices of children singing a hymn in the courtyard outside.

A plainly dressed sister entered the room, stared at him suspiciously until he introduced himself as a doctor who needed a household servant.

Her expression changed immediately. "I'm Sister Margaret. Please, would you take a moment to examine some of the children? I cannot pay you, but—"

He waved a hand to stop her pleading. "I have my medical case." He indicated his stout leather bag.

Her face relaxed. "Let me call the children."

An older girl, fourteen or perhaps fifteen years old, ushered a group of children into the room and they lined up facing him in the chair provided for visitors. She stood behind them, hushing

the smaller children who leaned against her, as they were afraid of
him. He knew they couldn't bear the scent of a Russian, his breath,
skin, the coarse odor of his body in a wool jacket. The Chinese
called Russians "the hairy ones" or "the red beards."

He felt clumsy as he bent close to a boy, listened to his shallow ex-
halations, asking him to cough. A lung infection. Nothing he hadn't
seen in an army barracks. The infected boy should be isolated, but
that was probably impossible here with so many children. He
promised to bring the boy medicine and he'd be better in a week.

One of the youngest girls began to cry.

"Close your eyes. He won't hurt you," the older girl said in Chinese and comfortingly stroked the child's shoulder. She was tall,
very thin, and her skin had a pale luster that didn't betray her troubled history. She looked straight at him and boldly repeated her
words in Russian.

The Baron's decision was immediate. It was simple to change a
life. Li Ju left the orphanage with him, to Sister Margaret's regret.
She had been sorry to lose a good worker.

He had made other choices in this manner, alert to something
that revealed a person's character. An animating spark. Sometimes
patients could be diagnosed in the same way, revealing themselves
with a word or an expression. He knew who could be saved or save
themselves.

That was his first encounter with his wife, Li Ju, and he could
never remember if she introduced herself, had said her name, and
it frustrated him, the only glimpse of her character before time and
intimacy shaped it like a folded page. He later told Li Ju that her
true heart was revealed by her tenderness with the children. She always giggled at this affectionate teasing. But when she had reached
a certain age, her rescue from the orphanage was never again discussed between them.

But he'd wanted to say, *You stood in line before.* Stood in line for other men and women, strangers who had come to adopt a Chinese child, choose a servant, slave, concubine, or prostitute. Other eyes had evaluated her, measured her for obedience, acquiescence. Her face and body.

"I remember our first meeting very clearly," he later said to her, not quite truthfully. "You comforted a child and caught my eye. So we left together."

"I was chosen." She clasped his hand. "My gesture must have been very graceful."

He was silent. He'd seen her make the gesture of someone who was drowning.

The Baron had been privileged his entire life and had tried to dismantle it. To some Chinese, he was a blue-eyed white devil. To the Russian community, he was a renegade and a mystery. He wed Li Ju and she became the Baronin. The aristocratic title meant nothing to her. Many Kharbinskiis believed that the Baron had disgraced his Russian heritage by marrying outside their circle. Even the czar himself did not approve of his wife. The marriage was scandalous not because of her tender age but because she was considered a pagan. A nonbeliever. An inferior Chinese. Certain individuals who had known the Baron for years as a solitary figure whispered he'd been bewitched by a young Chinese prostitute. He'd crossed too many meridians for them, with his foreign bride and fluency with the Chinese language. He ignored their gossip and hid his intimate relationship from critical eyes, unbending only to his wife and patients, to those who needed him.

But his title deflected criticism like a holy relic and after his marriage, he continued to receive invitations from high society, although it was expected that she wouldn't accompany him. These dinners and receptions were rarely entertaining, as he was constantly asked for medical advice, recommendations, and news about individuals in St. Petersburg whom he hadn't seen in years. Prominent Kharbinskiis were proud their sacrifices in Manchuria had built an empire for the czar and the motherland. They had little curiosity about China. Truthfully, he didn't mind that his wife was excused from social gatherings, as it was easier for him to socialize alone. There was her youthfulness and shy hesitation to speak, his apprehension that she'd be mocked.

It was unusual for a Chinese woman and a Russian man to be seen together, and they were constantly followed by stares, evaluating eyes. If Li Ju noticed, she said nothing. She welcomed encounters with the world.

Otherwise, the Baronin usually remained at home. She was always waiting. But the situation was familiar after her cloistered life at the orphanage. It was in the Chinese tradition, he told himself. She had little experience of choice, after all.

The Baron was a rarity—a Chinese-speaking Russian—and he practiced his Chinese-language skills in the Fuchiatien market, taller than the crowd around him. In fine weather, his Russian uniform of stiff broadcloth was exchanged for a traditional Manchu jacket, the *chang pao,* and trousers in plum gray or dull blue, the colors worn by older adults. At first, the foreign garments made him uneasy. He was unaccustomed to their logic—loose-fitting with four slits—and had the sensation that he was swimming in cloth. He felt unprotected without the wool swaddling of his uniform, the tight grip of belts and metal buttons.

Many Chinese believed he was a spy. He listened carefully, translating words overheard on the street, negotiating small transactions, the purchase of sweet rice or plums, surprising the merchants. Gradually, he was able to distinguish even the peddlers' voices from the clamor in the market. Their repetitive singing, shouts, and cries were punctuated with wooden clappers, whistles, jingling metal coins as they sold candied crab apples, congee, rice cakes, rolls of cloth, pewter pots, vegetables, blocks of rock salt. Hot tea was siphoned from a huge metal urn strapped to a vendor's back. He surprised himself, hesitating for a moment before drinking hot liquid from the china cup shared by many mouths.

He had witnessed the city and the railroad built at frantic speed by tens of thousands of Chinese workers. It was a city of men. The few women Kharbinskiis were either wives, servants, or prostitutes. It was unsafe for a Russian to walk without a weapon and a bodyguard in certain neighborhoods, among the opium addicts, drunks, beggar children, Bolshevists, anarchists, army deserters, smugglers, black marketeers. At dawn in the Pristan district, gamblers drunk on champagne stumbled from the Folies Bergère into the street, jostling and insulting the Chinese on their way to work on the tracks. The Chinese would never dare to harm the Russians, not here, not at this moment, when tardiness could cost a man his job.

The first year he'd settled in Kharbin, the Baron had stepped off the Sungari River ferry and noticed a man dragging two forlorn little girls. He thought perhaps the children had been sick during the voyage and observed them until the man came over and offered to sell him the girls, together, five rubles for an hour. Before he could answer, the man reacted to the look on his face and pulled the girls into the crowd. The Baron madly shoved people aside racing after them, but slow-moving porters blocked his way. He lost sight of them. His failure to save the two little children haunted him.

CHAPTER FOUR

The map of Kharbin in winter was radically different than during the rest of the year. Snow reorganized the city and entire areas vanished under thick snow, lost to observation. Streets were erased, buildings isolated, bridges cut off, landmarks unrecognizable. The snow smoothed over cinders spewed from passing trains, deposits fine as black lace along the tracks.

The flour mills, tanneries, distilleries, and warehouses near the wharves, desolate stretches of tracks, depots and signal stations, the deep ravine between Pristan and Fuchiatien, land around the barracks in old Pristan and the three cemeteries remained covered by snow, layer upon layer, until warm weather in May. Anything could be hidden in these places. Weapons. A body.

General Dmitry Khorvat squinted across the table at the Baron. The two men were working together in Khorvat's dining room, sharing small plates of appetizers: pâté, several kinds of pickled mushrooms, and vegetables. Even in his own home, the general remained in uniform. His white beard, soft as a woman's veil, almost hid the rows of military medals on his chest.

"How is your palace in Crimea?" The Baron knew the question would please the general, as it invited discussion of his wife and villa. A notorious miser, Khorvat sent all his money to Crimea, where an enormous home had been under construction for years in preparation for his retirement. The general shyly unfolded a small piece of white silk, and withered red petals showered over the papers on the table. The Baron smiled at dour Khorvat's whimsy.

"My wife likes deeply colored flowers. The bougainvillea will have grown well over the walls by the time I quit Kharbin for Crimea. There's a view of the sea from the terrace of our villa."

"Imagine the breeze."

"Crimea has everything that this place lacks. Sun and civilization."

In Kharbin, Khorvat lived in the Novy Gorod district near the foreign consulates and the offices of the Ford Motor Company, International Harvester, Skoda Industries. A wealthy man, Khorvat insulated himself against the vast emptiness of Manchuria by crowding his home with carved furniture, velvet curtains, carpets from Belgium, Venetian crystal chandeliers and mirrors, soap and stationery from London, silver platters, porcelain bibelots.

He was a benevolent dictator, the supreme authority in Kharbin, head of the Chinese Eastern Railway (known as the CER), which, in spite of its name, was owned and operated solely by the Russian government. Khorvat also controlled the police, courts, civil and municipal services, foreign relations, mines, timber concessions, the wharves, shipping, banks, tariffs, Russian newspapers, schools and nurseries, hospitals, churches, synagogues, and mosques. He could stop the newspapers, stop the trains, reroute a ship, imprison or exile anyone without cause.

When it was to his advantage, Khorvat ignored orders from St. Petersburg or claimed they'd never arrived. This was typically forgiven, as communication was erratic, mail delivery took months, and telegraph poles were frequently torn down and burned by Chinese, enraged by Russia's intrusive equipment on virgin grasslands.

The Baron routinely spent hours with Khorvat, translating documents from German, French, and Chinese into Russian. His knowledge of Chinese was viewed as eccentric but indispensable; no Russian officials were fluent in Chinese, as it was not considered necessary. This access allowed the Baron to witness the secret workings of empire, the skeins of loyalty and relationships, the maneuverings for favor, and assured his position with Khorvat, who could change a life with a nod or his signature on a paper.

This afternoon, while the Baron translated out loud, Khorvat's eyes were on his face, watching his expression as if to catch him in a deceit, a misinterpretation, a skipped sentence. In Khorvat's office, the Baron was occasionally forced to stand and silently wait in front of the general's desk while he arrogantly thumbed through papers. This breach of etiquette to a member of the aristocracy would never had been tolerated in St. Petersburg. Duels had been fought for lesser insults.

When Khorvat announced all the Chinese correspondence was now finished, the Baron was intoxicated with relief, released from the strain of translation. His shoulders sagged with stress.

Khorvat produced a small bottle, and two tiny glasses appeared next to it. The flourish of Khorvat's sleeve scattered the flower petals so that the Baron, in his fatigue, had the impression there had been a sleight-of-hand trick. The open bottle of *beryozovitsa,* a liqueur made from birch-tree sap, released a fresh resin scent.

"Springtime, eh? Makes one homesick."

"I do miss the seasons in St. Petersburg. Winter was more gentle there," the Baron said. "And the northern lights. I was fortunate to see the great aurora in 1870. There was a glowing line all along the canals where the lights were reflected on the ice."

"Lights on the ice? Food is the only thing about St. Petersburg worth discussing. Blinis and butter during Maslenitsa before Lent. I'd eat dozens in one sitting. The butter here isn't the same, although they claim it's imported. I should have someone check on it."

"In Beijing the food is truly excellent. If you have a good guide in the markets." The Baron immediately regretted his words.

"I cannot recognize most of what the Chinese cook. And I cannot eat rice." Khorvat changed the subject, describing certain shops in Beijing where passable copies of French furniture and German cameras could be purchased if you had currency the proprietor accepted.

From experience, the Baron anticipated Khorvat would begin a lengthy tirade about smugglers and Hutzul bandits who preyed on travelers outside the city. He pulled a Khorvatovki paper ruble from his pocket. The bills were printed with a red train, issued under Khorvat's order, bore his name, and were legal tender along with other currencies, the *diao*, traditional Chinese copper coins and ingots. Chinese workers refused the Khorvatovki rubles, insisted on payment in Mexican silver pesos, which were imported by the ton.

"I've always wondered why our Khorvatovki paper money doesn't have the czar's face."

"If you asked the archimandrite of the holy Russian church, he would say the czar, our Little Father, should not be associated with Kharbin, an ungovernable place of sin, a *zaraznaya yama,* an infectious pit." The usual sentence of allegiance. He made a dismissive gesture. "I decided no artist here had the skill to engrave our Little Father's portrait for the printer. So our money bears a locomotive because Kharbin was born of the railroad."

"A noble gesture. But some joke that dice, cards, and opium pipes should be on the ruble. Representing the infamous side of our city."

Khorvat shook his head. Not a smile on this subject.

The Baron calculated whether Khorvat was drunk enough for him to risk a blunter question. "A man was found lying in the snow by Churin's store. Unidentified. Presumed dead. Two other men were found dead at Central Station. Apparently they didn't die natural deaths."

Khorvat mimed a look of astonishment. "Who would do such a thing?"

"I was hoping you'd have an official answer."

"Blame a depraved anarchist. A Bolshevik revolutionary."

"At least one of the dead men was Chinese. A Bolshevik wouldn't kill a Chinese. They hate Russian officials and aristocrats."

"Perhaps it was a duel. A Chinese feud."

The Baron persisted. "A killing on the city's richest street?"

"The bottle, please."

"General, I don't know who's guilty. I cannot even guess at a suspect. But strangely, all the dead disappeared. No bodies were received at the Russian hospital. No death certificates were filed, since I was never notified. My wife spoke to the abbot at the Buddhist temple. He confirmed there had been no recent funerals."

"Perhaps the dead Chinese had converted to Christianity? God rest their souls."

"There were no funerals for any Chinese at St. Sophia or St. Nikolas Cathedral. Or at Dormition of the Theotokos. No burial services at Uspenski or the Jewish cemetery. Or the mosque in Pristan. No coffins were received at the CER shipping facility. And we know Kharbin has no morgue." He flushed at his audacity.

Khorvat's eyes, the opaque blue of enamel in an icon, slowly focused. "Perhaps the bodies are a plot to upset the situation here. The Chinese and Japanese want to drive us from Manchuria. We're outnumbered. You remember the riots a few years ago? Chinese workers found bones near the tracks and claimed the Russians had made a human sacrifice. Merciful God, they believe no act is too barbaric for Russians. Dr. Nikolaeva dissected a huge bear carcass in front of an angry crowd just to prove the bones were animal bones. His hands shook as he held up the bear's bloody leg bone next to the dirty bone they'd found. Identical. Bone to bone. The public dissection was necessary to prevent a riot."

"Autopsies aren't for the fragile." The Baron sipped at his glass of *beryozovitsa,* allowing its thickness to coat his teeth and tongue. It calmed him. "I wasn't informed about the dead men. If someone is trying to discredit me as chief medical officer, I want to be prepared to defend myself. I've served you and the czar honorably." He was sweating in his wool jacket and pulled at his collar. "The Chinese believe that a body left at a building puts a curse on it. Central Station. Churin's store."

"You've told me nothing that I don't know." Khorvat's patience had thinned. "You weren't consulted about the deaths because they didn't seem important. No slight to your professionalism. But it's better to avoid these conflicts. Don't make your sympathies too obvious. I remember your struggle with your young wife and the church authorities. A man must guard his reputation. Even in this place."

The Baron nodded to show that he understood.

Khorvat folded his hands atop the table and met the Baron's

eyes, a sign of greater-than-usual engagement. "Now. There's been another unexplained death. A merchant."

"Russian?"

Only the unexplained death of a Russian would be investigated. "Dmitry Vasilevich. God rest his soul. A soybean dealer. He'd just returned on the train from Mukden or Kaiyuang. His daughter, Sonya, has made wild accusations about who is responsible for his death. Blames her stepmother. The man died suddenly, probably apoplexy or brain fever. You should confirm this."

"When did he die?"

"Two days ago."

"And the body?"

"At rest in St. Nikolas cemetery. You will interview Sonya Vasilevna."

"I understand." The request was routine. He would create words to grace a paper and then seal them in a file.

"Good. Your answer will greatly comfort the daughter. I've also ordered a search for Dmitry Vasilevich's widow."

"Missing?"

"Perhaps fled. You're a doctor. Remember why I value your work. I don't value you as a cataloger of the dead." A flicker as their eyes measured each other.

The Baron was relieved Khorvat hadn't directly threatened him but only waved a flag of warning over the death of Dmitry Vasilevich. He rolled the bottom edge of his glass on the table, noiselessly crushing the scattered red petals against the white tablecloth.

The Baron had a calligraphy lesson each week with Zhang Boying, who had introduced himself as Xiansheng, Elder Born, a traditional title honoring his advanced enlightenment as an older gentleman and scholar. A reserved man, deliberate with his gestures, Xiansheng entered the Baron's study with the gentle stir of his robes, always plum, indigo, or dove gray, the colors of the elderly. In warm weather, he wore slippers of woven grass, and boots of Russian leather were his only concession to the severe Manchurian cold. The lessons were a ritual of courtesy and reflection, preceded by an exchange of bows and tea drinking. After the lesson, the Baron presented a sealed envelope to his teacher with a bow, holding it in both hands. Money must never be visible.

Before the calligraphy lesson, the Baron had accompanied Xiansheng to a stationery shop, a quiet space with walls of narrow shelves and an unidentifiable subtle odor, clean as water. The proprietor deftly slipped a piece of paper from a shelf, its flat surface reflecting light from the open door, a brief brightness that flashed like a wing in the room. They were shown papers flecked with mica, rose-pink and yellow-gold leaf, silk paper so fine that it became a transparent shadow when laid on the table. To gauge texture and strength, Xiansheng gently pressed his thumb against the papers, brushed them with careful fingertips and the side of his hand. It reminded the Baron of the way Chinese doctors used touch to diagnose a patient.

For the first lesson, the Baron had been instructed to close his eyes and listen to his teacher demonstrate calligraphy using different brushes. "Do not listen with the ears but with the mind," Xiansheng instructed, quoting a master. His brush moved in short sweeps, curves, straight lines, slashes, rough jagged shapes, dots. Each movement had an individual sound. One brush slightly resisted the paper, its bristles dry as whiskers, and another had a nearly silent silky glide. He was hypnotized by the soft rhythm of Xiansheng's work, the suspense until the final stroke, a horizontal line drawn unhesitatingly from left to right. When he opened his eyes, the Baron was astonished that the images on the paper did not match what he had blindly imagined.

The Baron was given a three-layered wolf-fur brush to create small strokes and dots. His posture was corrected, and his neck muscles tightened with tension. His hand trembled. He could wield a scalpel with delicacy but the brush was a clumsy twig in his hand. He struggled, powerless to control his movement, to calm himself.

Teacher told him to stop. "You must consider the brush in a different way. Release the brush."

"Put it down?"

"No. Release the brush while you hold the brush."

The Baron was confused, uncertain if his teacher was joking or if he'd misunderstood. Xiansheng was implacable. He instructed the Baron to sit with the brush for half an hour. It took fifteen minutes for his anger to subside. His teacher then read one of the principles of calligraphy that had been set down in the seventh century by a master Taoist calligraphist, Yu Shi'nan: "'If his mind is not tranquil, the writing will not be straight.'"

Xiansheng's expression was usually neutral, but occasionally the Baron caught a hint of the man's approval. Or perhaps this was just what he craved. During a lesson, he learned the character *ming*, for "brilliance," which merged the individual characters for *sun* and *moon*. Astonished by the beautiful simplicity of this word picture, he sought his teacher's eyes, stricken by the realization that he would never master this language. At that moment, Xiansheng's eyes shone with compassion.

News of Dmitry Vasilevich's death had passed from person to person at St. Nikolas Cathedral, where he worshipped. An elderly church member had confided to the Baron that the man had been quickly buried with little ceremony. A Russian Orthodox funeral usually lasted several days, concluding with a feast and alms to the poor. Vasilevich was in his grave even before the notice was in the *Kharbinskii Vestnik* and *Novoe Vremya* newspapers.

Dmitry Vasilevich had lived in a massive stone residence in Novy Gorod, the Russian quarter. The wealthy had segregated themselves here in newly built mansions of imported stone set in a naked landscape without trees or shrubs. Guards patrolled the area, searching every Chinese servant and tradesman with bags of produce for hidden weapons.

At the Baron's knock, a maid swiftly admitted him, asked his name, and vanished. Inside, weak September light was blocked by heavy drapes at the windows and across the doors as insulation, and he moved slowly, as if disconnected in a dream, to enter the shadowy parlor.

His footsteps were loud and clumsy across the floor, which was curiously uncarpeted, and the dark, heavy furniture seemed out of place on the bare boards. His feet cramped with the effort to quiet his boots. He stopped to peer into a glass-fronted cabinet, surprised it was cluttered with Chinese jade and porcelain figurines. Small carved jade and hard-stone decorative objects were also arranged on a side table.

"Please." The dark figure of a young woman silently materialized in the doorway. She introduced herself as Sonya Vasilevna and indicated two chairs near the tile stove. She sat down first and he settled into another chair, close enough to notice that her eyes were tender from weeping. He introduced himself as the city's chief medical officer, expressed sympathy for her father's death.

Sonya looked away and whispered a line from a prayer.

He bowed his head. As a doctor, he had created a series of sentences that were serviceable in a crisis. Unfortunate news was delivered in a neutral tone, as if held at an angle that prevented emotion seeping into it. "I apologize for disturbing you at this time. Your mother is not at home?"

She nervously smoothed her long blond braid. "My stepmother, Sinotchka, left Kharbin immediately after Papa's funeral. She hated this place."

"Where has she gone?"

"She didn't tell me. She left in a hurry but packed very well. Many things are missing from the house. My jewelry and an embroidered shawl. But it is a small price to be rid of her."

"I see. So I will rely on your memory and impressions for information."

"Information about what?"

"Your father's unfortunate death has been questioned by certain officials."

Sonya blinked. "I can't help you. I wasn't here when Papa died. Stepmother buried him against my wishes. I went to his gravesite alone." Her body straightened, indicating she imagined herself there again.

Sympathy would not make an ally of this young woman. He asked for an account of her father's last day.

"My father and stepmother took the train from Mukden to Kharbin. On business. September twentieth. First-class compartment."

"Was everything as usual on the train?"

"I remember Stepmother said Papa wasn't feeling well and didn't cross himself when they passed St. Nikolas Cathedral on the way home. I knew something was wrong. His belief in God was strong. The most important thing in his life. Stepmother left Papa at the Metropole Hotel. He came home late. The servants said Papa staggered in, coughing blood. Blood everywhere. Even in this room." Her hands flapped, mimed the chaos.

"May God rest his soul."

"Who dies that quickly? Tell me. How could he die just like that?" Sonya snapped her fingers. Her grief and anger had infected each other.

He shook his head. "Certainly his death was unusual. Hemorrhage, perhaps. I apologize for this painful question, but was his bloody clothing or bedding saved?"

Her expression was disdainful. "Your question is repugnant."

"I'm sorry. I'm a doctor. My questions can be uncomfortable but I make a diagnosis by asking questions. I believe an answer is a kind of salvation."

She laced her fingers tightly together and didn't respond.

He waited. Half the room was warm from the stove in the corner but the air was chill at the back of his neck.

"Some of his clothing was given to the servants. They stole the rest, even though it was bloodstained."

Clothing, any type of clothing, was valuable even in poor condition. "Are the servants here? May I speak to them?"

She laughed. "My stepmother dismissed all the servants. I don't know where they live. Some of them slept in the kitchen. They shopped and cleaned and cooked. It wasn't my concern to know anything about them."

"Even their names?"

"Their names? They're Chinese." After a moment, she said they were called Sasha. Azek. Boychick. Her manner was slightly apologetic.

So her family had followed the custom of giving Russian names to the Chinese servants. A lost thread. But he wrote down the false names.

"Thank you. Tell me, was the furniture taken from this room after your father died?"

Sonya said no, only the carpet had been removed, but her attention wasn't fastened on him. She appeared to be listening to something else. She abruptly hurried across the parlor and jerked open the door. The corridor was empty. She left the room.

He pulled a handkerchief from his vest pocket, spat into it, leaned over, and rubbed it over the two front legs of his chair. The handkerchief was clean. He quickly moved to investigate if there was a stain on the sofa legs. Nothing. But when he checked the underside of the seat on a second chair, there was a faint brown smear on the white cotton. "Blood," he whispered.

Sonya entered the room carrying a small glass jar. "Here. I kept the evidence. Before he died, Papa couldn't eat. He only drank tea she made for him. Stepmother put jam from this jar in his tea. She told me this herself." She sat down, flicking her long skirt around her legs. "She poisoned him."

Sonya slowly transferred her braid from shoulder to shoulder. "My father was a very important person. One of the wealthiest men in Kharbin. General Khorvat was his friend. You're obliged to investigate his death, although I know my stepmother is guilty."

She reminded him of a childhood playmate, a cruel, spoiled child who once tied his greyhound to a tree and threw stones at it. But that was another life. Sonya was the daughter of a rich man, but now that he was dead, she would lose her special privileges. She was simply a young woman without a family. She should marry quickly. Still, the passions were unpredictable. He slowly exhaled. "The truth, mademoiselle, can bring security. There is a line from a Chinese poem: 'A grain of sand contains all land and sea.'" He spoke the words again, translated back into Chinese.

"You speak Chinese?" Her face was creased with uncertainty.

"I do. Not with any ease."

She picked up one of the small carved objects, the figure of a scholar, from the table and handed it to him. "What do you think of this? Is it valuable?"

The stone was cold in his hand. He stroked its smooth surface and wanted to say that it should be admired for itself. "I'm no expert. But it is beautifully carved. I believe it has some age."

"You may take it with you."

He was startled by her generosity. "Thank you for this gift. But I—"

She interrupted. "When I'm alone, I like to study the objects. I placed them here so I could see them. Stepmother mocked me for collecting these Chinese pieces."

He was certain Sonya would marry a wealthy Russian and her home would be furnished according to his taste. Her Chinese objects would be put away. He nodded and thanked her again. "Tell me, how is your health? No fever? Cough?"

She faltered. "Nothing is wrong with me." The girl's arms were tightly folded across her chest.

The Baron waited, hoping she wouldn't weep. He wanted to unbend her arms, hold her hand in consolation, but he could only soften his voice. "Please contact me if there is anything you wish to tell me." He tried to radiate the energy of his smile, to bless her. He hoped General Khorvat's guards would be kind to Sonya.

So Dmitry Vasilevich's widow had fled. Evidence of guilt. Or despair. Her first choice for escape was probably the CER train. East, she could go to Vladivostok on the Sea of Japan. Or travel toward Beijing on the CER and the Japanese South Manchuria Railway. It was several weeks' journey by train between Kharbin, Europe, and St. Petersburg across Manchuria and Russia, a landscape that became impassable in the winter. Snow buried the tracks, swallowed up armies. There were boats and ferries down the Sungari River although the route was rapidly becoming icebound at this time of year. Pursuit of Sinotchka Vasilevna was tardy and would be haphazard, compounded by vast distances, undependable communication, untrained and unsupervised soldiers working in isolation to locate the woman. It was a fool's errand.

The Baron stirred the fire in the corner stove to warm the small laboratory in his office. On winter mornings, glass jars and metal implements had to be carefully handled, usually with gloves, as they became so cold overnight in the unheated room that they could injure the skin. Many mornings, the shallow water in the basin was skinned with ice. After half an hour, the room was warm enough for him to remove his gloves and work. His laboratory had minimal equipment: a British Beck microscope, an autoclave for sterilizing, platinum loops, glass slides and covers, test tubes of agar media, alcohols, needles, tweezers, syringes, swabs, surgical instruments, cotton, dark brown and transparent bottles that held morphine, chloroform, ether, oil of cloves, and other liquids for soothing or numbing pain.

If accurately described by Sonya Vasilevna, who had received the information secondhand, her father's symptoms were inconsistent with the most common forms of poisoning. Generally, the symptoms of poisoning were wide-ranging: vomiting, diarrhea, chills, fever, respiratory and heart failure, paralysis, cyanosis, hallucinations, unconsciousness. Cyanide caused the skin to flush deep pink. But vomiting blood was rare. The only citation he found that matched Dmitry Vasilevich's symptoms was the bite of an adder, which caused bloody vomiting.

Earlier, he had dissolved a little of the jam Sonya had given to him in a chloroform and sodium carbonate mixture and allowed it to dry in a small watch-glass container. A brownish deposit formed. A drop of Mayer's reagent was added with a capillary pipette. He waited for the drop to transform the deposit, create a ring around it to reveal the presence of poison. A chemical pointing finger. Negative. No telltale white or yellowish ring appeared.

He cautiously opened Sonya's jar and sniffed the contents. The still-fresh scent of strawberry. He swiped his finger around the rim of the jar, sucked it, instantly rinsed his mouth, spat, and waited. He figured this minute sample of jam wasn't enough to harm him. A tingling, numbed tongue would indicate aconitine. An intense bitterness was the signature of strychnine. Nothing. Saliva and a sweet taste of fruit.

Vegetable poisons, alkaloids, were difficult to identify in the body. For example, within hours of being ingested, opium left no trace. A spectroscopic analysis of alkaloids required special equipment, and they could also be identified under the microscope. However, his microscope wasn't powerful enough to break down the material into distinct crystals. Metallic poisons (mercury, arsenic, antimony) were detected by electric currents or spectrum lights.

He had performed each test with deliberate caution and attention to detail. All results were negative or inconclusive. His simple laboratory was not equipped for the challenge of more complicated tests of the evidence.

It was unfortunate that Dmitry Vasilevich had been buried without an autopsy. An accurate cause of death was impossible to establish since the dead man's viscera, urine, blood, vomit, hair,

nails, and teeth weren't tested. No autopsy had ever been performed in Kharbin, and there would be outrage if his body was
exhumed from the St. Nikolas cemetery.

His simple tests on the contents of Sonya Vasilevna's jar held no
authority. No proof of poison. But it was important to respect the
process. His time as an imperial army medic had taught him to answer the desires of officials.

He labeled the jar with the man's name, the date, and the tests
performed, then sealed it with wax and a strip of rice paper and
shoved it to the back of a shelf.

He wrote a letter to General Khorvat, praising his determina-
tion to uncover the truth about the death of Dmitry Vasilevich.
Citizens owed him their gratitude. He detailed the conversation in
which Sonya Vasilevna claimed her father had been poisoned by
his wife. He believed the girl's suspicions were unfounded, caused
by her wild grief. The inconclusive tests with the evidence were
described. The envelope for the letter was stamped with a carved
seal, numbered, and entered in the chit book used for messages.
Tomorrow, a Russian boy would deliver it to General Khorvat.

There were voices outside and the first patient of the day entered the office. The Baron politely questioned the laborer in Chinese. The man winced as the Baron unwound the dirty cloth, a
strip of shirt, that bound his fingers together. They were bent as a
brushstroke. Bruised black.

"I'll make a splint. Try to keep it clean. You should rest your
hand for a time." The Baron recognized this was unlikely, as the
laborer worked for the railroad. The man's expression confirmed
the situation. Perhaps someone could cover for him so that he
wouldn't lose his job?

"There is always work. I'm lucky." The man managed to smile.
"I have friends here from my village in Kuanchengzi."

He wanted to touch the man's arm to comfort him, but this would be disrespectful. There was no money or prestige in treating the poor and they were mostly charity cases. But the Baron didn't seek their gratitude. With his first Chinese patients, he'd quickly learned the words for "pain," "broken," "sharp," "help," "cold," and "hot." He tested himself by trying to translate what was said to him without watching his patients' faces. Expressions were grasped more quickly and fluidly than vocabulary. The language of suffering was simple to decipher. He always asked the patients to explain their past treatments to better understand the Chinese system of medicine, to discover a link, something potentially useful. If they shared information, he recorded their words in a notebook after they'd left his office. To write or be distracted in front of a patient aroused suspicion. *Wang er zhi,* to gaze and to know things, was the gift of the most skillful doctors.

The next patient, Chow Li, a man in his thirties, suffered from a lung infection that the Baron treated with applications of warm oil and camphor. As Chow Li dressed behind a screen, he described how people had been treated for smallpox in his village. A metal jar of small loose sticks was passed from hand to hand, and everyone selected one as a talisman to guard their health. Later, the villagers were actually inoculated against smallpox, mandated by the emperor, after which they prayed to the goddess Niang for twelve days to ensure its effectiveness.

Once, the Baron had observed an elderly Chinese doctor, skilled in traditional medicine, treat a young man suffering from *chungjing shanghan,* one of the most complicated diseases. The patient had chills, a fever, dry throat, dull eyes, a cold pain in his abdomen.

At that point, the Baron's grasp of the language was rudimentary, so the doctor slowly explained the process of diagnosis for his benefit, as if speaking to a child. The Baron was tense, alert to every word and gesture of the Chinese doctor.

The Chinese doctor quietly held the young man's hand, his delicate fingers pressed lightly against the inside of his wrist, and explained that it wasn't the pulse of blood in the vessels that he was monitoring. He registered *mo,* a flow that connected every part of the body and indicated the source of illness. The Chinese did not believe that the heart ruled the body but that the circulation of blood began in and returned to a small space at the wrist, streaming horizontally under the skin with a smooth or rough, faltering course. It wasn't Chinese medical practice to dissect a body. Diagnosis was based on the study of living people, not the dead.

The Baron quietly asked the doctor how he diagnosed the patient from the *mo* at his wrist.

"Each finger has a place on the wrist that corresponds to a part of the body. I use minimal pressure to diagnose the *fu,* the soft organs in the body. A harder pressure is for the solid *yin,* the viscera." He demonstrated. "Press the fingertips lightly, the weight of three beans, to diagnose skin and the lungs. Deepen pressure to six beans to read the blood vessels and heart; the third level is flesh and spleen. Fourth level is for the tendons and liver. The most intense pressure, fifteen beans, reveals the condition of the bones and kidneys."

While palpating the wrist with his fingertips, the doctor distinguished what he sensed at each pressure to make a diagnosis. Twenty-four qualities of *mo* were recorded in an early volume of *Mojing,* a revered ancient medical text. The descriptions of *mo* were poetic, mysterious, vague, allusive, built on metaphors that had been used for centuries. One type of *mo* was "a smooth succession of rolling pearls." Another *mo* was "rain-soaked sand." Faint *mo* was "extremely thin and soft as if about to disappear. It appears both to be there and not to be there."

Doubt and unease possessed him. The Baron didn't dare touch the patient's wrist, certain that he'd feel only a pulse, the common thunder of blood. The mysterious, elegant subtleties of *mo* were unintelligible to his fingers. An unknown language of sensation. Even the doctor's account of the symptoms of illness, the feel of the *mo,* the odors and colors of the body, its very solidity, were unrecognizable. He was humbled, realizing he would never comprehend the Chinese system of medicine. Even learning the language wouldn't enlighten him.

He had been blind to these perceptions and was shocked, as if the body suddenly possessed wholly unfamiliar characteristics. Some men looked at the sky and saw random stars while others deciphered a pattern, figures of men and beasts.

Sometimes he wondered if this new awareness had contaminated him. He kept his own counsel, didn't share this knowledge with other doctors or nurses. The idea that such fantastical concepts were worth consideration would have seemed ridiculous if someone had described it to him years ago, but in this place, with age and experience, the physical body had been newly revealed as miraculous.

The Baron shared his fascination with Chinese medicine with Li Ju. Occasionally, she sat beside him to interview traditional healers about their treatments and remedies. He marveled at her skill. When she was in the presence of these honored elders, her entire body became poised in alert but docile surrender. She made herself absent. It was admirable but he was also unnerved by her transformation. Once, after a lengthy conversation with a healer, it took a moment for her to respond when he spoke her name. *Where were you, Li Ju?* he wanted to ask.

Li Ju followed every stage of the moon, knew its schedule of brightness, half-light, and darkness. In Beijing, the buildings and streets were laid out so that the hour could be accurately told by the angle of the shadows they cast. Even a child had this skill. During his time in Manchuria, he had gradually become aware that he was surrounded by systems and information that were invisible to him.

The Baron crossed himself before an icon of Saint Xavier in the chapel. It was someone's brilliant strategy to place the detained train passengers in the Hospital of Mercy attached to the Congrégation des Missionnaires de St. Xavier, an isolated building with the inwardness of a shell, countless rooms empty of everything but the focus of contemplation.

Silence in the chapel was broken by the distant brush of footsteps. A sister emerged from a corridor in a white habit, the folds of her starched wimple angular as paper around her dark, severe face. A full habit curtained her body, hiding her posture and gestures. They had previously met at St. Sophia, and he remembered her unfavorably. The oldest sister at the convent, she had joined the order in Bombay and volunteered to establish the convent and its hospital in Manchuria, then sailed to China with the architectural plans.

"Sister Agnes, a pleasant day to you. I am Dr. Budberg."

"We live in the grace of the Lord. Praise be to God."

"I'm here to inquire about a sick man who would have been admitted a few days ago. He was found near Churin's store." His voice was reassuring and official, not judgmental.

"We have many patients." A moment as the sister blinked. Her face was almost blank with serenity. "I have no information about where the patients were located before they arrived."

Her composure was exasperating. Another sister glided silently over to Sister Agnes. He turned his attention to this younger nun, an unsmiling girl no more than sixteen, Russian or Slav, with green eyes.

"Sister Domenica, a doctor has come to visit." Sister Agnes granted her a half-smile.

He was patient. "The man is Chinese and probably unable to talk—"

"It doesn't matter. She doesn't speak Chinese," Sister Domenica said, interrupting.

"You see? What can I do?" Sister Agnes calmly opened her hands in a gesture of helplessness, although Domenica had clearly angered her.

He recollected a Chinese saying: The snare serves to catch the rabbit; let us take the rabbit and forget about the snare. Perhaps if he offered to pray with them they'd grant the information. He imagined sinking to his knees and their chill hands flattened against his bowed head in blessing. "Is the patient who was found by Churin's with you now?"

"No."

He struggled to twist her nonanswer. "But he was here at one time? That is correct?"

"Yes, I believe so." Sister Agnes's mouth was a grim line.

"And now he's dead?"

"There are no further details about him, I'm afraid." Relieved, Sister Agnes crossed herself, believing she'd escaped the spear point of his questions.

"Have any passengers from Central Station been brought here?"

Sister Agnes slipped her hands into her pocket. "Baron *le doc-*

teur, if you were meant to have this information, it would have been entrusted to you. I have no authority."

"Sister Agnes, there is no higher authority. I am the health commissioner for the city."

The younger sister pressed her fingers into the palms of her hands.

He sensed Domenica would talk but Sister Agnes might dismiss her at any moment and he'd miss his chance. He moved back a step to block the corridor. Calmer, he spoke slowly, deliberately, as if folding a piece of paper. "If you help me, your answer will benefit others. I share your struggle to care for the sick. I also lack supplies and medicine. I have patients who do not appreciate my effort. Patients who are unhappy."

"Yes, the Chinese believe that we trick them. Or want to steal their bodies."

Sister Agnes silenced the other woman's outburst with a simple shake of her robes. "I'm afraid Sister Domenica bears most of the unhappiness here, as she works directly with the patients."

The degree to which they—the sisters and the soldiers at Central Station—withheld information was a measure of its value. "Please, Sister Agnes, Sister Domenica. You obey holy orders. I'm a doctor. I have no wish to interfere."

"We simply care for the patients as best we are able. Our supplies are limited but we accommodate everyone as a compassionate gesture."

If she had been a government official, this would have indicated a bribe was expected, the usual gifts of goods, fresh meat, or boots.

Would she try to stop him if he suddenly raced past them into the patients' ward? He would not lose his temper with a pair of nuns. "Other officials may not understand or appreciate your mission. The government likes to meddle. I will try to keep them from becoming involved in your work. But as a disciple of God and a trained nurse, you know secrets do not heal. The heart festers."

There was an almost physical aspect to their silence.

Sister Domenica blurted out, "The Chinese man and the passengers are here. But they cannot leave."

"Enough." A rebuke from Sister Agnes. Her glance was an arrow.

The younger woman clasped her hands as if to protect herself. "Please, may I sit down? I'm not feeling well." She closed her eyes and fell into his arms as he stepped forward, surprisingly light despite her heavy robes. He set her gently on a bench against the wall but Sister Agnes swiftly pushed him aside, stared at Domenica for a moment, then slapped her face. The young woman cried out, and her body jackknifed over.

Sister Agnes swept around as if she intended to strike him. "You must leave."

"Sisters, God be with you." His voice croaked and his heart pounded in his chest as he walked away.

Was Sister Domenica truthful? What restraints or threats kept the passengers here, as no guards were posted outside the building? If the passengers were merely under observation, why were they kept hidden? Everything surrounding the situation blinded him to a pattern that was in place.

CHAPTER FIVE

Li Ju surprised her husband by insisting on accompanying him to the reception for the grand opening of the Railway Club. He reluctantly agreed, puzzled by her unusual request. Then she asked for permission to hire a servant, a Manchu woman, to spend that entire day at the house, assisting with a traditional dressing ritual. The Baron welcomed the Manchu guest when she arrived, carrying a small satchel, and he ushered her behind the screen where Li Ju waited.

First, the woman plucked fine short hairs around Li Ju's forehead so her hairline was perfectly even. Soot was stroked over her eyebrows to shape each one like a willow leaf. Her waist-length hair was smoothed with a resin mixture, combed, and twisted around ivory rods into large curls, thin as strips of silk, extending from the sides and the top of her head, the *liangbatou,* two-fisted style. Long pins with tiny jade ornaments and a silver stick, the *bian fang,* held her hair in place. White perfumed powder was dusted on the center part of her hair. Li Ju dressed in a stiff embroidered jacket, skirt, loose trousers, and short square-toed boots.

She stepped out from behind the screen and nervously stood before the Baron. Her thin white face and neck seemed hardly able to support the weight of her hair and the three dangling earrings in each ear.

"My butterfly," he said, hesitantly tracing her stiff curls with his finger. He touched the delicate quivering ornaments in her hair and on her ears.

Later, thoroughly chilled, the Baron slowly escorted Li Ju up the steps into the Railway Club. His feet were numb after traveling in a freezing droshky across the city to Kitayskaya Street. He entered the club as if cracked from ice, his body still stiff, fingers ten lengths of unfeeling flesh, the cold threaded inside the fibers of his evening jacket.

The club was lavishly furnished with leather armchairs, oriental carpets, bronze lamps. Walking through the rooms for the first time, the Baron could have sworn he'd been transported to the English club on Dvortsovaya-Naberezhnaya in St. Petersburg. The ballroom was overwhelming, cloudy with smoke from Lopato cigarettes, the men sweating in their heavy wool uniforms, the women fanning themselves, gold and silver flickering around their necks and on their dresses. The sideboard was set with several types of caviar in crystal bowls. It was a fasting day, according to the church, and fish was forbidden but caviar was allowed. The Baron spread a spoonful of osetrova on thick brown bread, noticed it was preserved, not fresh, since the eggs had a dull surface.

General Khorvat was the center of attention, surrounded by government officials and the men who had made fortunes in soybeans, timber, gold, smuggled goods, and weapons. He noticed Prince G. G. Kugusev, director of the Russo-Chinese Bank, the grain merchant Soskin, visiting Scottish dignitaries, German representatives from Krupp, and Americans from the International Harvester company. He didn't enjoy their company but it was in his interest to associate with the powerful men who ran the city.

Li Ju stayed close to her husband, silently smiling, earrings trembling, ignoring everyone's stares. None of the women spoke to her, the Baronin. The men barely nodded. Increasingly uncomfortable, the Baron took a glass of vodka from a waiter. Li Ju accepted no drink or food.

Bakai, the president of the club, stood nearby, grinning, his teeth discolored behind pale lips, accepting congratulations on opening the club.

The Baron made the introduction. "My wife, Li Ju, the Baronin."

Bakai nodded at her, his eyes on the Baron. "I understand you're married, Baron. A Chinese wife."

"Actually, my wife is Manchu." The Baron stiffened, helpless with anger over Bakai's mockery, afraid to involve Li Ju. Two of the three valued virtues determined by Confucius concern control of the expression, the *senan,* as a mark of the civilized person.

"Imagine." Bakai didn't lose his smile and moved closer with his drink, still ignoring Li Ju. "My own wife hasn't been feeling well. Perhaps you'd have a consultation with her, Doctor?"

Before he could speak, General Khorvat gripped his arm. A warning. "Certainly," the Baron answered and paused. "At a time convenient for her."

Bakai nodded. "I'm glad we understand each other."

The Baron shook off Khorvat's hand. "I want to be certain your wife wouldn't object to the close contact I have with my Chinese patients?"

"I'm certain you take every sanitary precaution. You are Kharbin's most renowned doctor."

His heart pounded and it dried his mouth so that words barely moved off his tongue. "I can't guarantee my sanitary precautions. But since he's never met you, my colleague Dr. Messonier is a better doctor for your wife. I wish her a rapid recovery, although you both probably share the same unpleasant characteristics."

Bakai blinked as the insult slowly came into focus. He hesitated, then turned away.

The Baron's heart rate slowly dropped. He didn't dare touch Li Ju or comfort her. To his relief, she was silent.

"Generous of you to send a new patient to Dr. Messonier." Khorvat's expression was strained. "Please be my guest here at the club anytime."

"May I bring my wife?"

Khorvat choked out a laugh and bowed to Li Ju. "Baronin, I am pleased to meet you. You bring grace to our evening."

Li Ju curtsied to General Khorvat since he was her elder. "Thank you." She answered in Russian. "The weather is cold tonight."

"Yes, gracious lady, I anticipate the cold will be with us for months."

The Baron marveled at the Baronin's armor. He finished the vodka in his glass in one burning swallow. He was pleased that Khorvat had been amused by his remark but uneasy he'd witnessed Bakai offending his wife.

The dwarf Chang Huai made his way across the room, a current of movement below eye level as men stepped back, women swept skirts aside allowing him to pass. A smiling woman leaned forward, revealing her décolletage as he kissed her hands, then angled his head to look up at her, emphasizing his small stature and creating the impression of trustfulness. She playfully tapped him on the head with her fan.

Chang Huai turned to address the Baron. "You've been set a task tonight."

"Myself and others. May I present my wife, the Baronin."

"Enchanted." He bowed respectfully.

She smiled in relief and the dwarf gave the Baron a thoughtful glance.

The Baron spoke in Chinese. "You have an amusing story? Or advice? What can you tell me?" He was tired and wished to avoid uncomfortable conversation.

"I couldn't speak freely when we met with Andreev. I was distracted. And the man has a reputation. But now I can tell you the body by Churin's store had been on the street all night. The watchman told me. I saw the men who took the body, but they were unrecognizable."

"How so?"

"Their noses and mouths were covered with a white cloth."

"Protection from the cold?"

"They also wore white clothing. Long white aprons. Gloves."

He gripped Chang's shoulder. "You're certain?"

Chang nodded, taken aback by his reaction.

"Please. I wish to go home," Li Ju murmured in his ear.

The Baron barely reacted to her words, lost in the scenario created by the dwarf's information. Men wore white uniforms for disguise or protection. He built the case for protection. They were most likely from the Russian hospital and had retrieved the body. He grasped Li Ju's hand. "You wish to leave? But it's early."

"I'll take the Baronin home. You should continue a conversation with General Khorvat."

A sharper look at Chang, his face impossible to read since it was only partially visible. "Thank you. I won't be long. It's a business matter."

From across the room, Andreev caught his eye, obviously drunk, gesturing excitedly at an officer, closing a deal or promising a favor. *How was this man admitted to the club?*

Aware that he was being watched, Andreev immediately became calmer. The man wasn't drunk but shamming for some scheme. The Baron sometimes felt clumsy around Andreev, earthbound, a slowness that came from a sense of duty and order. But this gave him an advantage. Andreev recognized only the type of behavior that was familiar to him. He must have read something in the Baron's expression and maneuvered his way over to speak with him.

"Good evening, Baron. You seem worried."

"Snow and cold conquers everything."

"Not everything. Tonight I've won." Andreev opened his hand to reveal a ring with a large red stone. "It belonged to an Englishman. Until he had a gambling loss."

The Baron had little patience for people who boasted about trinkets. "What pleasure to own such a fine thing," he said. His words had the effect of a dismissal, for Andreev swiftly put the ring away. "You've heard about the death of Dmitry Vasilevich? Yes? How did his widow, Sinotchka Vasilevna, escape Kharbin so easily?"

Andreev shrugged. "She escaped because no one pursued her. Or she crouched in an oxcart with her trunks all the way to Vladivostok. Or perhaps she caught a freighter to Canada."

"Could she have taken a ferry downriver?"

"Ice on the Sungari. Dangerous and slow. The roads are no better, nearly snowbound. Even a private carriage is too risky for a Russian woman traveling alone. There are Hutzul bandits. And criminal carriage drivers."

The Baron shook his head. "The train is the only way to escape Kharbin in winter. But our soldiers are garrisoned at all train stations."

"Unsupervised drunkards waiting for the Chinese army. As if they could stop an invasion. Or stop anyone." Andreev was humoring him. "Maybe the daughter, Sonya, killed her father and stepmother. Two dead Russians. Or perhaps the murderer followed Dmitry Vasilevich home from Central Station. See? There's your link to the train."

"Doubtful."

"You must be under General Khorvat's orders to even speculate about finding the widow. Curious, since a dead civilian matters very little to a general."

"Khorvat did ask for my aid. I believe it was a meaningless gesture, this searching for lost sheep, as the prophets say." The Baron nearly confessed his confusion. A simpleton's response. Andreev was not the person with whom to share the wavering-edged circle of his doubt. He spoke quickly to mask his anxiety. "Never mind. Tonight we drink with the highest society."

Andreev was quiet for a moment. Sometimes he pretended not to listen as the Baron spoke, or he yawned to show he wasn't impressed by the other man's title or position. He was free to be rude. The Baron could usually ignore this behavior. "High society? I prefer the people of Diagonalnaya Street to the Railway Club members. I go to the Fantasia cabaret. The Japanese bordellos. People know me." He grinned. "Sometimes I gamble. Or watch."

"Whom do you watch? The gamblers?"

The question amused Andreev. "Ah, my dear Baron. Here we are, two men of the world in the most godforsaken corner of the world. You can see things that are unimaginable anywhere else."

"I'm a doctor. I've seen everything." He tried to match Andreev's authority.

Andreev's laugh was brief, a dry bark. "Yes, but your patients show their bodies to you willingly."

He struggled away from the cruel images raised by the other

man's words. He turned and glimpsed Sonya Vasilevna speaking with an elderly man. No. He had mistaken another young woman for Sonya. Then Khorvat's deputy Diakonov waved at him.

The Baron walked over to join Diakonov and Khorvat. The deputy grudgingly stepped aside when the general indicated that he wished to speak with the Baron alone.

"I need you as a witness, Baron." Khorvat raised his voice. "Deputy Diakonov, bring the doctor's coat."

The clean warmth of vodka was still on his tongue as he strode after Khorvat and Diakonov down a bright corridor, wincing when the door opened into the darkness outside. A force of frigid air as he struggled into his sheepskin coat.

"We're not going far." Khorvat charged ahead of them, his unbuttoned coat flapping.

Outside, the landscape was empty, unbroken by trees. The cold space was a block of pressure that they slowly traveled through, dark moving lines against the snow, isolated in their heavy furs. Their figures seemed diminished. The crisp, bitter sound of their footsteps overlaid faint music from the ballroom behind them, a *schottische*. In the distance, a lantern threw a generosity of light on the squat shapes of two men. The scene reminded him of an execution. Closer, he noticed one of the men was drunk, and his shadow swayed with his unsteady movements, hugely elongated.

A cloth had been loosely thrown over the irregular shape of a corpse on the ground. The Baron immediately dropped to his knees, his posture an arc of tenderness as he leaned toward the still body, unerring as a figure in a holy painting. He sensed the other men turn away, embarrassed to witness this intimacy. He crossed himself, then pulled up a corner of the cloth, motioned for the lantern, and a hard geometry of light, blue at the edges, en-

tered the shadow cave of the blanket, revealing the upper half of
a body. Another twitch of the cloth revealed the side of a face, a
white cheek, barely shaded with stubble. A young man. No visible
marks. Blood on his chest.

"A Chinaman."

Someone cursed and laughed nervously.

"Of course he's Chinese. Russians don't drag the dead out into
the snow."

A flood of irritation at Deputy Diakonov's words. "Mother of
God." The dead man's exposed hand was rough and callused. A laborer, probably a servant in the kitchen. The man's arm was bent
across his torso, solid and unyielding, as the sleeve was frozen in
place. The body must have been here for hours. To examine the
corpse, he pulled off his bulky mitten.

"Don't touch him!"

The Baron stopped at Khorvat's shout. He waited for an explanation, but Khorvat smoked a cigarette, silently staring down at
the body. He exhaled a great stream of tobacco smoke as punctuation. Uneasy, the men shifted their boots in the snow.

The Baron instructed them to stake a tarpaulin over the corpse
to protect it from animals. No one answered.

"Gentlemen, when we return to the reception, forget what you
have seen here." Khorvat lowered his voice. "The ladies would be
alarmed by talk of a corpse near the ballroom." A card had been
played and nothing else would be revealed.

"We walked outside to look at the moon," Diakonov said.

"To share a cigar," another voice added.

Behind the men, the snow churned up by their boots was cast
into relief by the harsh lantern light. They should have been told
to walk on fresh snow, not over the first set of footsteps made by
witnesses or the murderer. A mistake. But the Baron was a doctor

and his expertise was with the living, not the landscape around a dead man.

"General Khorvat, I should examine the body at the hospital tomorrow. A formality, to establish cause of death. An account must be recorded. Especially since the corpse was found here at the club."

Deputy Diakonov, impatient with the process, thumped his gloves together. "Why are we talking over a dead Chinaman in the cold? Let's finish the vodka."

"You'll follow the doctor's request tomorrow at the hospital."

"He'll have his corpse." Diakonov hissed his acknowledgment.

They returned to the club, and servants knelt at the men's feet, drying their wet boots at the door.

The Baron calculated that the frozen body lay in a direct line from where he stood. He imagined that his weight balanced the dead man on the opposite end of a scale. A step, any movement, would upset the balance and the dead would win. His eyes closed.

Khorvat directed him into an alcove. "You tell the servants here to stay silent about this death."

So he had been ordered to threaten the servants. Did Khorvat really believe that they would keep a secret? "I can't carry around threats like a stick. I'm a doctor, not a policeman."

"Surely you'll survive the loss of your credibility with servants." Khorvat spoke quietly so they would not be overheard.

"That's my decision."

"Information does not belong equally to everyone."

"I'm a doctor and a health official. I need to evaluate how this unexplained death affects the city. Am I to stay blind and mute at your request?"

"The body will be delivered to you at the Russian hospital."

"And the other bodies left on the street?"

Khorvat demonstrated his lack of concern with a shrug. "Why am I always answering to you? We don't have enough soldiers to follow the trail of every dead Chinaman. I'd like to launch an investigation but who would back my decision? St. Petersburg? No. Only the *dao tai* has jurisdiction over the Chinese. He must act."

"The bodies were discovered in the Russian districts." He drew back, conscious that Khorvat was carefully studying his face in the light from the open door, and his cheeks reddened as if he had confessed to a fault.

"The bodies will soon be forgotten."

"Even Dmitry Vasilevich? His widow seems to have completely disappeared. Sonya Vasilevna, her stepdaughter, knows nothing. Unless there's news you haven't shared?"

"I grant you, the widow's behavior was peculiar. She fled without proper mourning. Unless she committed suicide from grief in a discreet place. If the widow had stayed in Kharbin, she'd get a hundred offers of marriage. Baron, what type of woman walks away from that security? There are few women here. Kharbin is a paradise for widows. It's suspicious. But what damage can a widow, a single woman, cause?"

"Dmitry's body was quickly buried. All evidence of his death was stripped from his home. The servants vanished." He watched Khorvat but sensed no willful deceit, only impatience with the conversation.

"Perhaps the widow had a jealous lover."

"An ideal solution, since we have no witnesses. No autopsy report."

Khorvat directed his entire focus on the Baron. "No. It would be ideal if Dmitry had been murdered by his Chinese cook. The *dao tai* would administer justice to the accused Chinese citizen and then the mercy of an execution. No Russians involved. End of case."

The Baron made his expression carefully neutral as if in agreement. This wasn't the place to issue accusations and demand answers. Khorvat's heavy hand was suddenly warm on his shoulder.

"Baron, it's to everyone's advantage to keep the system operating. Put Dmitry Vasilevich's death in perspective."

"The police?"

"I don't anticipate any conflict." Meaning they would follow Khorvat's orders.

They entered the ballroom. The Baron sensed they'd been marked by contact with the corpse. Or did he only imagine that voices became hushed, that people moved away as they stood in the doorway together? Khorvat recognized it too but quickly signaled to a waiter, and the tense atmosphere in the room was broken, the swell of music and conversation returned. They saluted each other with glasses of vodka.

The Baron managed to slip away. He hurried down a corridor past the dining room, following the noise of clattering dishes. The cooks didn't look up from the stoves as he entered the hot kitchen. He shouted in Chinese above the din, "Who is sick?" Startled, the kitchen workers stared at him.

"Who are you?" A rough voice.

"A doctor. Someone is sick here. The club will pay for treatment."

The uneasy kitchen workers were silent. One of the younger cooks stared at the floor.

"A worker is missing from his job in the kitchen. Who is he? Who saw him tonight? Does anyone know what happened to him?" It was pointless to threaten them to keep silent about a dead worker that no one would acknowledge existed. These wit-

nesses would never speak. The men in the kitchen shared the fear
of dismissal from their jobs, fear of an outsider speaking their language. "There's a reward for information about the missing man.
No harm will come to anyone who helps."

No one broke the silence.

If he'd spoken with them one by one, something might have
been discovered. No one confesses before an audience.

He returned to the ballroom. His vodka glass, a cold solid shape,
shook in his hand. He abruptly pushed his way through the room,
barely noticing the blur of faces around him. He slammed the rear
door of the building open, staggered into the snow. He squinted
into a pattern of white thrown by the wind, the snow flattening the
landscape, unable to distinguish the dark blanket over the body or
the tracks of a vehicle that he was certain had stopped to pick it
up. Bitter-cold air was driven into his nostrils, inside his throat.
Breathless, he flailed through the snow back to the building, closed
the door, and discovered that the glass had mysteriously vanished
from his hand.

Later that night, the Baron waved away the worried servant
who stumbled to meet him at the door with a lantern. He walked
through the house in darkness. His legs were stiff and he felt his
age. In the study, he lit a candle, and a slant of light crossed the
brush, inkstone, and paper on the table. He placed a thin transparent paper over a sheet of calligraphy written by his teacher. Stroked
the brush on the wet inkstone and held it poised above the paper,
waiting for his mind to settle into blessed calm. The first mark the
brush would make on paper, the *luo bi,* was the most important.
But the characters he formed were slippery, elusive as his brush
stroked them. He couldn't focus on the work. He cursed his lack of
control. His lack of courage with Khorvat and Bakai. He struggled
to quiet his breath. Let his eyes absorb the blackness of the ink.

His concentration was broken by an image of a body in snow. Black and white.

He was called by this image of the corpse as if he were a madman who reads sentences in a newspaper and is certain they're secret orders for him to follow. A grain, a black dot of suspicion, began to form.

CHAPTER SIX

The Baron asked whether tea might be prepared.

"My dear friend, I have always underestimated you. You are a mind reader." Dr. Francois Messonier transferred an unsteady pile of papers from table to shelf in his office. Two tiny cups, rimless as bells, made a dry, delicate sound as he placed them on the bare table. He lit the *daisu,* a small, traditional rectangular metal stand on four legs that held the kettle over heat. The Baron watched, soothed by these familiar preparations.

The two men frequently shared tea in Messonier's office at the Russian hospital or dinner in one of the better places, Felicien's or Palkine, for discussions, sometimes in French, about restaurants in Paris, the shortage of medical supplies in Kharbin, the endless bureaucracy, lack of trained assistants, their patients' distrust of treatment. Friendship broke their cold sense of isolation, as they were both critical of the ruling Russian establishment.

Before he accepted a position in Kharbin, Messonier had been head of the hospital in Mukden, where all Western doctors and the medical schools were under Chinese supervision. The French doctor had worked well in this situation, as it wasn't his character to directly challenge Chinese authority. He'd gradually mastered a halting, rudimentary spoken Chinese, which helped him survive the Boxer massacre in 1900. A young woman whom he'd once treated had hidden him from rebels in the woods.

"I've saved something for your special attention." Messonier cradled a small blue-and-white ceramic container.

The Baron smiled back at him. "Caviar? Imported hair pomade?"

There was a scraping noise as Messonier unscrewed the lid and produced a roughly wrapped thin packet tied with string. "Please do the honors, Baron."

He fumbled with the string and even before it was unwrapped, a strong earthy scent rose between them at the table. Inside the paper was a coarse brown disk that resembled tree bark. He closed his eyes and inhaled.

"This is *pu'er* tea," Messonier explained. "Very rare. The tea is one hundred years old. So they claimed. Fermented. Pressed into shape with a stone. Packed in a lead-lined leather trunk sent overland from Yunnan Province. Transferred to sampan and then steamboat up the Sungari to Kharbin."

It was a pleasure to share Messonier's bounty. A few months ago, he'd received a box from France and they'd divided the mirabelles, pâté, cognac, chocolate bars, and a tin of mustard.

The squat iron kettle reached a rattling boil on the *daisu*. Messonier poured water from the kettle over tea leaves in an unglazed clay teapot. Then he immediately emptied the water from the pot but saved the tea leaves. A second kettle of boiling water was added to the teapot. "Exactly twenty-five seconds to brew." He softly counted out loud.

Finished, the tea was poured into *gai wan,* small porcelain cups, each with a lid and saucer. "Count to five before you drink it."

The Baron sniffed the steam from the cup as he raised it to his lips. *Pu'er* had an intense mushroom aroma, woody, a damp forest, musty like clean dirt. Drinking and inhaling the tea was a single sensation, as the fragrance rushed into his nose and mouth, filled his entire head. He felt transported, as if he had opened a door into another season.

"I was told that *pu'er* can be infused ten times. The last infusion is the longest, ninety seconds."

He blinked with delight. It seemed the scent of the tea radiated from the surface of his skin. He felt himself slowing down. Only with an effort did he return to Messonier at the table, smiling beatifically. "Do you have a teacher? A master of tea?"

Messonier looked as if he'd been caught cheating. "A patient honored me by sharing her knowledge of tea."

"Payment for services?"

He smiled, raked the pale hair off his forehead. "No. It was purely a kindness." Inside the closed pot, tea leaves furiously unfurled in the third pour of hot water.

"I heard that another doctor taught patients recovering from tuberculosis to sing hymns in English. There you have payment in kind."

"Our church has forbidden the practice of indulgences." Messonier was a devout Catholic, unmarried, and so saintly that there had never been rumors about him with any nurses.

"Perhaps singing was part of the healing treatment."

"Perhaps hymns are required to fill beds at certain hospitals. I would not give such orders."

"The Scottish missionaries at the orphanage taught my wife to embroider and read English."

"What kind of life were they preparing her for?"

The Baron shrugged. "Li Ju left the orphanage when she was very young. She's continued her English lessons."

"She's fortunate to have a home," Messonier said, then swiftly added, "Not that she isn't perfectly happy with you."

The Baron was silent for a moment. "At times I find my wife profoundly puzzling. She always surprises me. She is a marvel." He was suddenly self-conscious about speaking so intimately to this man, a friend who was ten years younger. "I don't mean her beauty. Don't misunderstand me."

Messonier studied him, his eyes of a peculiar opacity, the irises like yellow lines, finer than stitches of embroidery. "There's no preparation for an enigma."

"My wife insisted on attending the reception at the Railway Club. Everyone ignored her except for Chang and General Khorvat."

"Always a gentleman." With the graceful gesture of frequent practice, Messonier again inclined the teapot over their cups. "You'll be delighted to hear I interviewed the sisters at the Hospital of Mercy as you requested. They are reluctant to disclose information. This you know."

"The capable Gorgons. No, I apologize. Forgive my words."

Messonier continued. "The sisters did acknowledge that several passengers from the trains had been admitted."

"The trains again. Do the passengers share a common ailment? Or are they simply held by the sisters under someone's orders? An arrest?"

Messonier slowly filled the two *gai wan* with tea while the Baron shifted impatiently in his chair. "The sisters wouldn't reveal the number of passengers, why they're under care, or who ordered them admitted. The contagious infections that could have affected passengers at this time of year are familiar to you—pneumonia, tuberculosis, whooping cough, scarlet fever. Unfortunately, the sisters wouldn't allow me in the same room as their passenger patients." He gently set the lids on the *gai wan* cups and handed one to the Baron. "But I was allowed to pray for the anonymous patients. Perhaps they're in quarantine."

"Mother of God." The Baron leaned closer, the cup in his hand precariously balanced.

Messonier's expression changed and his eyes narrowed with pleasure. "I hope you appreciate the elaborate lie that I spun for the sisters. Here is the name of the doctor who visited the patients. He also needs the intercession of the saints. Pray for him." He handed the Baron a folded paper.

Now he admired Messonier's strategy and his neat black handwriting: *Dr. Wu Lien-Teh.*

"Dr. Wu Lien-Teh is vice director of the Imperial Army Medical College of Tientsin. A graduate of Cambridge University. He recently arrived. Sent to Kharbin by the Chinese government, the grand councillor Na Dong, and the councillor of the Foreign Office."

"I don't know this Dr. Wu."

"You'll be introduced. Doctors can't avoid each other in this place."

"Dr. Wu may also be a surprise introduction for General Khorvat." He crumpled the paper. "A body was discovered outside the Railway Club during the reception. A Chinese man."

"Foul play?"

"I don't know. Khorvat promised the body would be moved to the hospital for a postmortem, but it was lost en route. Blame the snow, the cold, the lack of competence. Or something more deliberate. No one is responsible for the disappearance of the body, apparently."

"Do you believe it?" Messonier sipped his tea.

"I believe something is happening. I told you about the body outside Churin's store. And two bodies found at Central Station."

"Unusual number of homicides, even for Kharbin."

"Homicides? I'm not certain." The Baron fixed his gaze on the bookshelf behind Messonier. "Why wasn't I notified about the bodies? Is there a secret about the identities of the dead men? Cause of death? Some clue left with the bodies? There must be a common thread."

"Did you hear two dead men were found in Manchouli and Chalainor at the train stations? Deaths were also reported in Hailar and Puhudu. A friend at the Mukden hospital told me."

"No, I hadn't heard. Manchouli is north of us, several days away by train, near the border of Outer Mongolia and Russia. How did they die?"

Messonier shrugged. "Under investigation."

The Baron's eyes widened. He ticked off names on his fingers. "Manchouli, Chalainor, Hailar, Puhudu. The angel of death moved from town to town along the railroad. Then the angel brought death to us in Kharbin."

Messonier cupped his hands around the teapot as if to anchor himself. "But what is the angel? Or who is the angel?"

"Someone hid the evidence from us."

"From you. You're the only one that noticed a pattern. It couldn't be coincidence." His voice trailed off. "You're the chief medical officer. But someone isolated you from information. Perhaps someone from the CER or a government official made a decision without fully considering the implications. Or without consulting General Khorvat."

"Or perhaps in consultation with Khorvat."

"What next?"

"We try to stop the angel."

"She was dressed in a pink kimono, lying on a tatami on planks in the main room. All the servants and guests at the inn had left." The dwarf Chang sat across from the Baron in his office, waiting for tea, chair angled to catch the warmth from the corner stove. In another two hours, their breath would be visible in the large room after the balls of clay and compressed wood that burned to provide heat had cooled. "My source said the dead woman was an innkeeper on Koreyskaya Street. A Japanese woman."

"Who's your source? Who told you about this woman?"

"The cook. He entered the inn at number five Koreyskaya Street through the kitchen door. No one noticed him." Chang paused to dramatize his account of the story.

"Then?"

"Then he watched from the kitchen and saw the men huddle around the woman's body. Four men."

"Russian or Chinese?"

"He couldn't see their faces. They didn't speak Chinese."

"Maybe they spoke dialect. Or a code."

Chang laughed. "The cook wouldn't have the wit to notice a code. He was too frightened." He struggled to shape his next sentence.

The Baron waited, affected by the other man's unease.

"After the men left the inn, the cook crept out and looked at the woman. They had cut her open. Made a slit down the front of her body and then sewn her up."

The Baron bent forward as if released by a spring.

"Then three strangers came in dragging a wooden coffin. The cook ran back into the kitchen. The men knew what to do, went straight to her body. They dropped the dead woman in the coffin and threw the bloody mat on top of her."

The Baron's gulp of tea was automatic. A warmth in his mouth without taste. "I heard what you said but don't understand it." The mutilation of a corpse wasn't innocent. "You don't know how the woman died?"

"No. But if she had been Russian, not Japanese, there would be an inquiry."

"That's certain. Did the men take anything from the inn?"

"The cook didn't mention anything had been stolen. But he wasn't the best witness. He's afraid the woman's ghost, her *gui,* will come back and haunt him."

"You trust what he said?"

"I've watched expressions all my life. Who means to harm me. Who would mock me. No face is neutral. I say this not from complaint but because I'm a skilled observer."

"Can I speak with the cook?"

"Vanished. Probably working at another inn."

"So he won't be found." Another sip of tea. "Fortunately, whoever ordered the body cut up is unaware they've been discovered. We hold an advantage." Although he focused on the dwarf's face, his mind held the terrible image of a dead woman in a pink kimono.

"You have my silence." The dwarf's pledge was conditional, as it was likely he'd later embellish the story. "Maybe the dead woman was the mistress of a prominent man? A woman with secrets, murdered by order of an important official? Maybe the shame of pregnancy?"

The Baron made a decision. "The woman was dissected by someone trained in anatomy. A center vertical cut that opens a body takes skill. Bones protect the heart." He drank again, slowly, to stimulate thought. "The body was mutilated in secret because what they did was wrong. Disrespectful. Chinese tradition forbids opening a body. Once their work was done, it was easy to get rid of the corpse."

"Put a corpse outside and it will stay frozen until May."

"Snow aids those with something to hide. But the body was dissected at the inn, so there were no witnesses, which wouldn't be the case if it was performed at the hospital. The question is, who ordered servants and guests away from the inn? Someone knew to empty the place of witnesses."

The dwarf hunched down in his chair. The room had grown slightly less warm. "The cook told me others had vanished from the inn before the woman died. A kitchen boy. A guest who paid for a week in advance then disappeared after two days. Without collecting a refund. Then the lady innkeeper. People on the street say Russians will kill all the Chinese in Kharbin by infecting them with a secret sickness. Or poison. They say many deaths have been hidden. The Chinese feel threatened."

The Baron's hand tensed around the teacup. His immediate impulse was to argue against these claims, but there would be time and information later.

He pictured a diagram of the situation. A large circle contained everyone who knew about the dead woman. A second, inner circle contained those who mutilated the woman's body, placed it in a coffin, disposed of it. In the center circle was the organizer, the string puller, trap setter. Likely a Russian.

Early morning, an overcast sky, the Baron entered the inn at 5 Koreyskaya Street. Unlocked, the door opened into a dim central space. The lanterns were unlit. He sensed the room was large, judging by the temperature. He walked back and propped open the door with a chair so there was more light but there was no discernible change in temperature with the sweep of cold air into the

room. The large unrecognizable shapes on the floor became overturned benches and a table shoved at an angle against the far wall.
Dishes were scattered on the packed-earth floor. A scene of previous violence. The Japanese innkeeper's body would have been
situated here, in sight of the kitchen, directly under his feet in the
center of the room. Blood would have soaked into the floor. What
evidence did he imagine would be discovered? Perhaps a witness?
He cursed his optimism.

He called a greeting in Chinese. No answer.

He entered the corridor cautiously and moved toward the first
room, curtained with heavy fabric. It folded into stiff angles as he
slowly pulled it aside and ducked into the room. A small altar, a
stack of bowls and mats against one wall. He knelt to examine the
altar, the edge of the curtain brushing his shoulder. A rustle behind him in the corridor and a man blocked the doorway.

"Are you the cook? A guest here?" The Baron stood up very
slowly, keeping a distance between them, snugging the hood of his
coat around his neck as protection.

The man's breath heaved and his arms flailed as if he were
drowning inside his body. He gripped the curtain to steady himself
against the wall. Even in the faint light, his face was visibly flushed,
a dark liquid smeared over his chin. The Baron edged toward
the door to get past him, avoid being trapped in the room. The
stranger coughed repeatedly and gasped, clawing at the Baron's
coat. He twisted free, covering his nose and mouth, and blindly
shoved the stranger into the wall, flimsy as a bundle of cloth.

Wind had stripped and tattered the cloth flags in front of shops
along Novotorgovaya Street but sturdy signboards had been ham-

mered into storefronts, the walls of buildings, fences, wagons, and secured with rope around newspaper kiosks and lampposts, all of them advertising fortune-telling, *fu-ji* divination, *I-Ching* readings, magic charms, cures for fever, chills, aches, coughs, ailments. The messages were like holes made by weapons, proof of battle.

The Baron and Li Ju walked down four streets and she counted thirty-five signs. They stopped to read a large wooden board, its painted letters legible behind the snow that streaked across it. "A woman recently arrived from Tashinchiao has remedies for lung problems." The next sign promised a healer from Tientsin would cure all ill health. Fortunes told by a lady from Dairen. Fortunes told by a doctor, teacher, astronomer, scholar, priest.

She turned to him in fury. "Why didn't you tell me about these signs?"

Several people on the street stopped and stared, shocked that a woman would speak to a man in that tone of voice.

"I didn't wish to make you unhappy."

"Something is wrong. Did you think I'd never see the signs myself? I can read. I'm not a child."

He was silent to temper his reply. Not to meet anger with anger. In winter, conversation was fractional. Breathing in was a stab of cold air followed by a freezing rim around the lips as the voice was pushed out. Condensed moisture circled the nostrils, froze the inside of the nose. Ice formed on the eyelashes and eyebrows. He angled his head so Li Ju couldn't see his face behind the fur hood of his jacket. He'd give her the thinnest reply. "Superstitious fools. Trying to stir up business for themselves."

Li Ju answered with an exhale, an angry steam of breath.

Later, at home, their discarded boots wet on the tile floor, the troubling signs on the street were still between them.

"Explain the signs to me. They all offer help. Explain what I read." Li Ju's face solidified into a patient expression. "You know something. Or have suspicions." She'd detected his unease.

"The healers and fortune-tellers are making money from ignorance. The signs are just signs. One sign creates another. Like bubbles." His words were simple Chinese. When he was under stress, his command of the language faded; he grasped at words, forgetting the inflections at the end that could completely alter their meaning.

"People are frightened. I've heard talk in the market. They say the Russians kill people and steal their lungs, stomach, the guts from the dead, to make medicine. Is this true? Tell me. I'm not afraid." She could provoke him into a response or confession with a threat of independence.

The servants were shadows outside the room, listening, waiting to take their coats, mop the wet floor. He lowered his voice. "A group of doctors and nurses from St. Petersburg and hospitals in China will soon arrive."

"So they're here because of what the Russians have done?"

"General Khorvat isn't obligated to announce the new medical workers' roles. The hospital staff will expand but it isn't clear why this is necessary." A kind of shame, a lack of confidence, made the skin around his eyes wrinkle. "I was told another doctor has been appointed to the Russian hospital here. A Chinese, Dr. Wu. Educated in England. With his background, this new doctor could be a peacemaker between the Chinese and Russians. The fighting cats and dogs. I just observe for now, since their plans work around me. I don't know where in the circle I stand."

"Will you lose your position with the hospital?"

His eyes dropped. "Everything will pass." The gesture of his open hands was typically Russian, a silent code for her to decipher. She helped him remove his coat, pulling off the stubborn sleeves one at a time. The bulky, wet fur coat weighed down her arms. "What if the signs are true and there is something to fear?"

He swung around to face her. "Five bodies have been found in Kharbin. Chinese, and possibly one dead Russian. One of the servants, a kitchen worker at the Railway Club, was taken ill and found dead in the snow after you left the reception." He was surprised that he'd just described the man as ill rather than murdered. Was this a diagnosis? "Recently, a woman's body was found in Fuchiatien. She was Japanese, an innkeeper. Her corpse was brutally examined. I don't know how she died. But I'll find the answer." Distress in his voice.

Li Ju's eyes widened. "Who will help you?"

He ignored her indirect reference to his age, which was certainly unintentional. "Messonier has good counsel. We've speculated that all the deaths may somehow be linked. But we're only guessing." He deliberately didn't mention his conversation with Messonier about the deaths in Manchouli, Chalainor, and the other train stations.

The servants came in and bundled their boots and coats away, their faces impassive, although they must have overheard their conversation.

She closed her eyes, considered this for a moment. "You're concerned about bodies but not the dead. Because the five unfortunates weren't buried in their ancestral graves, they'll have no peace in the afterlife. They are cursed to wander forever as ghosts."

"*Gospodi-pomiluy,*" he whispered. "God have mercy."

"Let's go to bed."

"I have work to do at my desk." He kissed her, then left her alone with news of the woman's strange death.

Very late that night, the Baron assembled the tools for calligraphy in his study. He daubed the brush on the inkstone. Waited to relax his shoulders, steady his hand. He was overwhelmed by a formless sensation, almost vertigo, and his hand trembled. The brush fell from his fingers and rolled across the paper, trailing black ink like a violent slash. He stared at the black spoiling the white.

Anxiety was familiar, like a vine inside his body, holding him upright. He wanted to quit, set the brush aside, as he'd once wished to leave during a lesson when unfairly criticized by his father, but he stubbornly remained at his desk to hide his unhappiness.

Fate had taken the lives of four men and one woman but they didn't fall randomly as leaves. It wasn't coincidence. It was a warning. Their deaths might never be solved. Perhaps it suited the individuals who controlled or monitored the situation.

After a moment, he picked up the brush, cleaned it, let it slide from his fingers. He stared at the black water, dissolved ink from his brush in the rinse jar. Opaque, deep as a well.

Andreev was his companion at Central Station, the two men dressed identically as the crowd around them in bulky sheepskin coats, their faces half hidden by immense fox-fur hats. Andreev had confirmed the shipment would arrive on the afternoon train from Mukden and the Baron was eager to collect medical supplies ordered months ago. They had spent over an hour in the train station, watching the crowd, drinking tea, their damp coats steaming in the heat from the immense blue-and-white-tile stove in the corner. The Baron resented waiting for the perpetually late trains but Andreev wouldn't risk the goods being pilfered and then resurfac-

ing later at the market at a higher price. He broke off a chunk of
bubliki, a hard roll, and offered it to the Baron.

"The bread is firm enough to reset your jaw after breaking your
teeth. To your health."

He waved away Andreev's offer of bread with a glum expression.

"Have you made peace with the new corpse?"

The Baron stared back at him.

"The corpse at the Railway Club reception. In the snow."

"Hardly peace. May God have mercy. *Gospodi-pomiluy.*" Of
course Andreev would know about the death. He was a hovering
tiny eye, a fly, a shadow present during secret situations. "I'm prepared for the investigation promised by General Khorvat."

"Any progress with his promise?" By the tone of Andreev's
voice, it was obvious he was aware nothing had happened.

"There is always another official who lost the paperwork or
didn't receive the paperwork."

"We should just get on the next train and leave Kharbin. I
doubt the situation will improve." Andreev dodged a woman dragging a heavy pigskin suitcase. He made no offer of assistance.

The Baron encouraged this change of subject and asked
Andreev if he'd traveled in Manchuria. He'd once mentioned
visiting the remote northern territory, the ancestral home of the
Manchu.

"Yes. I made an expedition with a guide. We encountered the
Buryat, Oroqen nomads, and the salmon-skin tribe, who wore
clothing made from the cured skin of giant river fish. The kaluga
sturgeon were enormous. They said some were twice as long as
a man. But the worst terror was blackflies. Black clouds that
swarmed with a terrible noise like a machine. Our faces were covered with cotton masks, we put thin silk over the eye- and mouth

holes, but the flies still got in. We barely uncovered our mouths to eat. The stinging flies drove the horses crazy. It was a wilderness. No place to leave our mark." Andreev had been focused somewhere else but now his attention locked on the Baron. "Northern Manchuria is no refuge from Kharbin."

"Are you considering another expedition?"

"Only if desperate."

The Baron sensed his evasion clearly as if he'd made an about-face. "Now I'm curious."

Andreev tossed his head, stirring the feathery thick fur on his hat. "My contacts told me Russian officials have ordered a great quantity of barbed wire."

Andreev's words stuck like tacks in his skin.

A whistle blast simultaneously brought a low vibration under their feet as the train shook its way onto the tracks behind the station. The crowd immediately swept toward the huge double doors, a force of movement linking the entire room. A wedge of cold entered when the station doors were flung open by a uniformed soldier.

The waiting room had cleared and the Baron pointed at a figure slumped against the far wall. Andreev turned, but the Baron was already moving quickly across the room.

The Baron knelt by the still figure, pulled his jacket aside to check his neck for a pulse. His hand was batted away by the end of a rifle, and he turned toward two soldiers. He stood up too slowly and they shoved him away. A blanket was thrown next to the man on the floor and the soldiers grabbed his arms and legs, still slightly flexible. The man's arms flopped when he was dropped on the blanket. They carried the body, sagging in the blanket, toward a side door. A few people made the sign of the cross as the soldiers passed.

Andreev came over to him. "You should have given the soldiers orders. You're a doctor."

The Baron silently hurried after the soldiers, Andreev following.

Outside the station, they waited a moment for their eyes to conquer the glare on the snow. There was a narrow pathway, almost a tunnel, at the side of the building, carved in the deep snow by countless passengers. At its end, the soldiers were partially visible, swinging a long bundled shape into the back of a wagon.

Andreev raced ahead and the Baron struggled behind him, as slowed by the snow as if it were a thickness of blankets around his legs. Andreev reached the soldiers first, demanded to know where they were taking the body. The soldiers ignored him and yanked the tarp tightly over the corpse, secured it with rope at one side of the wagon. Andreev shoved a soldier and his fist swung back; the two men slipped and fell in the snow without injuring each other. Andreev staggered to his feet, swearing, wiping his wet face. Unconcerned, the soldiers drove away.

Andreev shoved the Baron into a waiting droshky. The driver whistled and they sped down Bolshoi Prospekt following the soldiers, the ice and mud thrown back by the horse stinging their faces. The cold air entered the Baron's throat like a screw driving in, his breath condensing into hard rivulets of frost on his beard and collar. The soldiers' wagon, tarp flapping, was just ahead of them and they expertly steered around an overturned cart. With evident pleasure, the Baron's driver slowed to watch Russians and Poles furiously arguing over the cart in the street until Andreev shouted and pummeled his thick shoulders.

The driver reluctantly set the droshky in motion, steering recklessly until they hit deep ice ruts and tilted wildly to one side, the horsehide blanket sliding off Andreev's legs. The two men clutched the seat for balance until the vehicle jolted upright. The soldiers' wagon was far ahead, past the Iverskaya Church, but they quickly narrowed the distance until their wheels caught in a thick snowbank. The chase was over.

The Baron looked at Andreev. Two idiots. Risking themselves for what?

"They must be preparing to unload crates from the train by now."

In the Baron's mind, the dead Japanese woman had the peculiar frozen luminosity of a saint in distress, her hair loose and untidy, her soiled pink kimono pulled open roughly so that the men, the doctors, could access her heart and lungs. Her face serene above their cuts and knives.

He'd just confided this vision to Messonier. "She haunts me. I know the woman was already dead, but I pray that the men who cut her open laid a cloth over her eyes to hide their work. To be merciful."

Across his cluttered office, Messonier waited for the kettle on the *daisu* to cool slightly. The warming teapot, filled with hot water, waited on the table behind him.

"Her body was cut up by a madman or a doctor," the Baron said. "From the description, it sounds like an autopsy. An autopsy without consent is a violation. A sin."

"An ugly incident. But who did the deed? And why?"

"The answer to *why* is that someone wanted to discover the cause of the woman's death. Make a diagnosis. Who made the cuts on the body? Surely a doctor." The Baron continued, his attention wandering from Messonier's process of tea making. "I went to the inn at number five Koreyskaya Street, where her body was found. The place was disordered and I thought it was empty but a man attacked me. Nothing serious. I wasn't harmed." He grimaced. "But I noticed his face was unusually dark red and splotched. He was obviously ill."

Messonier considered the Baron's description. "Perhaps he was an opium addict?"

"No. That would have made him lethargic, not aggressive. And his skin color was symptomatic of something else."

"Infection? Rash? Let me argue against you. Your attacker was drunk. Face flushed from alcohol." Messonier filled two cups with pale golden tea.

"Perhaps. I'm ashamed to admit it, but I didn't try to help him. I fled."

"You acted from instinct. You'd certainly never avoid helping someone. It's not your nature."

"Thank you, Messonier. In truth, I was afraid of the man. We were alone in the inn. All I know is that these events seem to have no answers when closely examined." His focus turned to the cup on the table. "By the way, the tea is very fine."

Messonier brightened. "*Luojie* tea. Mountain-grown. Did you notice its faint grassy scent? The tea leaves are unusual, pale yellow with thick white veins." He cradled the teacup in his hands. "By the way, Dr. Wu and a team of Chinese doctors, nurses, volunteers, and translators begin work at the hospital soon. Weather delayed some of their trains."

"Khorvat won't bow his knee to Chinese authorities. I know he wasn't pleased to have their new Chinese medical staff installed in his territory."

"The Chinese would never allow Russians to show them up. Dr. Wu has yet to put in an appearance but there are rumors he's been granted a laboratory in the Chamber of Commerce building."

"A bold choice." The Baron was incredulous.

"Yes. A strange location for a laboratory to test something unknown and potentially contagious. They said Wu wanted privacy to work. And there were no vacant spaces at the hospital."

"It's a marvel."

"Dr. Lebedev, one of the new doctors, is reluctant to discuss the situation. She claims the Russian doctors are in Kharbin only for training." Messonier hesitated. "I don't believe it. A great deal of money was spent transporting them here across Russia and Manchuria. They're on leave from their own hospitals. It makes no sense."

"Morning is wiser than evening, as they say." The Baron finished his tea. "I heard the hospital just placed an order for quantities of disinfectant, carbolic acid, gauze, soap, and rubber gloves."

"Curious. There's no evidence of typhoid or cholera at this time of year."

"Preparations for another Chinese rebellion? You'd think officials would notify us," the Baron said.

"Andreev is your source?" He'd once delivered an order of scarce high-quality gut and surgical needles to Messonier. The doctor had spontaneously embraced Andreev, rejoicing that the supplies would save lives, but the man had recoiled from his gratitude.

The Baron's expression confirmed this. "Officials have also ordered a shipment of barbed wire."

Messonier stood blinking for a moment before taking a vodka bottle from the cabinet and pouring it into the empty teacups. *Smorodinovka* vodka, slightly bitter with black-currant leaves. "I need something stronger." The drink marked a change in the conversation. He hunched over the table toward the Baron. "What could it mean? Barbed wire. Perhaps they anticipate an insurrection. A battle."

"They use barbed wire to mark territory. To keep out or keep in citizens."

"I predict they're gathering supplies for a siege. Or war casualties. A mission is under way." Messonier was glum. "Do you know if the barbed wire has been used in the city yet? Or anywhere?"

"No." The vodka's strong intensity of fruit on the tongue always surprised him.

"So we wait."

"If it so pleases God. We're here to be of service."

"Yes, serving at risk."

"I have a question." The Baron had heard rumors about Messonier and, under the influence of vodka, wondered if he'd confirm them. "Do you share your prize teas with someone else?"

Messonier's blush spread across his face and up into the roots of his pale hair. "Sometimes I share a cup with Dr. Lebedev. Dr. Maria Lebedev."

"I wondered. I saw you with a woman on the third floor."

"She speaks French like a native." Blushing again at the Baron's grin. "Studied in Switzerland."

"How does one conduct a courtship in Manchuria?"

Messonier lost his reserve and became very animated. "We meet at the hospital canteen for lunch. And dinner whenever possible. Our schedules are difficult. I gave her a can of chestnut puree, the last of my gourmet hoard for the holiday. Dr. Lebedev is so gracious that she almost refused my gift. I had to insist."

"Andreev can usually produce luxury goods. Gifts for fortunate ladies."

Messonier smiled cryptically, nearly demure. "The only goods I dare order from Andreev are for emergencies."

Vodka heightened the Baron's enthusiasm for his friend's tender new relationship. "It's a blessing you met each other. A miracle in Manchuria. I also found my wife here."

"We haven't spoken of marriage." Messonier's face was not as severe as his words.

Later, the Baron puzzled over what he'd learned about changes at the hospital. Perhaps it was foolish to wait until Khorvat or the authorities spoon-fed them information. Perhaps by that time it would be too late for an individual to develop a strategy for survival or escape. He had only hearsay and rumor and guesswork. Who had laid a path of clues, mutilated a body, cultivated secrets? A system that was fully confident about its power.

The only tangible fact was that Messonier had fallen in love.

Calligraphy was a forest. No, a labyrinth of spikes where a man could be lost. A sanctuary of discipline. The soft slide of his brush on paper released the Baron's anxiety. Each brushstroke demanded his focus and skill, but lack of control was evident at the feathery edges of characters where bristles separated, producing streaky ragged-textured lines known as "flying white." At a certain angle, he could see his moving hand reflected in the shining wet black lines as if it were disconnected from his body. A black shadow on black.

"Move your brush without fear," Xiansheng had instructed, quoting the master Li Ssu. "When you move the brush gradually toward the end of the stroke you will feel like a fish who enjoys swimming in the running stream." The Baron blinked, shook his head, and took a deep breath, as if he were a diver going underwater.

The Baron dreamed that night. There was a tunnel, its curved sides painted with Chinese characters. The tapering irregular forms and flourishes of the brushstrokes were tall as his body. He was overwhelmed by this calligraphy, unable to translate it. When he touched the surface with his hand, the jagged strokes were rough, coarse, and the contact woke him. *What were the words written in the dream? What was their significance?*

The Baron crossed the ornate foyer, tracks from his wet boots marring the freshly scrubbed marble floor. The night cleaners would soon eradicate evidence of his trespassing. He'd expected soldiers would be guarding the Chamber of Commerce building so his coat was open to reveal the sober Russian uniform underneath. It was usually enough authority to stop any questions, but if challenged, he would respond by offering a bribe—rarely unsuccessful—or threaten to report them for some infraction. This was standard in Kharbin.

Upstairs, the corridor was cold and the wall lights wobbly pinpoints in order to save electricity from the generators in the evening. He walked the length of the second and third floor until finding the door with Dr. Wu's name written in Russian, Chinese, and English in heavy gold letters, a ceremonial weight. He stood outside, listening, his breath irregular, tracing the pound of his heart into his arm and hand. His unease was located in the center of his chest, an aching pressure, as if he'd inhaled smoke from a fire. Perhaps age brought this symptom. A younger man would ignore it.

He took his pulse. It was elevated, but not dangerously. The laboratory was silent and the door was unlocked. He pulled a cloth from his satchel and swabbed the water on the floor from his boots.

Inside, he stuffed the wet cloth along the bottom of the door to block the light. He swiftly removed his thick sheepskin coat and draped it over a chair. For a moment, his eyes charted the surfaces in the room, the bulky dark shapes of desks and tables, thin reflected light from glass cabinets. Two cautious steps and his foot nudged a bucket, splashing a liquid across the floor. Water? This puzzled him until he realized there was no plumbing. A laboratory without running water.

The odor of formalin was traced into the adjoining room, where the laboratory was located. He switched on a table lamp, and light struck a wall of shelves lined with small covered glass specimen containers. Closer, he saw that each one was methodically numbered and labeled with a schoolboy's precision: JAPANESE FEMALE, NO. 5 KOREYSKAYA STREET, KHARBIN. The last line: DR. WU LIEN-TEH. The doctor had collected the body of the dead woman. Blood sucked from her heart with a needle, skin sliced thin as paper, guts opened and sampled, bones sawed. The fortress of the body destroyed by scalpel and knife, flesh pressed into petri dishes, slivered into containers, flattened on glass slides, divided under numbers and letters.

He was surprised by his tenderness for the woman's remains. The glass containers scraped against the metal shelves as he gently pushed them aside one by one, uncertain what he was searching for, using a pencil to avoid contaminating anything or leaving a fingerprint.

His sleeve brushed against a test tube in an upright stand, knocking it at an angle. He automatically reached to straighten it, then stopped his hand and awkwardly nudged the test tube back into place with the pencil. The drawers in the laboratory desk contained neatly packed equipment, all of it new: empty glass containers that softly chimed as they rolled against each other, pipettes, metal instruments, gauze, pencils, fountain pens, brushes, paper, ink pads. Innocent supplies. He turned to the immense cabinets lined with rows of leather-bound books, their spines tooled in gold.

Before opening the door of a cabinet, he carefully examined it for trick devices. His professor in St. Petersburg had tied small bells to the bookshelf doors in his library to prevent students borrowing books without permission. This policy ended when the students brought tiny bells to class, hidden in their pockets. On cue, jingling filled the lecture hall, their mocking laughter unnerving the professor more than the bells.

He pulled a random book from the shelf and opened it. It was blank. He angrily rifled through book after book, all of them identical, blank, to be filled with Wu's future research. He began to understand the way the man's mind worked. A book slipped from his hand, slammed flat on the floor. The sound seemed loud enough to blast the pages loose and send them flying. His head swung toward the other room as he waited for footsteps, the twist of the doorknob. Ten breaths. Silence. His fingers slowly unclenched.

In this calm state, he recognized a wish to avenge the dead woman. To humiliate Dr. Wu, prove his research incorrect, false, dangerous. Should he sweep his arm across the shelves and destroy the evidence? No. He'd respect the process. He was a witness who'd take only information, disturb nothing. Only his gaze would tamper with the order in the laboratory. His investigation was a precautionary measure, an extension of his work as chief medical officer.

Where were the autopsy results? Where was the diagnosis? The cause of the woman's death? The lab logbook?

He stood still, his awareness fanning out across the room. His hand shaped a curve; his arm described a wider curve.

Two thick black books were discovered in the drawer of the desk in the front room. He congratulated himself until he noticed his sweating palms had smeared the covers. The first book had only a few lines of cramped handwriting in English, an unrelated case history. The second book was written in Chinese and English.

Autopsy of a Japanese Woman. The District of Fuchiatien, Kharbin, Heilongjiang Province, Manchuria, China. November 1910.

Female corpse, thirty to thirty-three years old, well nourished, found on earthen floor in an inn. The room was cold. The woman's chest was cut open with little loss of blood. Death estimated ten hours previous to examination of body. Cartilaginous area / joints removed. Syringe (wide-bore) inserted into right auricle. Blood sample taken. A second long vertical cut exposed internal organs, lung and spleen. Sample taken with platinum needle. Two-inch-square pieces cut from lung, liver, spleen, and stored in 10% formalin solution. The remaining organs replaced in body cavity. The flaps of cut skin on torso sewn together. Corpse sponged clean and redressed in kimono.

The most recent entry dated three days ago:

All specimens from female Japanese corpse stained with Loeffler's methylene blue. Results confirmed after examination under microscope. Bacillus pestis. *Plague.*

His hands shook and he leaned against the desk to steady himself against the vise of this terrible discovery. An accident, a spill, and plague would free itself from the fragile jars and devour him.

Back in the lab, he stood before the shelves of glass specimen containers, the remains of the woman's body. He sensed something bright, an intelligence reflected back at him. Something with multiple eyes, like a hall of mirrors, a fractured consciousness watching him. A hypnotic command gripped him. Was it Medusa?

Frightened, he shouted to drive the vision away. He stepped back and spontaneously made the sign of the cross.

CHAPTER SEVEN

G od help us, we've been blind fools."

The Baron stood in Messonier's office, his open sheep-skin coat dripping melted snow on the floor. Messonier urged him into a corner chair and the Baron slumped in the seat, water puddling off his boots. "It's plague."

Messonier stared at him, uncomprehending, his tortoiseshell spectacles dangling forgotten from his fingers.

"The bodies of the dead on the street were hidden because they were evidence. It's a plague outbreak." His fingers tugged at his hair. "Have you vodka? Yes? Good. I don't have enough courage for tea."

Messonier quickly retrieved a bottle from the cupboard. "Who told you?"

"I entered Dr. Wu's laboratory. Without permission." He described the unsecured laboratory, the preserved specimens from the Japanese woman's autopsy. "Results of the Loeffler's test on the woman for plague were documented in Wu's logbook. They were positive."

Messonier stood in the middle of the room, holding the vodka bottle.

A sense of foreboding filled the Baron's head like music. "Like an idiot, I entered the laboratory without proper protections." He kept talking, reassuring himself, perhaps braiding a noose. "The Japanese woman was the only confirmed plague death. But everyone at the inn could be infected. And those who handled her body. Who knows how contagious it is? I trespassed but it was critical to know the truth." Was it his imagination or did an expression of fear flicker across Messonier's face? There was an invisible presence in the room. "I wouldn't be here if I believed it was a risk for you. I touched nothing that could put me in danger. Everything in the laboratory remained just as I found it. I didn't handle the specimens. I only read the logbook."

Vodka was poured and Messonier handed a full glass to the Baron. Then he fished a thermometer from a jar of disinfectant, held up the tiny silver wand, his expression a question. "This is probably overly cautious," Messonier murmured. He inserted the thermometer in the Baron's mouth and waited, counting under his breath, scrutinizing his face. "Time is up."

The Baron squinted at the thermometer, and its red line was within the normal range. He swallowed the shot of vodka, then dropped the thermometer in the empty glass with a sharp *ting*. He nodded at the other man.

"Welcome back. Even if you were ill, I wouldn't recognize your symptoms. I have no experience with plague."

The Baron noticed Messonier's slight hesitation. "So you won't order me into quarantine?"

"*Dieu.* You're the only doctor who has the ability to do something here."

"Now that you've cleared my good name"—he waved aside Messonier's protest—"let me make a prediction. The deaths at

Chalainor, Manchouli, Hailar, Puhudu, and south of us in Mukden were plague deaths. The infection must be spread by passengers on the train, station to station."

"The corpses from all the stations should be tested. We could learn how quickly plague spreads. Maybe the dead men were acquainted. Or they occupied the same train."

The Baron gulped another vodka. "Exhume the bodies. Freeze them. Ship them to Kharbin in lead-lined caskets."

"Even so, it isn't safe to transport them by train."

"Agreed. It would be a disaster if one of the esteemed shipping clerks on the CER train was curious about the casket contents. Perhaps deploy soldiers to escort the caskets here."

"You have General Khorvat's ear. But I imagine that tracking the bodies is probably impossible by now." Messonier looked stricken. "I just remembered Wu invited several men into his laboratory for a tour."

"What? Who?"

"The *dao tai,* the magistrate, and the chief of police."

"Holy Mother of God." The Baron imagined the men crowded into the small laboratory, curious innocents carelessly touching everything with bare hands, politely marveling at bacilli under the microscope's glass eye without comprehension. It was a fine theatrical show for Wu. A performing bear in a cage. "The men should all be isolated and watched."

Messonier raised his eyebrows. "Tell me which official would be willing to issue that order."

If the honorable officials had been infected during this foolish laboratory inspection, it would actually serve a purpose, creating alarm, bringing aid and money into Kharbin. If he survived, Dr. Wu would be elevated to prominence. Everything—rule of law, civic duty, a doctor's oath—was expendable.

The Baron groaned aloud but didn't realize it until he caught the concerned expression on Messonier's face. "How could Dr. Wu expose anyone to live plague bacilli?" he said.

"He's foolhardy. Or ignorant. Or a gambler. The new medical team arrived in Kharbin to counter the plague. Wait and see how it's announced."

"Doesn't matter. The plague has the next move." The Baron was swept by panic. He felt his jowls sag, mouth droop, brows join in a frown. He checked to see if Messonier had noticed that his features—eyes, lips, nose—had been pasted on a mask of fear. His next swallow of vodka was automatic, unstringing the tension in his body, and he experienced a momentary fleeting spaciousness from care, followed by dull apprehension.

For the first time the Baron sensed he was being watched. His calculations, the information he'd gathered in the laboratory, encounters with the sick, and rumors of the dead were known to others and had been tallied. Perhaps it was the dead woman in the inn who watched him. According to Chinese belief, those who were murdered, who were suicides, or who had no surviving male descendants to provide for them in the afterlife become *gui,* hungry ghosts condemned to wander for eternity.

Two bodies abandoned on the tracks at Central Station in Kharbin. A man's corpse on the street by Churin's department store. A partially clothed woman's body at a Fuchiatien inn. A man's body at the Railway Club. Some details of the corpses were similar: no broken bones, cuts, or visible injuries. Faces discolored. Clothing showed evidence of bleeding. Bodies may have been moved after death. All but one of them frozen. Cause of death: unknown ailment or misadventure. Only one body had been identified. No witnesses.

A massive red wax seal, blind stamp, and a tricolor ribbon were affixed to this official report. Without signing it, the Baron refolded the thick papers, careful of the wax seal, and gently returned it to General Khorvat. He'd been requested to review the document in Khorvat's office. Now he understood the loophole that the general wanted closed. He placed his fountain pen on Khorvat's desk to show he didn't intend to sign the report.

Khorvat ignored this. "Baron *le docteur,* once you've signed the paper, it will be translated from Russian into English and delivered to Dr. Wu. I believe in full cooperation with the Chinese. Any objections?"

"Please explain how the bodies found on the streets disappeared. Where were they taken?"

Khorvat snapped, "I won't rehearse my decisions with you. It's not for you to judge." His thick finger jabbed in the Baron's direction. "The five deaths are mysterious but don't merit extraordinary concern. Perhaps the dead were suicides. Took poison. Miscalculated a dose of opium. Or were drunk and froze to death. Not uncommon."

The Baron couldn't allow Khorvat to build a case for random deaths and then disagree with him. He'd risk insubordination and the general would look like a fool. His throat tightened with anxiety as he prepared to speak. "I visited Dr. Wu's new laboratory."

"And?"

"*Bacillus pestis.* Plague. The dead woman at the Fuchiatien inn was infected with plague."

"One infected woman. One. In a city of tens of thousands. A single confirmed death is sobering but not of great consequence."

He'd had a forbidding sense of recognition before Khorvat had spoken, anticipating his answer. "Yes, one woman. But everyone around her, the guests, former guests, and workers at the inn, should all be examined for symptoms. Residents from surrounding buildings should be questioned."

"We have no authority to investigate in Fuchiatien. No Russian soldiers, no officials are allowed in Chinese territory governed by the *dao tai*. It's their problem. I have other concerns."

"The residents of the Chinese district travel throughout the city every day. Fuchiatien is only two verst from your office. Anything contagious will immediately spread from there to here."

"Baron, I'm a soldier. I have a grasp of what's going on. I can recognize an ambush."

"General, I don't question your ability. I'm a doctor. I can anticipate the spread of infection."

Khorvat resisted. "The most qualified doctors and disease specialists are now in Kharbin as a precaution. They'll be apprised of the situation, and a plan will be unveiled. Everything has been considered. Once this sickness is identified—"

"General Khorvat, it is plague."

"We can make a policy. Until then—"

"You put the entire city in danger. Your decisions are ineffective until we know how plague spreads and how to contain it."

"You're an alarmist. I've been told it is spread by rats."

The Baron continued as if he hadn't heard him. "How contagious is plague? How is it treated? Who's susceptible?"

Without breaking eye contact, Khorvat lounged back in the chair, his confident posture enhanced by an unyielding uniform. "I simply cannot barricade everyone inside Fuchiatien. We depend on the laborers to run the city."

"The only option is to enlist Chinese officials to help. Search for the sick, set up a clinic, distribute information."

"No. We can't hand over responsibility to the Chinese. It's not our policy. A delicate situation. We must protect the balance of power. Better to avoid circulating too much information. It could cause panic."

"The dead Japanese woman at the inn was a warning. More deaths will follow."

"If there are any additional deaths, we will manage. A warning serves to keep us on guard. A window was opened but it will be closed."

The Baron was a stone.

After a few moments of silence, Khorvat asked the Baron what he was proposing.

He toyed with the fountain pen. "The Chinese trust me. I speak the language. I can go into Fuchiatien. Check the rooming houses and inns. Visit the eating places. Count the sick. Note their symptoms."

"Very well. Meet with this *dao tai* and request permission to inspect Fuchiatien. Be discreet. I don't want this information shared with other medical staff or doctors. Russians ask too many questions. Avoid them."

"Until?"

"Until a better time." Khorvat kept his finger on the scale. "In future, stay out of Wu's laboratory."

The Baron's grimace signaled his acknowledgment.

"Now. Enough of this miserable business." Khorvat pulled a bottle from under his desk. He nodded at the glass-fronted cabinet and the Baron retrieved two glasses behind the six thick volumes of the CER Annual Report 1909.

A generous pour of *zubrovka,* vodka steeped with stalks of buffalo grass. The fresh scent wafted into the room over their words of death and unknown death. He inhaled deeply and drank. One gulp. A tiny rim of heat around his lips. "What news of your villa in Crimea?"

"The last letter from my wife took five weeks to be delivered. She reported sultry weather. The workmen have completed the terrace. I picture myself sitting there. At a table. On the table is dinner. Roast veal with caviar sauce."

He could tell Khorvat was on the verge of inviting him to visit, his courtesy as host automatic. He couldn't imagine the general as genial host, wearing a thin shirt in the heat, his long beard blown by wind off the Black Sea.

"The blue sky over Crimea. I hope you'll be privileged to see it someday."

"Seems that more than distance separates us from that sky, General." The Baron signed the document with a flourish.

Khorvat poured vodka. "*Pust' angely tebia privet stvuyut.* May the angels greet you."

After another drink, the Baron left the CER building and walked into fresh snowfall. It was a dusting, not enough to hold the imprint of a boot on the ground.

In the Chinese Eastern Railway Club, a table the length of the grand assembly room was draped in white linen and set with over a hundred large and small plates of zakuski to welcome the new medical workers. The banquet was in the Russian style, so guests served themselves from huge cut-glass bowls of black and gray beluga, sevruga, and osetrova caviars, cold salmon, raw herring, anchovy paste, smoked eel and sturgeon, goose *en croute,* wild-fowl sausages, *pashto* made with boar, roast pheasant, suckling pig, and huge crabs from Vladivostok, their two-foot-long legs thicker than a man's thumb. Dishes of pickled mushrooms, preserved fruits, freshly grated horseradish, and mustards were arranged near twenty kinds of flavored vodka and two sherries for the women.

Most of the men, except for the newly arrived student doctors and nurses, wore dark Russian uniforms. The few women doctors and medical workers were in sober-colored civilian dress. It was a gathering of foreigners, nearly all strangers to one another, and there was an edge of tension that vodka didn't ease. Only the young volunteers at the far end of the table were lively, joking about the weather and the inadequate housing in the local hotels. The room was hot, humid, and smelled of roast meat and wet wool.

At the main table, Dr. Wu Lien-Teh, in a sky-blue Chinese uniform, had the place of honor between his young translator, Zhu Youjing from Soochow, and General Khorvat. Dr. Boguchi, the CER hospital supervisor, Mr. Kokcharoff, a government official, and Lin Chia-Swee, a tall Cantonese, were seated across the table.

The Baron arrived late and slipped into a seat next to Messonier, nodding to Dr. Iasienski, a Pole from the medical service of the CER. He surveyed the table and whispered, "I see General Khorvat has assembled the ark here."

A spoon chimed against a wineglass and General Khorvat stood up, towering over the table. He saluted the czar, "our Little Father," welcomed the medical staff as Kharbinskiis, praised future cooperation between Russia and China. Dr. Wu Lien-Teh was introduced as the chief medical officer, a position created for him.

Unsmiling and pale, Dr. Wu spoke a few halting Russian phrases thanking General Khorvat for his hospitality and assistance, then switched to labored Chinese, acknowledging Councillor Alfred Sze, representing the Ministry of Foreign Affairs; the *dao tai;* the superintendent of customs; and the *waiwubu,* head of the Foreign Affairs Bureau. He abruptly sat down.

The Baron exchanged a look with Messonier. "Dr. Wu isn't fluent in either language? Russian or Chinese?"

"He was born in Malay. Fluent in English, French, and German. Wu's assistant, Dr. Lin Chia-Swee, was his student at the Imperial Army Medical College in Tientsin."

"Dr. Wu is accomplished but he can't be more than thirty years old. How much experience does he have? But with the obstinacy of youth, he'll serve tirelessly as chief medical officer. General Khorvat can't be pleased that the Chinese sent their own man with an entourage."

Messonier frowned and flicked a finger over his glass to stop the waiter's pour of vodka. "I would wager that the Imperial Throne calculated that a Western-educated doctor would be acceptable to Russians. And who benefits?"

"We do. China maintains their illusion that Dr. Wu controls the situation for them. Who could criticize Khorvat for cooperating with a Chinese doctor at Beijing's request?"

"And our General Khorvat stands back, allowing the Chinese to make the errors."

"Clearly it's political. Not medical."

Messonier's chuckle was muffled by his napkin.

General Khorvat called for their attention. "Gentlemen and ladies. You may be aware of the recent unexplained deaths at Manchouli station, the intersection of the two great rail systems, the CER and the Trans-Siberian Railway. One week later, there was a second death at Chalainor, the station closest to Manchouli. Bodies were then found at Hailar, Puhudu, and Mukden, less than an hour away by train. Three, possibly four deaths here in

Kharbin. We suspect an outbreak of plague caused the deaths but this isn't confirmed. Plague has occurred in this region over the years. But Kharbin will be spared this misfortune because of our timely vigilance." Applause stopped his speech briefly before he continued. "Three patients are currently in the Russian hospital under treatment by"—he consulted a paper—"Dr. Wu, Dr. Mesny, and Dr. Lebedev. The patients are recovering under the doctors' excellent care. I myself have visited the ward. I would never hesitate to put myself in danger for the benefit of our citizens." He bowed slightly and stroked the length of his beard during the prolonged applause.

"Thank you. You're here in Kharbin, sent by your respective governments. In the unlikely event there are additional infections, everyone will be informed immediately. There's nothing to fear. Kharbin will continue to prosper with the blessing of the czar and the Imperial Throne in Beijing." Everyone at the long tables stood up to cheer.

The Baron observed there was no sense of menace at the mention of plague but a pleasurable swell of excitement, as if a plan to explore new territory had been announced. A plan of conquest. An opportunity to perform heroic work. The risk of failure or death was distant lightning.

The zakuski course was finished and the guests slowly moved, in a haze of intense conversation, to dinner tables in the next room.

The Baron spoke quietly to Messonier. "The situation is more serious than Khorvat admits. He does nothing but make a bloodless speech. And he ignores two crucial points."

"Which are?"

His voice was low so as not to be overheard. "First, how contagious is the plague? Second, look at the numbers. The new medical personnel outnumber the patients."

"You say we're overstaffed?" Messonier joked, his words a moat to keep fear away.

"Obviously, they anticipate an explosive increase in the number of patients. Numerous doctors and nurses will be needed."

At the table, the Baron switched place cards so he was seated next to Messonier. "Judging by the extravagance of the banquet, we are in crisis. All the years I've lived in Manchuria, I've never seen Russians and Chinese share a table."

For the first course, the waiters offered a choice of hot or cold soups, *botvinia, okroshka,* with tiny dumplings, or *pirozhki.*

Messonier's eyebrows lifted. "I believe my appetite has been diminished by your speculations."

"Enjoy yourself. This feast is unlikely to be repeated."

Noting Boguchi's quizzical expression, Messonier avoided his eyes and slowly dredged his spoon through the thick *okroshka* in the bowl.

A yellow wine, *huang-jiu* from Shaoxing, was poured as a concession to the Chinese, but the Russians ignored it for quantities of vodka. The entrées were elegant and substantial: sturgeon in champagne sauce, partridge fattened on juniper berries, roast saddle of goat, suckling pig with cream and horseradish. Strong punch marked the introduction of lighter fare, cucumber salad and cauliflower with sauce Polonaise. Dessert was a towering *babka yablochnaya.*

The Baron murmured praise for the dinner and introduced himself to the translator Zhu Youjing and Dr. Iasienski.

The waiter inserted a tray of fruit ices between them. The hours-long dinner was nearly finished.

Afterward, the Baron waited patiently with other officials for an introduction to Dr. Wu. Up close, the doctor was very boyish in a collared jacket and trousers tucked into high leather boots. Vodka had made the Baron careless and he automatically addressed Dr.

Wu in Chinese, a standard pleasantry of welcome. The translator Zhu Youjing quickly answered but Wu had lost face in front of officials and his cheeks flushed. The Baron hastily apologized in Chinese and then awkwardly in English.

Cold-eyed, Wu accepted his apology. "We can speak in English, German, or French, as you wish, Baron." They agreed to meet again the following week.

The Baron joined his hands in front of his chest and bowed slightly, making the *gongshou* courtesy.

"I will make arrangements for your meeting, as Dr. Wu is very busy." His translator's Russian was excellent, his *r* sonorous.

The Baron noticed Messonier edging his way toward a blond woman in the group gathered around two polite young men, medical students from Peking Union Medical College, a missionary institute.

Wang, the tallest junior doctor, was clearly excited to discuss his first assignment in Kharbin. "We'll monitor arriving and departing passengers at Central Station, where we're most useful. We watch for those who seem uneasy or sick, check their symptoms, and take their temperature."

Several men praised their sacrifice.

"Sacrifice?" The second young man's face creased with worry until a waiter approached with glasses of vodka on a tray.

Someone asked him about the sanitary measures in the train station.

He looked blank until Wang broke in. "Thermometers will be sterilized in alcohol after each use."

"You'll need rubber gloves and hot water. A mask. Memorize *shidan suan,* the word for carbolic disinfectant." The Baron's voice was gentle. "You'll be at risk, exposing yourself to so many people day after day."

"Especially the many foreigners at the station. The dirty Chinese." A Russian drunk spoke from the crowd.

Dr. Wu didn't change expression at this insult and Messonier looked at him in surprise.

"Anyone can carry an illness. Anyone can be infected." The Baron challenged the speaker, who was drunker than the others. "No weapon or shield can protect you."

"Not true. Imperial Russia protects you. Every measure is taken to safeguard your health. No need to be concerned." Dr. Iasienski addressed the two young Chinese doctors but his eyes were on the Baron. A warning.

"You see? Your safety is guaranteed by one of Kharbin's highest medical authorities." The Baron's gesture was expansive and mocking. Possibly at this point, some of his colleagues marked him as insufficiently loyal.

The blond woman addressed Dr. Iasienski. "I'm Dr. Maria Lebedev. Is there a report about the exact dates and the pattern of contagion, since the train stations are under surveillance?" The pale braids circling her head were harshly sculpted by electric light from the sconce.

"Only vigilance and caution will subdue the beast," said Dr. Iasienski, then added, "God willing."

Messonier cleared his throat but Dr. Maria Lebedev ignored him. "I assume an official report will be distributed at our first general meeting?"

"Let's not review medical issues here. It's inefficient gossip after a banquet," interrupted Khorvat.

"The most accurate information sometimes comes from unofficial sources." Dr. Maria Lebedev smiled at Khorvat. Because women's opinions were generally ignored, only a woman would dare challenge the general.

The Baron resisted the urge to kiss her hand.

An awkward silence as they waited for Khorvat's response until Messonier spun a comment. "Dr. Lebedev just arrived from Switzerland. A volunteer."

Khorvat's voice boomed. "Welcome, Dr. Lebedev. Impressive that you wish to immediately begin work."

"The situation seems to require immediacy." She didn't back down.

"We are absolutely ready if a crisis should arise." Khorvat's eyes flickered over their faces to see who dared disagree. They were silent and only the slightest movements, a hand in a pocket, an exchange of glances, betrayed their unease.

Messonier's thin laugh. "I'd best go home and prepare for battle."

"Or prepare a last will and testament. Depending on your faith," Iasienski joked.

"No. That would be bad luck." Dr. Maria Lebedev touched Messonier's arm.

When Khorvat was alone, waiting for a servant to bring his coat, the Baron approached him. "Dr. Wu is very young. But spirited."

Khorvat was benevolent after vodka and his favorite caviar. "Wu has Alfred Sze from the Ministry of Foreign Affairs as a supporter. Sze has Grand Councillor Na Dong as his patron. They can speak directly to the throne in Beijing. Although we'll see if it's an aid or a hindrance. The Chinese dream that they can battle an outbreak of plague alone. They don't recognize the peril of their position. If they don't stop the plague, Russia and Japan will help them."

"With their armies?"

"There are many kinds of help. But the important thing is that Dr. Wu cooperates with us."

"He will be embraced by the hospital. We've always been under-staffed." Not the correct answer but vodka would smooth over the general's memory.

The Baron heard indistinct voices, a pattern of orders and ac-knowledgments, as he entered the magistrate's audience hall. The *dao tai,* who represented the Qing imperial government, was a hunched silhouette in an elaborately carved chair, his jacket stiffly embroidered with waves and twisting figures of beasts, their intri-cate rainbow colors diminished in the hall's light. Attendants stood beside his chair.

As a mark of respect for the *dao tai,* the Baron had pulled his sleeves down over his hands and made the courteous *gongshou* bow. The *dao tai,* unblinking, registered no surprise as the Russian made the usual courtesies in Chinese. He was allowed to continue.

"Your Honor, a mysterious illness has taken the lives of several Chinese. I beg permission to inspect inns, homes, and eating places in Fuchiatien to find others suffering from the sickness."

The *dao tai* nodded and slumped forward. His attendants glared at the Baron as if this discourtesy were his fault. The *dao tai* abruptly jerked his head up again. "Will the sick receive treat-ment?"

"Yes. They will be taken to the Russian hospital." If the *dao tai* refused the request or asked for time to consider it, Russian sol-diers would probably conduct an inspection without permission. The *dao tai* would be foolish to risk losing face for the sake of a few poor laborers. Possibly he expected a bribe.

The Baron continued his role as a supplicant. "The situation needs your strength and wisdom." He believed these words at the moment they were spoken. "We also ask for doctors to monitor passengers departing and arriving at Central Station. We must be vigilant." This request was purely a courtesy, as CER trains were owned by Russia and their soldiers would enforce inspection at the station.

Unfocused, the *dao tai* blinked and slumped deeper in his chair. The Baron realized he was an addict. Opium. The wait for his reply could be lengthy. He shuffled his feet.

What was he doing in this role? Standing between two corrupt systems, a negotiator like his father, the diplomat. No escape from family or the past, even here in Manchuria. He'd sworn to avoid situations where he would represent the government, the instrument of empire.

The *dao tai*'s soft voice offered an agreement. With the slightest motion of his hand, he granted the Baron and those he represented power over his most vulnerable subjects. Letters of agreement would be exchanged with Russian officials to permit inspection of Fuchiatien. Men could disappear in the space between the two countries.

Perhaps this agreement would allow the Baron to save a few unfortunates. He was the worm in the bud, a broken thread in the official fabric. Perhaps his father had also recognized his own helplessness.

Afterward, the Baron met Chang in a teahouse on Kitayskaya Street in the Pristan quarter. The place was crowded and its smell of damp shearling, sweat, and burning wood was familiar.

"Yes, better now." Chang rubbed his jaw, a gesture to soothe his nerves. His fur hat leaked moisture from its dusting of snow onto the table next to the Baron's cup. "My droshky got stuck. Tipped at an angle in the snow. I was dumped out. I walked from Novotorgovaya Street here to the *chaynaya* teahouse. The snow wasn't cleared away even in front of the stores. Would have been easier for longer legs."

"I'll order tea for you." The Baron gently waved in a waiter's direction and turned back to Chang, his face displaying his concern.

Chang continued talking as if he hadn't heard the Baron's offer. "Sunlight glared off the ice in the harbor, so the street was blinding white. Then I see a hand sticking up from the snow. Right in front of me. This close." His arm stretched across the table. He spoke quickly, an exorcism to free himself of the experience. "I started shaking. The hand was so white I could hardly see it against the snow except for its shadow. And blue fingernails."

A waiter shoved the teapot on the table between them and hurried away.

"Doctor, do you have anything to help me sleep tonight?"

"Perhaps." The Baron automatically checked the teapot, stalling for time while his thoughts raced. He imagined locating the buried corpse, testing it for plague, presenting his discovery to doctors in the hospital. "You didn't touch the hand? The corpse?"

"I wouldn't have touched the hand even with a shovel."

"I'll file a report. Can you remember the location of the body?"

Chang was gratified by the Baron's serious attention to his story. "Between Kommercheskaya and Kitayskaya Streets. Tell me what you'll report."

"A body was found." The wooden table was so rough that the teapot scraped as the Baron pushed it across to Chang.

The dwarf was puzzled. "That's your report?"

"It's enough to launch a search for the body. Once it's found, the cause of death can be determined."

"The mysterious sickness?"

The Baron was careful. How to warn without alarm. "A meeting has been called tomorrow for the entire medical staff. I'll have more information. What steps will be taken. What I can do."

"I'm not a fool."

The Baron's nervousness stopped words in his throat. "I'm told there's no need for alarm. I've told my wife the same thing. Has anything changed at Churin's?"

Chang frowned. "Churin's store wishes everything to appear the same during this crisis so shoppers have confidence to spend money. So I remain at the door."

"I hope they've increased your pay."

"I'll probably die before I'm paid. But what are my chances of meeting someone with plague? I hear gossip. Terrible rumors about unexplained deaths."

The Baron tightened his grip on the cup. "Ask your fortune-teller."

"I may start to cross myself each time I open the door for someone at Churin's. Ask for a blessing. But I'm lucky to work. I wait inside the warm store, step outside only to open the door for a shopper. I keep my distance. There's plenty of fresh Manchurian air between me and the customers. But the rich are probably healthy."

"Anyone could be infected. Beggars, officials, newspaper sellers, the elegant Polish woman who sells fur coats. They're all dangerous."

"You're dangerous."

The Baron felt Chang's words had the weight of stone. "God have mercy, yes. I know. I'm afraid to leave Li Ju alone or send her away."

"Li Ju knows your indecision. Chinese women are superior judges of character. They gossip and observe, since they're mostly restricted to the home."

The dwarf had wild tales and a wealth of superstitions from his patchwork life. The Baron had once dismissed him as an exaggerator but now eagerly sought his opinion. He laid the template of Chang's words against his knowledge of his wife like transparent paper to see if it was true. Li Ju grew up under care of the sisters at the Scottish mission. Perhaps they had instilled in her shyness, a sense of not-belonging, a lack of place that was like homesickness. She usually deferred to his decisions. Surely plague wouldn't choose her as a victim. She'd achieved happiness after a struggle.

"Tomorrow at noon I'll burn mugwort in my courtyard. Mugwort drives away devils that bring misfortune." A belief gathered on Chang's travels.

"Devils may need something stronger than a burning herb."

"No." Chang lifted the teapot lid and inhaled. "What's in here? Silver Needle tea. Possibly *baohao yinzhen*? Needs another minute to brew. Listen to me. I'm proof that these charms work. If I had been born a girl, with my short legs, I would have been drowned. I was nearly drowned anyway. Fortune rescued me. And now I'm in uniform at Churin's every day. A gentleman's job. My hands are clean."

"Truly good fortune. But have you noticed anything unusual?"

"People seem cautious these days. A woman told me that her husband told her to avoid crowds. No shopping. But she does as she pleases when he's away. She likes to spend his money. She knows her value."

"There are so few women in Kharbin."

"Women are a problem. Did you hear that the wives of Russian officials complained about the prostitutes on the train? Somewhere between St. Petersburg and Transbaikalia, the wives refused to sit in the same car with them. Maybe it was the women's conversation? Or their perfume? So now unmarried women who travel

to Kharbin sit separately from the married women on the train."
Chang grinned. "Russians scorn the Chinese. Now they scorn unmarried women. Russians are very cautious citizens."

In the room behind them, men began to shout at each other.

The Baron raised his voice. "Russians also hate the Japanese."

"Wise choice. You may pour the tea."

The Baron carefully filled two cups. "Russians weren't wise
enough to avoid battle with Japan six years ago near Vladivostok.
Now we have hundreds of Russian veterans wandering our streets,
still carrying guns. Trying to live on miserable pensions."

"I've seen them. I see everyone come and go from Churin's.
Watching is my work. I know when someone will sneer, mock me,
when a hand will become a fist. I have my own revenge for these
betrayals." He delicately sniffed the steaming liquid in the cup. "I
used to be stopped by people who thought I was a child, a boy, because of my size. Men called to me. I would skip, wave, pick up
stones to toss like a child to lure them. I admit I was excited. I allowed men to follow me, then I'd shout at them in a deep voice.
Or whirl around to show my face to see them jump. To frighten
them. They learned a lesson from me." His expression was mocking. "Although some men were furious at being tricked and threw
things, chased me. I never walk on an empty street. Mercy, no.
Some men did pay me. Their guilty coin."

The Baron was troubled by the other man's—what? Calculation?

Chang stared at the Baron, slightly reluctant to continue. "I had
the idea to punish these men. Let them get close, then a little flick
with a knife. Maybe my lesson would save a child from a bitter experience. You understand?"

"If you arrive bleeding in my office, no questions will be asked."

"Don't tell me to be careful."

"Never."

Chang leaned forward. "I'm certain I was approached by a Russian official. I recognized him a few days later when he walked into Churin's."

"Did he see you?"

"It's difficult not to notice me."

"What did he look like?"

"Everyone looks tall to me. He had a pale mustache. A fur hat. About your age."

The Baron felt his face fold into sorrow. What could be done? Kharbin was a city of men, not mothers. "Every week, the ferries deliver women and children to their new masters, who meet them at the wharf. The newspaper reports this slave dealing but there are no arrests. No protests. Nothing boils."

"Change has a fixed path. The poor slaves met their fate." Responding to the Baron's expression, he said, "There's another old saying: Life commands us to climb a mountain of knife blades."

"Yes." The Baron's fingers pressed against the teacup but he didn't feel its comforting heat, his thoughts elsewhere, mind separated from body.

The Baron watched the hands and face of Dr. Wu Lien-Teh across the table in the hospital conference room, trying to anticipate the man's strategy, waiting to see how he was revealed by fleeting expressions and movements. Wu rested his folded hands on the table, a schoolboy's gesture. It was traditional etiquette for the Chinese to show their hands with great discretion. The Baron was ashamed of his judgment, his immediate assumption of superiority. Gazing around the table, he knew several of the other doctors—

Zabolotny, Lebedev, Messonier, Mesny—were locked into an un-spoken alliance against Wu, the foreign interloper. Their shared hostility was clear as ripples in water.

They hadn't anticipated China would appoint their own rep-resentative as health commissioner to manage the epidemic. It was unprecedented. Dr. Wu had been given unusual power and then inserted it between them at the Russian hospital. But his youth, inexperience, and the fact that he wasn't fluent in Man-darin or Russian reassured them that he was a puppet figure, someone to dismiss, work around. Wu had stepped into a cold winter.

Without hesitation, Wu confidently introduced himself in three languages, explaining the meeting would be conducted in English, the language shared by the majority. Zhu Youjing, his interpreter, would translate into Russian, Chinese, and French for benefit of the interns, medical staff, nurses, and volunteers seated along the sides of the conference room.

He continued, "Many questions about the plague can't be an-swered at this point. But the first approach to any puzzle is to look at what surrounds it. Why were bodies of the plague victims aban-doned? Was it self-preservation? Or because the bodies couldn't be buried? Do the bacilli enter the body by contact with an infected person, hidden in their saliva or breath? Is it transferred by a con-taminated object, such as bedding or clothing? Or a bite from an animal or insect? The situation is grave but we can control it at this early stage."

Dr. Gerald Mesny, a French surgeon and professor at the Peiyang Medical College in Tientsin, immediately offered an an-swer. "Two years ago, I served as the official medical expert in Tongshan, where rats spread bubonic plague. Rats and their fleas also caused epidemics in Cochin-China, Hong Kong, and India.

I worked in these locations. The plan is simple. Exterminate rats and plague will vanish."

"I have another point of discussion." Dr. Danylo Zabolotny had arrived in Kharbin five days ago from St. Petersburg. "I was told about a donkey whose owner died of plague in Kharbin. A second man purchased the animal, touched its bloody muzzle, and he died the next day. The terrible chain of infection will be stopped only by killing all animals contaminated with fleas, not just rats." Zabolotny, a renowned bacteriologist from the Imperial Institute of Experimental Medicine, was a short-tempered man, vain about his appearance.

"Kill the mules, pigs, cats, and dogs that live with the dirty poor. Close the Chinese markets. Raze these filthy places. Every Chinese hovel in Fuchiatien must be burned." Mesny sat back in his chair, polishing his spectacles, pleased with his drastic solution.

"For the love of God, we have no right to destroy homes. Where will you shelter thousands of people? Who will pay for their property?" The Baron's stare circled around the faces at the table.

Zabolotny said, "We're doctors. Housing isn't our jurisdiction. The government must organize sheltering the homeless. A task for General Khorvat."

"He's correct. We do whatever necessary. Save your sympathy for the dirty poor." Mesny directed his comments to Wu.

Uneasy murmurs from the others around the table. Maria Lebedev didn't hide her anger.

The Baron said he had a story to illustrate his point. "I'll talk you through a map of how plague spreads. I heard it from a friend. A woman brought a fine sable coat into a pawnshop. Five days later, the man at the counter died of plague. Then a second employee died of plague. The policeman who guarded the shop died. In twelve days, thirty-five people traced to the pawnshop died of plague, including the proprietor—a millionaire—and his entire family. The plague spread from person to person because of their close contact, not from fleabites. They infected each other. If you don't agree, tell me your theory."

Zabolotny crossed his arms against this challenge. "Simple. The sable coat was infected with fleas. The fleas carried plague, since they'd previously bitten rats infected with plague. Fleas jumped from one person to the next, bit them, and they all died."

"Wrong." The Baron kept his patience. "We can discuss theories about how this plague spreads, but nothing is yet proven. We're guessing. But it's urgent to protect the uninfected to break the chain of infection. Let's start with this room. We—the medical staff—need masks, gloves, and disinfectants in order to work."

Mesny made a show of dismissal, tapping his fingers. "A mask won't protect anyone from the bites of infected fleas."

The Baron waited to discover if he had any allies besides Messonier, who finally broke the silence.

"Even if rats spread plague—and that is pure conjecture—it's possible our epidemic isn't bubonic. As you know, there's more than one type of plague. Or perhaps it's an outbreak of septicemia. There isn't enough information. The bacteriologists must analyze how plague attacks the system. How it kills. But regardless of its type, preventing it from spreading is crucial." Messonier nodded at the Baron.

Zabolotny was exasperated. "It is a matter of terrible urgency. The plague must be stopped before it reaches the Great Wall at Shanhaiguan. It could then strike Beijing and spread to Japan, Korea, and Russia. Millions could die—"

"Meanwhile, all our patients are dying here," Dr. Maria Lebedev interrupted.

Wu ignored her to argue with Mesny. "There's no proof that the plague here is the same type you previously encountered in Tong-shan, Dr. Mesny. You said it was bubonic plague spread by rats and their fleas. However, not one of the patients I've examined have swollen glands or buboes in their armpits or groins. Where is your medical evidence? Your proof?" The young doctor's arrogant confidence didn't make it easy for the other doctors to accept him.

Mesny angrily answered Wu's challenge. "I am totally confident of my analysis. Dr. Wu, I've worked as a doctor practically since you were born. You're twenty-nine, thirty years old? You're the novice here. You have no expertise. You'll do better to listen and observe. That's the way we work in the Russian hospital. What can you tell us about plague tests?"

With little enthusiasm, the translator repeated Mesny's words in Chinese, his tone of voice clearly expressing his opinion. Tempers simmered while they waited for him to finish. How long before Wu interrupted this endless posturing? No one would take advice, respect another opinion, unless it was based on fact. But there were few facts.

Wu's anger was subtle. He'd studied bacteriology and his reply was easy. "Let's not debate expertise. A patient's sputum was recently cultured and analyzed in a laboratory here. The sputum was placed on a thin layer of agar jelly, inserted in a glass tube, sealed with cotton wool and paraffin. After twenty-four hours in an incubator, a thin crust of live plague grew on the jelly. Billions of bacilli. Highly infectious. That small glass container held the most dangerous thing in the world." Wu's posture relaxed slightly, confident the debate was closed. The autopsy performed on the Japanese woman wasn't mentioned. "Several government officials also viewed the bacilli through a microscope."

"As if government officials knew what they were doing," Mesny muttered.

The Baron studied their faces. Surely some of the doctors were aware Wu had obtained the plague bacilli sample from the secret autopsy on the Japanese woman. Who had collaborated with him, used a scalpel on her body? The doctors had traded sentences with each other, back and forth, like cards laid on the table, each with a different value. Wu had no allies.

Wu caught the Baron's sympathetic look and frowned. "I met with the consuls general of France, the United States, Great Britain, and Japan yesterday. They fully support my decisions. Now, let's continue." His expression betrayed the slightest anger as he waited for the translator to catch up. "I need to be briefed about what steps have already been taken to control the outbreak."

The doctors were silent until Zabolotny responded. "We've closed a public bathhouse. Six people possibly infected with plague are now under strict surveillance. There are also five patients at the Russian hospital, isolated in a special ward, and there's room to accommodate a few more. Dr. Lebedev and Dr. Mesny are in charge."

Wu asked if the patients had all been tested for plague.

Lebedev answered that she was a doctor, not a microbiologist. She turned to Zabolotny for an answer.

Wu ignored her pointed gesture. "Tests will be ordered immediately. Let's agree this outbreak has been unquestionably identified as plague. But there's still the crucial question of how it's transmitted. Our strategy hinges on how the infection spreads."

The Baron continued the discussion. "What do the infected have in common? Are they related? Did they share a bed or a meal? Is there something that makes them susceptible to the plague? How contagious is it? What's the incubation period? Bear with me for a moment. I say we don't know the face of our enemy. It's as if we're trying to identify something while blindfolded. We feel the presence of heat but cannot identify the source. Bonfire, stove, samovar?"

"Exactly." Messonier acknowledged the Baron. "We must work around the gaps in our information." He addressed Maria Lebedev. "Dr. Lebedev, were you able to interview your patients? Any clue about incubation time before their symptoms developed? How they were infected?"

She opened a thin file on the table, her posture as rigid as her blond braids. "I apologize, but the few patients I've treated were either too unstable to speak clearly or refused to speak. Language is a problem, since there's no Chinese translator in the hospital. I suspect patients withhold their names and addresses to protect their families."

"Wouldn't give their names? And they're in our hospital? Extraordinary." Mesny sat back in his chair.

She leaned forward and locked eyes with him. "The Chinese patients were forcibly brought to the hospital. I think," she said slowly for emphasis, "it isn't unexpected that they wouldn't cooperate. They fear that their families will be taken and imprisoned. Why would they trust us? Our patients' mortality rate is one hundred percent. Some patients die immediately. Others linger for a day or two."

"I've never heard of an illness that's one hundred percent fatal," Mesny answered. "No, that cannot be correct. It's the doctor's skills that are at fault. Poor treatment."

"You should apologize to Dr. Lebedev for that statement." Messonier sat straight up in his chair and glared at Mesny.

Voices were raised in protest and repeated more loudly by the translator. Mesny pushed his chair back as if to leave the table.

"Gentlemen. And Dr. Lebedev." Wu's quiet words calmed the room.

The Baron regretted the doctors' abrasiveness; it was a sad lesson for the young medical staff observing them. "Everyone shares the same goal, Dr. Mesny."

It was impossible to dissolve Maria Lebedev's composure and she continued as if there had been no interruption. "I could make suggestions about how to improve conditions for patients."

Zabolotny insisted the patients must be made to talk. "We have an explosion of infections and you're concerned about the patients' comfort? What kind of treatment is this? Everyone infected must be hunted down."

Messonier spoke up for her. "Give us your analysis of the illness, Dr. Lebedev."

"There are several types of plague, as we know. Our plague may be a type of virulent pneumonia. The lungs are affected. At its last stages, the patients have high fever, rapid pulse. Cyanosis. Breathing is labored. Coughing fits with considerable bloody sputum. Death is quick."

They agreed to quarantine all infected patients in the ward at the Russian hospital and additional beds would immediately be brought in. Sick travelers discovered on the trains would be transported from Central Station to the hospital for observation. General Khorvat would be asked to organize a citywide measure to eradicate rats, to placate Mesny. These decisions broke the tension in the room.

Zabolotny joked that he had nightmares about men invading his home and dragging him away. "I take my own temperature eight times a day now." The others restlessly thumbed through papers or leaned back in their chairs, betraying their unease. This uncertainty was a shared and familiar experience.

Someone called for the boychick to bring tea.

"Are we awake, or asleep and dreaming at this moment, can you please tell me?" Maria Lebedev's voice was a whisper.

After the meeting, the Baron recognized that his role as chief medical officer had changed with arrival of the new doctors. He felt a curious absence of anger. His skills as a doctor and translator familiar with the Chinese in Kharbin were more valuable to General Khorvat. He'd turn this to his advantage and help those who were suffering. Dr. Wu didn't have his loyalty. Not yet.

Li Ju's fingers on a cup of blue-and-white porcelain, a pattern of water and a woman in a boat. As the cup tilted up in front of her face, the image of a curved blue fish met her lips. After the Baron's hours in the hospital, the childish blue figures and his wife's smile were simple pleasures. A brittle clink as her cup was placed on the table in their kitchen.

"Li Ju, what's wrong?"

A frown narrowed her eyes. "The servants were telling stories."

"About you? About us?"

"No, no. The kitchen servant bought fish in the market and heard a man died in a house nearby. Then his wife and their two children died."

"The entire family dead? Perhaps the stove was blocked and they died from fumes. It's a common accident."

She answered with an unfathomable look. Her silence was a question.

"I'm certain there's nothing to worry about. I'll make inquiries." He pictured a diagram: One infected person returns home and infects everyone else. All die. He wouldn't share his concern with Li Ju, as she would silently betray her nervousness to the servants. They would spread the story. Information from a doctor carried weight. Made an echo. Calligraphy taught him that the Chinese had tools to unlock even a foreigner's state of mind.

Li Ju abruptly left the room and he asked the kitchen servant for a cup of water. When the young man brought a pitcher to the table, the Baron asked what he'd heard about the deceased family.

"A poisoned well. Their water was poisoned."

"Do you know which house? No? Who poisoned their water?" the Baron asked.

"They say the Russians poison wells to kill the Chinese."

"Why? To take their property?"

The servant hesitated. "To cut up Chinese bodies for medicine. To take their guts, their stomachs and lungs."

"This story isn't true." It was better to give information that didn't create unnecessary speculation or fear. Even the smallest act could contribute to the general happiness of citizens. This was a Russian official's duty. He gave the relieved young man a coin and urged him to report rumors of deaths or missing persons to him.

People can be reassured by a tone of voice. By a touch. A gesture. Even if the voice and gestures are false, the innocent person meets the liar halfway to complete the lie. It's a partnership.

He turned to find Li Ju standing silently in the doorway. "Remember the surprise I promised you several days ago? Yes? Go dress warmly. Wear your trousers lined with rabbit fur," he instructed. "We'll be outside in the wind."

They slowly carried the lightweight iceboat between them from its storage berth to the riverbank. Li Ju stepped cautiously backward onto the frozen river, blindly guided by her husband's spoken directions, until they set the boat's sharp metal blades on small wooden blocks that would keep it upright and immobile.

The Baron loosened the sail as she shoved the boat off the blocks, and it thudded down onto the ice. He stepped into the unsteady boat, ducked under the mast into a half-prone position, and grasped the tiller. Wind whipped open the thick canvas sail, propelling the boat forward on the ice. Hampered by her thick boots, Li Ju trotted alongside the boat, afraid to clamber in.

"Jump now. Now."

She swung one leg over the side and he caught her arm, pulling her aboard as the boat wobbled under their uneven weight. Sail flapping overhead, they nestled together as the boat gathered speed.

An area of river ice, marked by red flags, had been scraped flat, and sunlight whitened the ice so the tiny figures of skaters appeared to move across blank paper. The Baron sharply swung the tiller to change direction, and a fine curled frond of ice droplets arched over the skaters, their laughing faces turned up to catch the glittering blessing.

In the cocoon of the boat, secure as two clasped hands, Li Ju was protected. Nothing could catch her. She was oblivious to him, hypnotized by the shuddering speed of the boat, eyes focused on the distance as the stark white grain elevators, the few tall buildings along the skyline, swiftly vanished behind them. If she were thrown from the boat at this instant, her death would be a continuation of flight.

It was just after noon and faint sun was already leaking into twilight when they docked the iceboat at a remote wharf to stretch their legs. They giddily embraced, their hands and faces too numbed by cold to feel the other's touch.

"Is that your finger on my cheek? My nose?" they teased each other.

No one had walked near the warehouses recently, since the snow was unmarked by footprints or tracks of vehicles. Several huge pyramids shadowed a long row of warehouses, their monumental scale out of place against the surrounding smaller buildings. In this unoccupied silent area, he had the sense of being watched. He had a vision of their figures as if another eye hovered at a great height, observing them stiffly moving through the snow like awkward animals.

Curious, they slowly circled the first pyramid, four sides without doors or windows, softened and thickened by snow. *What are these structures?* His arm cleared away the snow, uncovering canvas stretched over a lumpy surface. The pyramids were frozen soybeans, rock hard, stored here over the winter.

She walked ahead around the massive structure and he followed her dark coat. Then she disappeared.

"Li Ju?" The echo of his voice ricocheted between the pyramids, distorting his sense of direction. *Sound travels more slowly in cold.* His breath steamed up around his head as if to obscure his vision. He stopped, bent over, breathed more slowly. He followed Li Ju's footprints until they were crossed by a second set of footprints. "Where are you? Where?"

"Here."

He turned in a circle, disoriented by the towering, identical-angled shapes that barred his way. His leather mitten scraped through snow, making a huge *X* on the ground. A mark in the labyrinth. An anchor so as not to lose himself. His hands and arms were cold, heavy. He shouted her name again and again. Silence was a huge block that fit between the spaces.

It was growing darker, the snow blue-tinted as he struggled around one pyramid and then another. He positioned himself between two pyramids, arms open wide to hold them back, their edges seemed to shift and blur. He'd walked in circles, walked over his original footprints. Something visible against the snowbank, a figure, Li Ju's coat. She was teasing him, a child's game of hide-and-seek. He fixed his eye on the place where he saw her and moved forward, his left hand tracking a line in the snow across the structures as a guide.

A woman in fine clothing sat cross-legged, her back against a pyramid. In front of her, the snow was bright with red, yellow, and green stains, and burned candles had melted into blackened ice-filled holes. She was dead, eyes closed, frozen upright. Someone—probably her family—had surrounded her with paper replicas of food, money, clothing, a horse, to provide for her in the afterlife, and their fragile colors had dissolved into the snow.

CHAPTER EIGHT

Three figures—identically dressed in white cotton coveralls, aprons, and close-fitting caps—waited outside the patients' ward as if for some strange ceremony. The Baron and the doctors Maria Lebedev, Paul Haffkine, and Gerald Mesny were nearly unrecognizable in their cumbersome protective garb. Smiling, Maria Lebedev offered the Baron rubber gloves and officially introduced Dr. Haffkine, recently arrived in Manchuria.

"Welcome to Kharbin." The Baron brought up Haffkine's distinguished medical family. "Your uncle developed a remarkable vaccine to treat bubonic plague in India."

"Thank you. I've also been working on a plague serum. It's ready for trial here. I intend to make my mark." Haffkine poked a wisp of dark hair under his cap.

The Baron wondered at the difficulties of a medical trial staged in this chaotic situation. "We certainly need a cure. Or a miracle."

Haffkine didn't appreciate the Baron's attempt at humor and briefly wished him good luck before hurrying to another meeting.

Mesny led them along the corridor to a door posted with a warning sign, QUARANTINE, in Russian, Chinese, English, French, and German. "All the floors and walls have been completely sealed with metal strips to keep out rats. No one will be infected—or re-infected—by rats in this hospital."

The Baron stopped. "I need a face mask."

"A mask? No, a mask isn't necessary. I don't wear one. There's little risk of infection." Irritated, Mesny opened the door and entered the patients' ward, reluctantly followed by Maria Lebedev. It was a breach of protocol to challenge a senior doctor.

With his first step into the room, the Baron cursed that fool Mesny for shaming him into compliance. Then he cursed himself. He should have worn a mask. Yet he didn't leave, didn't turn away, as if powerless to change his fate.

The white figures of the two other doctors moved ahead of him, as isolated as candles in the poorly lit ward. There were six iron beds with patients, separated at a distance from one another. The ward smelled of unwashed bodies and the bitter chemical odor of formalin. Someone coughed intermittently. He sensed the contamination that haunted the room, filled the thickness of the air, was layered on every surface, spread across his open eyes, entered his nose, his body. It was constant, invisible, like a vibration or music. Each bed held danger. His breath became irregular and he began to sweat in his bulky coverall. Certain he was using up a lifetime of blessings, he swore never to put himself at risk again if he escaped infection this time. This clarity shook him. He whispered, "God have mercy. *Gospodi-pomiluy,*" as if these words were a charm against plague.

They stopped at the bedside of a pale young Russian man who didn't seem to be in distress. He promptly sat up and quietly joked as Mesny listened to his chest and back with a binaural stethoscope.

The Baron noticed that Maria Lebedev maneuvered her clipboard like a shield to protect her from the patient. She recorded the patient's pulse, rapid at 110 beats per minute, and his temperature, elevated at 38 degrees Celsius. "According to the chart," she said, "his pulse increased fourteen beats per minute for each degree that his temperature rose. Breath slightly labored."

"Good day, sir." The Baron fought a feeling of dread and addressed the young man without getting too close. "Your name? Nikolai Ivanovich Popov? Yes? What is your profession?" Popov was a soldier who patrolled Central Station.

"Don't bother with your questions," Mesny directed. "All his information is in the file." His harsh voice disturbed the patient, who moved fitfully under the blanket.

"You'll have the file later." Maria Lebedev fidgeted with the clipboard.

Mesny handed the stethoscope to the Baron. This was his test. Under intense scrutiny from the two doctors, he fumbled with the stethoscope, bent over, placed it on Popov's chest. He angled his face away to avoid the man's breath, trying not to touch him. The pounding of his own heart was louder and faster than Popov's in the stethoscope. Disoriented, he immediately stood up, relieved the patient hadn't coughed or sneezed.

The Baron managed to smile at the man. "Tell me, Nikolai Ivanovich, do you have pressure anywhere? A heaviness in your body?"

Popov's fingers fluttered near the center of his chest, his expression anxious.

"Your chest aches? I will make a note. You have courage. It will help you through this time." No platitudes, *You'll be fine, you'll recover, God will bless you.*

Popov rewarded him with a wavering grin. The Baron met his eyes, which was his gift. No one likes to look directly at the dying.

The Baron stepped away from the bed so the patient couldn't

hear the doctors' discussion. "Can his fever be broken with cold compresses?"

"We've tried." Mesny was increasingly irritated.

"That's certainly very general. What specific measures were taken?"

Mesny frowned. "We have nothing but generalities to guide us, according to our expert colleagues. Unless Haffkine's new medicine proves to be the nectar that cures. And brings him a medal from the czar."

"God willing."

"Yes. Then we can leave this place."

The Baron asked Maria Lebedev about the patient's current treatment.

"After the first major symptom of plague appears, he'll have injections every six hours. Camphor, caffeine, or digitalin intravenously and subcutaneously. Oxygen or champagne can also be given."

"These injections are successful? They ease lung congestion?" The Baron wasn't convinced.

Mesny appeared less confident for the first time. "We haven't treated many patients. But at the next stage, I anticipate Popov's symptoms will become more severe. Coughing, bloody expectorate, high fever. Then we use stronger measures—morphia, argentum, unguentum Credé, or adrenaline."

"Very resourceful." He didn't question Mesny's choices. Morphia for pain. Argentum as a disinfectant. Unguentum Credé, a salve containing colloidal silver, distilled water, wax, and benzoinated lard, for bacterial inflammation. A compassionate doctor would reassure the patient there were many options for treatment. However, the Baron knew from the witches' brew of injections that they were simply trying everything in hopes something would be effective. It was proof of desperation. He sensed Mesny was on the verge of telling the patient how much longer he'd live.

Maria Lebedev was also quick to anticipate Mesny's potential blunder and suggested that they check the next patient.

As they approached an older Chinese man, they saw his breathing was spasmodic, guttural, and then he broke into loud, convulsive coughing. How could such a frail body produce such a wrenching sound? Exhausted, the man collapsed against his pillow. His face was ruddy, his lips pale blue, cyanotic. The Baron stepped back, refused Mesny's invitation to check the patient's respirations and heartbeat.

Mesny's face locked into a scornful expression and he roughly pulled the patient into a sitting position. The sick man didn't protest but was clearly uncomfortable as Mesny pushed aside his shirt and pressed the stethoscope to his chest. "Breathe."

The Baron spoke a few words of greeting in Chinese. The sick man looked up with dull, wondering eyes and the Baron had the wild thought to apologize for Mesny's brusque examination.

Outside the ward, he spoke quietly to Mesny. "You should protect yourself. Clean your hands after each patient—"

"That's enough. I know how to conduct myself. I've had years of experience with epidemics. Neither of you should be offering an opinion here." His head tilted toward Maria Lebedev.

"Dr. Mesny, the hospital isn't a place of competition." The Baron walked away.

Afterward, at the nurses' station, the Baron stripped off his rubber gloves and poured half a bottle of carbolic over his hands, wincing as it stung his skin, the stink burning his nostrils. He washed his face and neck with harsh green soap and hot water.

After he'd dressed, he approached Maria Lebedev in the corridor. "A word with you?"

"Certainly." She was cordial but distant.

"Dr. Lebedev, it was a mistake not to protect myself in the patients' ward."

"I was equally foolish."

He spoke more quietly. "How long will the patients live?"

"I haven't treated enough patients to make a prediction."

"But if you were to guess?"

Her pale eyes blinked. "Dead within a day. The onset of the severest symptoms happens very quickly." She changed the subject. "Would you teach me a few words of Chinese? For the patients. They're surrounded by Russians."

"God bless you. It's said that hearing is the last sense to go before death. There are simple Chinese words of respectful address I can teach you." He considered what to say. "But you cannot promise the patients health or hope. Nor sympathy or pity, because you won't be believed."

"But what can I say?"

What could be said? Words were such poor tools. The words that would comfort a dying Russian weren't suited to the Chinese, who avoided the direct mention of death. "Let's discuss it later. I need to think through my vocabulary, thin as it is." He wished Maria Lebedev good day, then walked down the corridor and up two flights of stairs to Messonier's office. It was unlocked, unoccupied, and he sank into the largest chair, exhausted. In winter, there were few opportunities to be solitary inside the hive of the hospital. Everything took place in the presence of others near the heat and smoky scent of the wood-fired stoves.

He picked apart his unease, mocking himself: *Should I make a list of my faults?* His inability to comfort the patients. The risk he'd taken in the hospital ward, touching the patients, sharing breath and space with the infected and dying. His resentment of

Dr. Lebedev's uncomplaining obedience and Dr. Mesny's hostility.

To unstring himself from this, he imagined warm weather, a walk by the Sungari River watching boys with burning bamboo torches guide passengers from the ferries. By morning, the decks would be littered with blackened husks of the torches, like pits of discarded fruit.

He surveyed the shelves of Messonier's precious teas, rows of metal, lacquer, and ceramic containers, each with a gummed paper label identifying the contents in Chinese and, underneath, the doctor's curved handwriting in French. Messonier must have been drilled in cursive as a child in Paris; the scrolled loops of his *F, D,* and *P* arched artfully as feathers. The quantity of stored tea filled the room with a dry, slightly musty welcoming fragrance. In the past few days, he'd noticed unfamiliar odors in the hospital, a faint floating ghost. Even Zabolotny had commented on it. "It's the smell of the sick. The blood of the plague-infected."

The Baron traced the odor to newly arrived shipments of antiseptics, sterilizing supplies, crates of cotton towels and sheets. He'd torn open a large box of black rubber gloves, shaken off the white powder that kept them from sticking together, lined them up like hollow fish on the table.

Messonier quietly entered and swept his arms wide in greeting to find the Baron sprawled in the chair. He immediately offered him a drink then noticed the Baron's expression. "Something has happened." He slowly unbuttoned his white coat and hung it on a peg.

"I went into the patients' ward with the doctors Lebedev and Mesny this afternoon."

Messonier began to prepare tea, quietly pouring water from a flask into the kettle, giving the other man time to regain his composure. "Do you wish to talk?"

"Dr. Mesny is a reckless man. You must urge Dr. Lebedev—Maria—to protect herself when she's with the patients. She must take precautions and not be swayed by him or others."

"She knows her own mind."

"Yes, but I was also foolish. I was in the patients' ward without protection. I'm ashamed I didn't speak up. I'll be sleepless thinking about it tonight."

"An hour with patients is unlikely to be fatal."

There was no proof for his statement but with the bloom of Messonier's sympathy, the Baron sensed something easing inside and he felt lighter, unguarded. Then he became aware of a hunger, a beseeching presence that craved comfort and attention. It was a familiar state, carried like an offering in his hands. *Have I always been like this?* he thought or spoke out loud as Messonier swung around and stared at him.

In the silent room, icy pellets of snow drove against the window, thrown like rice, a hard, irregular tattoo.

"I'm making you tea."

Messonier had absolved him. Salved his conscience. Hot tears brimmed in his eyes and he couldn't look up or they would leak down his cheeks. He tightened his face to keep control. Haltingly, he began to describe the dead woman sitting in the snow, the objects set around her for the afterlife. "When I first saw her, she seemed to be a statue. A goddess surrounded by offerings."

"Yes."

"I believe her family feared her sickness would be discovered so they abandoned her in an isolated place."

"Remember, she was likely infected with plague. A bomb."

The Baron ignored his comment. "Li Ju fell on her knees before the woman and wept. She forgot her prayers. I made the sign of the cross over the body although I immediately regretted it. The dead woman didn't need my Russian blessing. Always inserting myself into my wishes for others."

Messonier stood with a spoon poised above the tea canister. "A blessing is a blessing. Forgive yourself."

Water boiled, a loud rattling shake of the kettle on the *daisu*. The interruption broke their connection and the two men quickly backed away from their fragile exposure to each other.

"What do we drink, sir?" He hoped Messonier wouldn't notice his voice was husky from emotion.

"*Huangjin gui*. Osmanthus tea. A special oolong from Fujian with rolled leaves. One of the nurses has a brother stationed in Anxi. She gets the tea before the British traders. At a price. It's too subtle for the British. They prefer pedestrian black tea." Messonier busied himself with the teapot and utensils. "Should the woman's death be investigated?"

"I reported the location of the body. The soldiers found nothing."

"Seems impossible."

"Lazy soldiers. It was too cold for them to investigate. General Khorvat prides himself on rule of law. But as Chang the dwarf said, 'Baron, a lack of bodies keeps the crime rate down.'"

"A system is in place. Fill your cup, Baron?"

He nodded. "If Khorvat's men are picking up plague dead, someone will eventually become infected unless they take precautions. It's dangerous for them. For everyone."

Messonier cradled his cup. "This is guesswork. Until it is confirmed—"

"I hope my suspicions are uglier than the truth. If it please God. I beg you, friend Messonier, be cautious until the facts about plague are known. Our truth, not their truth. Who knows, perhaps the teapot we just shared is infected. I touched the patients.

I touched the teapot. An infection could spread from me to you. Anyone, any object could be dangerous. We're wringing our hands at the edge of the volcano."

"The volcano is still somewhat unofficial." He raised the teacup to the Baron. "À la guerre."

"To war!"

Messonier watched the steam wreath up from the spout of the teapot, white in the chilly room. "Is there a future for the type of medicine we practice here? The Chinese are slow to accept new medicine. May never accept it."

"I've been here almost seven years longer than you. And I still haven't decided." The Baron's fingers tenderly circled the hot cup. "Chinese don't seek treatment with me unless it is accompanied by free rice. I'm not critical. I understand this. I'm grateful when they ask for my aid purely from optimism. But at times it seems so futile. I showed a young man how to disinfect a cut with iodine. But then he vanished with the bottle. Probably to sell on the black market. Probably to you." He grinned at Messonier.

"Or to a soldier to drink."

"The young man must have thought that I was mad. *Bacteria?* The word doesn't exist in Chinese. I didn't have language to explain it to him without sounding like an evil spirit, a *domovoy*. Or a quack."

A clink as Messonier set down the empty cup.

"Did I tell you about my consultation with a Chinese doctor? I was allowed to observe him with a patient. It was confounding." The Baron held up his cup for more tea. "Here's my suggestion. I'll propose to the doctors at the hospital that we form an alliance with the Chinese doctors to fight the plague. They have traditions and knowledge to share. It's hardly a gamble, since we have no solution as yet."

"I admire your plan. But I don't believe the others will be receptive."

"I can only try."

"Tell me what the Chinese doctor did with his patient."

The Baron disliked uncertainty and felt unable to accurately describe the experience, even to Messonier. He set down the cup. He pressed his fingertips against the inside of his wrist. "Here. The doctor diagnosed the patient by touching the *cunkan,* a narrow spot, about an inch at the wrist. He said that palpating the wrist is *qiemo.*"

"So he monitored the patient's pulse?"

"I don't believe it's the pulse he monitored. But what is it? A vibration? Temperature? Mind reading? The doctor called it *mo.* It's something else. Perhaps he makes a diagnosis from the pressure of the vessels? There are twenty-four different qualities of *mo.*" He leaned forward, now eager to share what he'd learned. "I asked what his fingers sensed at the wrist. The Chinese doctor said the *mo* can be rough or smooth. Even slippery. I know, you smile. So did I. These descriptions are from an ancient text, the *Mojing.* Listen. Rough *mo* is 'like sawing bamboo.' Tense *mo* is like 'palpating a rope.' Faint *mo* signifies poor health, 'extremely thin and soft as if about to disappear; it appears both to be there and not to be there.'" He sat back in the chair. "How could a doctor apply this description to a body? What is this skill that he has? It is not a diagnosis as we know a diagnosis."

"'To be there and not to be there.'" Messonier slowly repeated his words as if trying to memorize them.

"My knowledge of Chinese is too primitive to understand this subtle concept. My medical knowledge is too blunt. Too coarse. Like you, I was taught to recognize only hard and soft. But the Chinese are aware of many other states. Degrees of states. It's as if the body possesses qualities—or transformations—that we can't recognize. I couldn't even ask the doctor an intelligent question. I'm provoked, mystified, and also enchanted, I must confess."

"Could what the doctor felt and described possibly be true?"

"I believe so. But it seems miraculous to me. Like a saint's miracles." The Baron sighed. "You know what I believe? I believe that I was blessed by this experience. The Chinese doctor's generous gift."

"Faith."

"Many kinds of faith."

"As one description of love is unlike another." Messonier hesitated. "I prepare tea for Maria Lebedev. I try to distract her from the hospital. What else can I offer? I have nothing. This city is without comfort. I never imagined courting a woman here. I came only to work." His face reddened. "My residence is near St. Nikolas Cathedral. Our first morning together we woke to bells. She was blissful. Said it was our blessing. She's very devout."

When the Baron walked outside the building, he carried the aroma of the tea inside his mouth and nose. He exhaled and it was dispersed in a ragged cloud. Lately, he'd been troubled by strange thoughts. An image of his face and beard coated with ice, the plague bacilli preserved inside, particles finer than pollen, a bee swarm of contamination, ready to be released by melting. Then the familiar clutch of anxiety. He shook himself as if waking from sleep. It wasn't a hallucination. It was caused by overwork, brain fatigue. Or was this ill feeling the beginning of an infection, the first symptom? Messonier understood his momentary lapses into silence, occasional lack of focus. Was he also distracted by bizarre images? Should he confess to Messonier?

Every night, he hungered for an object, something safe to touch that had no risk. Eyes closed, he would smooth Li Ju's hair, exposing the nape of her neck. He knew she felt cold air before the warmth of his mouth on her skin. She coiled her arm back around his head. Locked him safe.

"Forty new patients were admitted to the Russian hospital with plague symptoms. Ten new corpses were discovered in the Chinese district. Some were buried in snow and others abandoned on the street." The Baron spoke quietly to Messonier as they walked to the conference room. "I heard Dr. Mesny's six patients died just ten hours after my visit to the ward."

Messonier made a low whistle. "Sobering numbers. But just wait. Mesny will blame the patients for their own deaths."

"Or he'll blame Dr. Lebedev."

Messonier exchanged a sharp look with him. "Now we have a battle ahead of us around the table and only weak tea to accompany it. I wish you well with your proposal, Baron."

"It's a death parade in the conference room."

The hospital staff meetings were dreaded, as there was always a sense of uncertainty and, underneath it, fear. One doctor after another reported their unsuccessful attempts to save lives and the steadily increasing number of patient deaths. Their failures. It was as if a clock silently ticked away during the meeting. Many theories, hunches, and observations about the patients' treatment were debated. One sick child had no fever but a cough. Treated with morphia, his condition slightly improved. Was this a possible solution? Yesterday a young woman's prognosis seemed promising and it was hoped she'd be the first to survive the plague. But a few hours later she was dead. Scores of new patients were admitted every day but died so quickly that the numbers remained at the same level.

The Baron and Messonier greeted Mesny and Zabolotny, followed them into the conference room. *We're pallbearers,* thought the Baron. Dr. Wu, Dr. Iasienski, and General Khorvat were already seated at the table.

Dr. Wu opened the meeting by focusing on what was known about the various stages of infection. "One of the unusual effects is that patients appear fairly healthy, with only a slightly elevated temperature and cough, until the rapid onset of catastrophic symptoms, quickly followed by death. We now can estimate the incubation period, the time between exposure to the bacilli and symptoms, at three to five days. Exposure could come from an infected person, animal, an object. A bite from an infected flea. A contaminated blanket or room. Nothing and no source can be ruled out at this point."

"Rats are being eradicated all over the city under General Khorvat's highly successful bounty program." Zabolotny gestured at Khorvat, seated at the head of the table with Wu and his translator.

Khorvat acknowledged his praise. "The latest tally reported nearly five thousand dead rats have been collected. There's great progress conquering the vermin problem. The streets will be made safe."

"The effectiveness of the extermination will be demonstrated by a decline in the number of cases."

Iasienski was increasingly impatient. "There's another important issue to discuss. What procedure is in place for burying plague corpses?"

Wu's response was immediate. "The dead won't be returned to their families. It's a risk to move corpses around the city. They're infectious."

"A field outside the city has been marked as a common grave," Khorvat said. "A few rat hunters have been recruited to drive corpses to the field."

"It's fine to bury the corpses," Mesny said, "but we need blood.

We need tissue and samples from infected lungs and the lymphatic glands. Scrapings from the mucosa of the bronchi should be examined. We must autopsy corpses to determine how bacilli act."

"Autopsies are against Chinese tradition. Opening up a body is prohibited. But Dr. Wu certainly has more knowledge than I do." The Baron turned to assess Wu's reaction and watched him glance at Zabolotny.

Several doctors were obviously relieved that Wu ignored the Baron and allowed his comment to pass.

Then Zabolotny widened his eyes in mock astonishment. "No autopsies? We risk our lives for this epidemic and we're stopped by a quaint custom? What century is this?"

The Baron placed his hands on the table as a platform for his words. "Unlike Western medicine, Chinese medical practice doesn't rely on autopsies. There's no history of autopsy in China, so you can understand why it isn't accepted. Their conception of the body is entirely foreign to us. It's truly unimaginable. That's not to say it has no basis in fact. The Chinese have had an established system of medicine for a thousand years."

Mesny jumped in. "I welcome your lesson about Chinese medicine, but we're here to stop an epidemic with our medicine. The Chinese have a proven history of failure with epidemics."

"I'll remind you, Dr. Mesny, that we have no cure for the plague," the Baron said.

"Dr. Haffkine reports great progress with his serum."

The Baron didn't take Mesny's bait. "On the street, they say the bodies of dead Chinese are harvested to make medicine for Russians. Any Chinese who suspected their bodies would be eviscerated after death would refuse treatment in our hospital. This also relates to their religious beliefs. Without rites and a proper burial, they're condemned in the afterlife. We're all familiar with the concept of eternal damnation. We cannot solve this epidemic without their cooperation. There could be violence."

Mesny dismissed his words. "Then we'd better cozy up to the Japanese for protection."

"You joke, but the Chinese vastly outnumber Russians in Kharbin. Only a few years ago, Chinese mobs killed foreigners during the Boxer Rebellion. I hid in the woods for three days—" Messonier was interrupted.

With a gesture, Khorvat swept him aside. "Let's finish the meeting. Time is wasting. It's unlikely the Chinese will kill Russian doctors. Imagine how that would look to the world. They will lose face. China already struggles with foreign criticism, since no one believes they can manage the epidemic without international aid. That's why doctors were brought in from several countries. Remember, the only hospitals in China were built by missionaries. That said, the Chinese look for any excuse to rid this place of Russians. This talk of harvesting Chinese bodies could incite protest. There aren't enough Russian soldiers to contain hundreds of rioters. The situation is volatile."

Khorvat's point had a sobering effect. Messonier said the general's warning should be respected.

But Mesny had burned through his patience. "So we accept these ridiculous restrictions about autopsies? I strongly protest. How would the Chinese even discover the autopsies?" His eyes were on the Baron and Wu.

"Now that I've heard everyone's opinion, the best strategy is to petition the Imperial Throne for permission to conduct autopsies." The disdain in Wu's voice was apparent.

"The Chinese government will never support your request to violate their own traditions." Mesny's voice was querulous. "You like to gamble, Dr. Wu. If permission is denied, what will you do? Resign?"

Wu's reaction was barely perceptible. "I'm confident the Imperial Throne will accept my petition."

"Let's hope their answer will be swift."

Wu continued as if Mesny hadn't spoken. "Once the Imperial Throne gives permission, unidentified corpses will be autopsied in secret to avoid alarming the Chinese."

"Do you truly believe autopsies can be kept secret? We'll be acting like murderers, trying to hide the mutilated corpses. No, the solution is obvious." The Baron controlled his voice in spite of his anger. "It's unethical to autopsy Chinese corpses. So we'll autopsy Russian corpses." Messonier flashed a grin as Khorvat pushed back his chair and called for order over the angry voices.

The Baron kept talking, refusing to be shouted down. "We need to work with Chinese patients and doctors." Even before he'd finished his sentence, he sensed their disapproval but continued. "Who knows where the cure for plague will be found? Perhaps the Chinese already possess it." He was breathless.

"I disagree." Wu's voice was cold. "Chinese doctors practice folklore, not medicine. They would undermine our work at the hospital. One of their treatments for plague is to wrap a chip of horse bone in red cloth and wear it in a small bag around the neck."

"A horse bone? You must be joking." The doctors permitted themselves shallow smiles. Messonier wasn't amused.

The Baron kept his focus. "Dr. Wu, it's obvious that not every remedy has potential. But how can we determine which treatments are acceptable? We need all types of knowledge. Why not expand our circle of information? Some of the most unlikely remedies have been proven effective. It's a schoolboy's lesson, but even smallpox vaccine, cultivated from infection, was rejected at first."

"There's no time to explore Chinese superstitions."

Iasienski had been quiet but now thumped the table for emphasis. "I've heard about these superstitions. The Chinese make medicine from powdered deer hooves. They grind up pearls and insects. Fungus from trees. You're a modern man, Dr. Wu. Better to dismiss it."

The Baron persisted. "What harm is there in meeting Chinese medical men? It would ease mistrust between us. Bring them to the hospital. Discuss what they know about the plague. I will gladly translate for them."

"Translation may tax your ability. If the prefect of Laichow were here, he'd tell us to throw black beans into a well during the last watch of the night. Everyone who drinks water from the well will be saved from plague."

The laughter was audible this time.

As Wu spoke, the Baron realized he used his mockery of Chinese medicine to form a bond with the Russian doctors. It was the way to court their praise and acceptance. To eliminate the distance between them.

"Gentlemen." General Khorvat loudly called for attention. "This discussion is also pertinent for my announcement. The merchants in the Chinese Chamber of Commerce have contributed funds to open a hospital in Fuchiatien. It will be staffed with Chinese doctors who practice traditional medicine. We suspect that the Imperial Throne is behind it and money was funneled from Beijing to support their effort."

"Of course the goal is to prove their medical practices are legitimate." Zabolotny looked to Mesny for support.

"A rival hospital is an insult to our hard work."

Khorvat sketched a vague expansive movement with his cigarette.

Wu's gaze moved around the table, avoiding the Baron. "I believe that I speak for everyone here. We will not cooperate with the Chinese medical men." He turned away from the Baron as if to block him from the others at the table. A wall had been assembled. The Baron could sense it, almost touch it.

"The Chinaman has made a wise decision." Mesny was oblivious to the disrespect in his comment. "Imagine if our colleagues heard we were advised by these so-called doctors."

"I'd be mocked from my position at the Imperial Institute."

"The Chinese probably hold the same scorn for our medicine," the Baron said.

"You would defend them. You may find yourself chanting alone in a Chinese temple someday."

Wu added to Mesny's comment. "Baron, if you intend to practice unorthodox medicine here, please keep me informed. Not all the patients will welcome your experiments."

"I imagine even a sick Chinese would refuse his care. They come here for Russian medicine, not some concoction from lotus pods and rainwater."

Sounds of appreciation for Wu's barb. He had skillfully isolated the Baron.

The Baron's breath was measured. He wondered how Wu thought this mockery would aid their work.

Messonier began speaking in a reasonable tone. "I must point out that a crisis strains everyone's nerves. Judgment becomes impaired. Some of us speak and act carelessly. Almost as if we're drunk. Everyone here is at risk and it's crucial to support each other. It could save lives. Even our own." Because he wasn't angry and his words were careful, they created space in the room. The doctors had been called to account.

The Baron wished Dr. Lebedev were present to witness Messonier's tour de force. His own proposal for working with the Chinese was lost. He couldn't see the arc of the epidemic but sensed a vast shape that they would try to name and control with their evidence. Build a fence of hypodermic needles.

Dr. Wu did not forget Mesny's insults. He immediately sent a telegram to Alfred Sze at the Ministry of Foreign Affairs in Beijing, offering to resign as health commissioner. It was intolerable to work with Dr. Mesny, a foreigner who did not respect his position.

In private, the Baron began to criticize Dr. Wu, his English clothing, the thick tweed jackets and waistcoats. His inability to speak Chinese. His need for a translator. Wu was arrogant, constantly miscalculating the effect of his words and attitude on patients. This was an unforgivable flaw for a doctor. The Baron had lived in Manchuria for years, was fluent in the language, and respected the Chinese. Yet Wu didn't ask for advice or recommendations. Never shared a cup of tea. The man seemed to represent everything that was wrong with the system.

Standing onstage, Dr. Broquet waved a pair of floppy black rubber gloves overhead so they were visible to the Russian hospital staff in the assembly room. "Cover and protect yourself. Always wear rubber gloves." His dark hair gleamed with pomade under the spotlight. Dr. Zabolotny, seated at a table next to him, watched the presentation. "Wash hands before and after you wear gloves." Broquet's voice was tremulous, as he was obviously uncomfortable speaking to a large group. Flustered, he dropped a glove, and Zabolotny made no effort to pick it up.

Broquet retrieved the glove and caught his breath before continuing. "Your life may depend on your face. A mask shields nose and mouth from plague bacilli circulating in the air. See here." He held up a mask, pale, glowing, translucent as honey. "This mask is made of mica. Lightweight. It's one piece, without holes so the mouth and eyes are covered. Visibility is affected." He slipped the mask over his head; his features became tightly flattened and distorted behind its slightly glittering sheath. He turned left and right before awkwardly removing it. "After each use, sterilize the mask in boiling water. It can be worn several times."

A question from the audience. "Dr. Broquet, will the mica mask protect us? What are the disadvantages?"

"Face moisture condenses inside the mask." Broquet's hand flapped. "It's useless in the colder hospital wards. I wore this mask in the patients' ward and was blinded by ice on my eyelashes."

A young woman in the third row stood up. "I've heard it's important to protect the eyes. Can plague bacilli infect the body this way?"

Broquet shared his hesitation with Zabolotny before answering. "Possibly. Probably. We aren't certain."

The young woman persisted. "Obviously, goggles would offer better protection?"

"The problem with goggles is that there are no goggles." Broquet was exasperated.

A sympathetic murmur from the audience. "A shipment of goggles will arrive very soon," Zabolotny calmly announced from his seat onstage. "We're under enormous pressure to analyze plague bacilli and conduct experiments during this crisis. Small animals, rats and guinea pigs, had their eyes dusted with powdered dry bacilli to see if airborne particles can cause infection. It's one of many experiments. Few doctors have ever faced such an enormous challenge without properly equipped laboratories."

Another question from the audience. "The masks protect medical staff but how do we stop the sickness spreading between patients?"

"We're not certain at what point infected patients are contagious. Many facts are still unknown."

"I have proposed that all patients wear masks," Zabolotny answered. "Let the burden be on the sick. Gauze can be draped over patients' heads to catch discharge and sputum when they sneeze and cough. This is standard in India."

"But there's a shortage of gauze." Broquet stared at Zabolotny, challenging him to defend his proposal. "Here's another option." He waved two long strips of fabric as if deflecting attention from his previous ill-judged comment. "This mask is so simple a child can make it from two pieces of fabric." He spread the cloths flat on the table. "First, fold a three-foot-long strip of thin wool inside a piece of gauze of the same length. Cut three small slits at each end so it's less bulky. Cut two holes for the eyes in the center of the strips. Dr. Zabolotny, allow me to demonstrate on you. Hold very still, please."

Peevish, Zabolotny stood while Broquet wrapped the fabric strip over his eyes and across his face, tied it at the back of his head.

Broquet continued, "A second fabric strip goes over the top of the head to hold it in place. There we are."

His head clumsily wrapped in the bandage mask, Zabolotny stepped from behind the table, stumbling slightly, as his vision was impaired, to face the audience and make a stiff mocking bow to applause.

Broquet gestured for quiet. "These cotton masks are contaminated after exposure to the patients. Burn them after use."

In the first row, a middle-aged man raised his arm for attention. "I need more information to better understand the situation.

What's the time span between infection and the appearance of symptoms? How do we know when it's necessary to wear a mask?"

Zabolotny awkwardly loosened the cloth strips from his head, and they dangled around his neck. "We believe it's only a day or two at most between infection and the first symptoms. But no facts are definite yet."

Another questioner: "Does the treatment begin when the infected patient is admitted? How long does it delay the onset of symptoms?"

"Records of patients are still being compiled." Zabolotny was increasingly restless and batted at the hanging cloth strips.

"What is the patients' recovery rate, Dr. Zabolotny?" The audience hushed.

Broquet answered for him. "We don't know." His face was shiny with sweat, and his voice rose. "*Recovery* isn't a word that we use. I'll speak plainly. You must always be on your guard with the patients. If you wish to stay alive, treat the patients as if they mean to harm you. Never expose your bare skin in the hospital. Touch nothing without protection."

A murmur of astonishment at Broquet's outburst rippled through the assembly room.

Afterward, the Baron and Messonier stood near the stage, speaking quietly about the pall Broquet's last comment had cast over the assembly. The Baron could hardly restrain his anger at the doctors' haphazard and evasive demonstration. "We've just seen two conjurers demonstrate poor magic tricks with pieces of cotton."

"Nothing that can't be explained away by reason." Messonier was distracted, watching Maria Lebedev across the room.

"Who could feel secure knowing that cotton is the only thing that protects you from death?"

Messonier's eyes widened. "Remember, that's not yet proven. Regardless, we've accepted it."

"As an acrobat accepts a tightrope."

The two doctors joined the small group gathered around Broquet. Messonier praised his informative lecture.

Broquet thanked him. "I regret Dr. Wu didn't approve the second mask I'd proposed. I copied the mask worn during the plague epidemic in Florence from a fifteenth-century illustration. The mask was a hood that completely hid the face and covered the shoulders."

"Perhaps it was impractical?"

"No. Dr. Wu was concerned the hood would frighten the patients." Broquet shrugged, turned to speak to a student.

"This could be the last group assembly," the Baron said. "It's too dangerous to bring all the medical staff together in one room. Dr. Wu is a fool to take this risk." He turned away at Messonier's stricken look.

"I overheard your comment," Wu said. He and Zabolotny stood behind the Baron. "If you have criticism, discuss it with me face-to-face. It's disrespectful of my position."

"I apologize, Dr. Wu."

Zabolotny smiled. Messonier pretended he hadn't heard their exchange.

"Good afternoon, gentlemen." Wu left the room. His translator, Zhu Youjing, stayed behind and spoke with Maria Lebedev. A few minutes later, she found the Baron and Messonier.

"Wu dismissed Dr. Mesny." She gripped Messonier's arm.

Messonier struck his fist into his palm. "He made an example of Mesny. No disagreement is acceptable. A warning for others."

"*Gospodi-pomiluy,* God have mercy." The Baron shook his head. "The man was quarrelsome and opinionated but we need every pair of hands. Dr. Wu has robbed us of a valuable ally."

"The patients will suffer for this." Maria Lebedev's voice was steady but her eyes were thick with tears.

As Xiansheng entered the Baron's study, his fur-lined coat steamed from the lingering effect of the cold outside. The servants removed his garment, a bow was exchanged, and he accepted a cup of *tieguanyin* tea before the calligraphy lesson.

Xiansheng silently observed the Baron carefully set out brush, inkstone, ink, and paper—the *wenfang sibao,* Four Treasures of the Abodes of Culture. The rinse pot was filled with water. The paper was unrolled on the table and weighted with small stones. The wet brush was stroked on the inkstone. The careful ritual of preparation usually calmed the Baron, but this afternoon he was possessed by restlessness. It had been five days, perhaps a week, since he'd last practiced calligraphy.

Xiansheng had written the character *jen* for the Baron to copy, explaining it represented goodness, the virtue that must unite men. "When you work, remember each brushstroke must have vitality, life. Otherwise, it is *baibi,* a defeating or dead stroke. An empty stroke is a fault."

He straightened his body in the chair at the table, his neck aching. He balanced the brush between stiff fingers, its quivering bristles finer than feathers. He tried to summon calm to his fingers, to his wrist. His awareness of his hands expanded, bones inflating inside the flesh of his fingers like a glove. *I cannot make the first mark.* He tried to focus but his eyes continually slipped off the paper, sliding across it without the anchor of a black brushstroke.

Then he became angry. He was a doctor, an aristocrat, intimidated by the silent regard of a man whose language he imperfectly understood. A dead stroke? Was he at fault for not understanding? No one could understand. It was a trick, a puzzle.

He glanced at Xiansheng, aware that his expression was defiant. *He thinks I'm a barbarian.*

Xiansheng answered his look. "When I was young and studying calligraphy, my teacher took away my brush to help me."

The Baron was confused. "No brush?"

"I had practiced and practiced. Many considered my brushwork excellent. But my mind was unsettled. My teacher quoted the Taoist master calligraphist Yu Shi'nan: 'In the transformation of his mind, the calligrapher borrows the brush. It is not the brush that works the miracle.' He instructed me to write the characters without a brush, to only imagine using it. I did as he said. My teacher was unable to tell if I had followed his direction, but my hand became freer."

The words seemed simple, but as the Baron struggled to understand them, their meaning became more dense and tangled.

"The brush isn't the tool. A famous calligraphist used a brush the size of a cabbage."

By the time he translated this sentence, the Baron was smiling, pulled from the web of his thought. The spring wound inside him loosened. Uncoiled. His hands relaxed and the brush made its first mark, *luo bi,* on paper.

"Judging by your nervousness, I'd imagine you were preparing a banquet for the czar." Messonier watched the Baron pace around the table in thick fleece slippers.

The Baron barely acknowledged him, checking and rechecking the place mats arranged over the table. For Messonier's pleasure, he'd persuaded Chang to conduct a tea ceremony. "I've been cautioned about the amount of water required to make tea. There are extra mats in the wardrobe over there." They rummaged together through the shelves and found the stack of mats.

Messonier lowered his voice. "I make tea for Maria every day and take great care with the preparations. She believes I have expertise. But I'm certain my knowledge is very rudimentary compared to Chang's learning."

"I don't believe you need to be concerned."

"I've no wish to make a fool of myself in front of Maria. I don't know what to expect. What if Chang asks my opinion of the tea? Quizzes me?"

The Baron glanced at Messonier. "Chang is a stern master but he won't embarrass you. If you fail his test, it won't change Maria's opinion of you." Strange to comfort Messonier when he needed comforting himself. But he was relieved by the Baron's answer and they joined Maria and Li Ju at the table.

But the Baron was restless, uneasy with everyone's closeness. He calculated that, between them, the three doctors had treated over fifty patients in the hospital earlier that day. Li Ju had wandered through the busy market. One of them might have met a symptomless carrier of plague, someone at the stage when the infection was ripe and could be transmitted to others. One of them might have brought the bacilli to the table.

There was no protection. Everyone was suspect. But for the moment, they had the shroud of innocence and he would trust it. He wouldn't draw attention to his concern. He banished his calculations. They were simply friends sitting at a table. Companions of tea, *chalu*. He forced a smile to his lips, extended it to his eyes.

But Maria Lebedev was studying him. Startled, he busied himself as if guilty, straightened a dish on the table. Was she also uneasy? Did her expression mirror the worry on his own face?

Maria turned her attention away. Her wet boots had been left at the door and she swung her stocking feet as freely as a child, her thick skirt folded up over her knees. Messonier was delighted at her playful ease. So many doctors were unable to step away from the rigidity of service, the constant role of an observer.

Li Ju had just met Maria for the first time and giggled shyly at her boldness. She was quiet, slightly uneasy in the company of her husband's older friends. Her eyes moved hesitantly from face to face, but she was generous with her smile, even when their talk seemed strange or difficult.

Maria pivoted into conversation with Li Ju, admiring the embroidered sash at her waist, tracing the intricate thick threads with her finger. Li Ju was pleased by Maria's attention, the other woman bending toward her with kindness. The Baron knew his wife would unbuckle the jade button and present the sash as a gift to Maria. But Maria anticipated this courteous offer and was already shaking her head no, her hand extended to stop Li Ju's generosity. To receive nothing for herself. Li Ju insisted, and the gift was made. Maria clasped Li Ju's hand, the two women smiling at each other.

A lovely pantomime, the Baron thought. What significance might the embroidered sash have for Maria one day in the future, a bright piece of cloth perhaps pulled from tissue paper in a drawer, a memento of an hour when she drank ceremonial tea with her lover and his friends? Perhaps she would even turn to Messonier, if they had made a life together, and hold it up, ask if he remembered that afternoon.

A sweep of cold air from the door announced Chang before the stamp of his boots on the threshold. He called a greeting, handed the servant a wooden box, and hurried back outside. In a moment, he returned holding a bowl heaped with snow.

"Melt this over heat," he said to the servant. "Just to the boil."

The servant took the bowl of snow and vanished into the kitchen. Chang turned and nodded in the direction of the group at the table. "I've brought you a very fine tea." A second servant, a boy, helped Chang remove his coat and boots. The boy waited awkwardly as Chang stepped onto a stool and clambered into a chair at the table, uncertain if he should assist.

Chang unpacked the box on the table in front of them. "Today we drink wuyi, a rare *yancha* tea grown on the mountains in Fujian." He opened a metal canister and, with a practiced tap, spilled a measure of dry tea into a tiny blue-and-white bowl. "Together we will share the five phases of tea: dry leaves, the dry leaves when heated, wet leaves, scent of a cup, flavor in the mouth." He handed the bowl with dry tea to the Baron to pass around. "First, observe the size, color, and texture of the tea. Then appreciate its aroma."

The Baron studied the loose tea in the bowl, dark twisted leaves fine as threads, then sniffed them. Not a familiar scent. It was vegetable—no, the odor of a location, something grown. Dry ground in a northern forest.

How to memorize the scent, lock it to this moment as he touched Li Ju's fingers handing her the bowl? The scent frail, an intangible aura shared between them. His unease returned. He placed his hand on his wife's arm to reassure himself and Messonier caught his eye, recognizing his gesture.

"We use two sets of cups for the tea ceremony. One set is slightly smaller." Chang gently lifted a bundle of wrinkled red silk from the box and unwrapped five tiny cylindrical cups without handles. A second nest of silk held five slightly larger cups, also without handles, bowls, and a large plate perforated like a sieve. He held up a teapot the size of a small gourd, a rich brown-purple color, for them to admire. "My prize Yixing pottery. Yixing teapots are always unglazed. This is the natural color of the clay. It suits black or semi-fermented oolong tea." Chang angled the teapot, display-ing its interior for them. "Never clean the inside of a teapot. Each time tea is brewed, oil from its leaves adds subtle flavor. A teapot layered with years of these deposits is valuable."

The Baron held the teapot carefully, peered at the dull film in-side, and hesitantly touched a finger to its unexpectedly rough interior. He handed Messonier the teapot.

"A subterranean view." Messonier squinted into the teapot, his voice slightly muffled. "Or a cave. I will never drink tea with the same innocence."

The Baron took responsibility for this. "You may turn to the usefulness of vodka. Like the Russians." He addressed Maria. "Dr. Lebedev, you must watch Messonier very carefully."

Amused, she focused on Messonier, and he grinned. Some pri-vate joke between them.

Chang waited for Messonier to pay attention. Then he placed the perforated plate over the bowl and set the cups in a circle around it. "A proper tea ceremony requires a flood of water inside and outside the teapot. A repetition of water and tea." The teapot was carefully balanced on top of the plate and bowl. "Where's our hot water?" Irritated, he hurried from the room in search of the kettle.

They waited in respectful silence until he returned, walking ceremoniously toward the table balancing a hot kettle. He dra-matically filled the teapot until it overflowed, the steaming water draining through the perforated plate into the bowl underneath. "A scholar claimed the Nanling water of the Yangtze River was the most superior in all of China. But even here, in the dirty wilder-ness of Kharbin, we can drink the purest water from melted snow." In five seconds, the teapot water was emptied into the bowl. "Now the teapot has been heated. It's ready for the tea."

A spoonful of dry tea leaves was sprinkled into the empty warmed teapot. After one minute, Chang lifted the lid, handed the open teapot to the Baron. "Smell it."

The teapot was a warm globe in his hands, and, eyes closed, the Baron inhaled the aroma of the slightly damp tea inside. The scent possessed the steady clean familiarity of straw, leaves, dirt—rounded, comforting yet strange.

Li Ju was next. She tilted the dark pot up to her white face, inhaled, slowly exhaled. "It's earth." Her eyes met her husband's over the teapot. "I'm in a field with my cheek to the ground. It's an autumn afternoon." She blushed.

Chang's solemn nod was her reward.

Hot water was again added to the pot, cleaning the tea leaves and removing impurities. Chang immediately decanted the water into the five cylindrical cups, about two inches high, arranged in a circle. They watched him track the time and in exactly half a minute, the water in the cups was discarded into the bowl. "Now the cups are warmed." He rubbed his palms together. "Such work for my clumsy fingers." This was an exaggeration, as the dwarf's hands were completely steady.

They praised Chang but he gestured away their words. "The tea isn't boiled. Unlike tea from your primitive Russian samovar, made like soup."

The Baron laughed. "Friend, if you celebrate Christmas as our guest, I promise you an exquisite Russian feast. I set a fine table. We break our six-week fast on Christmas Eve with fellowship and delicacies."

Chang nodded briefly and added the final infusion of hot water into the pot to steep the tea leaves. After a few minutes, he poured the finished tea with a single circular, fluid motion into the five warm cups. The tea was then transferred from the smaller cups to the five reserved larger drinking cups. "This part of the ceremony is called 'Guan Gong inspecting the city,' as each cup is equal and each guest has equal respect. Pick up the first warm cups, the empty ones, and sniff them. Quickly, quickly, or the scent is lost."

Maria laughed, delighted by this unusual request and reverently held the cup to her freckled nose as if taking communion. A soft breath. She blinked. "Ah. A hollow that is empty, yet filled."

"A paradox in a cup," said Messonier. "Thank you, Chang."

They sat together in momentary silence. The Baron watched Li Ju put their comments into order for herself.

Chang was beatific. "The tea fragrance in the empty cups is called cold aroma, the essence of tea after it's swallowed and floats into the nose and throat. Now hold your cup of tea. Inhale. Wait thirty seconds. Inhale again. Wait one minute. Inhale a third time. Each inhalation will be different. Like the changing of clouds. Sharing the many essences of tea is called 'Han Xin mustering the troops.'"

They held the teacups, heated to the comfort of skin temperature, ready to drink, but Chang was in no hurry to release them.

His voice softened. "Before you drink, observe the color of the tea. Swallow it slowly. Delicately. Notice how the flavor changes in different areas of the mouth. Notice the encounter."

Scented warmth filled the Baron's nose, sinuses, wisped into the spaces under his cheekbones, mouth, throat. His thoughts slowed; his hand unclenched in his lap. The measure of his delight surprised him. He felt light-headed. He looked at Li Ju.

"How beautiful," she said, returning his gaze.

The tea drinkers had been altered; their expressions were tranquil, sleepy. Chang pinched the used wet tea leaves with wooden tongs and removed them from the bottom of the pot. The tea utensils were wiped clean with a cloth and he sat back in his chair, finally relaxed. "The tea ceremony is a ritual of observation and pleasure." He closed his eyes. "I don't have a poet's gift but I have memorized a poet's words." He recited for them:

Washing the bowl, cultivating a vegetarian diet, brewing buds of tea,
In the mind of the way float silent dust and sand.

After a moment, the Baron left the room and returned with a small bundle wrapped in blue cloth for Chang. "Here. Everything you need to survive."

The bundle contained green carbolic soap, formalin liquid, gauze, rubber gloves, and a dozen masks. A letter on official hospital stationery, with the Baron's signature, guaranteed the bearer of the letter safe passage from Kharbin.

"You can sell the letter if you don't need to use it."

That night, he made a confession to Li Ju. "I should leave home, avoid you. I may bring the sickness here. There's no way to tell if I'm infected until it's too late."

She held his gaze. "Never. We would become sick together."

But she was young and he would never hold her to this statement, made from ignorance and love.

Someone running in the hospital corridor. The Baron quickly stepped out of his office, nearly colliding with Maria Lebedev, who was out of breath, coat hanging from her shoulders.

"Mesny's ill. The Metropole Hotel. I have his injection."

"Where's Messonier?"

"I don't know." She fumbled an arm into the coat, her fine hair loosened from its braid, falling over her face. "Zabolotny's waiting downstairs." She left him, half-stumbled down the corridor.

"I'll go to St. Nikolas. God be with you." He backed into his office, hastily threw masks and rubber gloves into a satchel, pulled his sheepskin coat from the peg.

When he reached the main doors, Maria's droshky was already rounding away down the hospital drive. He flagged another vehicle and the driver waited outside St. Nikolas while he raced through the church to find elderly archpriest Father Simeon Orchinkin.

In the droshky, both men were silent, the wind and rattling of wheels canceling conversation. The world had condensed around them. He visualized Mesny ill in a hotel room like a miniature in the glass globe of a paperweight.

In the Metropole Hotel, the Baron helped Father Orchinkin navigate the lobby, moving so slowly that snow had puddled off their coats and boots by the time they stood in front of the sullen desk clerk.

"Third floor." The desk clerk pointed at the staircase, guessing their mission. The hotel had few visitors.

Outside Mesny's room, the Baron handed Father Orchinkin a narrow strip of white cotton fabric. Puzzled, the priest held the limp cloth until the Baron fastened a strip across his own face.

"It's a mask. You must wear it."

Orchinkin frowned. "No, no. I won't hide myself. I must be able to pray."

"Father, without a mask, you could become infected by Mesny. You'll infect everyone in the blessed church of St. Nikolas the Wonder-Worker. You must believe me."

The priest grudgingly allowed the Baron to fit a mask on him, and they entered Mesny's room still wearing their coats.

"Welcome." Mesny's voice was a soft liquid croak. He was

propped up on pillows, and at first glance it appeared his skin had absorbed color from the blanket on the bed, as his lips were faintly blue and face darkened from cyanosis.

Maria Lebedev stood at the bedside next to Zabolotny, holding up a hypodermic. "He's ready for a second dose of morphine."

The Baron strode across the room and jerked Maria away from the bed. Without protest, she waited while he rummaged in his satchel to locate a pair of gloves. She silently extended her arms and he worked the gloves over her fingers like a limp, black second skin. Finished, he softly gripped her hand for a moment. She blinked, her eyes tired behind the coarse holes in the white fabric mask.

Zabolotny hovered over Mesny with a thermometer, but Maria quickly waved it away. "I'll give you morphine now to ease your symptoms."

"Morphine? Where's the plague serum?" Mesny whispered.

She gently pulled Mesny's nightshirt up, swabbed his stomach with a cotton pad, pinched a fold of skin, and slid in the hypodermic needle. Mesny groaned and slowly grew calm, passing into sleep. She stroked a strand of damp hair off his forehead.

Zabolotny indicated a second hypodermic on the bedside table. "Shouldn't we try the serum?"

She held her finger to her lips. "Speak softly. Let's wait. The morphine seems to have had an effect. Let him rest. He's comfortable."

Zabolotny lowered his voice. "The serum will save his life. I insist we use it."

She shook her head and sat next to the bed. "It hasn't been proven effective. It could worsen his symptoms. Wait a few minutes."

"His condition is deteriorating. His temperature is elevated and his pulse is rapid. This is the perfect situation to test the serum." Restless, Zabolotny dug into his medical bag. "I don't agree with this waiting. It serves no purpose. Let the medicine do its work." He addressed the Baron. "Should we try Haffkine's treatment?"

"Let's all be in agreement with each other. I'll follow Dr. Lebedev's decision."

Maria Lebedev wrung a cloth in a pan of water and laid it on Mesny's forehead to bring down his fever. "You're not alone," she murmured to him. She found Mesny's hand under the blanket and held it.

The men carefully maneuvered chairs close to Mesny's bed. A wisp of smoke as Father Orchinkin lit a candle and began to pray under his breath, a soothing repetitive murmur.

Mesny jolted awake, dazed, and flung Maria's hand away. His coughs became deep and racking, jerking his shoulders forward. The pillows were speckled with his pink-tinged mucus.

Without changing expression or interrupting his stream of prayer, Father Orchinkin moved to avoid the spume of blood droplets coughed up by Mesny. Maria fumbled for the vial of morphine. The Baron and Zabolotny found towels and wiped blood from the bedclothes and furniture. Everyone was in motion as if evacuating a sinking ship. But in mask and gloves, they were blunted against the suffering patient, the sharp acid brilliance of his blood, its deadly slipperiness the thing they warily avoided.

Zabolotny swore. "See? Now we may be too late." In a fury, Zabolotny grabbed the hypodermic and turned aside to load it with a vial of serum.

Mesny's coughing was violent, joining the energy of all the muscles, forcing his body into great rolls and shuddering waves, firing in spasms, blood erupting from mouth and nose. He was turned inside out by plague.

The shots of morphine and the serum had no effect. Mesny bled so profusely that it seemed he'd been stabbed, spattering the white-masked figures around him. During a brief respite, he stared at his witnesses, panting, breathless, bewildered by the blood soaking his clothing, the bed, the walls, the floor. His room a canvas for a gaudy crimson display. Finally, blood was more alive than the figure in the bed.

Father Orchinkin whispered Mesny must confess in private. The doctors reluctantly stood in the corridor in their blood-stained clothing, fearing discovery by a hotel worker or guest.

After they were readmitted, the priest recited *kondaks* and *irmos,* short psalms and verses, in a low voice. "'My soul, why sleepest thou? The end is nigh, and prayer is needful for thee.'"

Their vigil soon ended with Mesny's death.

CHAPTER NINE

The Metropole Hotel on Kitayskaya Street was made from imported stone so pale that the sand blown from the north in the summer settled nearly invisibly over the building, erasing the fine carved ornamentation above the doors and windows.

Swords drawn, Russian soldiers swept into the hotel lobby, their boots depositing snow over the ornate carpet. They were followed by five men in masks and loose-fitting white coveralls, the uniform of the plague worker.

"Everyone out!" a soldier yelled at astonished guests sitting by the fireplace. "The hotel is closed."

The bewildered desk clerk waved his hands in protest but the soldiers shoved past him and ran upstairs. The chandeliers shivered as the soldiers sped from door to door, shouting orders. At first, some guests laughed in disbelief at the white-uniformed figures, believing it was a prank or an absurd Chinese demonstration. But then the guests were allowed to grab only their coats before they were hurried down the stairs and outside.

A woman screamed at the white figures reflected in the tall mirrors at the end of the corridor. Belligerent drunks and businessmen were hauled from their rooms. An angry German was forced out at sword point and a second young man, unregistered, was discovered hiding in his wardrobe.

After guests were cleared from the hotel, the five uniformed plague workers entered the room where Dr. Mesny had died. The windows behind the heavy curtains were unsealed, and the insulating sand between the double panes flowed onto the floor. The men worked quickly, as the room rapidly became freezing. Clothing, cushions, towels, and bedding, stiff with red-brown stains, were rolled up in the carpet. The bed, chairs, and wardrobe were splintered with hammers. When the room was empty, a carbolic acid mixture was haphazardly swabbed over the walls with mops as snow blew through the open windows. The disinfectant and the water on the walls and bare floor gradually froze, transformed into an icy shimmer.

All the refuse was carried downstairs through the kitchen into the alley behind the hotel. The furniture in the pile quickly burned but the mattress smoldered for a day, unnoticed, as the Metropole was empty.

A sharp bang as a firework rocket was shot from a window and then descended, wobbling, into a Fuchiatien market stall. Then explosions shook the small building, transforming it into a lantern filled with brilliant red and blue stars, a cascade of yellow arrows. The next explosions lined the windows with flowing silver sparks, quicker than rainfall. Someone had died of plague on the second floor and the sulfur fumes from the fireworks were disinfecting the building. The light, fire, and pattern of the fireworks had no power over contamination.

A child laughed loudly but the Baron hadn't seen any children in the crowd watching the fireworks around him. Unnerved, he stepped back, colliding with a stranger as several frightened people hurried away through the clouds of gunpowder, bitter gray smoke hanging over chalky snow. It seemed the snow, even the air itself, had become strange, foul, poisoned. He imagined snowflakes erupting from a seedpod, a malignant container, spreading plague across the city, whirling furiously into every crevice and corner, sticking their spiked edges into skin, drawing blood. There was no protection, no safety.

Each morning, plague dead appeared on the streets like carnage from a secret battle. The plague-stricken crawled from home to die alone. Others were dragged outside and abandoned, or their bodies were hidden. Many of the dead were naked, stripped by thieves who stole their clothing to sell or wear. Snow buried and reburied the corpses but drifts betrayed what they concealed. Shadows formed in the hollow of a bent arm or leg. A head was exaggerated by a helmet of thick ice. A dark shape on the ground could be the sleeve of a dead woman's coat, a foot in a boot, a hand in a glove.

Like a dreamer confronting an absurd situation, the Baron carefully scanned the ground before he took a step, afraid his boot would strike a body frozen in the posture of death. He was more secure here on trampled snow where others had already walked, making paths around bodies. He felt like a sleepwalker but there was no waking.

He gulped cold air to jolt himself into movement and leave this place. He shouted for the droshky driver, then clambered into the vehicle. Exhausted, he fell back against the thick bearskin rugs and ordered the driver to Central Station.

Reluctantly, he left the comfort of the droshky and walked through the waiting room. He stopped at a small shrine where a group of Chinese women crossed themselves and bowed before the icon of Saint Nikolas. The Chinese had adopted "Grandfather

Nikolas," convinced the Russian saint brought travelers luck, and left him offerings of incense, candles, coins, food, tea, and paper money heaped on a red cloth below his icon.

There was shouting near the departure gates and then the abrupt movement of bodies. Following the noise, he hurried across the waiting room as if his name had been called, dodging passengers burdened with baggage.

At the departure gates, Wang Xiang'an, a young doctor in a white uniform, and another intern held a struggling man as passengers jostled them, angered by the man's rough treatment. Wang held the flailing man's chin, pinched his cheeks, and poked a thermometer into his mouth. Frightened, the man bit down then spat out bloody glass pieces. The two doctors loosened their hold on him, moved back to a table set with medical supplies, gloves, and jars of disinfectant.

"Give him water. Rinse your mouth." The man spat bloody water on the floor, wiped the red from his face with a sleeve.

The Baron hesitated, reluctant to interfere. Where were the soldiers? More men were needed to keep the situation under control and prevent passengers from storming onto the train.

"The glass stick isn't poisoned. Look here." Wang's voice carried over the crowd. He confidently dipped a thermometer in a jar of clear liquid, wiped it on a cloth. "You see? Nothing to fear." He momentarily held up the thermometer, then inserted it in his own mouth.

The crowd murmured as if he'd revealed the secret to a magic act.

Wang produced a fresh thermometer and waved it in front of their stubborn captive's face until he accepted it between his lips. After a minute, Wang removed the thermometer, studied it, and smiled. "You're not infected. You may go."

Dazed, the man wandered in the direction of the departure gates and the lone waiting soldier.

"No one boards the train until they're tested," Wang announced and grinned at the Baron, visibly proud of his success.

He answered the young doctors in French. "Where are your masks? You should be protected."

Wang dismissed his concern. "It's difficult to talk and handle the thermometer wearing a mask and gloves. And there's always a fight. But we study each passenger carefully."

"Carefully? You're too confident. Symptoms aren't always obvious. It's like gunpowder. You can smell it but the time of explosion isn't predictable."

Wang briskly prepared a thermometer for the next passenger in line. "We've tested hundreds of people this week. A good number were sent to the hospital with fever or a cough. There's always a passenger who argues."

"Move aside. Move aside." A tall blond Slav in a shaggy fox coat swung his arms as he led a family—a gentleman, his wife, and four small children in identical black fur coats—toward the departure gates as if claiming a table at a fine restaurant. The crowd parted for the wealthy family. The Slav stalked past the doctors' station toward the soldier at the gates.

Wang shouted after them. The passengers in line weren't surprised. A voice jeered: "Money gets you on the train."

The doctors, grim-faced, seemed diminished in their white uniforms, uncertain how to control the unruly group. "Shall I find another soldier?" The younger intern was panicked, but there were no soldiers nearby.

The Baron threatened the Slav. "I order you to halt."

The Slav wheeled around, furious at this challenge. Fine hair, colorless as powder, fringed his pockmarked face; his pupils were pinprick circles. An addict.

"This man cannot board the train. He's in possession of drugs.

Opium." The Baron beckoned to the soldier, who winced, reluctant to provoke a rich man's fury and lose a generous bribe.

The gentleman flushed with anger. "My servant is stopped on whose authority?"

"The city health commissioner's."

The gentleman scornfully studied the Baron, an official in a thick, worn sheepskin coat, a cotton mask wrinkled around his neck. The Baron knew he was an unprepossessing figure. No one of account. But he spoke for all the passengers. "On whose authority are you boarding the train without medical clearance?"

The gentleman frowned. "Very well. The servant stays here."

"Please hand me your papers." The Baron took a thick envelope from the gentleman, unfolding it carefully so as not to dislodge the wad of rubles inside. A letter stamped by General Khorvat, wax seal, ribbon. It appeared authentic. The Slav took advantage of the Baron's distraction to slip into the crowd.

"Baron Rozher Alexandrovich, can we help?" Wang played the nobility card.

At the mention of the title, the gentleman straightened and studied the Baron with an incredulous expression. "I am Sergei Ivanovich Zhirmov. Our fathers were friends in St. Petersburg."

"God have mercy. Why are you in Kharbin?"

Zhirmov relaxed. "I opened a timber concession here. My wife's mother is very ill. We're traveling back to visit her." He leaned closer, edging for sympathy.

The Baron understood Zhirmov's unsaid message. The watching passengers were a pressure behind the little group.

"Sir, my friend, my mission is to save your life and the life of your children—"

The wife interrupted. "It's urgent we leave immediately."

The woman had a pleading expression and something else, hidden knowledge, a calculation. Perhaps she suspected one child was ill. If so, the entire family would be sent to quarantine. A doomed situation. The Baron cursed his own thoroughness. He imagined a long line behind the family, those they would infect and who would infect others in turn. A chain of infection. There was no choice. No exceptions. "Let the doctors check you and your family. After this single test, you'll never need worry."

Wang, hovering behind them, stepped forward and presented a thermometer to Zhirmov, who scowled but allowed it between his lips. The intern swiftly distributed thermometers to the other family members. The last child backed away and hid behind her mother's long skirt. Wang knelt, coaxing the child into cooperation, while the intern read the thermometers from the rest of the family.

"Everyone is within the range of health. Their temperatures are normal."

They gathered around the little girl, waiting for the glass stick to declare her family's fate. The mother exchanged an anguished glance with the father and he leaned over to rummage in his satchel.

Does he have a weapon?

Even suicide to avoid the purgatory of quarantine seemed reasonable. Betrayed by only the slightest tremor, the Baron slipped the thermometer from the child's lips, turned it over. "She's fine."

The mother closed her eyes. The group smiled, a burst of exuberance.

"Give my regards to the Neva and Vasil'evskiy Island. Years since I've been there. I wish you a pleasant journey."

Relieved, the Baron embraced Zhirmov. The other man laid his gloved hands on his children's heads and ushered them toward the gates.

The Baron turned to Wang. An impressive young man.

"I interrupted you. I hope I acted correctly." Wang was uncertain.

"I applaud your quick thinking. The situation was difficult to anticipate. It could have been deadly. Now, I have another assignment for you. We go to Torgovaya Street. A sick man was discovered by an innkeeper. But first, scrub your hands and put on fresh gloves. Otherwise, we ride in separate vehicles."

The Baron and Wang Xiang'an stepped into the inn, and the door slammed behind them. They stood in a murky room, suffocatingly hot, the walls and ceiling layered with smoke from lanterns. A group of men were gathered around a table and a small stove, their figures stern black silhouettes that turned toward the intruders.

It was customary to weave a narrow strip of red cloth into children's queues to ward off evil spirits who brought smallpox. The Baron wished for a similar protective charm as he began the inspection. "I apologize for interrupting you after a hard day's work." The surprise of a Russian speaking Chinese momentarily held the men's attention. "We're doctors. We're here to find someone who was reported ill. The sick person must be treated."

Faces unmoving as a wall. The men muttered and shifted uneasily. No man would betray another. The Baron was a Russian telling lies, his Chinese words a trick. He was seeking prey. Why would he help a Chinese?

"If one person is sick, everyone here will become sick. This is truth." The Baron spoke softly to Wang as he set up a small lantern on the table. "How can we make it clear that the sickness jumps from person to person?"

The young doctor's face creased with impatience. "They're too stupid to understand. You might as easily explain a microscope.

Lie to them," he sputtered. "Frighten them. Force them into co-operating."

"We're outnumbered."

Wang shouted for silence. "Your lungs, one of the five yang organs, guards your vital breath. *Feng*, the empty wind, possesses the body only when the body is weak. We will check for signs of weakness in the yang organs."

This was familiar, and the tension in the room eased slightly.

The two doctors cleared space around the lantern, unpacked a medical kit, and placed thermometers, a jar of alcohol, and cotton masks where they could clearly be seen. The Baron held up a tiny wand of glass, a thermometer, then slipped it into Wang's mouth. After a moment, the thermometer was removed, dropped into the jar.

"See? No harm." Wang smiled. "If anyone is sick, they will be taken care of in the hospital without fee. They will be fed."

The doctors spoke quietly, explaining their actions as they buttoned long white jackets over their clothing, concealed their hands with rubber gloves, secured cotton masks across their faces. White was the color of death, traditionally worn by Chinese mourners at funerals. But it seemed the doctors hid their faces behind masks to prepare for a sinister ritual.

A wave of hostility and several men in the back of the room stood up. The clamor of angry voices. "Throw out the foreign devils!"

The Baron hesitated, then boldly walked between the tables, hoping his presence would calm the situation. He was slow and bumbling in his clumsy uniform, his voice and vision muffled, but if a blow came, the extra clothing offered some protection. The laborers watched him move among them, no one daring to touch the stranger in white. He searched their faces, noticed a man with a long queue under a fur hat hunched over the table, gently asked him to stand. Scowling, the man lifted his legs over the bench with an effort, his sullen expression vanishing as his body shook with coughing. The others edged away from him.

"Come with us, little brother." The Baron took the man's arm, guided him to a seat by the lantern. The man's defiance vanished as if he'd confessed to a crime. His temperature was high. He was obviously unwell.

The rest of the men reluctantly cooperated with the doctors' rudimentary examination. None of them showed signs of fever, a flushed face, or a swollen tongue. The Baron couldn't look at them without a sense of betrayal as he checked them for symptoms. He was repeatedly overwhelmed by a wave of tenderness, a longing to stop this process, to explain the situation, turn them aside from their fate.

Gradually, the Baron became preoccupied with the fact that he could carry the thread of sickness. He scoured and cleaned his contaminated hands, wished they could be peeled raw like an orange or a lemon, the dull thick skin. The rough whorls of his fingerprints should be uncoiled. They were dangerous patterns that trapped bacilli, deposited it on everything he touched, the back of a chair, his pockets, bootlaces, a spoon, circumference of a teacup, edges of a tray, the wadded silk coverlet on the bed. Perhaps he'd unwittingly tracked infection across the pages of calligraphy, bacilli from his fingers embedded in ink, the weasel-hair brush, water in the jar that dissolved the ink. Perhaps his fingerprint on a glass was a charm of infection, waiting to contaminate the innocent touch of Li Ju and the servants.

He usually recognized and dismissed these disturbing thoughts as fantasies formed by despair and fear. Still, people reacted in unpredictable ways when they were frightened. Patients had been known to strike at doctors in fury when they were ignored or in pain. One of his patients had smashed the glass in his office door after a poor diagnosis.

He began to hoard rubber gloves, even those that had been worn and discarded, certain that in the future they'd be scarce or unavailable. Gloves were valuable; like gold, they were a hedge against misfortune.

The locations where the plague dead had been found were converted into red dots on a map behind General Khorvat's desk. There were identical maps in the offices of the doctors Boguchi, Iasienski, and Haffkine. Dr. Wu was the only Chinese who possessed this information. The Baron leaned close to study this view of Kharbin, its cluster of deaths telescoped into code on the map. His two fingers covered all the red dots, the greatest number concentrated in Fuchiatien. Four bodies on Bazarnaya Street. The dead were also found at 238 Mekhanicheskaya Street, 19 Torgovaya Street, and 8 and 20 Yaponskaya Street. With his Chinese contacts, he'd helped build this map, searching boardinghouses, brothels, barbershops, inns, and eating places for the plague-stricken and the dead.

The Baron turned to face Khorvat. "This map is a fraud. The number of dead is far greater."

Khorvat's benign expression barely wavered into disagreement. "There's no proof of your statement. The dead are removed by corpse carriers. They tally the bodies. I assume they're reliable."

"Have you seen the corpse carriers?"

"No. But I make decisions based on information I receive." Distracting and placating others is one of the liar's skills. "Last night, I was confronted by a woman at the Railway Club. Can you imagine? She wants a flag flying over Central Station to warn about the level of danger from plague. Claimed it was the system for a yellow fever outbreak when she was in India. My wife has greater inconveniences in Crimea. I dismissed the woman immediately."

"They're hiding bodies."

The Baron's statement fixed a bewildered expression on Khorvat's face.

"Families, innkeepers, even shop owners hide the dead so you won't burn down their buildings. Or take everyone in the place to the hospital for observation."

"It's fortunate that with few exceptions, bodies were found in Fuchiatien, one-third verst away from us here in Novy Gorod. So there's no need to panic. God forbid there's a corpse near the British American Tobacco Company or John Deere headquarters. We'd have an international crisis. The consuls would flee Kharbin."

The Baron ignored his comment. "A corpse freezes solid in less than a day. The Chinese hide the frozen body, later return it to their village, and bury it with the ancestors. Even plague victims. It's their custom. Plague will spread across the country."

Khorvat dug a crumbly Crimean cigarette from a small tortoiseshell box and offered it to the Baron with a sour expression. "Baron, ask anyone in my office if they've seen a corpse. The answer is no. I plan to keep the situation quiet until it's conquered. There's order on the streets."

"Order? It's temporary. A false peace. There are bodies under the snow on the streets." The Baron recognized he was verging on disrespect but recklessly continued. "Picking up corpses won't stop the epidemic. You're sweeping the floor while the wind blows in leaves and dirt."

Khorvat lit the cigarette and then slowly exhaled fragrant pale tobacco smoke over his desk, an action meant to keep his temper in check. "My soldiers do what they can. They can't peer under every rock and into every cart in Kharbin looking for corpses. The first twenty buildings registered as contaminated by plague were burned to keep the infection from spreading. Other buildings were fumigated with sulfur or carbolic acid solution. Even the Metropole Hotel was fumigated."

"Mother of God. Would a thunderbolt strike sense into your head? The plague is out there in the street. It's a live thing, a beast with a strategy for survival, for spreading infection. For killing us."

"What do you offer? What will you put in my hands to help, Baron?"

"Yesterday we found one sick man at an inn on Torgovaya Street. By tomorrow there'll be ten sick men. That's how it works. People will panic as more bodies are discovered. There will be mobs in the streets. More soldiers will be needed."

"We have limited options. I don't have enough soldiers to patrol the city even under ordinary circumstances. If the number of dead goes up, our weakness will be exposed. Unfortunately, the newspapers *Kharbinskii Vestnik* and *Novoe Vremya* and two Chinese papers have reported Dr. Mesny's death from plague. I couldn't stop them. Why frighten civilians when the situation is being handled?"

The Baron slumped in his seat, stared at Khorvat as if he'd just recognized something familiar. "So it's in Russia's best interests that bodies are hidden?"

"The czar would gladly send more soldiers to Kharbin but the Chinese would regard it as a provocation. This is what they wish to avoid at all costs."

Khorvat momentarily forgot the Baron and muttered calculations. "Unless, of course, the Chinese ask for our help controlling the epidemic. Then our soldiers move in with their permission."

"But soldiers will help keep order. Lives will be saved. How could the Chinese object?"

"The Chinese believe every Russian soldier is a foreign invader in their territory. I predict the Chinese will refuse help. Even if millions die."

"So we're unable to obtain any kind of assistance?"

Khorvat moved away from the Baron's question. "We have a delicate peace. We must keep this illusion and hide our teeth. Our position is unstable. Japan wants Manchuria. They have a military quarantine along the Korean border. They built iron barracks, although they call them quarantine stations, along the CER train tracks, each accommodating one thousand to three thousand men. The Japanese Eleventh Division arrived from Hiroshima to relieve the Fifth Division in Kharbin. I don't approve." He waved his hand, delicately dropping cigarette ash over the papers on his desk. "But any Russian military action against Japan would be interpreted by China as infringing on their sovereignty. So the Japanese army waits like a cat for a mouse. At the right hour, they move into Manchuria and seize the Kharbin station and its network of trains. They'd be pleased if all the Russian soldiers died of plague, leaving Kharbin vulnerable to invasion. We're the gateway to the world. Why do you think I've been posted here?"

"To be honest, I've never considered what determines a general's location."

Khorvat paid no attention to his comment, clearly enjoying spinning his argument. "We have a treaty with Japan. Secret, or it was secret. The presence of the Japanese army is to our advantage since they keep the Chinese in line. China hates Japan more than it hates Russia. China plays Russia against Japan. You see? The three armies checkmate each other."

"But the Japanese also built their barracks along the railroad from Tientsin to Dairen. There are thousands of Japanese soldiers. They could easily be decimated by plague."

"The Japanese have their own medical personnel. It's out of my hands. I suppose the Japanese generals are convinced guns are a greater threat than plague. I understand this logic. Better the death that you know. But some generals take chances that surprise me. I predict China will welcome American aid, believing that they're no threat."

"So if we survive plague," the Baron said, speaking slowly, as if examining something unfamiliar, "we could be attacked by the Japanese?"

Khorvat made a dismissive gesture. "The military would never target doctors or civilians. But I assure you, there are plans for evacuation in the event of a Japanese invasion."

The general's answers outlined the parameters of a trap. The Baron fixed his gaze on the rows of gold buttons on Khorvat's uniform to help neutralize his expression. "There's another battle in the hospital. Dr. Wu. He's young and inexperienced. He can't manage this situation. It isn't just tending the sick in hospital beds. Wu has no loyalty from the other doctors. It's hurting our patient treatment. He doesn't understand—"

Khorvat interrupted. "Dr. Wu represents the Chinese government. He must be obeyed. One angry telegram from Dr. Wu to the emperor would end Chinese cooperation and perhaps bring their army into our streets. It can't be risked."

"Wu is incapable."

"This isn't just a feud between doctors. It's a claim of national territory. You try to convince Wu that your analysis is superior to his own. But I won't save your skin once he turns on you. You remember his dismissal of Dr. Mesny."

The mention of Mesny stirred bitterness, as Khorvat had never properly acknowledged the doctor's suffering. Mesny had sacrificed his life. The Baron struggled against his anger but failed to keep it in check. "So the only protection for everyone is the throw of the dice."

Khorvat's reservoir of sympathy had run out. "We wait and trust merciful God. I will forgive your disrespectful address to me, your superior. My job is to keep order. You tend the sick. We meet in the middle."

"Better meet in the middle than at each other's sickbed. Good day, General Khorvat."

During the silent ride home in the droshky, the Baron remembered threatening dreams in which he'd been unable to move, had been trapped in place. Mesny's death was like that dream. He had been powerless to save the dying man, to stop the remorseless force pumping blood through his veins until it gushed into the world, a shapeless liquid.

At home, he shook wet snow from his boots and his sheepskin coat, ridding himself of everything he had carried past the door. Without waiting for the servant to bring hot water, he angrily scrubbed his hands in the icy basin until they were bright red. Irregular surfaces that couldn't be easily cleaned were suspect, invisibly veiled with contamination: his rough hands, carved furniture, the folds of a fan, buttons, books, embroidery. At night, he visualized everything he'd touched that day as if they were clues linked to a future catastrophe in the same way others worried about an unlocked door or an untended fire.

Li Ju brought his felt boots and sat close to him at the table.

He felt the slight pressure of her body against his, remembered she and Chang had been planning to visit a fortune-teller that afternoon, although he'd cautioned her against it. He feared predictions might bring misfortune, a cataclysm of bad luck opening around them inexorably as a flower.

"What did the fortune-teller say? I hope there were no predictions of illness."

"No," Li Ju said quietly.

"Did she predict happiness, long life? A child?"

"First the woman offered the choices. She could tell my fortune by a coin toss, casting lots, or chopsticks in a bowl of water. Or cards and two shaped blocks of wood, *buguo*. She could read my face and head or the joints of my fingers. In spring, she interprets the cries of birds."

"What was your choice?" He was relieved Li Ju so easily shared the information with him. She kept no secrets. Still, he disliked himself in the role of questioner.

"The *I-Ching*. The woman threw the forty-nine yarrow sticks on the table. She studied the sticks for a long time. I waited and tried to be still. Chang almost made me laugh; he kept making faces. Then she read a hexagram from the *I-Ching*. I remember one, nine in the second place."

"Tell me."

Li Ju was straightforward, a good child reciting lessons:

One kills three foxes in the field
And receives a yellow arrow.
Perseverance brings good fortune.

Kill three foxes? the Baron thought. The fox was associated with the supernatural. He had an old man's nervousness, the bitter awareness of his own mortality. Had Li Ju carried his fear to the fortune-teller? "How did she interpret the hexagram?"

"The foxes are sly. She said I must battle the power that they hold and kill them. The yellow arrow's a weapon to use in the future. It's my reward. The color is harmonizing. Its message is to avoid the tangle of extreme passion."

"Passion? She said avoid passion?" He was bewildered. He'd been secretly convinced the fortune-teller would praise him to his wife, celebrate their union, how well suited they were to each other.

"I think so. A warning of excess."

He didn't trust Li Ju's answer; she seemed evasive. Perhaps she didn't believe the prediction, although she'd heard nothing about death. Any future threats seemed conquerable.

"But what was the fortune-teller's expression when she spoke to you? Do you believe she was truthful?" He continued to question her although she backed away from his pursuit.

"I've told you everything I can remember." She frowned, struggling to describe the encounter. "The fortune-teller was tired. Many people were waiting. It was a small crowded room." Uneasy, she twisted her fingers together.

"Nothing else?"

"No."

"Was Chang pleased with his future?"

"Yes. He gave me a gift. See." Chang had brought a colorful printed paper titled "The Chart of Disappearing Cold" with nine rows of nine circles to mark eighty-one days from the winter solstice until spring. A count to carry them through the bitter season.

"Very pretty. What did the fortune-teller say to Chang?"

"'There is no escape from the unchangeableness of change.' *Xuanxue* is the dark law of mysterious things."

That was no comfort. He carried the words like a closed book to bed. His body slowly eased into a familiar position and in the moment before sleep, Li Ju slipped in beside him and found his cold hand under the quilt. Her fingertips playfully pressed the inside of his wrist, pretending to read his *mo*. She wasn't trained but had memorized the twenty-four descriptions in the ancient lexicon for him. The loving connection of *mo* was part of their intimate play. He hoped this didn't mock or betray the tradition that he regarded as profound. To her, the *mo* was poetry, direction, joy. What he desired. A touch and an incantation, mysterious and strange, linked to pleasure.

She communicated her desire to him in the language of the *mo*. Sometimes she instructed him to be rough with her, like "rain-soaked sand." At other times, she desired "a smooth succession of rolling pearls." He was certain their imaginations never matched but arousal was mutual.

When she was younger and he first took her to bed, he was uncertain, afraid that something in her education or background would make her reject his tenderness. He exposed his nakedness to her only gradually, wearing a loose robe, understanding that his large hairy body with loose fatty flesh was totally foreign to her. The *mo* was their game, a coaxing seduction.

"Sand over water," she whispered in his ear.

A line of ink on paper was irreversible. Skin was more forgiving. Skin changed with the touch of a finger. He dedicated his calligraphy to his wife. Her body was the paper; the brush traced a pattern of intimacy. Pressing memory into a line with the ink. If he had explained this to her, she would have smiled, made a gesture of dismissal.

Xiansheng, his teacher, didn't recognize this tribute, his secret state of mind. The Baron felt himself a deceiver. But his teacher had once stated that the *cao shu*, the delicate, lively grass-style calligraphy, could be successfully learned only against a background of quietly rippling water or by witnessing snakes as they writhed and fought.

The Russo-Chinese Bank was a palatial building with chandeliers and marble floors. The serenity of the main room was interrupted by an echoing *click-click-click,* steady as the noise of insects, as each clerk at a desk worked with an abacus. Overhead, ceiling fans delicately vibrated in the hot air radiating up from the blue-and-white porcelain stoves in the corners. The Baron stamped snow from his boots on the threshold mat and noticed Andreev across the room, finishing a transaction with a clerk. The Baron handed a chit to the teller behind the window and was issued a stack of rubles and a few heavy silver pesos. He decided to wait for Andreev on the upholstered settee and savor the pleasure of a warm room.

Andreev bundled up his papers, bowed to the clerk, and greeted the Baron. "A cold day for business. My shoulders ache from walking outside in this frigid temperature. Like a clenched fist." He shrugged his shoulders, stretched his arms, and nestled into the plush cushions next to the Baron.

"December weather." The Baron had just started relaxing in the heat.

"I don't need reminding. You've probably already started preparing for the Great Lent."

"Not yet." The Baron wondered if Andreev should be invited to dinner before the fast started. Was he hinting at this? He peered at the man's face but sensed he was already distracted.

"I heard the gold is stored upstairs." Andreev glanced up at the open gallery circling the dome of the building.

"Gold?"

"Prince Kugusev persuaded the Upper Amur River Gold Mining Company to deposit their ingots here. See the guard?" His eyes followed the dim figure of a man pacing with a rifle on the open gallery above them. "The guard marched around the gallery until the prince complained his boots were too noisy. Maybe the soldier is barefoot now." Andreev's face wrinkled into a grin.

"All quiet today. But how do you have information about this gold?"

"Talk drifts downriver."

"Seems very innocent."

"I recently supplied two men who went north as far as Manchouli in Manchuria. They hunted birds, strange fierce animals. I saw the skins they brought back. I introduced Alexiovich, the Russian hunter, to his Jesuit guide. Alexiovich came back with a collection of dead animals, swore he'd never return."

"Jesuits were the first explorers allowed in Manchuria by the Imperial Throne, over two hundred years ago."

"Manchuria is barely settled but it has dangers that make Kharbin seem like a cradle. Hutzul bandits swoop in on horseback, kill entire villages. The Russian said they'd walked into a village where everyone had died of a sickness."

The Baron's attention flared like a match. "A sickness?"

Andreev was startled by the Baron's interest. "All I know is they found one man who was still alive. Blood everywhere. They thought it was a Hutzul massacre. The Jesuit priest was too late to save his soul."

"What was this sickness?"

"I don't know."

"Where can I find this Russian, Alexiovich?"

Uneasy with the Baron's insistence, Andreev put on a false

smile, attempted to take back his words. "He told me very little. What I heard, I've mostly forgotten."

"But you must know how to contact him, since you delivered supplies for his expedition."

"My men made the delivery to him. I don't drive goods around Kharbin."

Their exchange became jagged, stressful, as both men recognized it had decayed into evasion and falsehood. *The superior man is master of his demeanor.* The Baron relaxed his mouth. "I see. You might recollect the information later."

"Yes. I might."

"And the Jesuit priest, Alexiovich's guide? Who is he? Where is he?"

"Lost in Manchuria. Never returned."

There was some reason for Andreev to withhold information about the Russian hunter and his guide. Alexiovich was probably a prominent businessman or official who could afford a lengthy expedition. Andreev might know about a scandal, potential blackmail that involved this man. Alexiovich. A common name. A hare's chase. But he couldn't afford to dismiss Andreev for keeping this secret. Friends, anyone, could die within a day. A lapse of judgment could be forgiven. Even an insult could be forgotten.

Andreev returned his attention to the Baron. "There's something you should see. Follow me."

Outside the bank, the wind caught them and they doubled back on Konnaya Street. Andreev turned into a narrow alley and grabbed the Baron's arm.

"There. See," Andreev hissed softly, pointing at two shadowy figures standing so still they seemed embedded in the courtyard wall. One of them had something draped over his arm, perhaps a cloth or net, and they both held stout sticks.

"Don't move," Andreev whispered.

One of the silent figures stepped cautiously forward, then stopped. Another step and a pause. Then he leaped forward and smashed his stick into the ground several times.

The Baron turned for an explanation, but Andreev's hand gestured for quiet. The two figures edged along the wall, waiting motionless for twenty breaths, then chased something back and forth, furiously slamming their sticks down again and again, churning up the snow. Then they slowly searched the ground, stabbing their sticks to impale small dark objects, dropping them into a sack. Finished, they stopped and pulled back their fur hoods. Two women.

"Rat hunters. Each dead rat gets a bounty from the Kharbin government," Andreev said. "Thousands of rats are killed every day. People are desperate. There's no work. The railroad dismissed all the Chinese workers, thousands of men, fearing they'd spread infection. But the Russians are still employed."

So Dr. Mesny's rat-collecting program had survived his dismissal.

A man pushed a cart over to the women rat catchers and they swung their heavy sacks into it.

"Rats are saviors of the starving. Some hunters boast they can strangle rats with their bare hands."

"You're well informed about rat hunters, Andreev."

"I'm always interested in new markets."

"You're considering work as a rat catcher?"

"Broker and importer." Andreev made an expansive gesture. "I have wagons and carts loaded with dead rats moving from Kirin, Hulan, and Shitaochengtzu to Kharbin. The rats are packed frozen. Flattened. Easy to transport here for the bounty payment. There's no proof of origin."

The Baron felt something like admiration and the absurdity of the situation bubbled inside and erupted. His laughter was a white cloud between them.

They walked past the opera house and the Standard Oil office, Andreev waving at patches of dirty snow and bright red ice patterned with spatters of blood from the clubbed rats.

Andreev hailed a droshky and they drove past the sites haunted by rat hunters stalking their prey in alleys, garbage dumps, cesspools, wells, burned-out buildings, warehouses stacked with timber, and flour mills. By the tanneries, footsteps marred the snow around foul black pools, the waste from skinned goats, lambs, and horses, scummed over, crusted, never frozen.

"A tour of hell." The Baron pulled the fur collar up under his nose as the smell penetrated even inside the droshky.

At a collection point, the driver stopped and they watched a steady stream of men, women, and children line up with bulky sacks and baskets balanced on poles across their shoulders. The dead rats were dumped out, counted. The hunters were paid. A row of wagons, guarded by soldiers, transported the dead vermin to a warehouse in Staryi Kharbin, about five miles from the Sungari River.

Next, the droshky driver took them to the stock exchange building, where three soldiers loitered near the door. One of them lifted his rifle and slowly swung around, tracking something moving on the ground along a stone wall. He fired once, triggering a faint high-pitched squeal, and then he ran forward and thumped his rifle butt into the snow, finishing off the animal.

Andreev grimaced. "They kill cats and dogs since they also carry plague fleas. I begin to think everything that moves is infected. There's one last place to show you."

Daylight was fading. Snow hid a vast mesh of train tracks around a warehouse so it appeared stranded in a field of smooth snow. The droshky driver refused to go farther. The two men jumped from the vehicle, moved unsteadily toward the warehouse, their legs plunging deep into the snow, unable to judge its depth. At the warehouse, the guard acknowledged Andreev's salute and the Baron followed him through a low door. Inside, a terrible stench, and he clapped his cold glove over his nose, shaken by the howling and barking of dogs. He stepped back from the hundreds of dogs locked in cages, row upon row stacked above his head.

Andreev had blocked his nose with a cloth and gestured toward the door. Outside, they fell back against the wall, gasping, gulping fresh air. The Baron wanted to throw himself in the snow, roll and roll to suffocate the memory, the smell of the place.

"Why did you bring me here?"

Andreev's eyes were fixed in calculation. "The men who raise the animals for skins and meat smuggle in food for the dogs. They buy scraps to feed the animals from several sources to avoid raising suspicion. If this place was discovered, all the dogs would be slaughtered, since they have fleas that might carry plague."

The Baron staggered upright, waded through snow in the direction of the droshky, moving so slowly he felt it was the suspension of a dream. Then Andreev helped him stand up although he didn't remember falling. "I want you to report this place. For the sake of the dogs."

"But the animals will be killed." The Baron was bewildered.

"It will be a mercy. The poor beasts suffer."

CHAPTER TEN

Wu fiddled impatiently with his spectacles while a boy moved around the hospital conference table, deftly serving everyone hot tea from the samovar. The Baron recognized this was not an empty moment and prepared himself during the wait, correcting his posture, settling calm into his breath. *Stilling the heart,* as his teacher had described. It was a relief to be free of the bulky protective clothing, the white mask, and sit face-to-face with the others. But the smooth wood table, the metal chairs, shelves, the scattered papers, offered no defense against the bacilli that haunted them. He imagined the hospital empty, the soft bodies of the doctors and patients vanished. Was anyone else uneasy? Zabolotny, Iasienski, Lebedev, Haffkine, Wu?

Wu wished them good morning, called for their attention. "A few points of business to begin. After Dr. Mesny's untimely death at the Metropole, the hotel was fumigated and temporarily closed. Unfortunately, his death also prompted a neighboring hotel, the Grand, to evict all the doctors and medical workers who were guests. Until there's an alternative, we'll rent private homes or rooms for the displaced. Never discuss this with anyone outside the hospital. Certainly never speak to newspapers or representatives from foreign countries. Rumors harm us."

Messonier raised a hand. "Dr. Wu, with all respect, Dr. Mesny's death touched everyone."

"His death was a tragic warning."

"I'd like to offer silent prayer in honor of Dr. Mesny." Messonier lowered his head over his folded hands and the rest of the doctors followed his example.

After Messonier had finished, the Baron broke the silence. "Glory to God. Thank you, Dr. Messonier. You spoke for our hearts."

Only the slightest flicker betrayed Wu's relief that the prayer had ended, as if he'd somehow been excluded, and he immediately filled this space with words. "The Red Cross has organized insurance. In the unlikely event of death, they'll provide for the families of all the doctors." He paused, interrupting the glance between the Baron and Messonier. "Now Dr. Haffkine will brief us about his anti-plague serum."

"A supply of the serum to treat the disease was just delivered here from Fort Alexander in Kronstadt. The shipping expense was considerable."

The Baron had questions. "My Chinese contacts said Japan ships two thousand doses of Dr. Kitasato's plague vaccine to Manchuria every day. Anyone—Chinese, Russian, Japanese, German, Slav—can be vaccinated immediately without charge. So why are citizens not being inoculated when a free supply is at hand, Dr. Wu?"

Wu was serene. "The viceroy of Manchuria is aware of Dr. Kitasato's plague vaccine. But to inject Chinese citizens with a Japanese vaccine? Never. The Japanese are not trusted. The viceroy has forbidden Kitasato's vaccine. It is too risky. Japanese, Russians, and everyone else may make their own choice about this vaccine."

"Dr. Kitasato is a recognized expert at the Tokio Institute for the Study of Infectious Diseases. He's studied plague for years. But I believe I understand your position." The Baron's words were drawn out, calculated as a brush on paper. "The viceroy of Manchuria cannot allow the Japanese vaccine to succeed."

"I'm not authorized to discuss the viceroy's decision with you."

"So national pride is what determines the use of the vaccine. Not the needs of the people."

An uncomfortable silence bound everyone at the table. Maria Lebedev struggled to keep her expression composed.

Wu ignored the Baron. "Your opinion, Dr. Haffkine?"

"Yes, of course. The patients are treated with my serum when the first symptoms develop. I anticipate it will slow the progress of the sickness. For those exposed to plague but without symptoms, the infection can be stopped with the vaccine."

The doctors shared smiles of relief.

"Your claims are very positive." The Baron set his cup on the table, the movement jerkily animated by anger. "I'm curious to hear what type of trials were conducted to test the Haffkine serum's effectiveness?"

Haffkine avoided his eyes. "Just recently in the Russian hospital, four plague-infected Chinese were treated with various amounts of the anti-plague serum made from pure plague endotoxin. Two hundred, three hundred, four hundred, and five hundred ccs were injected subcutaneously into their abdomens. A second group of sick patients received no treatment. We wait for the results of this trial but it seems promising. Everything is well documented."

"Were the patients informed that they were receiving this serum?"

"No."

"No?"

"It wasn't considered necessary."

"No?" The Baron recognized this game of charades, the players asking question after question to identify the hidden answer.

Haffkine's fingers tapped against a folder in front of him. "How could the concept be explained so these illiterate patients could understand it? No translator was available. It was simply more expedient to administer the medication."

"More expedient?" Iasienski spoke in a whisper.

Dr. Wu said, "There was no plot against the patients, as you and the Baron seem to imply. It was a decision that I approved."

"Of course they'd want treatment that would extend their life." Zabolotny nodded. "Anyone would make that choice."

The Baron turned to Haffkine and unfolded his challenge. "Mother of God. You claim the patients couldn't understand life and death? Shameful. And you support this decision, Dr. Wu?"

With Wu's backing, Haffkine was bold enough to show his exasperation. "I'm not making excuses, but these risks are necessary to save other lives, Baron. Some decisions are guesswork but must be made quickly before we all sink. Deaths are counted by the dozen every day."

"It's a state of emergency." Zabolotny raised his voice. "The city collapses if the epidemic strikes. If we fail here, the consequences are disastrous. Should plague spread inside the wall at Shanhaiguan and Tientsin, Beijing is threatened."

"Yet you refuse to consider Kitasato's vaccine." Maria Lebedev gestured violently with both hands. "We all desperately wish for a solution and a cure. Every minute we make this wish. But we shouldn't foolishly dismiss other possibilities, other answers. Or abandon our honor."

"At this point, there's no proof Haffkine's injections have saved a single life." Messonier opened his hands palms up on the table, as if this vulnerability would soften his statement.

"Say what you like." Haffkine finished with his argument. "My serum is the only therapeutic measure that offers hope. I believe that when this crisis has passed, my actions will be viewed positively. I will be praised."

The Baron fought his anger, trying to give space to the others at the table who were afraid to show him their support. "I sense you view this situation as an opportunity to experiment. It's death by plague or death by injection. Toss a coin. But unlike the patients, we have a choice about death."

"With luck." Wu moved his head and light sliding over his spectacles blocked his eyes. "Bold words, since you lack any knowledge about vaccines."

Messonier gasped.

Wu continued, "Let's adjourn for today. Your differences can be settled with more information, which Dr. Haffkine can provide at our next meeting. In the meantime, he'll arrange for your inoculation with the vaccine."

The doctors slowly pushed back their chairs and stood up, woodenly, clumsy in one another's presence without the security of the table between them. They were numb, as if their dialogue, all the planning and strategy, was simply a useless vanity.

He was driven home. Bitter cold on his cheeks. A life in rags of disorder. He fell into bed after disinfecting his hands and face. In the dark, he was unable to see Li Ju reach toward him until she touched his mouth, her fingertips like cold coins. She should be locked in a tower. How could he work, touch the infected, and return home if he carried a fatal souvenir, a hidden weapon that could cause her death?

*   *   *

The hospital was filled with hundreds of new patients. One after another, the sick were carried or stumbled in, some barely conscious of their surroundings; others walked as if spellbound from the effects of their illness. The largest ward was a plain rectangular room, the beds crammed close together as if they had been forced there by an upheaval of the floor. The plague sick in the beds weren't silent, as blood was violently expelled with choking, heaving gasps, red stains branching like coral across the white sheets, bedclothes, the thick towels held to their mouths. The floors and walls were spattered with blood, a record of suffering. The room appeared to be an execution chamber. As the doctors moved from patient to patient, their feet constantly struck pans, spittoons, and buckets filled with bloody sputum.

In the hospital disinfecting room, two attendants stripped off the Baron's day clothes and roughly bundled him into overalls, a long cotton coat, a close-fitting cap, a mask, gloves, and galoshes. He stood patiently during this process, waiting for the mask to be positioned across his eyes, a barrier that partially blocked his sight of the patients. He was ashamed of how quickly he had accepted this limitation. In this cumbersome white uniform, his senses were blunted, his movements slow and clumsy, as if directed from a distance. He was transformed into an uninfected living soul in a uniform that hid his health. What did patients imagine as he towered over them, a ghost-white figure, unidentifiable, featureless as a column?

The Baron recognized the shape of the thing that occupied the hospital ward, dulled the patients' eyes, filled their lungs, stole their breath and substituted blood. He could smell it. Plague burned quickly through their bodies. Pain could be muted with morphine but there was nothing that halted the trajectory toward death.

He was suffused with tenderness for the afflicted. When he could steal a few minutes, he spoke calmly to those who could tolerate conversation, who were coherent. A few patients sat up in bed and spoke amiably or were even strangely exuberant. Others died in anger, revealing the chain of their illness, naming loved ones, friends, or acquaintances, recently deceased, who had infected them. Many victims died anonymously, refusing to reveal their identity or place of residence, fearing their families or coworkers would be hospitalized, their homes destroyed.

There was also a web of purpose. Snow was cover for the dead. Dressed in their finest clothing, the dead were hidden outside, frozen solid, waiting until spring for a proper burial. It was a curse to be buried away from the ancestral home.

"Why am I here in this place?" a man whispered. "I have only a slight cough. Others are sicker."

"Yes, perhaps there's a mistake," the Baron said. The man had a temperature and his pulse was rapid, symptoms typical of plague. The onset of the most severe symptoms arrived with unpredictable suddenness.

"Tell me about yourself. How you arrived here in the hospital."

"I was a cook at the Metropole Hotel."

The Baron's face contorted in fear behind his mask. Perhaps the man had been infected by Mesny before he'd died at the hotel. Was there a connection? He marveled at the uncanny neutrality of fate. Plague was passed by the crossing of two lines. An infected person sat with a friend or family at a table, sharing a cup of tea, a conversation, spreading the infection. Perhaps the bacilli had leaped between them, lip to lip. Who knew how plague spread, how it ravaged the systems of the body? What were the conditions for infecting another person, an entire roomful of people? "Do you know anyone else who is sick? Someone at work, at the hotel? Anyone who died? A relative? Neighbors?" he asked the man. Many patients lied, believing this would keep others safe, away from the hospital.

"I'm the only sufferer."

"Did you touch anything that might have been infected? Food or an animal?" The Baron made halting notes in a logbook. Perhaps this information might help someone else, the observations and guesswork salvaged from this circle of hell.

The man shook his head. "Will I be released soon?"

The Baron continued taking notes to avoid his question. "Has medicine—or anything at all—eased your symptoms? Tea, incense, a charm? Prayer? Opium? A needle?"

"Nothing." A calculating expression transformed the man's face. "But I know a secret for a cure. A special tea. We can make an agreement. Let me leave and I'll tell you everything."

The man bargained with death. "Little brother," the Baron said, his voice warm, accepting. "This is a valuable offer. Guard your secret a little longer and I'll talk to the other doctors." Give him hope. It could extend life. If the man survived three days in the hospital, he'd be cleared of plague. If not, his ineffective secret for a cure, if there was one, would perish with him.

The Baron left the ward. In the corridor, his foot struck a pail, splashing bloody mucus on his pants and boots. He swore. "*Gospodi-pomiluy.*"

Two hours later, he returned to check on the man who'd claimed to have a secret cure. The patient was sitting up in bed, eyes closed. The Baron hesitated, then touched his shoulder, and the body toppled from the bed to the floor.

When his rounds at the hospital were finished, the disinfecting process took over an hour. First, the soles of his galoshes were dusted with powdered lime. He stood unmoving while a medical student sprayed his uniform with carbolic acid solution, eyes squinting against the chemical fumes. In the dressing room, he gargled and spat a foul pale liquid disinfectant into a basin, then stripped, and two men sponged him with antiseptic. He was briefly immersed in a vat of slippery sublimate lotion before clambering into a wooden tub of hot fresh water. He finally relaxed, his flesh shriveled and wrinkled.

Dr. Iasienski slumped on a bench in a blood-streaked uniform, waiting his turn to undress. The Baron could judge how long the doctors and nurses had been in the ward by the amount of blood on their clothing. "I've been here all day and half the night. Fifty patients dead in the last twenty-four hours," Iasienski said.

The Baron closed his eyes. "God rest their souls."

"They died about sixteen hours after being admitted. Some died quicker." Iasienski continued, his voice dull with fatigue. "I cannot understand the Chinese. Many seem resigned to dying. They accept it. They don't fight. But the young doctors and nurses blame themselves for the deaths. Their lack of experience. Or faith. But we know better."

It was useless to respond. Iasienski talked to himself, heedless of anyone else. The man needed sleep and vodka. No. Reverse that order. Vodka first. The Baron felt he was dealing with a sleep-walker. "Did you get vaccinated?"

Iasienski finally looked up at the Baron, his face haggard. "No. Had no time. I'm thinking about it. A few new arrivals from medical school were vaccinated. I know Wang was vaccinated." His hand waved away the thought. "They say Mesny caused his own death. He was careless. Took risks. Not me. But I'm exhausted and afraid I'll make mistakes. God, to die like that. Like Mesny."

The Baron's mouth was dry, foul. He couldn't speak the usual platitudes, soothing words that filled space until the problem became lost. How could they be a strength for each other? "I know. I fear it too."

The Baron had discarded his bloodstained uniform but still felt marked by his passage through the patient ward. He clumsily moved from the disinfecting room into the corridor, barely aware of his surroundings. Someone took his arm. He recognized Messonier, and ten steps later, the door to his office closed behind them.

The Baron collapsed in the worn leather chair. "You're stronger than I am."

Messonier shook his head. "I went down to the canteen. I avoided the patients' ward. Forgive me." He smoothed back his thin blond hair until it peaked over his forehead. "The discussion with the doctors about the vaccine and serum was troubling. I think of the sick patients, innocently waiting for Haffkine's needle. Waiting in hope. But it's hopeless. Just a roll of the dice. And us? One mistake, we're infected and we gush like Mesny. Sodden in our own blood. I'd rather have my neck wrung like a goose." He took a deep breath. "No. Forget my words. I'm tired." He blinked, straightened his slumped shoulders. "There was an early explorer in my family. He sailed to the island of Bourbon. But I never imagined I would weep in a hospital in Manchuria, this godforsaken place. But I've learned to respect the Russian use of vodka here."

The Baron studied Messonier's face. "My friend, there's a history of undistinguished vodka drinking in France. Some hidden purpose brought you here to encounter vodka. Take it as a good omen."

Messonier's face creased with anxiety. "I tell you, Maria is also a weight on my mind."

"It's a blessing that you found each other."

"Is it? I'm wrenched between joy and fear. I've never experienced such intensity." He shyly studied his hands. "It's difficult to embrace the two simultaneously. When we can be together, we stay in bed under fur blankets. She talks about Warsaw. The plum trees in her family's garden. The color of the stones in the garden wall. We talk about Paris. Touring the gardens at Monceau. I serve tea." His smile was lopsided. "I asked Maria to join me in Paris. Imagine the freedom. The warmth. To love someone without fearing their death. She said yes. But not until work here is finished." He bit his lip, close to tears. "I'm afraid to continually risk my life. I dream of carelessness. To touch a patient—anyone—without fear. Am I a coward?" He turned to the Baron, an expression of shame on his face. "In this crisis, nothing seems to have any value. Except companionship." He moved away and began to silently rummage in the cupboard for drinking glasses.

The Baron watched him. "We'll stay and trust one another. We'll tell stories to survivors." Messonier didn't answer and the Baron sensed he was weeping. "There's some comfort that our battle is an exalted one. The plague is a thing of genius."

"More lethal than any weapon of war. If the goal is to rid the earth of human life."

The Baron raised an eyebrow at this statement.

"The infected have few symptoms—fever, racing pulse, blue lips, bloody expectoration—until shortly before death. So the infection swiftly passes from person to person like a secret." Messonier held up the glasses. "How does it spread? Contact with blood? Is it in the air? On the skin? Here, let me pour."

"That's the puzzle. One thing is certain. There's no point at which the infection can be stopped. Except for it not to start." The Baron made a gesture of benediction. "It's a diabolical maze. We can only quarantine the infected from the uninfected."

"If you can find them in time. At first cough." Messonier stared into the sharp clear liquid in his glass. "If there's no successful vaccine or treatment, what do we have to work with? Nothing but fever and blood and bodies. Where's our crutch, our staff? We're outwitted and outmaneuvered." He swallowed the vodka in a single gulp, then loudly exhaled. "There's little protection for us if the situation spirals out of control. Maybe it's the end of the world."

"No. That isn't true. According to Wu, the plague cure has been delivered by Haffkine."

"I admire that you can challenge Wu."

The Baron frowned. "He's young enough to be my son. But that doesn't matter. I've watched him with patients. Arrogance is his flaw. We're expected to blindly obey him when there's nothing solid, no real information behind his decisions. It's all false hope. Wu has authority only from the Chinese. It's certainly not from his experience. Or his fine English tweed suits."

Messonier's usual caution was jagged from drinking. "Still, our positions depend on Wu's favor." He poured two fresh shots of vodka.

"Everyone's at risk in the hospital. I speak up only because I still have General Khorvat's support. If I become less valuable as a translator and an inspector of inns, he could send me into exile. His soldiers would deliver me straight to the train without a hearing."

"They could do worse."

The Baron fixed him with a quizzical look.

"He could throw you in quarantine."

"If that should happen, swear you won't search for me."

"I swear." Messonier's promise wasn't made in good faith.

The Baron embraced Messonier and left the office. At the end of the corridor, a young nurse crouched on the floor by the supply closet, her back shaking with sobs.

"What's wrong?"

The nurse didn't respond. The Baron stooped to comfort her but first peered at the cloth in her hand to see if she was coughing blood. He recognized his transformation. Fear had become automatic.

"Wang Xiang'an is dead." Her face was wet, splotched red from crying.

"Mother of God."

She hiccuped violently. He helped her stand, half-carried her to a chair, and shouted for someone to bring water. Or vodka.

It was fifteen below zero when the Baron left the hospital. As soon as he took one step out the door, cold was a pressure against the two exposed inches of his face; the moisture in his skin stiffened like sap, the inside of his nostrils stuck together, his hair crackled. Skin turned white when it was frostbitten. Once bitten, it eventually blackened. But the dark areas of skin could be cut away and the body would heal.

Wang's death was a blackness that couldn't be excised. Only calligraphy, the writing of characters, was a refuge, blank tunnel, the infinite edge of a line made by his hand.

That night, the Baron sat facing a blank paper spread on the table. The hard carved chair was a knot at his back, the brush a pressure in his hand. The paper was a waiting white abyss. Grinding the dry ink stick into the water on the stone released a faint scent of soot.

Now.

He struggled not to direct the brush but continued its movement, stroking characters on the paper. It was a paradox, this disengaging. For a brief instant, he didn't question or interpret what he'd written. He felt suspended above the four corners of the paper, and the black characters became a floating pattern below him. Exhilaration filled him like breath. He knew the brush and his hand held the entire work that would follow.

He had kept vigil in the Russian hospital's quarantine ward most of the night, arriving home at daybreak. A messenger came to the house, handed the Baron a summons from General Khorvat. It was eight o'clock in the morning. He dressed quickly and returned to the hospital.

He crossed the lobby, recognized by the char lady as *chumore,* a plague doctor. The woman moved away, shifting even her gaze to avoid him. As he passed, she muttered and crossed herself, invoking the holy against harm, against the death figure who walked the corridor, carrying sickness, stinking of disinfectant.

General Khorvat, Wu, Zabolotny, Messonier, Haffkine, and Lebedev were seated around the conference table and barely looked up when he entered the room. Tension was woven around them. The doctors' protective masks, wrinkled strips of white cotton, lay on the table like surrendered weapons. How had it fallen to these six men and one woman to stop a catastrophic epidemic? Their knowledge was nothing but theories and guesswork propelled by fear. Their efforts were so puny. A fist against a wave, a wall of brick.

The group at the table were the most dangerous people in Kharbin. Was someone among them already infected with plague, their symptoms hidden? Could a single unprotected breath, a cough, infect everyone around them, cause their deaths? The Baron imagined one of them coughing, a droplet of infected blood spattering on the table, bubbling as if heated, magically condensing into infected smoke that rose and forced itself into the others' bodies, entering their throats, their moist lungs.

He was relieved when a young Chinese nurse carried around a

tray with small folded towels, and they each cleaned their hands with one of the formalin-soaked cloths while she waited behind their chairs. The strong smell revived him.

Khorvat impatiently tapped the table and the nurse bowed her head, scurried from the room with the crumpled towels. "Good morning. Dr. Wu, will you kindly start the meeting."

"Thank you, General Khorvat. First, I regret to announce that all the Chinese doctors in the Fuchiatien hospital died with their patients. Every one of them."

"The fools." Zabolotny broke the silence after Wu's statement. "I knew their hospital was rubbish. Chinese medicine is nothing but quackery and folklore. Bear bile and children's urine aren't cures. This tragic failure is proof."

"God rest their souls." The Baron had secretly hoped Chinese medicine would be effective against the plague, humiliating the Russian doctors.

Even after an expression of grace, Zabolotny was relentless. "The Chinese are against us. Sabotaging our fight against the epidemic. The patients refuse to give information about how they were infected. Or name others who are sick. We're only trying to cure these people. What's the advantage in lying?"

"The Chinese tell the truth when it suits them," said Wu. "It's characteristic passive resistance."

"It doesn't help that the Chinese hide their sick." Khorvat glanced around the table for confirmation. "Entire families become infected. We've found inns filled with bodies. My men also found hidden corpses." He grimaced. "The corpses are frozen as solid as marble. Then the Chinese wrap them in blankets and hide them in wagons or under stacks of firewood or in the stable. They sew bodies into bags and bury them in snowdrifts."

"In the face of death, desperate people will try anything." Maria

Lebedev tried to ease the tension, although her frustration was obvious. "Are we so different with our trial injections?"

Messonier caught Maria Lebedev's eye. "Only desperate doctors blame their failures on others, including their patients."

"They hide bodies to save their families from being thrown into quarantine." The Baron's voice was mild from fatigue. "It perpetuates the epidemic. But it's not hard to understand their desire for self-preservation."

Zabolotny grimaced. "We know you're a Chinese lover, Baron. Always an explanation."

"The Baron has searched many inns for plague victims. A dangerous mission no one would willingly choose." A rebuke to Zabolotny from Khorvat. "He's saved lives."

This answer didn't please Zabolotny, but he didn't waste energy arguing as the Baron continued.

"The situation is complex. The Chinese won't cooperate because they're certain everyone in quarantine is forced to drink poison and eat disinfectant. They believe our goal is to rid the city of Chinese. But they're not against just the Russians. They claim Japanese poisoned all the wells with disease. People drink and get sick."

Haffkine pointed out that several Japanese pharmacists had recently arrived and set up a laboratory in Pristan, probably to peddle cures.

"No law against Japanese who treat plague." Messonier remained calm.

"They probably hope to become rich from selling cures." Haffkine waved his hand. "Always profiteering in a crisis."

"I wonder how long the Japanese will remain healthy," Zabolotny said. "The Chinese hospital didn't last long."

"I welcome Japanese medical personnel unless they're escorted by the Japanese army." Khorvat was grim. "Now, let's get to the numbers. I was told there are one hundred dead every day. And the count is going up."

"Yes," Wu responded. "The actual numbers are probably higher. It's difficult to get figures from the buildings around the city where patients have been dispersed." He measured his words. "As you know, a boys' school, a theater, a department store, a bank, and two inns have been converted into hospitals and quarantine wards. Messengers with supplies go back and forth between these locations but communication is erratic for many reasons. We've lost many messengers. Large amounts of supplies have been stolen."

"The reason is simple. No one will go near the plague victims." Zabolotny expanded on Wu's explanation. "We've had to pay Chinese workers double wages just to get them to take supplies from the train station to the quarantine ward. Of course, they must undergo a disinfection process each time."

"Thank you, Dr. Zabolotny, for sharing that information." It was difficult to tell if Wu was being sarcastic. "The team of microbiologists who just arrived from St. Petersburg have set up a laboratory and living quarters in a stable. The largest stables on Artilleriaskaya and Pskovskaya Streets were converted into laundries, disinfection stations for mail and vehicles, eating halls for corpse carriers and plague-wagon men. Needless to say, there was resistance from the owners of the buildings when they were ordered to relinquish their property. But the general's soldiers were very persuasive."

"My soldiers are dependable." Without looking up, Khorvat searched through the papers on the table for his cigarettes. "The new arrivals—five hundred men—are quartered in Bogoslovsky's mill by the Sungari. Conditions, I admit, are not optimal. But they're temporary." His expression showed his unease.

The Baron stared at Khorvat. "Five hundred soldiers in the flour mill? It's not possible. One infected man and the plague spreads like fire." He turned to Wu. "You've allowed the men to live in these conditions?"

"There's no proof infection spreads from close contact, Baron. The cause has yet to be determined. There are many theories. But we're in crisis. There isn't enough housing for hundreds of soldiers." Wu recited his words as if reading from a textbook.

"Your hopeful calculations don't change the risk to these poor soldiers. Plague thrives where people are packed together. I've seen it in the inns. One death. Then three deaths. Then everyone else."

"The history of medicine is filled with risk. It's the only path to progress." Haffkine was severe.

"You're unreasonable. The soldiers are provided with masks, soap, and water. Disinfectant is spread on the floors by the latrines."

"Yes, unreasonable. It doesn't matter what proof I present. Death will fix their accommodations." The Baron checked the faces around him to gauge their reactions. "God have mercy. *Gospodi-pomiluy.*"

"We can only make our best choices." Wu's voice was as flat as if he were discussing the weather.

The Baron, reacting to his composure, violently pushed back his chair and left the room.

He stood outside the door to quiet his breath. His hands trembled. Messonier would search for him but he needed to drain his anger, so he began to move slowly down the corridor. He passed an open door where interns, all of them young, probably Li Ju's age, made face masks, yards of cotton and white gauze draped over three tables. He noticed a young woman drop the fabric she was holding and slump over in the chair.

The Baron rushed into the room, straightened her body in the chair, and felt her pulse. Normal. Then he jerked his hand back, remembering she might be ill. No, her skin had felt cool. The young woman had fainted. Her eyes blinked. After she had mumbled a few words, he walked her to a comfortable chair near the nurses' station, brought her a cup of water. She stared at the cup in his hand, wouldn't accept it.

He understood. He dug the rubber gloves from his pocket, pulled them on, and filled a second cup with water.

"Thank you," she whispered, taking the cup from his hand.

"Tell me your name."

"Gaidarova Manzhelei."

"What's wrong?"

"I'm fine."

"Don't worry. I'm the only one who can hear you."

"I'm afraid of the room. Someone could be infected. No one wore a mask. I wanted a mask but I couldn't be the only one covered, you understand."

He nodded. In a few minutes, he coaxed her to return. They entered the room, interrupting a young man mocking Gaidarova for her weakness.

The Baron gently addressed him. "Your name? Stepan? I would listen to Gaidarova Manzhelei's advice. She understands the perilous situation here. The number of people in a room multiples the chances someone is infected." He took a finished mask from the table and tied it around his face. Everyone in the room silently followed his example.

Rude, fatalistic jokes and superstitions were survival tools in the hospital. Washing hands three times in succession guaranteed immunity for a day. A broken thermometer meant a broken promise. The Baron remembered this type of behavior from his wartime service, when soldiers clung to coincidences, and the smallest things—a knot in string, a lucky pencil, a specific number of steps across a room—were a guarantee against misfortune in battle. Every Russian child receives a small metal cross on a thin chain that is worn for life. Several days ago, he'd caught his own chain on a shirt button and realized it had snapped only when he felt a slight tug on his neck. There was little blood from the fine cut. Was this a warning of future ill fortune? Had he broken a charm, angered the gods?

Nothing could be trusted. Not the visible or the invisible world. What offered protection? Not gloves or a mask of cloth. Not vaccine in a needle.

Some doctors and nurses realized they were outmaneuvered by the plague as the infected emptied their bodies of blood, their last strength pumped the veins dry. The more experienced caretakers blocked their emotions, pulled themselves back from grief and the patients. Others blindly ignored the hopelessness of the situation, lying to themselves and those stricken with illness. Many became withdrawn, insomniac, overworked to the point of angry exhaustion, their focus narrowed to the raft of the patients' medical charts. A few doctors and nurses turned to vodka or morphine or opium as a charm, a way to cope.

Dr. Wu, barely thirty years old, in a position of high authority, never praised his staff's valuable work and sacrifice or relieved the ache of their isolation. It was not his nature.

The doctors distracted themselves, passing around a new crime book by Dr. Edmond Locard, a renowned French police investigator. Locard's philosophy of investigation was *every contact leaves a trace.* Unconsciously, they followed his rule and avoided speaking the word *plague* out loud, as if it would leave a fatal trace on the tongue. They were all stalked by the same predator. "It is a bacillus," they whispered.

The Baron, Li Ju, and Chang traveled by train to Kirin for Dr. Wang Xiang'an's *kaitiao*, to pay their respects to the dead. On the long drive from the station through town, the Baron noticed the depth of snow in the streets surpassed even that in Kharbin. Then perhaps he dozed off, as the vehicle stopped and he was startled by a tall red pole in the snow, like sinister punctuation, outside the gate of Wang Xiang'an's family's house.

"What does it mean, that pole? Is it a warning?" he asked Chang.

"When a man dies, a red pole is placed at the left side of the gate. For a woman's death, it's on the opposite side."

Chang's explanation—symbolic order—didn't soothe his unease. Red represented an alarm. He reached for Li Ju's hand, immobile in her lambskin mitten.

They walked through the great entrance gates, solemnly opened by servants pulling on white cloth sashes attached to the latches. They followed another servant through a large courtyard paved with smooth stones that narrowed into a covered corridor. Servants dressed entirely in white, the color of mourning, crashed cymbals, drums, and gongs along the temporary walkway as they passed into a large inner courtyard and entered the house. Two large paper lanterns, painted with the family's name, guarded the door of the room where the coffin reposed. There was a strong odor of incense.

Wang Xiang'an's elderly father, his hair disheveled, barefoot in rough white clothing, stood next to the coffin, which rested on a draped bier in the center of the room. He was surrounded by mourners. A lama and Taoist and Buddhist priests loudly prayed and chanted at altars against the wall. None of them interrupted their ritual to stare at the three strangers.

Wang Xiang'an's father bowed once after each guest's three low bows to him. The Baron murmured the customary Chinese expressions of mourning and scanned the man's face for signs of blame or anger but found none. He bowed three times.

The Baron was relieved the coffin was sealed, as he was concerned about the possible spread of infection. He crossed himself. Chang had explained that Dr. Wang Xiang'an would be buried in his best robes; a fan, handkerchief, and willow twig to brush away angry demons would have been placed in his hands. Dr. Wang's body was never left alone. At night, the family took turns sleeping behind a black curtain near his coffin at the end of the room. Later, the coffin would be moved to a small separate building until it could be properly interred.

After forty-nine days of mourning, there would be a formal funeral procession with a long line of mourners, musicians, and priests, white lanterns on poles, banners, and servants carrying small painted pavilions containing incense and food. A tablet would be erected at the ancestral grave after burial.

The dwarf handed gifts to the servants, who added them to the table where paper replicas of houses, automobiles, horses, food, dishes, gold and silver ingots, clothing, and fancy umbrellas were displayed. After they were ceremoniously burned, each item crossed from smoke into the next world to serve and give comfort to the deceased doctor.

The train returned to Kharbin with only minor delays.

Outside the station, a man approached, and the Baron waved, thinking he was a droshky driver. But as he moved closer, the stranger walked stiffly, rocking back and forth as if his knees wouldn't bend. The man fell forward onto the pavement. Li Ju stepped toward him but the Baron stopped her.

"Stay away."

Chang hurried in the other direction, frantically looking for a droshky in front of the station. From the corner of his eye, the Baron saw a second still figure sprawled in the snow. If he turned the two men over to check their vital signs, there was certain to be evidence of blood. He had no protection. A small black object rapidly moved toward them, rolling end over end through the snow. With a cry, Li Ju jumped aside as the man's fur hat blew past.

An ungainly wagon emerged from the fuzz of snow thickening the air. The plague wagon appeared to have been built upside down, as the large slatted cage in back made the vehicle top-heavy and hard to maneuver. Two soldiers, identical in white clothing, leaped down from the wagon and cautiously approached the man sprawled on the pavement. The soldier with a bayonet prodded him with a foot. He didn't move. They dragged him around the side of the vehicle and roughly threw him in the cage on the back of the plague wagon.

A droshky pulled up. Chang was inside, frantically gesturing to them. The Baron felt Li Ju help him lift one leg then the other leg into the droshky, and he fell heavily onto a seat. The vehicle jerked forward. They nestled together under an immense bearskin rug, Li Ju warm against the length of his body. In the uneven light from the driver's lantern, her face was a white circle, and the points of the coarse fur were jagged as grass.

"No one is safe on the street." He gripped her hand. "The plague-wagon men could have seized us. This was a warning. If anyone tries to arrest you, give them my name. Or General Khorvat's. Or Dr. Wu's. Never leave the house alone. Will you promise? Will you remember?"

The names were her catechism. Her lips silently repeated the charmed words.

"You must always dress well. Wear your best fur coat. The cape from Scotland. Your gold earrings."

"How will this protect me?"

"They won't arrest the rich. They believe only the poor have plague. Only the poor are helpless and disappear. Chang, you must also remember these names if you're threatened. They're your passport. Understand?"

"Yes, Baron, but not everyone listens to a Chinese. I might as well say I'm a friend of the czar."

The Baron didn't answer. He had nothing else to offer.

At home, he and Li Ju were surprised to discover Andreev slumped in a chair by the stove. His lank hair covered one eye and he was unshaven. "Good evening, Baron."

"You're never idle. Unusual to find you relaxing here."

"This is a commercial venture. Although the warmth was worth the wait." He grinned, pulled his hair behind his ears.

Li Ju disappeared into another room, as Andreev wasn't a favored guest. But the Baron welcomed him as a distraction after the day's events. There was always a sense of circling with Andreev, as he positioned himself as the bestower of information and favors. The Baron raised his voice, asked the servants to bring vodka. "So you're delivering a commercial proposal?"

"I've come to the aid of your cook. First, I urge you to order extra caviar, smoked sturgeon, and eel. They keep indefinitely in storage, as we know from our sainted Russian mothers."

"Please continue, Andreev." There was pleasure in recollecting food shared at the family table.

The servant brought vodka and two glasses on a tray.

"Also order pickled beets, mushrooms, and cabbage. Hard cheese. Horseflesh. Dried apples, berries, peaches, apricots."

"I understand vodka never spoils. Is there a reason to hoard anything else?"

Andreev raised his glass to the Baron. "Many reasons. I'm a

fortune-teller. I predict opportunity. It's as clear to me as a sunrise or a cheating heart."

"My wife consults fortune-tellers. She collects good-luck charms. She'd worship a saint's relic if there were one at St. Nikolas Cathedral."

"There probably isn't a genuine saint's bone in all of China."

"So you're the pious man who can separate a true from a false relic?"

"For a fee. Or I could have a relic made for you. Guaranteed." Andreev enjoyed his own joke.

Perhaps he could explain how to recognize when luck vanished or changed direction. Could this be learned or was it innate, like right- or left-handedness or the ability to identify scents? "People follow any lucky sign these days."

"Don't trust luck. Listen to me. I tell you as a friend that things will become scarce soon. Prepare for uncertainty. The hospitals and government officials have ordered enormous quantities of supplies that fill up the CER trains. There are restrictions and inspections. Bad weather slows deliveries."

"It sounds as if the world is ending."

"Only Kharbin as we know it. Word spread about Dr. Mesny's death from plague. And other deaths. When people who work for the CER railroad learn about the number of dead here, there will be trouble. Engineers and trainmen will refuse to deliver food or wood or anything to Kharbin."

"The government has a way of forcing cooperation."

Andreev laughed. "I hear the only cure for plague is death."

The Baron's expression revealed no information.

"News will spread," Andreev said. "Mark my words."

He made a decision. "The poor are deliberately kept ignorant. Officials try to keep the deaths hidden. The Chinese and Russian governments believe there are no consequences. General Khorvat fears only protest or riots, because there aren't enough soldiers to keep control."

"That's why General Khorvat ordered a huge supply of barbed wire."

The Baron swallowed his vodka without tasting it. He struggled against a feeling of exposure. Perhaps that was the way the bacilli entered the body, exploiting a weakness just as the wind finds a crack in the wall. "I'd like you to do something for me." He went to the table where he practiced calligraphy, searched through the papers, and returned with a notebook. "I'd like to place an order. I need alcohol, lime powder, rubber gloves, green soap, cotton gauze, carbolic acid, hypodermic needles, cotton operating caps. A sterilizer from my usual supplier in Germany."

The Baron paid Andreev a small amount, not enough to entirely compensate him for all the supplies and his discretion. Like other Kharbinskiis, Andreev operated on a system of *guanxi*, credit based on trust and honorable relationships. Their unspoken agreement was the Baron's access to medicine and mercy if Andreev should become sick. He would turn up, like a black pebble.

Andreev nodded. "Good. I'll double your order. I'll keep a single order of everything for myself in reserve for the future. Make space in your storeroom for the shipment of foodstuffs. You won't regret it. The dried apricots are especially sweet this year."

"Our cook will be pleased."

"Now I have a favor to ask of you." Andreev leaned forward in his chair, nervously turning the empty vodka glass in his hand. "An innkeeper told me a stranger had hidden something outside near his building. It could be valuable. I need your help to recover it. I trust you."

The Baron quickly agreed just to escape this conversation. The vodka had loosened a raw state from his fatigue. It was late. Andreev would spend the night as his guest, as it was too cold to travel home. They'd hunt for Andreev's mysterious treasure in the morning before the Baron went to the hospital.

The next day, after a brief negotiation, the innkeeper accepted Andreev's payment, a fistful of rubles and yen. He led Andreev and the Baron through the claustrophobically low-ceilinged inn, unlatched a back door, and waved at a small structure, a shed, in the field near a neighboring building.

"You'll find what you seek there." The innkeeper handed Andreev a lantern.

Andreev frowned. "We also need a second lantern, blanket, and rope." The innkeeper agreed to follow them with the extra equipment, then quickly shut the door behind the two men.

The Baron tightened the fur hood on his jacket. "He probably has a grudge against the neighboring innkeeper."

They crossed the field, the Baron first, Andreev behind him, his head lowered against the wind, fitting his boots into the other man's footprints in the snow to ease his passage.

They reached the shed, made of boards roughly nailed and stacked together. It had no windows, no door. Andreev kicked at several loose boards until they toppled silently backward into the snow, forming a dark nimbus.

The men squeezed through the small opening between the boards into the shed.

Andreev whispered, "There's a well here." Then he cursed himself for his caution. The lantern grated against the thick stone wall around the well as he set it down, its light magnifying their shadows on the boards behind them.

A winch held an ice-covered rope that made a taut line into the well. A faint, cold odor radiated from the silent space.

Still breathless, they leaned into the well, white puffs of their breath filling it like a cauldron. Andreev held up the lantern and its slant of light revealed an indistinct pale shape suspended deep inside the well.

"Andreev, whatever is down there cannot be saved. There's no treasure here. Leave it."

"You made a promise. Let's finish what was started. It will be quick work. Then tea and vodka. Or just vodka."

"Someone stored provisions in the well. Or a bag of rice." The Baron knew that Andreev expected to discover something valuable, wanted to possess it himself.

The Baron pulled on the winch handle until the frozen rope stubbornly rolled up, ice splintering off it in a transparent shower. The heavy burden at the end of the rope scraped the side of the well, setting off an echo.

The men cranked the winch handle hand over hand together, fearing the strain of the weight would break the rope, thin and frayed in places, as it slowly moved.

"Gently, gently. But quickly, quickly."

The mysterious suspended object spun lazily, struck against the well and bounced to the other side. They gripped the winch to hold it in place, then wound it faster, ignoring their aching hands, the strain on their arms and shoulders, as the weight dragged up.

"There must be a board or a piece of metal attached to the thing. The treasure." The Baron gasped for breath.

The innkeeper silently wedged himself into the narrow space, ice beaded on his thin mustache. He dropped the blanket, balanced a second lantern over the well, and peered in.

The Baron didn't need to translate the man's shout of excitement. The thing was nearly within reach. They were locked in movement together, struggling to get footholds, to brace their boots in the mushy snow as the bulky shape gradually emerged above the well. Under a thick armor of ice, a curved, cloth-wrapped bundle glistened and revolved in the lantern's sharp light.

Andreev grabbed the blanket, threw one side across the well to the innkeeper. Each held an end as they looped the blanket under the hanging bundle to cradle it, then struggled to haul it closer. Andreev carefully stepped around the well until he stood near the innkeeper.

The two men tugged but the heavy bundle slipped and smashed into the opposite side of the well. Chunks of ice tumbled down. The blanket fell, snagged on a stone in the well. Andreev clambered on top of the well, his balance dangerously unsteady, and reached for the rope around the bundle as it swung precariously back and forth. He grabbed an edge of the bundle and fell to the ground, still gripping it, the rope uncoiling on top of him. He sprawled in the slush, exhausted.

The Baron released the winch handle and helped him sit upright. They stared at a lumpy shape the size of two cushions covered by a thick layer of ice. The surface was deeply cracked where it had scraped against the stones.

Andreev held the lantern close to the thing. "The lantern isn't hot enough to melt the ice. Let's carry the treasure back to the inn to thaw."

The Baron took a moment to reply. "No. It's safer here, away from prying eyes."

The innkeeper struck a board against the bundle, throwing off shards of ice fine as confetti.

"No, stop. You might break it."

Andreev chipped at a cracked area of ice with his Swiss army knife. "I can see cloth wrapped around something."

"Cut it. Carefully." The Baron's teeth chattered.

Hands shaking, clumsy from cold, Andreev hacked at the stiff cloth, tore away a strip. He stuck the knife under the fabric and worked to loosen it. His hand stopped.

"What?"

Under the cloth, a colorless ear. A fringe of black hair. A face with a line of eyelashes.

"Merciful Mother of God."

Two children dressed in white funeral garments were bound and frozen together. Plague dead, hidden until they could be properly buried.

Andreev dropped the knife as he crossed himself. The innkeeper wailed.

CHAPTER ELEVEN

The vespers service at St. Nikolas Cathedral ended with the Doxology and the *ektenia* of prayer, *Blessed is the entrance of the saints, O Lord.* The priest dismissed the congregation with a benediction. A brief silence as incense curved in the shadowed interior of the church, mingling with the stream of breath from the worshippers.

The Baron made his way to the sanctuary, where he'd noticed two elderly women holding handkerchiefs over their noses. He was curious, as few Russians protected themselves from potential infection, believing the sickness was restricted to those outside their circle.

"Good evening, ladies. The service was well attended this evening."

The women solemnly nodded. Their spidery, black-gloved fingers pinched at the handkerchiefs veiling their noses and mouths. They stood at a slight distance from the Baron so that he had to speak loudly for them to hear him.

"Too many worshippers before Christmas. We don't like crowds." The taller woman's voice was muffled by the handkerchief. "I am Polixena Nestorovna. This is my sister, Agrafena."

He introduced himself as a doctor and reached inside his coat for a card, but Polixena's gesture stopped him.

"*Nyet*. We don't need a doctor—"

Agrafena interrupted her. "But others are ill."

"It's the weather." He shook his head sympathetically, drawing out the conversation. The elderly don't appreciate quickness.

"It isn't the weather." Polixena frowned. "My son doesn't approve of us leaving the house. He doesn't know we're here at church. But the great Christmas fast is an important time of worship." The sisters' eyes, identical and slightly milky with age, studied him. "There's an illness. It starts with a cough."

Agrafena moved a little closer to the Baron, as she was deafer than her sister. "We know an entire family that died. One after the other. Fell quickly as stones."

"All their servants ran away. The house was empty. They left the front door open."

"Someone saw wolves inside the house."

"Sister, that's just hearsay." Polixena's handkerchief slipped down.

Agrafena was stubborn. "My grandchildren said the place was haunted by the *leshie*, goblins from the wood."

He kept his voice level, disconnected from the growing tightness in his chest. "Polixena Nestorovna, why did your son tell you to stay in the house?"

"He made us swear to protect ourselves. That's why we carry handkerchiefs." Polixena's voice was a whisper.

His hand reached to grab her arm but he caught himself. "Protect yourself from what?"

The sisters' gestures coyly mimed keeping a secret. Astonished, the Baron realized they were flirting with him. Flustered, he continued. "Your son is obviously devoted to you. To your health. He must be an honorable and distinguished man."

"He has a very important position. He travels constantly." Polixena was gratified by his flattery.

"In August, he went hunting in Manchuria with a Jesuit priest as his guide. They stayed in a hut with savages. Imagine." A faint giggle behind Agrafena's handkerchief.

"He told us many savages in the village were sick and died. When he returned from Manchuria, he wouldn't even sit at the table with us. He stayed in his room for a week. We were forbidden to leave the house. The children were cross."

The son could have been a plague carrier. He stared at the women, expecting crimson blood to bloom on their handkerchiefs.

"Who was your son's guide? The Jesuit?"

Both women shook their heads.

"Do you know where he traveled in Manchuria? The names of the places he visited?"

Polixena measured her words. "No. The towns in Manchuria have strange names. Not for the Russian tongue."

The women were becoming tired and fidgety from conversation. The Baron needed more information and made a decision in the time it took to escort the sisters to the door.

"Please, good mother, will you introduce me to your son? I'm considering a journey to Manchuria. I'd like to hear about his adventure." They stood at the church door. "Where can I find your son, Polixena Nestorovna?"

"He's the master of Central Station. Alexeievich Nikolaevich Nestorov."

He helped the sisters down the church steps. Polixena gave a little cry as wind swept away her handkerchief. He glimpsed the woman's exposed face before her hand covered her nose and he could have sworn Polixena held her breath as he helped her into a waiting droshky. Lately he'd found himself trying to memorize faces, like landscapes he wouldn't see again. He recognized that he carried this from the hospital.

He reentered the church and walked its length up to the iconostasis near the altar. The "throne"—a small square table that held a velvet-bound book of the Gospels—was being washed by two priests.

He watched them for a time in silence. "Father, may I have the sponges when you've finished cleaning?"

The priests solemnly nodded. They wrapped the damp sponges in paper and a bit of silk, then presented the package to him. They exchanged bows. These two blessed objects from the priests would guard their home from harm. Li Ju would be glad.

He considered stopping at Central Station to interview Alexeievich Nikolaevich Nestorov, but the hour was late and the man had probably left for the day. Home to a family and a vigil that only he had recognized.

Li Ju wasn't at home. The Baron waited, pacing from room to room, absently crossing himself before the painted icons of Saint Gregory the Theologian in the kitchen, Saint John Chrysostom in the study, and the Virgin Mary in the bedroom. He remembered his father had ordered small icons hung even in their stables, never leaving anything to chance. After a time, the images of the saints blurred together, dark still figures against a gold background.

Li Ju returned carrying a satchel. The Baron inspected her face for signs of infection as intently as if he suspected she'd been meeting a lover. She avoided his eyes. The hood and shoulders of her pale sheepskin coat were freckled with black dots, fine as pinpoints, and she smelled of smoke.

"One of the inns burned down." She still didn't look at him. "I watched the fire." The Baron undressed Li Ju as gently as if stroking a brush on paper. He urged her to wash her hands. She immediately obeyed and returned with a faint odor of rose on her fingers from the soap. There was salve on her lips to guard against plague, a jar of potion bought from a woman on the street, and he recognized the taste of ginger and animal fat on her mouth.

"Where were you today?"

"At the fortune-teller."

He was silent as if jealous but was secretly afraid. Every day the old woman probably sat with twenty or thirty people who sought answers and comfort from the future. The air over the fortune-teller's table and the air in the room would be poisoned with the exchange of infected breath.

"Remember, everything you inhale remains in the body," he warned. "If anyone coughs or sneezes or even laughs near you, turn away. Act as if they are a thief. The plague will steal your life."

"I'm careful. Chang was with me." She'd become more cautious since their encounter with the plague wagon.

"How does the dwarf have time to dawdle with a fortune-teller? Has he stopped work at Churin's store?"

Li Ju was puzzled. "I didn't ask. Chang was happy to visit the fortune-teller. She predicted long life for both of us. He always attracts attention."

"It's safer to pass through the streets unnoticed."

They could be mistaken for children because of their diminutive size, the two of them wearing nearly identical fur coats, faces blanked with clumsy, confining masks. As fear of infection spread, it seemed suddenly everyone on the street wore a mask, as if a single white line had been broken and re-fastened across a multitude of faces. Moisture from the eyes, nose, and mouth condensed in the cold, turning men's beards and mustaches into thick twists of ice and eyebrows into bristling spikes. Some wore masks with foolish bravado, leaving them to dangle uselessly from their ears or around their necks. Bundled in heavy furs, heads covered, faces hidden, men and women, Chinese and Russians, were indistinguishable.

The Baron was torn between the desire to keep Li Ju always in his sight and the need to have her remain isolated and secure, locked in the house. He watched as she silently unpacked her satchel on the table. She unfolded paper packets to show him silver fungus, mushrooms, bear paws, dried centipedes, mollusks, frogs' legs, and shark fins from the South Seas. Tiny envelopes held cardamom, licorice, saltpeter. Small dark pottery jars were filled with pig gall, wine made from tigers' tendons, quince from Canton. The most delicate materials—dried skins of field mice, velvet from stags' antlers—were stored in tiny tin boxes.

The Baron marveled at the display of precious goods on the table. "What will you do with these supplies?"

"They'll be useful medicine someday."

"But you don't know how to prepare them."

She stared at the floor, hands folded together in a gesture of respect, still smiling, but her mouth was tight.

He wanted to pry her hands apart. Break her repose. Where had he acquired this demanding impatience? This abruptness? He was aware of a sense of urgency, as if these were his last hours and days. The patients had become his timekeepers. "Forgive my words. We can find someone who knows how to prepare your materials from the apothecary." He touched Li Ju's shoulder and she blinked her agreement.

Li Ju pushed aside the packets and emptied a flurry of yellow paper strips from an envelope on the table. "You see? 'Jiang Taigong is present, a hundred evils are warded off' is written on each strip. Jiang Taigong was a legendary fortune-teller long ago.

We will paste the papers across the top of the door frame to guard against ill fortune entering our house."

"I also have something to show you," the Baron said. "For us. Blessed by the priests at St. Nikolas." He unwrapped the two sponges, still damp in the stained silk wrapper. Next to the silvery deer velvet and the parchment-thin mouse skins, the sponges looked ugly, coarse. But now they had an arsenal of charms against misfortune. To make amends for his earlier criticism, he surprised Li Ju with an invitation to an operetta at the theater.

Pleased, she dressed herself without a servant's help. A one-piece *dudou* of printed flannel was an intimate garment worn next to her skin, fastened at the waist with thin ribbon. A long fur-lined skirt was wrapped over two pairs of narrow flannel trousers, one of moleskin. On top, a tunic and a jacket lined with rabbit fur. Before they left the house, she put on a sable hat and a voluminous cape from Scotland, her husband's gift, made of wool felt pressed thick and dense as pine needles.

The Ves' Mir Theater was in Novy Gorod, but its decor was taken directly from St. Petersburg, with its chandeliers, red velvet curtains, gold-painted box seats, and exclusively Russian audience.

It wasn't until the Baron and Li Ju were seated near the orchestra that he panicked at the sight of so many bare unprotected faces. A few men and women had white cotton masks, and some discreetly held up handkerchiefs to their noses. Others used fans of silk or feathers, confident the rapid movement of air would stop the spread of infection, drive floating bacilli away from the face. At quieter intervals during the performance, the constant rhythmic whisk of fans was a tense counterpoint to the music. Still, there was a sense that the Russian theater was a refuge.

The Baron coughed. Coughed again. Heads immediately turned, searching for the guilty. *You? Are you sick?* The Baron began to sweat. He abruptly stood up, aware of Li Ju's distress, forced his way through the row of seats. In the lobby, he waited, breathing heavily, for the attendant to bring their coats. He would have been driven from the theater if the audience had known he worked with plague victims. His safety was compromised. He was *chumore,* unclean, a man who tended the dying. There was no protected place.

Li Ju followed him outside. The walk in front of the Ves' Mir Theater had been swept clear but the air was filled with blowing snow, thick as confetti. The Baron turned, squinting, at a fire burning in a huge barrel on the street and the dark shape of a vehicle beside it. A movement against the field of white as two men stepped forward. The snow was deep and they moved slowly as if with patient politeness toward the Baron and Li Ju. They didn't respond to his greeting.

The men were very close. "You have a fine coat. And the lady does too." Their words a challenge.

The Baron and his wife were silent; the space between them and the strangers held a waiting pressure. He automatically pulled her against his side, her arm stiff in his grip. An encounter in extreme cold required absolute clarity. Each movement must preserve the body's heat.

"We heard you cough." The taller man noisily cleared his throat and spat, the gob frozen as it arched into the snow. "You should be in quarantine."

Plague-wagon men. They'd moved into the wealthy heart of the city, patrolling for the infected and the opportunity to rob others. *Let them see your face.* The Baron pulled back his hood, slightly loosening his mask, and the frigid air had the force of a slap on his skin. "Vodka would be welcome now, wouldn't it? To break the cold?" Uncertain of the men's intention, his words strained to extend the measure of time. Perhaps the constellation of his fate waited to shift within the span of these seconds and minutes. The only stability was constant change, as his teacher claimed. It had a fixed course.

The Baron began to sweat inside his coat. "What are your names?"

The taller man said, "I'm Piotr. This is Sergei."

"What can I offer you?" *Should I tell Li Ju to run, now?* They were in an open space at the side of the theater. Trying to escape was useless, as they'd flounder in the snow. They must remain standing within the light from the theater lamps or no one would see them. He scanned the street for a witness, someone exiting the theater or a droshky. Unlikely anyone would leave the theater until the performance was over. "I freely give you what we have. Without argument." His hand reached inside his coat for money. "Let us walk away."

"What do you have worth that trade?" Piotr turned to Sergei, who was holding a thick net. "Take a gift from the sick? They want to leave. They seem cold here."

The second man shook out the net. "They'll be warm after being thrown in the wagon."

"But he's a doctor!"

Li Ju's error. Now the plague-wagon men must get rid of him, an official witness who knew their names, to stop him from reporting them to the authorities.

Piotr raised his voice. "You, infected stranger. How did you escape quarantine?"

"An infected person is a murderer. Infecting others," the other said.

"I'm a doctor. I know the cure for plague."

"You need a lesson, braggart."

For a moment, the Baron imagined suffocating Li Ju, holding

her head in the snow to spare her from quarantine, where she would die. Suffocation was a quicker death, the numbing thickness of snow. He shouted, refusing them.

He shoved Li Ju facedown in the snow. Confused, the two men didn't move. The Baron extended his hand to lift her up, waited a moment, then swung around and flung himself at the tall man's torso, sending him sprawling. Li Ju crawled forward and threw herself across the fallen man's legs as he struggled to stand. He kicked her off and she rolled in the snow.

The second man held the heavy net open in both hands, nervously shifting from side to side, waiting to toss it. Wheezing, the Baron staggered to his feet, unsteady in his boots, the snow untrusted as sand. Li Ju crept toward the burning barrel. She pulled off her face mask and thrust an end in the fire, and it instantly ignited. She hurled the blaze at the man with the net. He ducked but the net slowed his movement and his fur hat erupted into a fiery circle around his head as he stumbled, then plunged into the snow to extinguish it. Li Ju and the Baron struggled through the snow back to the opera house.

That night, he couldn't free himself from the encounter. A memory remained, like a reddened finger held too close to a flame. He embraced Li Ju but the dear intimate familiarity of her body had been altered. How could he protect her when he recognized his own fragility? It seemed his bones were draped with silk not skin.

Boxes of supplies were unexpectedly delivered to the Baron's house by Andreev. The two men watched Russians and a Pole carrying the goods into the house, tracking wet snow over the floor, closely supervised by disapproving servants. They unloaded bags of dried soybeans, mushrooms, and fish, jars of oil. Caviar. Tins of food from America. Candles. Kerosene for lanterns. A length of brocade for Li Ju.

"Where are your Chinese workers?" the Baron asked.

"Russians refuse to have Chinese in their buildings. They're afraid they bring the sickness. I had to replace them with Russians. They're drunken sods. Learned to be lazy in the army. But you can thank them for saving your servants. It isn't safe to walk among the crowds in the market. It's the last visit before the cemetery."

The Baron took Andreev aside when he recognized the Slav with the white-blond hair from Central Station. "Watch the Slav." He pointed as the man crossed the courtyard. "Not to be trusted."

Andreev shrugged. "He's got working arms and legs."

"Fine. You're the master."

Andreev turned aside the Baron's offers of money and gratitude but accepted a bulky package of folded white cloths from him. He was puzzled by the gift.

"My wife made them for you. There are enough masks for you and your workers." The Baron was unable to keep the scolding tone from his voice. "Your life will be saved by masks and disinfectants. Doctors won't save you." Andreev would probably throw the masks away or sell them. If there was time. Relationships, familiar situations, changed unexpectedly, as the end of life could arrive without warning, like a book with the last page torn out.

After all supplies had been stowed away, the Baron insisted they visit a nearby *chaynaya* for tea. Fewer lights interrupted black winter on the streets, but Andreev brought him to a good restaurant. Cautioning the Baron not to tell anyone he was a doctor, they passed the inspection of the guard at the door.

"I'm grateful you'll still drink with me."

The tables in the restaurant were widely spaced and without

white cloths. The chairs had no cushions that could anchor bacilli or dust. A few patrons wore masks, removing them only to drain a glass of vodka.

The Baron gazed around the barely occupied room. "I wonder what happened to the children who sold newspapers here? They've all disappeared."

A line of sweat trailed down Andreev's cheek as he tugged off his fur hat. He sneezed and the Baron winced, quickly turned away. "Some questions are better not asked. Another drink? Let me distract you." Andreev traveled with treasure in his pockets, a tiny pouch around his neck or hidden in a book. He pulled a jewel glittering on a gold chain from inside his coat. "This is a valuable from a German merchant. His soybean warehouse was forced to close. There's a strict new customs inspection for goods exported from Kharbin. Everyone is afraid plague hides in grain, blankets, furs, even bamboo baskets. The inspection of the German's soybeans was delayed, and the shipment rotted."

"To your good fortune."

"Don't congratulate me so quickly. I rescued the grain merchant. I paid him enough for the business to survive. Unless plague gets him first. And then I claim his entire warehouse." He slipped the jewel back into his coat. "Many precious things float loose these days. Brought back into exchange. Everyone is a sentry, guarding their snowy plot of land. Lucky if they have coin, gold bars, gold dust, and not fragile things, like paintings, that won't stand up to disinfectant. Merchants only accept payment in silver pesos these days, since metal can be sterilized in vinegar. You trade your paper money for coins as I advised?"

"Yes."

"A train ticket out of Kharbin will soon be more valuable than currency or gold. The price of a ticket increases with demand.

You'll see. Thousands of panicked people will try to escape. You remember during the Boxer Rebellion, people traded their jewelry for a place in a train?" Andreev leaned closer. "With bribes, the rich buy train tickets and pass health inspections at Central Station. Rich Russian ladies and gentlemen are too elegant to be infected with plague. Only the poor will be forced to stay here and die or get out any way they can."

The Baron was sobered by this mercenary vision but accepted it as truth.

"The passengers refused by CER trains will need transportation. I'm buying up wagons and carts as a new business. My drivers can go south to Beijing or east to Vladivostok, where you catch a ship. Secret routes. Anyplace to avoid plague and inspection."

"Who are your clients?"

"Restaurant owners and gamblers. Officials and their wives. Merchants. There are fur traders who trust my word. I get a large fee for supplying these escapes. I guarantee surviving this travel even during winter in Manchuria." It was vodka speaking for Andreev, who was gratified to have an audience. "Why stay here? You can do nothing. Save yourself and serve others elsewhere." The Baron didn't reply. "Friend, I can offer train tickets from Kharbin to St. Petersburg. Or Paris, Shanghai, Tokyo. Anyplace that puts distance between you and Kharbin. You'd arrive by New Year's Eve. Bring your wife and servants. A favorite nurse. I'm discreet."

The Baron had only to waver to say yes. "The Chinese believe fate is fate. The one unchanging certainty in the world."

"You talk to too many Chinese." Andreev was never interested in hearing about Chinese customs. He raised his voice, disregarding stares from the others in the restaurant. "Soon, Kharbin will be nothing but a death pit. Piles of corpses inside and outside the city with a few creeping survivors. No one left to bury the dead. What do they tell you at the hospital?"

Andreev's words struck him like a stone.

"At least save your wife. Send her away. Give her a choice."

"It's a war," the Baron finally managed to say. "I serve in the war."

Andreev pulled his hat back on his head. "Let's leave while there's enough light."

Outside, the snow reflected the sun and the two men blinked, dazed by its sharpness, standing without a sense of direction. There was an odor of burning, and a pale yellow glow was visible above the rooftops. They followed a few others to the next street, where the silhouette of a house was visible inside sheets of brilliant orange and yellow flame. The building stood isolated on a jagged black shape, an island, as the surrounding snow had melted from the fire.

The number of buildings burned in the city had rapidly increased, as it was more expedient to destroy them than disinfect them. But buildings that had been made uninhabitable, doors nailed shut, roofless like a mouth open to the sky, had their use: the plague-stricken crawled into these poor shelters and died anonymously. Fewer crowds gathered to watch the fiery spectacles, since they feared smoke carried bacilli, a gray and weightless veil of infection that breath drove deep into the lungs.

There was a struggle near the flames as dark figures and soldiers fought over goods salvaged from the house. The soldiers threw furniture back into the blaze. A man with a bayonet tore a bundle from the arms of an old woman.

"Why burn good clothing?" she cried, her fur coat whitened by intense light from the fire.

"They belonged to the plague dead. They're poisoned," the soldier shouted.

A boy grabbed a blanket off the ground and darted away with it. A soldier seized the child and shook him until he dropped it.

"Easy to throw you into the fire."

The Baron stepped forward and the soldier released the boy.

A boom as a supporting wall of the burning house collapsed, slid at an angle, raising a cloud of sparks fine as insects.

The Baron pivoted away from the fire and was immediately chilled.

"Look." Andreev nudged the Baron. "A corpse carrier."

A flat wagon carrying lumpy cargo under a tarp moved slow as a barge between two snowbanks. The crowd immediately turned away or fled in the opposite direction. Puzzled, the Baron waited. The tarp haphazardly roped over the wagon blew free, exposing dangling white arms and intertwined bare limbs, frozen together, the corpses shaking obscenely with every jolt of the wheels on the road.

Andreev's hand on his shoulder and his voice. "The fear is that you'll recognize someone's face in the wagon."

The Baron closed his eyes, wishing away the wagon and its terrible burden. Andreev continued talking. "I've seen families of the dead running after the corpse carriers on the street. They bribe the drivers to release the body. Or offer something in trade."

"It will bring their deaths."

"The corpse carriers are desperate railroad workers and servants who lost their jobs. Nothing else pays in Kharbin except picking up the dead or sick."

The Baron crossed himself and whispered, "Where do they take the dead?"

"Outside the city. Some corpses are dumped on an island in the Sungari. Others are dumped on the ice until the river thaws."

Andreev's face was barely visible inside the fur hood but his scornful expression was obvious. "The bodies must be destroyed or the dead will return to haunt us with plague." He proposed visiting another destination, where he said the Baron would see something of interest. They crossed the city without conversation in a droshky, stopping near a wharf on the river.

They climbed to the top of the Soskin grain mill, one of the tallest buildings in the city. From the small high window, they viewed the shadowy irregular line of the ravine obscured by dense clouds from twenty fires burning in Kharbin. It appeared that an artery had opened in the ground, gushing smoke. The Baron's focus moved. Several verst away, in an area of desolate land, train tracks patterned a net of black lines and curves in snow. Small figures moved around a stationary line of boxcars as a constant stream of carts, wagons, and other vehicles arrived.

The Baron turned to Andreev. "I expected to see the fires. But what's the activity around the train cars? Why are so many people in the field?"

"General Khorvat didn't explain? No? You've been blinded by your grief for the patients. What you see is Khorvat's solution. People with symptoms are picked up by the plague-wagon men and locked inside the train cars. If they survive three days, they're freed." Andreev's words, delivered in a patient mocking tone, had an undercurrent of fear.

The Baron felt the glass in the window would shatter under his gaze, that the tower couldn't hold his weight, that he'd plunge from this height. Flight was the only escape from this place.

During a calligraphy lesson, the Baron's teacher Xiansheng had once described a Chinese painting of a storm—immense thick clouds, lightning, rain, dark sky—that represented *lung,* the dragon. The monster was there but not his physical image. The dragon was present only for those who knew how to translate the significance of the visual clues. The Baron nervously scanned the sky, certain a dragon would emerge from the smoke of Kharbin's burning buildings, jaws unclenched, hungry for survivors.

Chang evaded the servants at the door and bustled into the Baron's sitting room, still wearing his coat. "Look. Kharbin has marked me." The dwarf raised his arm to display a red badge on the coat sleeve. "They've set up barricades. Divided the city into four quarters. Everyone must wear a colored badge according to where they live. Red, yellow, blue, or white. When you enter or leave your quarter, soldiers shove a thermometer in your mouth. If you have a temperature, you're arrested. You disappear."

So another system had been imposed. A vise tightened on the city. The poor would be imprisoned in Fuchiatien, the district with the greatest number of plague victims. A pressure across the Baron's forehead pulsed. He would put aside his concern for now. "What else have you brought us, Chang?"

Chang set his satchel on the table, ceremoniously unwrapped *yangxian* tea for Messonier, Maria Lebedev, the Baron, and Li Ju. "This tea escaped the vigilance of inspectors. A precious tea from southern Zhili." He'd feared this last shipment would be doused with disinfectant and ruined during customs inspection. "We might have a tea shortage someday but there's never a shortage of water," he said, indicating the sealed window. "Now I have a puzzle for you. Why is tea better than vodka in a crisis?"

Messonier answered first. "Tea isn't better. Vodka brings forgetfulness. Oblivion."

"Vodka is a dull liquid." Chang continued unpacking.

Messonier was puzzled. "The answer to your question, please."

Chang gracefully arranged the tiny cups around the teapot. "The aroma of tea brings memories. An escape to past pleasures. Tea leaves are alive, constantly changing in water as they do under sunlight. Tea changes in the pot and in the mouth. You must pay attention when you drink. No distractions."

"He reminds us that even during these dark days, we can still savor delicacy." Maria Lebedev was serene, supported by pale cushions on the only upholstered chair in the house. "Christmas was barely observed this year. St. Nikolas Cathedral was avoided by many who feared the plague. It was a somber place."

"Not for those who trust and worship God," Chang announced without looking up from his cups. He was a benevolent figure presiding over the table, cheeks flushed from the room's heat.

The Baron ignored Chang's comment, which was certainly not sincere. "When I was young, during *svyatki*, between Christmas and the end of the year, it was traditional to have your fortune told every day. To anticipate the new year."

"The fortune-teller was kind to me," Li Ju said, confidently adding, "She promised long life. I'm safe, so I can aid the sick."

"Li Ju makes dozens of masks every day. She has a gift." Her industry was a relief to the Baron.

"And a charmed life." Messonier smiled.

"Some people have only dirty cloths to wear over their faces as protection. I've seen them on the street."

Chang said he'd take a packet of Li Ju's masks and hand them out to the distressed.

The Baron was always startled, momentarily, when he returned home from the hospital and Li Ju and the servants greeted him with bare faces. An uncovered face was as dangerous as a weapon. A loaded gun. Everyone sitting here at the table shared a risk. Was one of them an assassin who would innocently infect the others, take their lives? Even the simplest interactions and those who were dearly beloved were suspect. He panicked, gripped by an urgency to stop the process he sensed unfolding around him. He stood up, glanced wildly at the others. Concerned, Li Ju tugged at his sleeve to bring him back to the table and their circle. His hand swung his empty teacup.

His breathing returned to normal. "*Nazdorovie,* to your health." He would put aside his concerns for now.

The dwarf immediately spoke to cover the Baron's odd behavior. "Yes, to everyone's health. I crave the wait before tea is poured. The anticipation." He shifted in his chair and described the three famous springs at Mount Huqiu: Sword Pond, Stone Well, and Tiger Running. "The water! Its clear brightness soothes the mind. Pure as a mirror. Like drinking a reflection. People make pilgrimages to drink tea made with the water. Perhaps we'll drink there together one day."

"I feast on your image of water." Maria Lebedev smiled and Chang grinned back, pleased by her teasing. His dark head and her blond braids moved closer together, inclined at the same angle over the cups in their hands.

"I wonder what they speak about," Messonier murmured to the Baron later when they were alone in the next room. "It's agreeable to watch Maria and Chang in conversation."

"You're not jealous?"

Messonier turned and his blue eyes widened. "Oh no. That's why I love her." He looked away.

"What troubles you?"

"Nothing. Just fatigue." He coughed.

The Baron studied his friend's face. "Let's sit down. Now tell me."

"I have no peace. I'm devoured by my worry for Maria."

She had agreed to monitor patients, mostly children, housed in a boys' school and a theater. The buildings had been fitted with rough plank beds, and tea and rice were provided, but the heat and disinfecting systems were inadequate.

Messonier slumped and he spoke directly to the floor. "Maria could have worked in the hospital with me and I could protect her. But she's in a primitive place that isn't properly equipped. Not even a hospital. Why would a woman voluntarily make this choice? Why?" He looked up and his face was anguished. She'd recently grown into greater independence, a reluctance to compromise, and he knew better than to plead or argue with her. She had no wariness, no guard.

The Baron chose a practical answer. "Maria is a doctor. She's careful. She knows all there is to know about disinfectants and sterile precautions."

"I'm a doctor. I can't live with this risk. With her risk. I want her to quit. Stay home. But she would leave me if I dared make that demand. Why can't everything be controllable? Fit in the palm of my hand? And I have other concerns."

The Baron understood he meant a possible pregnancy. Maria had quietly moved into Messonier's house after the medical staff had been evicted from hotels in Kharbin. Relations outside of marriage were a sin and she could have been dismissed, but many behaviors were forgiven during the crisis. Messonier was shy about their situation and, to protect her good name, never discussed it with anyone except the Baron. "All doctors are at risk," he said. "No need to remind you."

"I obsess about my own health every day. Every hour I ask myself, *Have I escaped infection?* I would gladly trade my life for Maria's if she was in danger. But how can I freely embrace her when she returns? Surely you fear carrying infection home to your innocent Li Ju?"

"The fear never leaves me." It was impossible for the Baron to offer comfort. Optimism was false.

Messonier blinked and looked away. "And yet, I'm happy," he

whispered. "She embraces even my sorrow. Here." A small box in his hand. Inside, a gold ring. "It belonged to my mother. It was shipped here from Paris, sealed in a book. For Maria."

The Baron smiled and touched his friend's shoulder. The contact brought a whiff of formalin.

"I wait for the right moment and place to propose. A romantic location. Not the hospital. The restaurants and public spaces are too dangerous. But Father Orchinkin promised the first wedding at St. Nikolas will be ours. Once this crisis passes. As surely it will."

"Bless thee and Maria."

Xiansheng announced that the day's lesson would begin with ink. The character for ink was written with *tu,* meaning "earth," and *hei,* "black." The Baron ground the ink stick with water on the inkstone, leaning close to examine the lustrous black liquid, willing himself to focus on this task at his desk.

Xiansheng had another instruction. "Hold the ink stick to your nose."

"Pine. Why, it has an odor of pine." The Baron had never noticed.

"Ink has been made from the same materials for hundreds of years. A hole is carved into the base of a pine tree. A small lamp is fit inside. The heat of the lamp encourages the resin to flow from the tree. After the resin has been drained, the tree is cut down and burned for several days in a kiln. The black soot is scraped from the kiln walls and mixed with glue made from animal hide or fish skin to make the ink. The different qualities of ink depend on the type of pine or fir that was burned. A skilled eye can distinguish between them. The finest ink is *dongquan,* made with dark amber-colored glue, molded into sticks, and elaborately carved. Rich men hoard these ink sticks like jade and never use them."

"I know the words for pine-soot ink. *Songyan mo*," said the Baron.

Xiansheng had gradually introduced the different brush-strokes used in calligraphy so as not to overwhelm his student. Always hold the brush vertically. Stroke it left to right, top to bottom. "Master calligraphists have described the three characteristic brushstrokes for calligraphy and painting. Long strokes are bones, muscles the short strokes, flesh forms the connecting strokes."

The Baron learned by copying, tracing the characters faintly visible on a second paper underneath the top sheet. He touched the brush to the ink. Every muscle in his back held him tense as he worked the brush. His fingers strained and tightened. He criticized himself. Frustrated and angry, he set the brush down.

Teacher offered little comfort when his student struggled but he acknowledged his decision to stop with a nod of approval. He waited in silence until he had the Baron's full attention. "There are beautiful ways to describe the act of writing," he said. "Li Ssu, a master who created a style of calligraphy, wrote, 'When you swing the strokes outward it is as if the clouds were rising from behind the mountain.'" After a moment, he recited another quote. "'A vertical stroke should resemble the stem of a dried vine myriad years old. A horizontal brushstroke should resemble a cloud a thousand miles long.'"

How could such a concentration of information be deciphered from small black lines? The Baron's focus wandered. He recollected a singing lesson when he was a child in which his music teacher instructed him by using metaphor after metaphor. *Sing as if your lips were soft as a cushion. Weightless. First, think the sound, because once it leaves your throat it's too late.* After a moment of hesitation, the Baron loaded the brush with ink. How simple to hold a brush. Not simple.

A brushstroke must be simultaneously spontaneous and deliberate. His awareness became joined to the movement of his hand wielding the brush as he wrote the first character, then another. He completed a line. He squinted at the brushstrokes he'd just made on the paper. Xiansheng made the slightest gesture of approval.

The intensity and anxiety of the lessons sometimes left the Baron exhausted. Occasionally, he felt a lightness, a growing exhilaration, but suspected even this state wouldn't have met with Xiansheng's approval. His teacher wanted something indefinable and elusive, and the Baron failed to understand this mysterious demand.

Sometimes the Baron believed that he created meaning with his hands as a healer. Brought peace to others as he desired it himself. He remembered a dream. He had stood next to a painted Chinese character—he couldn't read it—enlarged to the size of his own body, standing upright, solid as a statue, although flat and without depth. He had walked around this huge black character and had instantly understood the brushstrokes that created it as if some mechanical thing had been taken apart to reveal its workings. It was as clear and simple as the gesture of a blade, the movement of cloth in wind.

On the second floor of Central Station, Alexeievich Nikolaevich Nestorov, stationmaster of the CER, welcomed his visitor. The Baron introduced himself, squinting at Nestorov silhouetted against the wide windows overlooking the snow-whitened rail yards behind him.

"An honor, Baron. What brings you here? A quest for train tickets?" Nestorov was a large man with a reddened face and pale dry hair, evidence of long days exposed to the sun.

"No. Although perhaps I'll need your help later. Do you anticipate any travel difficulties in the near future? This winter?" He caught Nestorov's hesitation, quick as the dilation of the pupil.

"Only if something unexpected happens."

"Such as?"

"The whims of men. Of passengers. Crowding, yes, a lack of seats can be a problem in the winter, and trains suffer delays because of the snow. But you're with the Russian hospital. You'll always be accommodated. Others must wait."

"I had the pleasure of meeting your mother, Polixena Nestorovna, and her sister Agrafena at St. Nikolas Cathedral. We spoke about your travels in Manchuria."

Nestorov was delighted to discover a thread between them. "I believe the sisters were jealous that they couldn't join my expedition. But please be seated." He enthusiastically called for tea and beckoned at a leather armchair draped with a tiger-skin rug. The floors were also covered with animal skins, many boldly patterned, and the walls were filled with mounted heads of wild boar, black bear, and roe deer.

"I tell you, Manchuria is a Garden of Eden. I saw meadows of blue gentian. Orange lilies high as your shoulder. Rhododendron. Campanula and peonies. Fields of bluebells where no man has ever walked."

"You seem to be a hunter rather than a plant collector." The Baron's curious fingers had found the teeth on the tiger skin slung over his chair.

"We ate what we shot. Pheasant, pintail snipe, boar. They were practically tame, as they'd never encountered hunters. We also spotted the kingfisher and the rare oriental roller, *Eurystomus calonyx,* with its extraordinary green and blue plumage. I fancy myself something of an expert taxidermist. I prepared bird skins in the field, although rain made it almost impossible to keep the bodies from rotting." His hand waved at the stuffed birds arranged behind the glass doors of a case.

"I admire your spirit of adventure. You traveled far north as Manchouli, yes? When did you return?"

Nestorov lunged across his desk and yanked a stained journal from a shelf. "August. End of August. Or early September." His thick fingers tapped the book, and a heavy gold ring flashed.

A uniformed young clerk silently entered, balancing cups and a teapot on a tray. Nestorov quickly drank his tea with a sugar cube clenched between his teeth.

"Surely you had a guide in that wilderness?" The Baron worked toward his target.

"Father Jartoux. A Jesuit explorer. He'd crossed the territory years ago. Prayed as he hiked. Tiresome. But good to walk with a holy man." Nestorov abruptly dug under the files on his desk, pulled out a paper fan, and used it even though there was a strong draft from the unusually large windows behind him. "Now, if you wish to see something beautiful, I recommend Laolongwan Lake in the Pai Shan Mountains. You climb for two hours and at the top, there's a completely transparent lake in the crater of an extinct volcano. Water like crystal. There are seventy-two of these dragon pits, the *longwan,* in the area." His eyes narrowed with pleasure. "Why are you so interested in my travels?"

"I'm considering an expedition to Manchuria myself. Andreev, an acquaintance, described outfitting your expedition."

"Andreev? Has he been arrested?"

"Not to my knowledge."

Nestorov seemed disappointed. "He's a well-known smuggler, you know. Black marketeer. Appears and disappears. Reliable when it suits him."

"Your dealings with him were unsatisfactory?"

The stationmaster broke eye contact. "He always remembers certain people, his sources, with gifts."

Clearly there was something between Nestorov and Andreev. The Baron shifted in his chair, smoothing the tiger skin under his legs so he wouldn't crush it. "Andreev is a useful contact these days. But so are you, with the railroad under your command."

"Yes. If you plan to travel. Or escape." A nervous chuckle from Nestorov. "Andreev always told me he was in the business of selling animals to animals. His joke. He sold sable and tarbagan pelts, horn and bone. Bear paws. Live tiger and fox cubs. Perhaps the creatures were to be raised as pets in a brothel." He blushed. "I've heard of such practices."

"Your mother mentioned that you'd stayed with a native tribe?"

"The Buryat. They treated me very well. I've never felt so safe. Slept like a child."

The Baron ignored this and moved toward his target. "I heard there was an illness among the Buryat."

Nestorov's hesitation spanned a blink. "Father Jartoux, who spoke their language, was told about an illness that periodically returns." He was sweating profusely and the high collar of his jacket was ringed with a dark irregular line. He rubbed a handkerchief over his face and neck, studying the Baron in calculation. "You're a doctor at the Russian hospital?"

The Baron felt a prickle of fear, as if he were responding to a threat. He was surrounded by an aura of disinfectant, a warning to others. A death stink.

Nestorov fumbled in the drawer of his desk. "I met no one who was ill. No one."

"You lie."

A dry mechanical click and Nestorov's hand swept up holding a gun. "I knew I'd be tracked here. Did you come to arrest me, Doctor? I'm not sick. I won't be quarantined. Don't worry, I won't shoot you. The pistol is for my head."

The Baron sprang at the desk, knocked Nestorov's arm sideways. The gun thudded onto the floor.

Nestorov began to weep noisily, cheeks scarlet with tears.

Moving slowly, the Baron slid open the drawer in Nestorov's desk. It was filled with rows of neatly rolled gauze bandages, disinfectant, liquid morphine, carbolic acid.

"You're still alive, weeks after exposure to the sickness. The plague. You're not contagious. Trust me." The Baron waited for gratitude, as he'd delivered the man from a death sentence.

Nestorov was dazed. "All this time I was afraid. I waited." His voice a whisper. "Waited for the cough. Fever. Blood on my tongue." His broad fingers rubbed his jaw. "Then Andreev came here. Knew about the sickness, the Buryat tribe. Jartoux had told him everything. Andreev confronted me and I paid him. Otherwise, he said, the plague wagons would come for my family. Later, I realized that Andreev didn't believe I was sick. He stood here without a mask or anything to protect him from infection. I was a fool."

"You're safe now."

Nestorov's bluster returned. "I wonder if the plague is a Chinese plot." Then he sighed and leaned over his desk. "We found one Buryat man who was sick. He vomited blood. Father Jartoux started to treat the man in his tent but then refused to touch him. Even Jartoux's boots were bloody. He performed last rites outside while the man coughed and coughed in the tent." He grimaced. "What do you think the savages did next?" Without waiting for an answer, he continued. "They sewed the sick man inside the tent. Then they packed up camp and left him. Jartoux and I traveled back together, keeping a distance from each other. I was afraid of him, afraid he'd caught the sickness and would infect me. I wanted to leave but had no other guide. We shared no foodstuffs or water, slept in separate tents. All our equipment, the Kabul tent and supplies, was burned when we arrived in Manchouli. Others would gladly have paid for the stuff but I swear we destroyed everything. You believe me?"

The Baron nodded.

"I returned alone on the train. After a week, isolated at home, I was certain that I wasn't infected. I would die before exposing my family to any sickness. Then I heard about the deaths, the bodies in the Hailar, Chalainor, and Manchouli train stations. And bodies near Central Station here in Kharbin. I cautioned my family about crowds, forced them to stay in the house. Now I fear that this thing is among us in the city. But I'm not the carrier. I didn't bring plague death."

"I need a list of train passengers and staff on the day you traveled back to Kharbin."

"What will you do with the names?"

"Check the obituaries. One match spreads fire." But the Baron suspected this was a dead end. It was probably impossible to discover who had brought plague to Kharbin. He imagined the dim interior of the Buryat tent, walls wet with blood, hot, close, and stinking, the Jesuit priest leaning over the sick man, listening to his rasping cough, crawling backward out of the narrow space. A man of God despite his refusal, his turning away.

The Baron wished Nestorov good day and caught a droshky

outside Central Station. He woke abruptly, thrown forward when it stopped at the Russian hospital. In the lobby, a messenger caught his attention before he'd even removed his hat.

"From General Khorvat, Baron. Sir." The messenger was a young boy and he stood at a distance, obviously nervous about physical contact with a hospital doctor, a *chumore*. Still wearing gloves, he handed over the envelope.

"A meeting at the general's office?"

"I—I don't know. Sir." The boy stuttered. "I didn't read it." His face, reddened from the cold, blossomed scarlet. He took the Baron's coin and quickly left the building.

General Khorvat's letter ordered the Baron to negotiate with Father Bourles, a Catholic priest, at his church compound. The priest and his followers had amassed a store of food and barricaded themselves in the church to wait out the plague. They anticipated that faith and prayer would save their lives.

He found the droshky outside and wearily pulled the weight of a fur rug over his legs, its pungent odor sharpened by the cold air. At the church, a ragtag group of medics, a nurse, two soldiers, and Father Androvich were waiting for him by the high stone wall surrounding the compound. A soldier angrily kicked a clod of ice at the door in the wall.

"How long will we stand here?" The second soldier impatiently pulled the bell rope by the door. He leaned over, squinting into a crack above the door latch. "I see snow in the courtyard. No footprints. Nothing moves." He straightened up and studied the thick door. His ax splintered the wood around the latch and the door swung open.

The group crowded into a wide courtyard, a square of undisturbed snow surrounded by gray stone walls.

"Hello? Hello?"

Across the courtyard, a small figure appeared, so still that it seemed to have emerged from the wall of the building.

"Who is it? A child?"

The nurse took two steps forward but the Baron roughly pulled her back.

"Wait."

The child made a helpless gesture and collapsed. They struggled through the snow across the courtyard and gathered around the body of a small girl. Her face was lilac and her lips were blue. Her white garment was stained with blood.

"Don't touch the child."

Father Androvich pushed a medic aside and fell to his knees by to the body. "Where is thy mother, little one?" he whispered. He cleaned the child's face with his sleeve. "The earth is the Lord's and the fullness thereof, the wide world, and they that dwell therein." He made the sign of the cross.

Everyone crossed themselves, muttering, "God have mercy."

Two bodies were found near the stone wall. They were facedown, both of them in fur coats and partially buried in snow. Impossible to tell if they had died of plague or cold. The soldiers tugged at the frozen arms and legs angled stiff as branches. They rocked the bodies back and forth, pried them from the snow's grip, and turned them over. Two Chinese, a young woman and an older man, their faces speckled with bits of leaves, the skin blotched red-purple-green where blood had settled after death. With a gloved finger, the Baron gently touched the woman's cheek, surprised by its solid hardness. Flesh like stone.

He noticed a tall stack of wooden boxes against the wall. Not everyone had shared Father Bourles's belief in the curative power of prayer. The young woman and the man had attempted escape by climbing on the boxes to get over the wall.

"We should search the grounds. But there aren't enough men to help," the Baron said.

Father Androvich shook his head. "Wait until the snow melts."

A soldier responded, "If there's anyone left alive in Kharbin by springtime."

The Baron separated the group into four parties to search for survivors.

Inside the first building, their breath billowed around them, and the sound of their boots was amplified by the bare floors as they moved warily through the freezing rooms. Dishes and utensils were marooned in pools of ice on the tables in the kitchen.

"The bedrooms must be on the second floor."

The nurse and a medic followed the Baron upstairs. In the corridor, uncovered chamber pots were haphazardly set along the walls, and he angled his boots, careful not to tip them over, until he realized they were webbed with a scum of frozen crystals. There was no smell.

The Baron dreaded opening the door, the discovery of a suffering figure in bed, the frantic attempt to comfort or relieve pain. Or he'd find the dead, although there was no odor of decay. He tied on a mask, hampered by his gloves, and indicated that everyone else should do the same. He felt lopsided, the sense of his body blunted by the mask over his face.

He knocked on the bedroom door. He felt the fear of the others waiting behind him, and it was a struggle to control his breath, the tight pressure of anticipation in his gut. He was trapped inside a bell, a blind, suffocating place. Fear pulsed through his hand, and without waiting for an answer, he shoved the door open with a bang.

They'd expected to be welcomed as saviors, rescuers, but there was only a strange flatness, a sense of waiting, not peace. The silence, and the lack of greeting, was a momentary relief.

A dead woman lay in the first bed, a prayer book open on her lap, the linens stained black in the dim light. Her face had been cleaned, perhaps a caretaker's last gesture.

The Baron hesitated, sensing another presence. A cradle holding a still white figure was wedged next to the bed, the wall pinpointed with spots, blood from the infant's coughing.

Another room with rows of beds. A man's dark silhouette in the corner bed, dirty linens bunched up around his neck as if to hold him upright. Two men lay on the floor. Other beds held the rounded shapes of bodies covered with blankets. Better to die here, among familiar things, preserved by the cold, than locked in a train car for quarantine. "Nothing we can do here."

The nurse and the medic who had followed him into the room stepped back into the corridor. They decided to check the church for survivors. Their voices stilted and very loud in the quiet space.

The church door was unlocked and they entered the climate of familiar odors, incense, wax, cold stone. The echoing noise of their movements stopped as the medic fumbled with a lantern, filling the height of the center space with frail light above lines of empty pews. In front of the altar, coffins were stacked on long tables, fit together like a raft waiting to be launched.

"Mother of God."

The trespassers crossed themselves. The dead in the coffins must have been the first plague victims, their bodies stored here in the church for burial when the ground had thawed. Something caught the Baron's eye, and he crouched to examine the legs of a table. "Bring the light here."

Each table leg was wrapped with a large inverted metal cone to stop rats climbing up to reach the corpses inside the coffins. The lettering on the side of the coffins was barely legible and he leaned closer, reading several names aloud, his voice solemnly rising into the dim height of the church, a courtesy owed to the dead. He feared finding the name of a friend or acquaintance.

No one had an appetite for a meal, but they found tea and the samovar in the kitchen, heated snow until it boiled, and drank the hot liquid. Two bottles of vodka were discovered in a cupboard and a glass quickly poured for everyone.

When their share of the vodka was finished, the two soldiers left to continue searching the church and the outbuildings. The Baron and Father Androvich slumped at the kitchen table, waiting. Conversation was impossible.

Someone shouted that they'd found a closed room. The Baron and the priest hurriedly followed the voices to the door of the church cellar. The excited soldiers stood aside on the steps to let them pass, lanterns swinging in their hands.

The door at the bottom of the steps was sealed with metal strips and a thick plate was secured along the floor. Giddy from nerves and vodka, the soldiers joked about the gold and valuables inside the room.

The priest wearily leaned against the wall. "There's nothing precious behind the door. You'll see."

The Baron gestured for a lantern. "Here's a puzzle. The door is heavily secured but the key's in plain sight. Look." A key hung next to a crucifix on the wall.

The key fit the lock.

The door opened to a foul odor and a faint bitter smell of carbolic acid. Inside, the light from the lantern was a harsh eye on a disorder of heaped coffins, the tumbled long shapes of corpses wrapped in shrouds, blankets, rags. A catacombs. The suffocating air invaded the Baron's nose and throat, and his face was damp with sweat. He silently backed out of the room, the images unwillingly fastened in memory as if burned in place.

The medic and the nurse were dismissed after all the buildings were searched. Two hundred and forty-three bodies were counted and left in place. The door in the stone wall around the church was repaired and barred against looters.

The Baron joined Father Androvich and the two soldiers in the church. They replaced the candles in the holders on the altar and set a kerosene lantern on the front pew, sharpening shadows on the rows of coffins. The plague dead were a tainted burden.

The priest recited an epistle from Thessalonians: "Rest with the saints, O Christ, thy servant's soul, where there is no pain, nor grief, nor sighing, but life that endeth not."

The Baron hoped the presence of other believers had brought peace to the dying and that they had been tended and mourned. Perhaps, mercifully, many of them were unaware that Father Bourles and everyone else had died. The place would be cleaned and someday no trace would remain of the many who had perished here.

He didn't remember falling asleep in the church but woke in a wagon jolting back to the hospital. The streets were deserted. Was it morning or late afternoon? He could barely see his hand in the dimness.

He blinked, rubbed his eyes, needing the contact, the pressure of his fingertips as a connection to wakefulness, to convince himself that the events in the church hadn't been a dream. He was awake.

CHAPTER TWELVE

The plague's hunger had carved up the city. A layer had been stripped away, revealing hidden bones, barbed wire, metal, and wood that became barricades. Every road into Kharbin was blocked by men with bayonets against an invisible enemy. A cordon radiated out over the quarters—Novy Gorod, Pristan, Fuchiatien, Staryi Kharbin—dividing the city into four, then eight and finally sixteen guarded sections. Some Kharbinskiis felt more secure, as if plague could be held inside certain boundaries.

The center of Kharbin was deserted. The furriers on Kitayskaya and Mostovaya Streets were shut down first, as fur was suspected of harboring plague-carrying fleas. All the foreign-owned companies and the Chinese and Russian banks closed. Hotels refused guests who worked in hospitals or gave dubious answers when queried about their visit to Kharbin. Public worship was forbidden, and churches, synagogues, and temples closed. Schools closed. Libraries closed. The opera, ballet, and other theaters locked their doors. Restaurants and most *chaynaya* closed. The lumberyards, the Soskin grain mill, and Borodin's vodka distillery closed.

Pawnshops drew their curtains but secretly continued a flourishing business in certain goods, solid durable valuables that could be disinfected—jewelry, silverware, icons, jade and ivory objects, precious metals.

Pleasure was accessible for the brave or foolhardy. Opium dens and nightclubs defied the ban on public gatherings and remained open. As a dark joke, the young women selling cigarettes and cigars added a few thermometers to the offerings on their trays.

The Baron stared down the dim alley at the plague wagon next to the inn. Three reflected points of light indicated the bayonets held by the soldiers seated in the front of the wagon. The Baron spoke to the men's silhouettes. "Wait here. Let me enter the inn alone. I'll shout if I need help."

"Be quick with your inspection."

Lanterns illuminated the center of the low, overheated inn, and the faces of the laborers massed around the tables shone with sweat. It was like being confined in the belly of a ship.

He addressed them in Chinese about the sickness. "If one person becomes sick, everyone around him will become sick. Then you'll give the sickness to your families. In the hospital, you'll be made comfortable." His words were unconvincing.

A bottle was tossed from the back of the room. It missed his shoulder and struck the wall. Shouting, boiling movement as men rushed forward, but he didn't flinch. He'd suffered worse blows. The innkeeper waved his arms, and the men withdrew.

The Baron held up a thermometer, a brilliant white line of glass reflecting the lantern light. He allowed a few men to gingerly inspect the thing. No one would touch it. He slipped a clean thermometer into his own mouth to demonstrate its safety. After a moment, he removed the thermometer and tied a mask over his face. He stood still, waiting for them to accept his transformation, his retreat into a disguise. He was an object of fear and wished Wang were present to ease the situation. He moved very slowly through the room as if to diminish the threat of his grim task, examining each man in turn for signs of ill health. The laborers sullenly cooperated. Two men were found to be symptomatic, with high temperatures and rapid pulses.

He accompanied them outside, their few possessions bundled in a cloth, to the waiting plague wagon. A soldier leveled a gun at the frightened Chinese men and they drew protectively together. The other soldiers stood atop the wagon and fastened masks around their faces. It was a show of business, dressing before a performance. A soldier leaped from the wagon, seized one of the Chinese men, and dragged him, struggling, to the cage in the back of the wagon.

The inn door slammed open and a crowd of laborers streamed out. Shouting, they attacked the two men wrestling in the snow, kicking and punching the soldier.

At a gunshot, all the Chinese fled, wading clumsily into the thick snow then disappearing into the alley.

The Baron helped the bruised soldier stand. No broken bones. "Fools. Fools. Everyone who helped the sick men escape will die."

Shaken, the soldier clutched his arm. "What about me? I touched him."

The Baron cursed his own words, carelessly spoken. "Your name is Vladimir Vasily'vich, yes? Perhaps the man wasn't infected with plague. Medicine is never certain."

They clambered up into the wagon. A few minutes later he put his arm around the soldier's shoulder. "It may be wise to put yourself into the hospital. Just as a precaution. I'll watch over you." He directed the driver to take a route to the hospital.

The soldier Vladimir Vasily'vich was admitted for observation. The Baron wished him good night, didn't wait to see his first encounter with the doctors in their clumsy protective clothing. He would go home.

Outside, it had become so cold that snowflakes seemed to grind their edges together. Every footstep in the snow made a sharp brittle sound. The wheels of vehicles rolled with a crushing noise.

The Baron's droshky slid across a layer of ice on the street, and at the sudden movement, shadows around a half-buried body fled, the red points of their eyes caught by lantern light. Feral dogs or wolves, savaging a corpse. In daylight, he'd noticed places where snow had been disturbed, dug up around a body, recognized it as the work of animals or thieves that stripped the dead of flesh or clothing. *Never look twice. Make no attempt at rescue or salvage.* He made the sign of the cross and swore that the pounding of his heart was audible through his clothing.

The brush of calligrapher Zhang Huaihuan created dots "like balls of stone." The suffering caused by the plague was so catastrophic that it could not be written—the words would plunge through paper. The Baron wished that his eyes would become balls of stone, obliterating what he'd seen, two weights that punched memory into a black hole.

Xiansheng arrived at the appointed hour for the Baron's lesson.

"A thousand pardons, Elder Born, but everyone who visits must be tested." The Baron felt ragged shame for this request, but paranoia had made him the unhappy instrument of delivery. The plague had stepped inside his house.

The Baron slid a thermometer under his own tongue, handed

another to his teacher with a slight bow. Without the slightest hesitation, Xiansheng submitted to Russian custom, calmly folded his hands, and waited for the thermometer's verdict.

The Baron saw the future as a maze, imagined Xiansheng's illness as an inevitable vigil of suffering, death, and grief. He slipped the thermometer out of his teacher's mouth and looked at the red line, finer than a needle, encased in silvery-white glass that blurred and shook between his fingers. Nothing to fear. Temperature normal.

Teacher studied him solemnly and suggested tea, although it was an enormous breach of courtesy for a guest to make this request of a host. They moved to an adjoining room and a servant, accompanied by the sharp clink of porcelain cups on a tray, carried in the necessities. They were safe, drinking from cups that warmed their hands until they were ready for the lesson.

Calligraphy began with the familiar preparations. Fine goose-white paper, readied on the table. Ink stick, inkstone, brushes. A tall container of water.

The lesson was a single character, *qi,* representing breath, air, vapor, floating, expanding, and also spirit, vital force. When Xiansheng pronounced the word *qi,* it sounded like the release of breath. An exhale.

A smooth scratch as Teacher's hand moved quickly, his brush painting the character, which combined wavy curved lines, representing the breath, and *mi,* the character for rice or grain, representing sustenance. The Baron watched, gradually conscious that the man focused from a knot of stillness that he could never hope to experience in his own body.

Finished, Teacher straightened to study his writing on the paper. "The character *qi* is also described as the invisible presence of the calligrapher's spirit. But it cannot be deliberately placed in a work. It's only recognized by those who possess the right qualities."

The Baron's mind buckled with uncertainty. "*Qi* is the characters on the paper, but it's also a hidden code?" He joked to mask his bewilderment and anger that he was oblivious to this mystery. "How can *qi* be created if it's invisible?" He felt foolish, grasping. It was weak to allow anyone to witness your confusion. To lose face. Everything he'd hidden in a corner of his memory.

His teacher silently waited.

He struggled for control, a familiar sensation. Bowed his head. "I don't know. Tell me, Elder Born."

Xiansheng recited the words of the master calligraphist Zhang Huaihuan.

Mind cannot consciously give to the hand and hand cannot consciously receive from the mind. Both mind and hands are one's own but fail to grasp wonders when searching with intention. It is very strange indeed!

If the Baron allowed himself to weep, he'd be disgraced. He took a breath and turned to hide his face, lowering it over the paper. His hand shook slightly as he picked up the brush, stroked the inkstone. He hesitated as if approaching a precipice. The brush wobbled on the first mark. He made an error then another error but continued. He was aware of an edge of self-criticism and ignored it. Only his hand—his mind—made an error. Not the brush. For a moment, the bodily sensation of his hand holding the brush was lost and he floated with the black line of ink, completely weightless. He didn't experience pleasure but a kind of suspension, frail and delicate, that vanished the instant it was examined. Startled, he blinked, noticing Xiansheng's faint amusement, and he was unable to ask for an explanation of what he'd felt. The sense of the experience lingered like déjà vu.

After the lesson, Li Ju joined them at the table. Companions of tea. They needed nothing from the world outside their circle. The last of Chang's special wuyi tea was brewed, the rare spring-picked qingming.

Li Ju was unfailingly solicitous and the Baron sensed Xiansheng's quiet appreciation for her attention to their comfort, refilling the cups, requesting hot water, adjusting the chair cushions. He dared to broach an intimacy and ask his teacher a personal question. "Have you ever seen a fox spirit?" Then instant regret for his foolishness, the question irreversible as a brushstroke.

Unfazed, Xiansheng answered in a slow voice, as if he'd dipped a finger in ink and spelled out the story.

"Manchurians sacrifice to fox spirits in special shrines to court their goodwill. But these spirits must always be approached with caution. Even the character for fox spirit is never written on paper, as it would offend the animal. A character with the same spoken sound is used in its place. I will write it for you one day."

"Why do the fox spirits cause trouble?" Li Ju leaned forward for his answer, a lock of hair falling in front of her ear.

"The fox spirit can transform itself into human form, often as a beautiful young woman who leads mortals astray or causes misfortune." Xiansheng's expression was distant. "One night, when I was a young man, a fox spirit came into my chamber. It had glowing golden fur and an immense tail that was as full and waving as grasses. The fox spirit rested its head near my hand on the blanket. Its tail moved slowly back and forth like a woman's fan. I saw its green eyes, tiny pointed teeth, long silky whiskers, and knew the fox spirit meant no harm. The fox spirit's jaws didn't move, but it gently asked if I had a question. My mind whirled. I was too shy to answer. In an instant, the fox spirit vanished into a chink in the lattice. Sometimes I imagine the questions I should have asked and the fox spirit's possible answers. I could have had wisdom."

"You really saw the fox spirit? How do you know it wasn't a dream?"

"The fox spirit brought a gift."

"A gift?"

"The fox spirit allowed me to pluck one of its long whiskers. It was wrapped around my finger when I woke. It was not a dream. I kept the whisker folded in a gold paper until I had enough money to have it set into a special brush. I always carry it."

"Do you have it with you?"

Xiansheng nodded. "I brought incense, a carved tablet, and meat to the fox spirit's shrine. But the fox spirit never appeared again. Years later, in Tsingtao, I saw a woman on the street with fiery gold hair the same color as the fox spirit's. I hurried after her. She had green eyes but cruelly pretended not to recognize me. I couldn't speak. I lost my second chance to question the fox spirit. I later learned that the woman was the wife of a missionary. I knew where she worshipped. But you cannot provoke fox spirits or they will ruin your life."

Xiansheng looked deep into the tea remaining in his cup. The lesson had ended.

"A tiger?" Dr. Wu Lien-Teh stood in the doorway, his stoic expression changed to transparent wonder as he saw the taxidermied animal head hung on the wall. The Baron noticed Wu's momentary loss of composure.

"Siberian tiger. Rare. Shot at fifty paces." Alexeievich Nikolaevich Nestorov, the CER stationmaster, was flattered by the doctor's attention. "Extraordinarily difficult to travel with the creature's skin from the wilds of Manchuria. Over there, my bird collection." His heavy arm rose in the direction of a corner cabinet, the neat silhouettes of mounted birds faintly visible inside. The CER stationmaster welcomed General Khorvat and Dr. Zabolotny, keeping his distance, obviously uneasy with several *chumore* plague workers crowding his office. His expression faltered when he encountered the Baron, but he didn't acknowledge their previous meeting. The Baron wondered if Nestorov still had a hoard of medical supplies in his desk drawer.

Khorvat ignored the taxidermy and casually took the chair closest to Nestorov's desk. Wu hesitated. It seemed he would refuse the seat near the window because of Khorvat's deliberate lack of protocol. As a Chinese government official, he should have been seated first. The Baron watched to see if Wu's expression, his *yanse,* would show his anger, but the doctor's face was implacable. A superior man doesn't betray his emotions.

Behind his desk, Nestorov inched his chair back from the visitors. "These days, with the sickness, you wish for another way to meet. Speak from a distance rather than the same room. Could be safer."

Zabolotny dismissed the idea. "We've been thoroughly disinfected, I assure you."

"There's always a chance." Nestorov cleared his throat. "Gentlemen, how can I help you?"

Wu took charge. "There's concern about the effectiveness of the passenger inspection at the train station."

"Passenger inspection? Death is a passenger. Many die on the train. Bodies are thrown off between stations. It is strictly forbidden, of course," Nestorov snapped. "A few of my experienced train conductors have quit. Brave men, but afraid of Kharbin, city of the dead. That's what they call it. Trouble everywhere. You're aware of the huge quarantine wards built at the Chalainor, Manchouli, Tsitsihar, and Taolaicha train stations? A ward was even constructed at Imienpo for the timber workers. Hot water was poured on the frozen ground for half a day before the building posts could be driven in." He turned his attention back to Wu just as the increasingly impatient man prepared to interrupt.

"No inspection is completely effective. It's the nature of the epidemic." Wu shrugged off his concerns.

Nestorov opened his hands to indicate he was waiting.

"We will correct the situation," Zabolotny assured him.

"Nestorov, what's the passenger count on the CER trains? An average day?" Khorvat acted as if the others hadn't spoken.

"Several hundred passengers. Busiest railroad station in China. It's the gateway to Europe and the Americas. Everyone from China and Japan traveling to Vladivostok, Vancouver, Paris, Berlin, St. Petersburg, all major cities, stops at Kharbin's station. The greatest number of passengers is in January."

"January?"

Nestorov forced a thick book from the shelf and thumbed through the pages. "All Chinese travel home to celebrate New Year, even to the most distant villages. They take trains to Mukden, Shuangchengfu, Ashihoh, Kuanchengtze and then go by mule or wagon to remoter villages." He looked up. "Within two weeks, several thousand people will leave Kharbin on the train."

The doctors exchanged alarmed looks.

"The trains must be stopped." It pleased Khorvat to deliver this edict.

Nestorov gaped. "Impossible."

"You don't understand the danger. Plague is a bomb the travelers take into the world."

Nestorov sat back heavily in his chair. "A bomb? It's diabolical. Reminds me of Kuschei the Immortal, the sorcerer in the fairy tales. His secret power, a needle, was hidden inside an egg."

The Baron recognized that Nestorov was talking around the subject. *He's probably afraid that I'll say he was exposed to the plague while traveling with the Jesuit.* He caught Nestorov's eye to reassure him. "The plague has a brilliant strategy," he said. "It hides so those who are infected spread the bacilli to others without suspicion. It's a Trojan horse."

"Yes, it's a Trojan horse." Zabolotny nodded. "I heard a woman got it in a droshky, rode across town to the theater, and was dead on arrival, dressed in an evening gown."

Nestorov now allowed himself to acknowledge their alarm. "But I believed this plague was under control. Your doctors inspect all passengers at the station."

"We know more about this epidemic than anyone on earth." Wu's voice was barely civil. "But none of us have encountered anything like this plague. Once you're infected, you have a few symptoms until just before death. An elevated temperature, rapid heartbeat. You talk, eat, drink as if nothing is wrong. Until you cough blood. Your face turns blue from cyanosis. A few hours later, or the next day, you're dead."

Nestorov whistled, and his astonishment was convincing. "There's no cure?"

They waited for Wu to speak but he only shook his head.

"Why wasn't I notified sooner?" Nestorov stared at the doctors, one by one. "The city will starve without supplies. The CER railroad operates with certain principles. Serving the czar and the people. I can't allow the railroad to lose money. Not deliberately.

I need permission from Russia, not China, to make any changes. General Khorvat, can you give this order?"

Khorvat laughed. "Imagine how the Russians will react when they learn there's no escape from Kharbin. They'll push the locomotive from the station with their bare hands. By the time their complaints reach St. Petersburg, our city will be a graveyard. And I'll be one of the early burials."

Wu's posture indicated his disagreement. "Your plan is unacceptable. Let me speak plainly. If the trains shut down, it implies we have no control over the epidemic. There will be international panic. This isn't to China's benefit. Our standing in the world would suffer. There are also political situations—threats from outsiders—that are best avoided. The trains must continue to operate. Put more soldiers in place to screen the passengers."

"Thousands of Chinese passengers?" Nestorov's voice slowed to a patient drawl to tamp down his anger. "There aren't enough soldiers at Central Station to control the situation. It's already chaos. They bring pigs and chickens on board. There will be riots unless you provide more soldiers."

It was Khorvat's turn. "What kind of vise do you want to use? My soldiers are deployed at all major roads. They're at the barricades inside the city to arrest the sick. Our good Russian soldiers keep order on the train and in Central Station. Where do I get additional troops? It's hazardous to cross Manchuria in the middle of winter. We function on a thread and with God's grace."

"Lock up anyone who wants to leave Kharbin in quarantine. After five days, they're no longer infectious." Wu was exasperated with the conversation. "We issue them official travel passes after quarantine."

Zabolotny agreed. "The advantage to quarantine is that everyone is released after a few days."

"Or they're dead." Wu had the last word.

"You're mad with your petty travel passes." The Baron's voice was heavy with scorn. "We already shelter nearly five thousand people who were exposed to the plague. They're shut up in boxcars, for God's sake. There's no place to keep even another thousand people in quarantine."

"Only the cemetery can accommodate thousands of people." Zabolotny's temper rose.

"He's correct."

"Quarantine them on boats."

"Boats?" Khorvat's fingers stroked his beard. "Ridiculous. The Sungari is frozen. Even Chefoo has a seven-day quarantine for ships. Why not use spare rooms at the foreign embassies for quarantine?"

Wu smiled briefly. "The viceroy wishes to avoid alarming the foreign embassies."

"China can't stop this epidemic alone. It's useless to pretend otherwise." The Baron folded his arms.

"Pity that the weather is against us. Otherwise, the quarantined could be put in tents. Surely there are military tents left over from Russia's unsuccessful war with Japan." Wu mocked the military.

Nestorov called the boychick to bring tea. The men waited in uncomfortable silence.

Then they worked out a strategy in a few hours. Money was the solution. During the period of the Chinese New Year, first- and second-class tickets would became hugely expensive. The cheap third- and fourth-class train tickets would be eliminated. The poor and those most likely to be infected with plague would be unable to travel. Doctors and soldiers would patrol the train cars every three hours, searching for sick passengers.

Nestorov brought out *pertsovka* vodka to celebrate the plan. They'd nearly finished the bottle of peppercorn-flavored liquor when, as a joke, they splashed a little vodka over their fingers as disinfectant, a strange ceremony under the wild animals' heads, Nestorov's trophies.

Afterward, the doctors walked through the Central Station waiting room in their face masks, surrounded by others with masks or rags over their noses and mouths as protection. From habit, the Baron searched the crowd for anyone with the spasmodic shake of a cough, the hunch and gait of ill health. He had developed a rogue eye. Outside the station, he caught a droshky back to the Russian hospital with Zabolotny.

After pulling the fur rug over his legs, Zabolotny attempted a cigarette. "I need to smoke. I'm removing my mask. Don't you dare cough." He was noticeably tense.

By silent agreement, the two men fixed their gaze on each other, avoiding the windows and the chance sighting of a body or a group stripping a corpse on the street. Yesterday, the Baron had watched from a doorway as a solitary figure staggered the length of a building across the street and collapsed in the snow. A moment later, a woman and child calmly walked around the fallen man. He'd wished a death in bed for the stranger, the blessing of a raft made by men. He'd used up so many wishes.

"All the patients admitted yesterday will likely be dead when we return to the hospital." After a pause, Zabolotny added, "God forgive me but my hands are never clean. Never clean, never completely disinfected. Not in the hospital, not away from the hospital. Not anywhere. Not at the table when I eat. When I can manage to eat." Exhaustion had subdued Zabolotny, stripped his confidence and the need to challenge others.

"You're not alone. Dr. Broquet stopped shaving." The Baron was ringed by hazy cigarette smoke. "He's afraid if he cuts himself, bacilli will enter his bloodstream through broken skin."

"A beard is prudent. Tamara, the new nurse, will only open doors with her left hand."

"To avoid infection?"

"For luck."

At the hospital, the two men found a group of doctors, nurses, and interns standing listlessly in the third-floor corridor. The Baron stared at their faces, stern and lean as if the masks they wore had gradually altered their appearance. A tearful nurse in possession of a telegram told them Dr. Jackson had died in the Mukden hospital.

No one had met Dr. Dugald Jackson, since he'd arrived in Manchuria only ten days earlier. A twenty-two-year-old missionary doctor with the United Free Church of Scotland, Jackson had been monitoring passengers in the Mukden train station. Feverish on Monday, he died Tuesday evening. A stone marker would commemorate Jackson in the church where he'd worshipped twice. Viceroy Hsi Liang, the Chinese representative, had sent condolences.

Some of the staff had already decided to quit the hospital even before Jackson's death, fearing for their own lives, unable to face the constant threat. *Chiku nailao,* endurance in hardship. It was a virtue to even remember the words.

The Baron noticed Messonier had joined them. His sorrowful expression was unchanged even when he was away from the patients. Messonier closed his eyes and the Baron knew he was praying. Messonier surfaced from his devotion and signaled the Baron.

They met by the samovar at the nurses' station. Messonier poured vodka into teacups since someone had stolen the glasses they'd hidden in the cupboard. They drank a salute to young Dr. Dugald Jackson.

The vodka was sharp, purposeful. The Baron found its clarity a relief. "Dr. Jackson's death affects us although no one knew him. You wonder what mistake he made. Was he careless, overconfident, too young and untrained?"

"Haffkine's response was to ask if Jackson had been vaccinated."

"He's more sentimental than the microbiologists."

"Debatable." Messonier stared at the decorative pink flowers painted in the bottom of the teacup. "You know the Imperial Throne gave Wu permission to perform autopsies?"

"What? Where?" The Baron was astonished.

"An abandoned temple has been converted into an autopsy room. Near the Russian Orthodox cemetery. Wu set it up with Dr. Richard Strong, who just came from America. Recruited by the Red Cross but paid by the Chinese."

"At least they take the dead. There are rumors patients have been spirited away to secret nursing facilities by the microbiologists. But where do they find corpses for dissection? Here at the hospital? Or the quarantine train cars?"

Messonier hesitated. "I'm not certain. It's not discussed. But I heard they'd hired a Russian to find bodies and transport them for autopsies. They probably figure he's less likely to spread rumors than a Chinese."

The Baron swore softly. "The hospital is a laboratory for these microbiologists. The experimenters. Corpse hunters. The patients are just subjects for their observation and testing. We do the bloody work." He shaped his grudge, describing them as a group that trusted only petri dishes, test tubes, glass slides that held evidence, the promise of an answer, a cure. "They stoop and sniff at the keyhole. We're inside the room, listening to patients. Our intuition is as valuable as their experiments."

"Remember Zabolotny and Wu both studied under the microbiologist Metchnikoff in Paris. It's their area of expertise." Messonier tried to remain neutral.

"Yes, they're such experts that they blamed rats for the epidemic. It's not surprising that young Dr. Wu recruited microbiologists. Thinking of future fame rather than tending patients. These micros come in and demand help from the youngest doctors, who are too intimidated to refuse. They should take care of patients rather than swabbing them for samples and running to the laboratory."

"Who couldn't understand wanting to avoid patients? I don't mean to sound as if I'd like to neglect my duties."

"You'd never neglect a patient. But do I seem resentful? Paranoid? Old?" The Baron struggled with anger, freed by the vodka. "I'm not arguing for myself. My concern is for the patients. We're like two detectives debating which clue is superior, a fingerprint or a footprint. A hair or a thread."

"Meanwhile the body is sprawled on the floor, Sherlock," Messonier said to soothe him. "Nothing to solve here. Just look the other way. Move along. I've been troubled by my own experiences with these laboratory men."

"Not everyone can hold up under the stress. Maria Lebedev?"

"Still at one of the temporary hospitals. She isn't sleeping, stays there all hours. She's an excellent doctor but you might as well throw yourself under a train as do this work. I wrestle with myself because it seems pointless. Our patients need a priest, not a doctor. We cannot save anyone. We should at least save ourselves. There. I've said it. I'm not proud." His expression was rueful. "I have a silly dream. I find a magic carpet. I steal Maria away. We wake on the magic carpet on the grass in the Bois de Boulogne. Love follows." His smile was lopsided.

"Friend, I pray for your happiness. I'll speak with Andreev

about the magic carpet." He enjoyed the vision of Messonier's tryst in Paris. "And the gold ring? Have you given it to Maria?"

"Not yet. The right moment hasn't presented itself."

"The time will come."

"I carry the ring with me." Messonier pointed to his neck. "On a chain."

"You have courage. I'm afraid to touch my wife. The fear of infection. She's also wary of me, although she denies it. I should grow a shell. Everything smells like disinfectant to me. Even my wife." Embarrassed by this confession, he finished the vodka.

"What will we remember of this experience, I wonder."

"God help us."

The Baron returned to the ward, maneuvering around patients sprawled on cots, mats, and blankets crowded along the corridor. Some had turned their faces to the wall, claiming privacy for their suffering. His evaluation of their condition spanned a few breaths. There were so many sick. It was impossible to remember a patient's symptoms, the curve of a face, a name, a scrap of personal information. There were no talismans. It was as futile as trying to memorize a blade of grass in a field.

Five patients in one family had died that afternoon and the only survivor, a young girl, wouldn't live long. The walls were speckled with blood, fine as a growth of lichen. The Baron carefully pulled a sheet over her brother's body in the next bed, a ritual that should have been accomplished with more delicacy than he managed, his hands burdened in thick gloves. He hoped the girl would die before she realized her family was gone.

A medical assistant in a protective white uniform brought in two large buckets and dropped them on the floor near her bed. The Baron thought he was here to clean and, irritated by the intrusion, quietly told him to return later.

"No. This must be done now." The assistant stood by the buckets.

There was an abrupt movement inside the buckets. The Baron peered over and saw two small white rabbits. "What is this?"

"It's an experiment. We close the door, leave the rabbits here with new corpses for four hours to see if they catch plague." The assistant was impatient with his explanation.

"The girl is dying," the Baron hissed.

The assistant's shoulders moved up and down in a shrug. Sometimes it was easier to communicate by pantomime in the bulky uniforms.

The Baron calmed himself to avoid alarming the sick girl and slowly turned to face her. She'd managed to prop herself up on one elbow and looked down as the rabbits cautiously stood up inside the buckets. Frightened, she cried out and then fell back against the pillow, violently coughing.

"Get out."

"I have orders from Dr. Wu Lien-Teh and Dr. Strong." The angry assistant left with the buckets.

Speaking Chinese, the Baron reassured the girl, told her not to be afraid. Her face was pinched and her lips were a blue line. He called for a nurse to bring an ampoule of morphine. He swiftly gave the girl an injection, praying that it soothed her pain. Perhaps the spirits of the two rabbits would follow her into the next world. The mythical jade rabbit, associated with the moon, made medicine for the goddess Chang'e and brought good luck. He considered injecting the animals with morphine. A better death for the poor beasts.

The temperature had fallen to twenty below zero and he'd sleep at the hospital again tonight, restless on a cot near a supply room. Another day unmarked by sunlight in a closed world, moving between patients. The body of the city outside was lost to him. Veins of the streets, viscera of the markets. The *mo* of Kharbin.

The Baron studied the temple from the window of the droshky to confirm it was unoccupied. He'd waited to search the building until this particularly bitter day when it was too cold for the doctors to perform autopsies, as he was certain the place was unheated. The driver refused to accompany him so he asked the man to wait.

A chain across the road interrupted tracks in the gray ice from different vehicles and wider lines where boards had been dragged. The shutters over the windows of the temple were closed. At the side of the building, a splintered heap of pine coffins, their lids missing. There was no evidence of doctors or guards, but the outline of a glove was visible under a thin layer of snow on the steps. Perhaps it was a sign.

The massive front doors were unlocked. Nothing to protect. He began to hope that Messonier's information had been wrong and the temple was simply abandoned.

He walked cautiously through the first small empty room, his breath a playful wisp of fog. The next hall was a larger open space and he watched his boots, as the stones were in cracked disrepair. He imagined gray-robed monks cross-legged on the floor, listening to a priest in a five-faced crown, the yellow silk flag of the Buddhist trinity billowing over the carved doors.

Standing in the doorway of the next room, he smelled the chemical odor even before his eyes had adjusted to the lack of light. Gradually he distinguished lanterns sagging on wires over two bare tables in a windowless space. Ignoring protocol, he silenced the voice in his head that urged caution, convinced bacilli couldn't survive below zero, and snugged his scarf over his nose. His bare hand fumbled in his pocket, and he heard the familiar rattle of matches. He drew a lantern down to eye level, released it when the flame inside blazed. It bobbed crazily on the wire, its jerky pattern of light a violent disturbance in the room.

A row of dirty aprons hung on pegs against the wall. Whatever had been spilled on them, soiled them, had frozen the fabric stiff. A clue to the presence of doctors. A place of work. Glass-fronted enamel cabinets held a spiked collection of knives, scalpels, blades, scissors, and thin-handled saws on their shelves. An arsenal of tools for a single task, the taking apart of a body. There were no records, no identifying evidence in the drawers. He didn't touch the large covered metal bins, guessing they contained refuse from the autopsies. There was no odor of rot. It was too cold.

Under the lanterns, the two long tables gleamed with cloudy streaked ice. Small holes had been crudely hacked into their tops for drainage near a block of wood for the cadaver's neck. The edges of the tables were overlapped with lumpy ice and jagged icicles, black in the dim light. Puzzled, he snapped off an icicle and held it up to the lantern as if studying the translucent hidden pattern of a shell. Then he recognized the blackish thing as frozen blood. The overflow of a dissection.

He used another match to light a stick of incense, walked the smoke around the space, then left it propped up on the table.

Outside the front door on the stair landing, the Baron threw a handful of loose snow over the footprints he'd made entering the temple. Then he scraped the Russian Orthodox cross in the snow with the heel of his boot. Next to it, he made the Chinese character for *qi,* breath, just as he'd been taught.

After he was finished, he realized he'd gone over to the side of the dead against the living.

CHAPTER THIRTEEN

The Baron was alone in the hospital corridor, fumbling with his gloves. He was cold to his bones. He sensed a growing disconnect, dully surprised that the sickness came to him like this. To escape, he must accept that he was sick. He was infected. Carried his own death sentence. His heart pounded through a vise that imprisoned his chest, and the same pulse beat in his head. He stood still, trying to focus. He wanted only to fall into his wife's embrace, so ordinary.

Touch nothing. Speak to no one. He was terrified that a doctor, nurse, guard would recognize his symptoms. Take his temperature and throw him in quarantine. The doctors and medical staff constantly monitored one another. Scrutiny was self-protection. He must hide.

Praying that he wouldn't attract attention, he moved unsteadily along the corridors, angling his face away from others so as not to infect them or betray his sickness and panic. Medics and nurses passed him without stopping. Cautiously, as if his body were leaking, he slowly opened doors, covering the knob with his sleeve.

The Baron ducked into the supply closet, ransacked the shelves for disinfectants, filled his coat pockets. He jerked open a drawer, and the brown vials of morphine rolled around, escaping the chase of his clumsy fingers. A box held ampoules of Haffkine's serum. He broke the seal, filled a hypodermic. He rolled up his sleeve, secured a tourniquet, and when the vein inside his elbow popped, he twice tried to inject the needle with numb, shaking hands. He dropped the hypodermic, ground it with his boot. *Haffkine won't save me.*

The corridor was empty. The jars of disinfectant rattled softly with his steps, clear as the movement of a clock. A figure turned the corner and moved briskly toward him.

Dr. Wu looked up from a clipboard, checked the Baron's face, and half turned as if to avoid him. Surrounded by a haze, the Baron was unable to move away. His ghastly smile to the other doctor, lips pulled over a dry mouth.

"Why are you wearing a coat?" Wu's face was creased with concern.

His sympathy was more unbearable than criticism or anger. The Baron started to tremble. The two doctors stared at each other.

"You seem tired. You should be examined."

"Yes." He would surrender. The Baron's voice a croak. "The infirmary."

"Good."

Dr. Iasienski interrupted them. An urgent communication from the American consul.

The Baron was forgotten. He was a smuggler, leaving with his life. He fled. On the back staircase, trying to quiet his boots on the steps, he became dizzy, gripped the handrail, stopped to catch his breath.

He struggled with the side door, forcing it half open against wind pushing back like a live thing, and a fury of snow burst into the corridor, strange as fire in daylight. His arm braced the door, keeping it ajar, then he slid past it into blinding whiteness. Ten steps outside the building, he lost all sense of direction in the humming whirlwind, his eyes stinging, arms flailing in emptiness. His father once had a paperweight filled with suspended white dots, a blizzard inside a globe. He was walking into this glass stone now, snowflakes circling him, suffocating. He didn't have strength to turn back. He fell and was pivoted up as someone seized his arm. He stood shaking, peering into the snow at a man's dark silhouette.

"Lucky I caught you." A shouting voice.

"Home." Wind forced the word back in his throat. He pushed Andreev away, afraid to let him get close, but the man clutched his arm. Their bodies bent together against the snow, they moved slowly forward.

Andreev hoisted him into the droshky, gave the driver directions. The Baron fell asleep and then recognized the shape of the gate outside his house. An indistinct figure waved at him.

He stumbled over the threshold. "Get away."

Confused, the servant mumbled an apology, trailed anxiously behind as the Baron staggered, dribbling disinfectant over his melting footprints on the floor, cleaning all traces of his presence. He collapsed on the bed.

He isolated himself in the bedroom. No one could enter his quarantine. Food, water, kindling to heat the samovar was to be left on a tray outside. Soiled dishes must be cleaned in boiling water. He whispered that the servants should wear gloves, a mask. *Never tell anyone that I'm sick.*

Li Ju didn't weep but refused to obey some of his orders. "If I sense you're leaving me, if you're silent, I'll force the door and come to your bed. You won't stop me. I won't leave you alone if you're dying."

He was helpless against her threats. Others had crept to death alone to protect their families. But he feared dying alone and came home. The illness obliterated his sense of failure and shame.

The plague would show itself within hours or a day. He had only to wait for symptoms to unfold like a familiar piece of music. His mind raced through his body like a telescope, checking the lungs, the tough bronchial tubes that would become inflamed, expel a froth of blood. If a traditional Chinese doctor had treated him, the man's knowledge would follow the *mo* at the Baron's wrist through his entire body, the net of blood and nerves, the places where liquid threaded through muscle and the soft firmness of the organs. Monitoring the body's temperature with a thermometer was primitive in comparison.

First there was a cough. Then coughing became constant, the pain striking his ribs and back like blows. His body jerked as if pulled by strings, muscles tense. Exhausted, he waited for the next cough like an inexorable wave.

He made a tunnel around himself. In delirium, he spoke loudly, ordered everything burned. His books, letters, calligraphy, the scrolls and brushes. Clothing and bedding. His voice, even his mouth, seemed distant. Li Ju must hear him.

She had sealed the corridor along the bedroom against the invisible enemy with a formalin-sprayed curtain. Buckets of diluted chlorine were poured along the floor and steam rose from the warm water. Li Ju brought a chair to the far end of the corridor. For hours, she read Sherlock Holmes and *The Woman in White* aloud in English, sang hymns in the Scottish-inflected accent acquired at the orphanage. She whispered endearments. It was meaningless to him, her voice as indistinct and soothing as if she spoke from a well or behind a screen. He'd sleep and then jolt awake to find her singing had changed to a one-sided conversation or a description of a foggy London street. Sometimes he recognized her voice.

One day, he was able to sit up in bed. Li Ju slipped a paper from the *I-Ching Book of Changes* under his door, an explanation of Hexagram 13 by Confucius.

> *Life leads the thoughtful man on a path of many windings*
> *Now the course is checked, now it runs straight again,*
> *Here winged thoughts may pour freely forth in words*
> *There the heavy burden of knowledge must be shut away in*
>   *silence.*
> *But when two people are at one in their inmost hearts,*
> *They shatter even the strength of iron or of bronze.*

The dreams brought by fever vanished. The Baron's self-imposed quarantine ended. He had survived severe pneumonia. Plague had spared him. Illness had compressed sensation, and even lifting his arm took effort. Li Ju and a servant bathed him, helped him from the bed in slow stages. He wasn't strong enough to test the length of her body against his. Her mouth, her breath were a sweet weight. At any hour when he called her name she would appear at his bedside.

Li Ju tried to persuade her husband to listen to the fortune-teller who had just arrived and stood outside the bedroom door. "She's here. This is an auspicious time."

"No. It's not safe."

Unperturbed, the fortune-teller agreed to calculate the destiny of an unseen man, although for a higher fee, sitting in a fur coat outside his door. Li Ju anxiously knelt beside the woman as she placed three coins in a tortoiseshell. The coins had holes in their centers and the blank side had a value of three. The opposite inscribed side had a value of two. The coins rattled inside the shell, and were shaken out onto the floor. The fortune-teller opened the

Book of Changes to read the interpretation of the coins for dramatic effect.

"It is a time to resolve difficulties. This is a breakthrough. You should forgive the past and swiftly finish whatever task still lingers in your life."

> *The southwest furthers.*
> *If there is no longer anything where one has to go,*
> *Return brings good fortune.*
> *If there is still something where one has to go,*
> *Hastening brings good fortune.*

"Now I will read the image for the hexagram to you."

> *Thunder and rain set in:*
> *The image of Deliverance.*
> *Thus the superior man pardons mistakes*
> *and forgives misdeeds.*

Swept with relief, the Baron sank back against the bed cushions. He imagined Li Ju's smile, her bow of acknowledgment, handing the money to the woman in an envelope.

"You see? Nothing to fear." Li Ju's body was against the partially open door, her voice fitting through the crack. "Her words were a comfort."

He slowly walked to the door and leaned against it.

Her face was on the other side of the door, so close that he recognized the scent of her mouth. They played with their breath, in and out, a sigh of exchanging vapor as if it were the contact of their lips. Her hand pressed hard against the door and he felt its warmth.

*   *   *

Chang's spoon bit into green-gray tea in the container, organizing its loose crumble. He glanced at the Baron, who had gained enough strength to sit at the table for longer periods. Li Ju hovered restlessly around her husband, adjusting the light, his cushions, the angle of the teacup on the table.

The Baron didn't notice Li Ju, was pleased to see Chang, reassured that he hadn't been infected. "You have courage to visit my sickroom."

"I have no courage. According to the *I-Ching*, it isn't my fate to catch your illness. I risk nothing sitting here next to you. To mark your recovery, I will prepare a special tea."

The Baron recognized that he should respond to Chang's words but he still couldn't break the dull pressure that possessed him. A lingering effect of his illness. "I need more comfort than what's provided by leaves and water." He immediately regretted his words and apologized for his rudeness. "My health isn't fully recovered. Please continue."

But Chang took no offense. "There's a saying: *Bingzhong shi xin cha.* 'In sickness, I sample some new tea.' Tea makes the bones light. Tea is an aid to immortality. So say monks and poets and scholars. A cup of tea warms your hands, your throat."

Chang passed the Baron a shallow cup containing a few damp tea leaves. "Here. This young tea is delicate and slippery. Mature leaves are the opposite, firm and leathery."

"Show me too." Li Ju peered into the cup. Then she looked at her husband, huddled in a quilted jacket against the chill and the hard back of the chair. Neither of the men tried to bring her into the conversation, her husband curt because of illness and Chang distracted by concern for him. The Baron stared at the teapot on the shallow tray. Robust brown clay. A texture that held traces of the potter's hand. Earth. With an effort, he smiled at Li Ju. Relief curved across her face.

Chang was also relieved. "Sharing pleasure is valuable. *Chalu,* we are companions of tea." He handed her a tiny cup with the last leaves from the teapot. "Observe the oblong shape of the leaves. Flat leaves brew slowly. Crinkled and balled leaves release their flavor quickly because they greatly expand in hot water. Tea leaves can also be whole, flat, twisted, crimped, curled, needle-shaped, broken, granular, fanning. Like clouds that fill the sky."

He sent a quizzical glance toward the Baron, who nodded, imagining how Xiansheng would unlock the characters that might form this observation. "I've had little news during my quarantine," he said abruptly.

"No news from Kharbin is a blessing." Chang lowered his face to the teacup in his hands and slowly inhaled. Exhaled. "Lately, the only good fortune is at the pawnshops. I've bought many things that others have cast aside. Ivory boxes, jade. Even an icon of some saint with pearls and amethysts. Why not? A man needs luck these days. Even from saints. There's no work. People have no money."

"Have you abandoned your Churin's store uniform?"

"I'm no longer at the door. Too short to put a thermometer in the mouths of the Russian shoppers." The Baron's eyes widened and the dwarf laughed. "No. I'll return in spring. They predict the world will be healed by that time, although store owners aren't fortune-tellers. For now, there's a guard with a bayonet at the door, keeping away sickness and looters."

Li Ju silently toyed with a fan.

The Baron gently asked if stores had been looted.

"Only a few stores in Fuchiatien. Not enough police or soldiers to patrol the streets. They're stationed along the railroad tracks and roads from Kharbin. I saw them force a droshky to drive through burning sulfur to fumigate his vehicle. The pony panicked in the smoke. The city is closed. Unless you're rich."

"Bribes no longer work?" During the Baron's illness, events had unwound outside his knowledge as if in another country. Barriers were built. Soldiers moved into position.

"Bribes are the only currency." Chang's mouth sagged. "But some things are worse than a bribe. I recognized someone, a customer from Churin's, dead on the street. Lovely woman. She always smiled at me. I thought to put my coat over her but it would have been stolen. I brushed snow over her face to hide her from others. Then I went to Central Station and lit a candle at the shrine for St. Nikolas. Many people were there, weeping and praying."

Li Ju stared at the teacups on the tray. She very slowly stood up and left the room. Chang looked stricken. "Forgive me. Should I have stayed silent? I didn't think—"

The Baron interrupted. "I've tried to shield her. Don't worry. I'll speak to her later. I suppose it's better that she hear about it from you before witnessing so many corpses on the street."

"Don't leave your house if you wish to avoid death. Either you're dying or someone you know is dying or dead." The dwarf sipped his tea and savored it in his mouth before swallowing. "You cannot believe the things I've seen." He leaned forward, lowered his voice. "I have free time since I'm no longer at Churin's. I tell you, the imagination of the desperate is ferocious. I was in the Fantasia cabaret on Ofitserskaya Street near the wharf. I saw a man begin to cough. He had the sickness. The plague. He ordered champagne for everyone, for the entire cabaret. He gave his armband to the waiter. His fur coat to the cigarette girl. He drank and took opium, sang and danced. He performed shocking acts with women and men. His recklessness was irresistible and no one backed away from him. Finally he ran from table to table, asking if the sun had risen yet. Then he called for attention, undressed in the center of the room, and walked naked out of the cabaret into the snow. Knew he'd quickly freeze to death, drunk. Perhaps not a bad death. The farewell was unforgettable, a whirlwind of scandal. You met him. The Slav. Tall, with blond hair and a white fur coat. The owner of the nightclub gathered up whatever the Slav had touched. His clothing and the tablecloth. The chair cushions. Glasses. The bloody napkins he'd thrown under the table. Everything would be burned. As the Slav walked out, he gave me his top hat. Should I burn it?" He studied the Baron, expecting him to provide an answer. "I stayed well away from him. He tossed me the hat."

"God rest his soul." The Baron gently placed his teacup on the table. He explained that the hat would be ruined by treatment with disinfectant. "But leave it outside overnight. The temperature will kill bacilli."

After Chang left, the Baron pulled the jacket more tightly around his shoulders. *How do we move during this time? Stand up or sit down? What does a body do during a siege?*

The Baron had decided not to return to the Russian hospital but would tend patients at a temporary facility in one of the converted buildings. This decision was not discussed with his wife. When he began to pack medical supplies into a satchel, she pleaded with him to stay home. He still looked like a patient himself, gaunt, eyes troubled. An old injury from the war had returned and his hands shook slightly when he was chilled or tired.

"I can't wait at home while others suffer."

"They will suffer regardless. They will die with or without you. Stay here with me."

He agreed to stay. But only for a short time.

*   *   *

After his illness, the Baron transferred to a hospital in the Pristan quarter, converted from an elegant department store into a hospital for plague victims. Furniture, display counters, and cases had been removed but chandeliers and an elaborate clock graced the large open space crammed with wooden beds, rough as benches. The place was freezing. Patients huddled under blankets in their street clothes and coats. Occasionally, a man laboriously walked to the immense porcelain stove in the corner and pushed sticks of kindling inside. A flame briefly glowed red.

The Baron felt invisible, lacking the ability to treat the sick. Morphine was the only comfort. So he began to record the names of those who could talk in a small notebook, sitting next to their beds, an infinitely patient witness, waiting through their fevers, spasms of coughing that marked the pages and his clothing with blood. Many were unable to speak or refused to reveal their identities. He guessed at the spelling of some names whispered to him. Time passed slowly, measured by the breaths of the dying and the movement of his pencil, their last conversations on earth.

Page after page filled with names as the daily death rate reached two hundred. A cemetery had been established in the notebook, a monument to the lost. The final document of these lives was compressed into black lines in his spiked lettering, a mix of Russian and Chinese characters, fierce and tender. Black ink insubstantial as paper.

He feared the notebook with the list of dead would be misplaced or accidentally damaged by water, blood, or disinfectant. Someone moved the notebook while he changed in the disinfecting room and he erupted in a rage of weeping until it was found under a bench.

Li Ju painstakingly began to copy the names of the dead into a second book.

After he left the patients, he walked directly into the disinfecting station, joining a line of doctors, nurses, stretcher bearers, corpse-carrier attendants, and soldiers. He'd hoped to see Dr. Maria Lebedev but there wasn't a single familiar face in the room.

In the disinfecting room, standing on the sheet of black rubber, he pulled off his bloody clothing, leaving it crumpled in folds around his feet like stiff wings. He stepped to the sink and scrubbed his hands until they cracked and bled. He wanted to strip his hands of discolorations and scars, proof of injury, everything rough. He wished a horned surface could grow over his skin, translucent scales like a fish or dragon, as protection. Clothed in scales, he'd be safe here, even stepping into fire or water. He pulled off his mask, wet with perspiration and condensed moisture, raked his hair back with his fingers. He stank.

The odor of disinfectant clung to his skin. His wife wouldn't share the *k'ang* bed until she'd first walked around him several times holding a stick of burning incense like a wand trailing a cloud.

The cavernous room in the department store was always dim, a purposeful twilight believed to soothe patients. The large display windows on the ground floor along the sidewalk were blocked by immense stacks of coffins to shield pedestrians from a view of the sick in their beds.

The Baron bent over the bed of a new patient, a man swaddled in a coat against the cold, and gently straightened his blanket. The man turned his head, and Xiansheng's eyes found the Baron's face. He whispered his teacher's name: "Elder Born." His eyes fluttered. The barest acknowledgment.

The Baron ignored the explosion of grief in his chest. He pulled at his mask to reveal his face, stripped off a glove, sought his teacher's hand under the blanket. His beautiful dexterous hand, shaped by skill with a brush, ivory skin a fragile wrap for his fine bones.

He couldn't speak words of comfort or promise but prayed for a miracle, an intervention from Saint Nikolas or Guanyin, the goddess of mercy. He called the fox spirit. He visualized the black structure of calligraphy, horizontal and vertical lines, as if Teacher could escape, slip between these marks and escape.

When his teacher coughed, he wiped the red spittle from his face with a cloth. There was a cold compress for fever. He never released Xiansheng's hand, solid with cold and unchanged by warmth from his own hand. He focused on the gentle contact of his fingertips against Xiansheng's wrist and fixed his eyes on the distance, copying the Chinese doctors he'd observed. The evidence of *mo* at his wrist was the key to diagnosis. What did he sense? Confinement. He was confined in a liquid black tunnel that trembled with a pulse. He blindly followed it without a measure of distance, gradually aware of a tightening of space that led to the throbbing chambers of the heart.

Words came to him and he recited, "'In writing one sees the hanging needle, the dropping dew, crashing thunder, falling rock, flying bird, startled beast: it is heavy as breaking clouds, light as a cicada's wings, graceful as the new moon and dependent stars—it equals the exquisiteness of nature.'" Naming the things of this world. He recited the words again and again, making it a lullaby with the fullness of prayer.

Xiansheng met his eyes and his fingers stirred. He was gripped by rasping coughs, and blood covered the bedclothes. The Baron left his side to find another ampoule of morphine. When he returned, Xiansheng had died, his face now mute and unchangeable. The Baron carefully cleaned his face and hands.

Sorrow spread fire-fast inside his body. He stood up, swaying a little, pulled the blanket over Xiansheng. He stepped back for two men who appeared at the bedside, tightened the blanket around the body, and slid it onto a stretcher. The Baron numbly followed them from the building. Outside, the men eased the body into a flimsy coffin, their actions unusually gentle, since they were being watched. He wedged his glove under the coffin lid as a marker so he could find it again.

A man who revered words, his teacher would have hated to be buried without his name.

The next morning, the Baron was unable to locate Xiansheng's coffin outside the hospital. Identical coffins of weather-beaten gray wood were stacked higher than his head along the length of the building. He stopped the three corpse carriers shoving coffins into a waiting wagon.

"Did you take coffins away from here yesterday?"

"Yes. We took a wagonload to the field past the barracks."

Two men roped a canvas over the coffins to secure them in the wagon. The Baron waited until all the men were seated to hoist himself up next to the driver. One of the corpse carriers aimed his foot to kick him down from the wagon.

"Let him pay!" the driver shouted.

Another bribe. The driver shrugged. A fool's errand, but to honor his teacher, the Baron would accompany the corpses to the burial ground. He sat in front with the driver, ignoring the men's hostility. He snugged the hood tighter around his head, wrapped the fur blankets tighter around his body.

They headed north of Kharbin past the barracks into a wild unsettled area. The coffins slid and shifted noisily in back as the wagon navigated the icy tracks in the road, the snow unstable as water. The Baron huddled, as did the corpse carriers, the cold stripping their hands of sensation. Periodically, they checked one another for frostbite, telltale patches of white. The nose was especially vulnerable.

A long line of vehicles were stopped at a barricade near a railroad depot. They inched forward as several soldiers searched for plague-infected travelers and contaminated goods.

Other vehicles gave their wagon a wide berth, moved from the line to avoid them and the stack of coffins visible under the flapping canvas. Their cursed cargo.

Near the barricade, two masked soldiers slammed their bayonets against a fine carriage until the passengers, a bewildered man, three women, and several young children, slowly climbed down. A soldier herded the women and children together. He seized the smallest boy and, holding his coat, stuck a thermometer in his mouth. The father lunged forward but was held back by the soldier. He argued furiously until a bayonet was leveled at his chest. The children shrieked. The family was ordered back into the carriage but the boy squirmed from the soldier's grip and ran away, foundering in the deep snow. His mother followed him, slowed by her long skirt and coat. A soldier overtook the woman, grabbed her shoulder, and she tumbled into the snow. It seemed the soldier was ordering her to leave the child.

The Baron twisted around to jump from the wagon and bribe the soldiers, rescue the family.

The driver put out his arm to stop him. "The soldiers won't leave the child in the snow. There are too many witnesses. But before the family is locked in quarantine, the soldiers will rob them of everything. All their furs and clothing will be stolen. Surely the man has a gold pocket watch that's worth their trouble."

The most dangerous acts are those undertaken without consideration. Now the Baron was aware of his foolishness. The family could have been infected, and he would have perished if he'd left the wagon. The corpse carriers wouldn't have waited for him.

The family clambered back into their carriage. Driven by a soldier, it quickly sped away from the barricade in the opposite direction. When the corpse wagon reached the barricade, the soldiers waved it through without inspection. Death was always accommodated.

The road curved along the railroad tracks, overlapping them in places. The wagon shook, jolted over an intersection, the hard metal tracks uncushioned by snow. Irregular shapes were scattered along the train tracks. Corpses. The bodies of travelers who couldn't afford the train and died following the tracks as an escape route from Kharbin.

It was suddenly clear that the arrangement of the arms and legs of the sprawled bodies depicted the Chinese characters for *peace* and *tranquillity*. Excited, the Baron almost pointed out this extraordinary message to the men on the wagon but realized they were illiterate.

They stopped in an open field divided by a high irregular wall a distance from the road, extending for miles. The corpse carriers quickly shoved coffins from the wagon. The Baron slowly made his way to the wall through the snow, flattened and rutted by wheel tracks and the dragging of heavy objects.

The wall was a jumble of splintered wood and coffins that seemed to have been scraped across the field by a monstrous tide. Unflinching as the glass eye of a camera, he distinguished naked bodies embedded in this wall, frozen arms and legs bent at sharp angles like branches. Rags of clothing and shrouds fluttered in the wind. His teacher's body was lost.

At the far edge of the field, a line of black shapes swiftly approached, as if driven by a pulse. A procession of huge sleighs drew closer, their blades easily knifing through the snow, the horses' harnesses slapping. A shout from the corpse carriers, interrupted at their work, as the sleighs circled and surrounded them.

Soldiers helped Wu Lien-Teh, his translator Zhu Youjing, and the doctors Zabolotny, Iasienski, and Broquet from the first sleigh. They were joined by General Khorvat, the *dao tai,* the viceroy, and a few other Chinese officials and dignitaries. The Baron recognized Mr. Greene, the American consul, in a wolf-skin coat. The men gathered in the area where the snow had been leveled, their eyes locked, fearful of breaking the link that held them together, protection from the terrible wall of bodies. No one noticed the Baron, and when he walked toward them, they recoiled, as startled as if a corpse had been resurrected. A ghost in daylight. He stood silently outside the group. They could hardly ask him to leave, as there was no place to go.

Wu was the first to speak, addressing his translator Zhu Youjing. "Is it possible to dig a hole here?"

The translator repeated his question in Chinese to the corpse carriers.

The corpse carriers gaped at him, slow to answer. "The ground is frozen. Like stone."

"How deep?"

"Very deep."

"Deep as a man is high?"

The corpse carriers looked at one another, anxiously made confused gestures. Was this a trick question? "Deeper." They motioned depth, stretching their arms overhead.

Wu turned to the group. "There's your answer. The ground is frozen seven feet deep. The corpses cannot be buried. They must be burned." Wu's words were repeated in Chinese for the Manchurian officials.

The Chinese shouted that it was sacrilege to burn a body.

Zabolotny's arm jabbed at the Chinese. "Who will bury the bodies? You? The Russians? Japanese soldiers? There are no workers." His angry response didn't need translation.

"It would take months to bury thousands of bodies in these conditions."

"There are thousands and thousands of frozen bodies here. They're eaten by rats and wolves. The animals become infected and bring plague back to Kharbin. When the weather becomes warmer, the situation will be worse."

No one responded. The silent Chinese officials moved closer together. The wind flattened their thick fur coats in one direction as if smoothed by a giant hand.

"A petition for permission to cremate the bodies will be sent to the Imperial Throne and the governor of Kirin. Everyone here will sign it." Wu had forced their participation by bringing them to this grotesque stage. A brilliant strategy. But for the Chinese, the dead had been deprived of burial rites. Their spirits would never rest.

The Baron remained after the men departed in the sleighs. He lit incense and burned paper offerings. He was reciting the Russian and Buddhist prayers for the dead for his teacher when a pounding noise and the sharp crack of wood interrupted him. He turned to see the corpse bearers hammering a frozen body, breaking its arms to fit it into a coffin.

The snow broke crisply as lacquer when hundreds of men crossed the open field to the miles-long wall of the plague dead. During the few hours of available daylight, the laborers would dismantle the wall to prepare it for the mass burning. Under the pressure of its own weight, the terrible wall had compacted into a frozen mass, the bones of the dead hard and resisting, cemented in place by the filler of flesh and snow.

The wall was clawed and chopped apart with saws and hatchets. Huge sections were looped and bound with chains and ropes, then pulled by horses until they separated. When the temperature plunged well below zero, the wood and ice were wrenched apart with a shattering high-pitched noise.

Load after load of massive trees, timber, and logs were hauled in, bringing the raw scent of the forests in northern Manchuria to this bleak landscape. This new timber and the corpses were piled into twenty-two enormous pyramids, temporary tombs of gray and black, threaded with dirty tangled shrouds, white in places where fresh snow had settled. There was enough space for teams of horses to pass between them. From a distance, the jagged structures appeared to have been created from the ruins of many other buildings by a mad giant.

On a morning of unusual brightness, doctors from the hospitals, Russian and Chinese officials, and the curious arrived at the pyramids in the field. They waited in their sleighs, black droshkies, and carriages, warm under fur blankets, the white evidence of their breath hanging over them like a canopy. Icy snow struck their vehicles in scratchy bursts.

The Baron stepped down from the droshky, an anonymous interloper in the crowd, unrecognizable in his furs, only a small circle of face exposed through the porthole of his hood. He scanned the crowd, although he didn't believe any families of the dead were here to pay their respects. He overheard strangers joking about the weather.

"Thank merciful God, no snowfall blocks visibility."

"The light is perfect today. We'll have a good clear view."

There was General Khorvat in his distinctive white fur coat, his wispy beard unruly in the wind.

"Good morning, General."

Khorvat didn't recognize the Baron until he heard his voice. "You're here?"

"A witness, like you."

"A cold morning for a display. But the city will be rid of this pestilence."

"You mean the evidence of pestilence. Nothing's been cured." The Baron regretted his words. "Where's the priest from St. Nikolas?"

Khorvat was puzzled, but then his expression smoothed as he understood. "No priests were notified."

"No?"

"This isn't the place for a religious ceremony. We aren't holding a funeral."

"A strange claim, General Khorvat, since thousands of bodies are stacked right before our eyes. There are Russian dead among the timber. Our countrymen."

Khorvat's face, surrounded by feathery fur, appeared almost regretful. He understood the mechanics of an official operation. "Baron, in the midst of war—and we are at war—some details are overlooked. Survivors will mourn in their own way." It was as close to an apology as the general would deliver.

The Baron released the burden of argument. He was aware of someone next to him demanding attention. A slight man in a fox coat addressed Khorvat, his eyes darting back and forth to the pyres.

"General Khorvat, we're ready to set up the cameras. We need direction."

Khorvat indicated the nearest pyramid. "Stay back at least two hundred yards."

"We need more distance. The light will overexpose our photographs. It'll be brilliant as a desert here soon."

Khorvat addressed another aide and the Baron turned away to search for Messonier. The crowd slowly began to leave their vehicles and gather around Khorvat, sharing a tense excitement, the anticipation of a performance that held the risk of injury or disaster. They loudly greeted one another.

"We couldn't have a better day for the spectacle."

"This isn't the launching of a ship. Show some respect, gentlemen." Messonier quietly reprimanded the group of men. He touched the Baron's shoulder, and they clasped each other with surprising emotion. Only the pantomime of large gestures worked in bulky winter clothing.

"You're here, Baron. Still the outlaw at an official occasion."

"I'm a witness to this strange ceremony for the dead. Our patients."

Several fire trucks and wagons moved around the closest pyramid. Dozens of men filled buckets from the fire-truck hose and passed them hand over hand to others, who struggled to carry them up the dangerously unsteady piles of timber and coffins. Unskilled mountaineers, many slipped and fell before dumping their buckets and slowly descending. Someone shouted at them in Russian and Chinese to hurry and get down.

"What are they pouring on the wood?" The Baron was mystified.

"Kerosene. The fire trucks carry kerosene, not water."

Fire trucks circled a pyramid. Spray from their hoses was directed in a high arc over its sides, a bright veil that didn't freeze. The trucks moved on, spraying other pyramids along the row.

At a pistol shot, a crowd of men carrying burning torches, dots of light like a moving necklace, surrounded the first pyramid. Another pistol shot and pale flame spread quickly as wind over the huge pyramid. A great shout from the crowd. The fire's hunger increased and the color of the flames deepened. With a roar, the heat reached them, hot on their faces. Fur coats were opened and hats were abandoned in the searing cocoon of heat.

A man, drunk, ran to the flames to toss a vodka bottle on the pyre but was tackled and dragged back by his laughing friends. There were cheers from those watching.

Flames rose from the second pyramid. The photographer and his crew jerked the camera tripod from the snow and fled, comic silhouettes, hobbling figures weighed down by their awkward equipment.

The wind changed. Smoke rolled toward them, carrying a blizzard of particles, twirling specks of paper, bark, leaves, twisted threads from shrouds and clothing, an odor of wood and something foul. Panicked, the watchers pulled masks over their faces, fearing the spread of bacilli from the burning bodies. They fled as snow melted around their boots, trampling the sodden discarded clothing. A swarm of red sparks followed them like vengeance, directed by *xiefeng,* the evil winds that could strike mind and body.

CHAPTER FOURTEEN

Within minutes after she became chilled and her pulse raced, Dr. Maria Lebedev was swathed in blankets. By evening, her temperature rose and her face flooded with color as if she blushed. Her hand found Messonier's hand. A sentinel at her bedside, he had stripped off his rubber gloves, unable to bear their thick clumsiness, the barrier to her skin. His mask, forgotten, dangled around his neck. When Maria slept and he could slip out, he wept in the next room, away from her eyes and ears. His anger was more difficult to hide because it made him reckless. Messonier had poured a bottle of her perfume, Jicky, all around the room, on the floor, pillow, and bed linens, to hide the odor of disinfectant. Maria was still lucid. She murmured a request to be taken to St. Nikolas Cathedral.

No, no, no. Messonier slid to the floor next to the bed, gripping the linen sheet as if to wring the fever from her body.

It seemed cruel to expose Maria to the cold, but he followed her wish. Messonier hired a sleigh and made a nest for her, a thickly swaddled figure, unrecognizable in blankets and furs in the back of the sleigh. It was a slow, halting procession to the church as the road was rough with ice under fresh snow.

The side door of St. Nikolas Cathedral had been left unlocked. The Baron and Messonier carried Maria on a stretcher into the building, followed by Li Ju and Chang.

It was only slightly warmer inside the church, faintly lit by the wavering pinpoints of candles on the altar. An odor of burning wax, the pressure of deep cold against wood. Maria was gently maneuvered to face the iconostasis, the royal gates, the towering gold screens hung with icons, that hid the altar. The gates had been specially opened for the service of extreme unction. The ceremony was usually performed by seven priests representing the seven churches, but only four men had been found at short notice. Each priest covered his mouth and nose with a protective mask.

They were uncertain if she was aware of her surroundings. "We're in the church now, Maria. All of us." Messonier's whisper echoed in the space. He caressed her shoulder through the thick blankets.

The fine cloth placed over the lower half of Maria's face rose and fell with her labored breathing. She had insisted on this caution for the others. Messonier, Chang, the Baron, and his wife stood behind Maria, as if her stretcher were a raft that they would help guide.

A priest paced around them, swinging a censer back and forth on clanking long chains, leaving a zigzag trail of incense, gray against the dim light. The candles held by the witnesses flickered as the priest's full robes stirred the air.

In silence, Archpriest Orchinkin placed a dish of dry grain, symbolizing death and resurrection, on a small table covered with a white cloth before the royal gates. In memory of the Good Samaritan, a glass of oil and wine was set in the center of the dish. Tiny wooden sticks, their tips wrapped with cotton wool, were inserted in the dry grain and stood upright around the glass.

The priest read from James, chapter 5:

Is any sick among you? Let him call for the elders of the church; and let them pray over him, anointing him with oil in the name of the Lord.

Archpriest Orchinkin raised his voice over Maria's coughing as he read the psalms, litany, and prayers of benediction. He dipped a stick in the oil and made the sign of the cross on Maria's forehead, cheeks, nose, lips, and breast and over her folded hands. Her chest heaved with coughing and Messonier tenderly dabbed bloody foam from her mouth and face with gauze until she was quiet. The four priests surrounded Maria, one by one anointing her with oil as the Seven Epistles and Gospels for Unction from Romans, chapter 15, were read.

The mind governed by the flesh is death, but the mind governed by the spirit is life and peace.

Maria groaned softly. She clawed at the blanket around her shoulders and struggled to free herself. The Baron secured the mask over his face and helped Messonier lift her into a slightly inclined position on the pillow. Messonier held her shaking hand, making the sign of the cross. He nodded at the Baron, who placed something in Messonier's outstretched hand. A shine of gold as Messonier slipped the ring on Maria's finger and closed his hand over hers. She recognized his gift and her fingers moved, responding to his touch. The back of Messonier's hand was wet with tears.

Each priest grasped a corner of the Book of the Holy Gospel and held it open over Maria's head as they prayed.

You, however, are not in the realm of the flesh but are in the realm
of the Spirit.

Messonier tenderly adjusted the pillow behind her back. Her coughing was louder, deeper, racking her body with spasms. Blood flecked the pages of the Bible above her. They waited.

"I ask for the priest's blessing." Maria's words were torn by her gasping for breath.

Archpriest Orchinkin blessed her.

"I ask for everyone's forgiveness." Her voice was stronger now.

Everyone murmured consent for forgiveness.

Her eyes flickered with weariness and found Messonier. He bent to kiss her forehead, but with a flash of gold, her hand fluttered to stop him.

The space across Maria Lebedev's grave was narrow, but the snow flew with such force—furious white sparks—that the mourners were visible only as faint featureless outlines to one another. In voluminous layered robes, so heavy the wind barely disturbed them, the priest swept his arm over the grave and poured oil and ashes of incense reserved from the service of extreme unction.

Rest with the saints, O Christ, thy servant's soul, where there is
no pain, nor grief, nor sighing, but life that endeth not.

The beggars standing behind the mourners loudly wailed and wept, a ritual performance for which they were paid.

It was nine days after Maria Lebedev's death. Traditionally, a second remembrance ceremony would be held twenty days after her death and a third ceremony at forty days.

The feast of remembrance for Maria Lebedev was held in Novy Gorod at the home of Dr. Iasienski, head of the Russian hospital. Members of the medical staff were present and guests wore gloves and cotton masks or held handkerchiefs over their noses. Physical contact was strictly avoided. People stood apart from each other during conversation and the distance made them more animated, their voices louder. Because of the fear of infection, all interior doors were propped open to allow free circulation of air.

The sideboard was laid with small plates of zakuski, smoked fish, meats, and many types of vodka, each bottle wrapped with a napkin. To pour a drink, guests placed a fresh napkin over the bottle to avoid touching it directly.

Through the open door to the kitchen, the Baron recognized a familiar figure. Chang stood on a chair leaning over the table, hands deep in a bowl. Sensitive to observation, he turned and beckoned the Baron into the room.

"They practically boiled my skin before I was hired to cook." Chang's voice a hoarse whisper. "The women in the house inspected me. Boychick, they called me. I had to unbutton my shirt so they could see I didn't carry infection." He grinned, reacting to the Baron's expression. "No, no. They just wanted to look. I didn't mind. Wasn't the first time. Hand me the knife. Put your gloves on first." He carefully spooned caviar into a hole in the center of a pie crust. "Caviar is the surprise garnish in the fish pie."

"*Rastegay.*"

"Ah, you like it? An extra serving for you. There's also *selianka* with sterlet and sturgeon. Pickled tomatoes, mushrooms, and pumpkin. Beets and bog berries boiled with cinnamon and cloves. *Pokhobka*, potato soup. It was hard work to get the ingredients.

Provisions aren't delivered. You can't buy anything. There's nothing in the market but fear of plague. You wonder about my cooking skills? I was a kitchen apprentice years ago. Russian cooking is a challenge, although Chinese food is more complex."

Chang refused to discuss Maria Lebedev and wouldn't mention her name. "Now leave me, Baron, so I can finish."

At the table, *koutia* was served to guests. Archpriest Orchinkin bowed his head over his bowl. "This rice is the buried seed that will rise up again. The raisins, like Christians, will be reconstituted. Honey, like the Resurrection, is the sweetness of heaven."

After the archpriest's blessing, bottle after bottle of Russian Excelsior champagne and red wine from the Caucasus sent by General Khorvat were passed around the table. As they grew noisily drunk, guests casually loosened or removed their masks.

The Baron noticed Zabolotny and Wu standing with Messonier near the sideboard. Messonier said little, nervously turning a smudged empty vodka glass in his hand. The other two doctors didn't cross the room to speak with the Baron and soon left the house to return to the hospital.

The Baron brought Messonier a fresh vodka. "My friend—"

Messonier interrupted. "I don't want the burden of accepting her death. To be the taker of sympathy. Better to refuse sympathy and be alone."

The Baron laid his hand on Messonier's arm.

"The strangest transformation has happened. Everything in the house where I live has been replaced with identical worthless things. I saved Maria's teacup. Her last drink with me. Now I should boil her cup or swab it with alcohol. It's contaminated." His face was stiff with sorrow.

The wait for Messonier to compose himself created a physical ache.

"Maria was always impatient to drink and return to work. I'd say, 'Finish your tea slowly. Refresh yourself. Hurry only if you believe you can save a life.'" Messonier made a dismissive gesture. "Her sacrifice was useless. No one was saved."

"We cannot tally up a life." The Baron's consolation stuck in his throat. "I don't have faith to offer any comfort. The Chinese say the only certainty is change."

Messonier's wan smile. "I need more vodka. You? Give me your glass if you dare. I wear no gloves."

The Baron put his empty glass in Messonier's open hand.

All conversation took place inside. Outside, there was no direction a body could stand without encountering wind that suffocated sentences, cold that pressured lips and throat.

The Baron and Andreev slumped at a table in a *chaynaya*, one of the few teahouses still open. Andreev was ill at ease, disheveled, face shadowed by a huge gray fox hat, the stubble on his cheeks damp from the mask he'd just removed. He constantly wiped his nose.

"Do I seem well?" Andreev shoved up his sleeve, extended a bare arm, insisted his pulse be taken.

The Baron hesitated, noticing a fresh cut on Andreev's arm. One of the Chinese doctors had mentioned the diagnosis in an early medical book that if the lungs were healthy, the *mo* would be "quiet and whispering like fallen elm pods." If the lungs were infected, the *mo* would be "suspended, and one has a sensation of striking a rooster feather." His fingertips gently pressed against Andreev's wrist and he became lost in a jumble of signals. He kept the bewilderment from his face. Wait. There. A racing pulse.

"Your pulse is rapid, but it could be nerves." His finger against the wrist with slight pressure diagnosed the nerves. With slightly harder pressure, the viscera could be read. By increasing the pressure, the bones could be sensed. He was cautious about contact but placed his hand across Andreev's forehead. "Your temperature is slightly elevated. It's not a death sentence."

"A day never passes without fear of a cough."

"I live by those words. I'm resigned to the situation."

Andreev changed the subject. "The rich have left the city. The money is gone. Everything shipped into Kharbin is inspected, every crate opened by a medical officer and sprayed with God knows what foul stuff. Vegetables, feathers, paper, fur, hair and skins, rags. Even coffins and earth are sprayed. The disinfectant eats gold leaf from porcelain. Tarnishes silver. Ruins everything."

"How is your transportation business? Helping others flee the city?"

"I was running people south to Kirin, Dairen, and Mukden. The money was good. But several wagons were wrecked by a blizzard. Icebound. Lost three drivers. That's how the trouble started." Andreev's words tumbled out, and his fingers nervously tore at a napkin. Perhaps he'd taken a drug. "A woman died. And her children. Wife of an official. All her trunks were lost. I'm certain she died of plague, not conditions in my vehicle. Now her husband pursues me. Unless he dies of plague first."

"Surely your business will recover. Plague has no mercy." The Baron kept his voice quiet, attempting to calm Andreev. "People are desperate to leave Kharbin since the price of the CER train tickets was raised, thanks to the Russians."

"I'm in a hole. I have very little money. I can't officially work since I have only a wolf's passport. My creditors threatened to kill me."

"What do you need?"

Andreev asked for a loan, named a vast sum. "I swear it will be repaid honestly. Unless there's something you'd like to buy or order."

The Baron whistled. "Impossible. I'll give you money for a train ticket. You can escape."

"Escape? How can I escape? You said I have a temperature. I'll never get past the plague doctors at Central Station. I'll be thrown in quarantine. You've always been fair with me. I don't beg without reason. What's the saying? What's here today would scarcely have been believable yesterday?"

Andreev's eyes seemed to leave a mark as they searched the Baron's face. In self-protection, he angled his head away. "Come to the house tomorrow. I have more money there." He laid all the money from his pockets on the table. He felt himself slowing down against the other man's panic. Setting a distance was a way to resolve concern for others.

Agitated, Andreev stuffed the bills inside his shirt. "The city's on the verge of collapse. It's quicker to freeze to death than starve or die of plague. And possibly more pleasant. But tell me more about the sickness. The plague. If a sick person touches something and then you touch it, can you get infected? Is it true gloves protect the hands?"

The Baron patiently answered his questions. Probably not, and yes.

"Can you catch plague from a corpse?"

"I'm certain the bacilli die with the host body. Although some doctors disagree."

"Once the plague corpse is buried, is the dirt around it contagious?"

"No. A body would freeze before it could decompose in the ground. But why this concern about plague? You've always been so reckless." The Baron studied the other man for a clue, trying to locate the driving point behind his questions.

"I'm older. More cautious." His grin to signal a joke between them.

Then the Baron knew. "You're working for Dr. Wu. Taking bodies for autopsy. For experiments."

Before Andreev turned his face away, a fleeting expression betrayed his answer.

"*Gospodi-pomiluy*. God have mercy."

Andreev's fingers tapped the table as if the sound would silence the Baron's words. "I'm just a carrier. Move the dead from one place to another."

"Where do you get the bodies?"

"From the hospitals. The unclaimed corpses. Otherwise, they'd be dumped in a field. Isn't it better the dead help the living? But now they plan to take corpses from the cemeteries. All the bodies recently buried."

The Baron found his voice. "So they're afraid the corpses are contagious. So they'll dig them up." He made a silent vow. "But the churches won't allow it. This desecration."

"Who will come to church surrounded by the plague-infested dead in the ground? The priests at St. Nikolas can't stop soldiers with shovels."

"God have mercy. Pray for the souls of the dead." The Baron placed his hand over Andreev's hand. "Protect yourself. I'll do what I can to help you. You'll come to the house tomorrow?"

Andreev bowed his head. He drank from a bitter cup for survival.

The Baron checked the teapot, nearly empty, the sodden fragments of leaves in the bottom like torn shrouds on the dead. He feared the effect this news about the exhumation of the cemetery would have on Messonier.

That night, the Baron had a vision of decomposing corpses leaking into a subterranean network of infection, foul tentacles reaching underneath the city.

The Baron stood on the field where the twenty-two immense pyres of wood and bodies had been burned. The temperature of the fires had been so intense that the mounds of hot ash had gradually sunk into great deep pits, the earth softened to mush. The pits were surrounded by snow crusted with black soot, fragments of bone, cloth, charred wood, and the bare ground was glassy with ice where melted snow had refrozen. A landscape without trees or foliage, it stank of burning.

He couldn't look at the ground without visualizing the choreography of what had happened here. The bringing of bodies, their burning, the scarring of the earth.

He watched Li Ju and Chang picking their way across the field in front of him. Slowly moving figures, diminished by the damaged landscape, they approached a fresh pit of brown earth that had been carved out by dynamite to accommodate the newly dead.

Although certain no harm would come to them from this place and contact with the dead, the Baron had been reluctant to ask Li Ju and Chang to accompany him here. *It's for the good of others,* he had told them. *The only reason I would take this risk.* He shook out the blanket he carried and draped it over Li Ju's shoulders. "This won't take long. But be careful."

"I will." She stared up at him, eyebrows an unhappy line, and held out her hand. Steadied by his grip on her arm, he followed Li Ju into the pit. Bodies were scattered over the sides of the pit where they'd been dumped, fallen in their last posture, fixed under lacy snow. He felt her hesitation and uneven movement over the rough ground, frozen hard as marble, and wished to apologize, to carry her away.

The first corpse was a young girl, facedown, in a pale ragged robe. Li Ju threw the blanket open on the ground next to her. Braced against the angle of the pit, they bent over the girl, cautiously rocked her body back and forth to pry it loose. She was stiff, unyielding, and the Baron feared her face, frozen against the dirt, would be torn off by their crude effort. Gradually, with a muted cracking, the earth released her. They turned the body over. A white face with closed eyes, a tiny silver amulet—a padlock—around her neck for luck, to lock her to life. She was placed on the blanket, the debris brushed from her face. The Baron crossed himself. Li Ju was silent. Had the girl perished alone? Or was her body given up by her family?

Li Ju crawled farther down the slope to the tiny corpse of an infant embedded in a slab of ice. She kicked at the ice around the body, then clawed the loose pieces away. She pulled him free, the ice stuck to his shoulders as if he'd been pierced by a transparent wing. The Baron and Li Ju carried the corpses, sagging in the blanket, across the field back to the droshky.

Chang had unpacked a heavy wooden camera and struggled to mount it on the tripod, holding it with one hand while peering underneath to locate the locking device. The Baron hurried over to help him and the delicate piece of equipment shook slightly in the wind as they worked. They stuck the tripod legs into firm snow to steady it.

With a mechanical click, the Baron inserted the glass plate into position at the back of the camera. "Everything is ready. Just squeeze this bulb to take the photograph." He ducked under the black cloth hanging over the back of the camera and adjusted the lens, a cylindrical black eye.

The dwarf took the Baron's place behind the camera, standing on a box to peer at the glass plate that showed the image. The Baron sat down heavily on the blanket and Li Ju moved the dead girl so she faced the camera, half reclined across his lap like a board. Without removing her mittens, she smoothed the girl's hair, straightened her tattered robe. He pulled back the fur hood on his jacket, exposing his face, and held the girl's shoulder so she wouldn't topple over. The body was a cold, hard weight.

"Are you ready?" Chang waited behind the camera.

"Yes."

"I'm removing my mittens now. Be careful with the focus. It must be clear that my bare hands are touching her skin." The Baron placed his hand against the girl's cheek, surprised by its immobility, neutral as a stone, absent blood, nerves, an animating presence.

"Hold still." Chang quickly tripped the camera shutter before cold numbed the men's fingers.

The infant was simpler to photograph. The Baron again removed his gloves and cradled the tiny body, his arms and legs folded as if he were swaddled. It was like holding a block of ice with a human face.

"Finished." Chang stepped off the box.

The two bodies were wrapped tightly in the blanket. Li Ju and Chang held the ends of the blanket shroud and awkwardly carried it into the pit, teetering, half stumbling, until they could no longer stand upright because of the severe slope. They knelt, gently pushed the bundle, and it clumsily rolled down into the intertwined arms of the corpses at the bottom of the pit. It was hoped the dead would be safe from the reach of animals until they could be burned.

At the edge of the pit, the Baron recited a brief prayer, and in

her clear voice, Li Ju recited words from the Church of Scotland
service for the dead.

*Earth to earth, dust to dust, till that great day when earth and
sea shall give up their dead, and when the Lord shall change
our vile bodies, and make them like unto His own glorious
Body, according to the mighty working whereby He is able
to subdue all things to Himself.*

In a metal cup, the dwarf lit paper replicas of food, drink, clothing, gold and silver ingots, a horse, and a home to provide for the
deceased in the afterlife. Wind took the fragile burning papers,
flew them over the pit, twisting them into ash.

In the droshky returning to Kharbin, the Baron thanked Li Ju
and Chang for their brave assistance. "Now we have only to wait
three days for my theory to be proven. If the dead are infectious, I
will die. But I'm certain I'll be fine. I would never do anything to
risk those I love."

Li Ju stirred uneasily against him. "Risk? I will not throw you in
with the other corpses. My prayer was for you." She turned away,
buried her face in the fur blanket. She refused his words of comfort. Visibly uneasy, Chang also remained silent.

In the disinfecting station set up in the stable, Dr. Zabolotny angrily accused the plague-wagon crews of shirking their search.

"If you miss a single infected person, it could cause hundreds of
deaths."

Protected from one another by white cotton masks, their identities safely hidden, the wagon men shouted down his accusations.
It was impossible to verify their claim that fewer people were infected.

Later, Zabolotny met with General Khorvat and suggested a bounty be offered for each plague-stricken person delivered by the wagon men. The general refused, since his budget was already strained by bounty paid for fifty thousand dead rats.

In the Russian hospital, just over one hundred and fifty patients died every day, a number that had remained steady for weeks. But gradually, there had been a decreasing number of patients brought in by the plague-wagon men.

The medical staff quietly tracked the declining number of deaths tallied on the clipboards. But they anticipated something worse would happen, an ambush, double or triple the number of patients. Or the plague would transform itself, develop terrible new ways to infect and kill. The devil came in many guises.

"After an earthquake, everyone stands on the street waiting for the next stage of destruction," Wu reminded Zabolotny. "The epidemic has the shape of a curve. The end is still invisible."

Five beds in the plague ward remained empty for twenty-four hours. Then ten beds were empty for three days. This new pattern held over the next week. The medical staff cautiously identified a turning point in the epidemic. It was unsettling. It was considered bad luck to talk about the situation. Do not tempt the gods. The hospital workers were still in the grip of a siege, unable to dismiss their fears, grasp a rescuer's hand, escape through a door accidentally left unlocked. There was no celebration or self-congratulation. The doctors and nurses were only survivors.

It seemed the grip of winter had slightly loosened. According to the Chinese, the fresh east wind would mark the beginning of spring and have a positive effect on everyone's health. The Russians prepared for the fast for Great Lent, which began in February and continued for forty days, until Easter. All meat and animal products, including lard, eggs, milk, butter, and cheese, were forbidden by the

Russian Orthodox Church. The very devout also refused sugar and fish during the first and last weeks of the fast.

Holiday traditions were observed. Eggs were hard-boiled, dyed red with beet juice, and painted with geometric designs and inscriptions: *Take, eat, and think of Me. This present I give to Christ I love. XB,* which symbolized *Christos voskres,* "Christ is risen." Red eggs filled bowls placed in the conference room, the nurses' station, the doctors' mess, even on a shelf in the guards' box downstairs. The entire staff, Russian and Chinese, appreciated the shared offering, as red eggs were also a Chinese tradition, a gift at the birth of a baby.

"Red for good fortune," a Chinese nurse had quipped.

"Good fortune? The color gives me no joy," said her Russian co-worker, an intern from Tomsk. Red was the sign of plague, the bleeding that drained away life.

The devout claimed the blessing of the red eggs broke the plague. Others were convinced that it was prayer and the intercession of Saint Nikolas the Wonder-Worker, Kharbin's patron saint, that had delivered them from death.

Messonier remained in mourning. He occasionally worked at the hospital, was silent with colleagues, left after a few hours without signing out on the schedule. The Baron had no idea where he spent his time. Messonier was beyond criticism.

The Baron respected this gulf between them. But there was a gift he held for Messonier. He would make a plea to the other doctors that Maria Lebedev be allowed to rest in peace. Messonier was unaware of his plan. He resolved to practice self-effacement when presenting his case to the others, speak to them without overconfidence or scolding. Illness had stripped away a layer of the Baron's self-regard. He recognized this presence of mind had been initiated by his teacher.

A guard forbade the Baron entry into the Russian hospital. A smile, a recital of important names, and a generous bribe were provided. Upstairs, the conference room was crowded and noisy as the staff gathered in small groups, waiting for latecomers to the morning meeting. Few noticed the Baron had joined them and only Dr. Iasienski courteously greeted him. Dr. Wu called the meeting to order.

"Please forgive my interruption." The Baron stood up to speak, his manner apologetic. "I have an urgent matter that needs your attention." He walked to the head of the table next to Dr. Wu and Dr. Zabolotny. Wu graciously moved aside for him. "Last week, I entered the plague burial pit in the field north of Kharbin. Unprotected by gloves or a mask, I handled two corpses." He slipped the photograph of himself cradling the dead infant from a leather case and held it so that everyone at the table could see it.

No one spoke. He handed the photograph to Zabolotny, who immediately put it facedown on the table. Wu picked it up and turned it over.

"I'm no danger to anyone here in the room. I was isolated in quarantine for three days afterward. I have no symptoms. None. As I stand before you now, I'm perfectly healthy." The Baron showed them the image of the dead girl. "Without protection, I also handled the body of a young girl dead of plague in the burial pit." This photograph was also placed on the table in front of Wu.

"Baron *le docteur,* this is a surprise." Zabolotny's eyes swept the table to gauge the doctors' reactions. *Who will rid us of this man?* "A surprise and an outrage to bring these grotesque images here." He flicked a photograph with a finger and it skidded across the table. "Leave the room as a gentleman before you are forced to leave."

Protests erupted around the table.

"Let the Baron speak." Wu gestured for quiet. "Continue."

Zabolotny didn't hide his displeasure at Wu's request and the Baron was reminded of how the man enjoyed centering attention on himself. The aggrieved party. "Thank you, Dr. Wu. I admit my experiment was unorthodox, but it proved that those who died of plague are no threat to the living. Corpses aren't contagious."

"He's mad," said Dr. Haffkine.

"No, he's trying to be a hero."

The Baron agreed. "Yes. It was foolish to risk my life for a medical theory."

"Let's consider your foolishness. You've published articles anonymously—surely written by you—in the St. Petersburg newspaper criticizing our work. Our sacrifices." Zabolotny looked to Wu for confirmation.

"That's not the issue under discussion." Wu's stern voice. "What do you propose, Baron?"

"Leave the plague dead undisturbed in the cemeteries. There's little chance infection will spread from the bodies, since the ground stays frozen until May. There's time to test my theory. Be thorough and logical. It's less work and disruption than digging up the cemeteries. Let's not act without consideration."

"There's no time for the luxury of guesswork," said Dr. Boguchi. "I say remove the infected dead before there's a new epidemic. It's dangerous not to eliminate the problem. The dead are a time bomb buried under our feet."

The translator had a stricken look but Wu had remained calm in the storm of scornful dismissal. "Baron, as you explained, the corpses are frozen. But once they thaw, it's possible bacilli infesting their bodies could still be alive. Perhaps the bacilli are only in a suspended state, hibernating inside the corpse. We don't know. The plague could reemerge and strike Kharbin again."

The Baron tried to retain a neutral expression despite the escalating hostility. "There's another issue. You need the blessing of the Russian Orthodox Church to exhume the cemeteries. It's sacrilege."

"Who could argue against the dead?" Zabolotny acted as if he'd been unjustly accused. "Respect the dead but not at the cost of the living. The priests will be reasonable."

"You would watch your families and friends taken from their graves? Betray them without protest? Maria Lebedev is buried in St. Nikolas cemetery. Surely you'd spare Dr. Messonier, her fiancé, this anguish?" The Baron's words pulled a momentary silence from the room.

The mood shifted against Zabolotny, as there was little enthusiasm for digging up dead Russians. The cemeteries of other faiths wouldn't be defended.

"Perhaps an exception can be made for Dr. Lebedev," Wu suggested.

"Although Dr. Lebedev had a woman's soft heart, she wouldn't agree with this sentimental decision about her grave." Zabolotny's anger built a wall for benefit of his argument.

The Baron couldn't let this pass. "Now you speak for Dr. Lebedev?"

"There may be another solution. We can discuss it with the archdeacon at St. Nikolas. Let Maria Lebedev rest in peace," said Haffkine.

"No, Dr. Haffkine. No one should shelter a poisonous body in the churchyard. The entire cemetery is festering. Thank God it's sealed under snow, although snow is no disinfectant, regardless of the Baron's wild claims." Zabolotny's lips curved with distaste. "It's expected you would defend the dead, Baron, when you're not defending the Chinese. A pity that your medical knowledge is less than your sympathy. Someone should step in and protect you from your own experimenting."

The Baron was ice. "God's mercy, have we survived the plague, witnessed countless deaths, to behave with such a lack of grace toward each other?" He gripped his hands together for courage, checked the other faces at the table for support. "Dr. Zabolotny, your insult is not to be borne. Sir, I challenge you to a duel."

The room exploded with shouts.

Zabolotny's voice was louder than the others. "Baron, even if you were half your age, I wouldn't consent to a duel."

The Baron gently excused himself without anger or haste. No one followed him from the room or urged Zabolotny to apologize.

Inside St. Nikolas Cathedral, the Baron steered Messonier up the shallow steps of the sanctuary. The church was unlit, had been closed for over a month, and they were trespassing. They walked through the royal gates in the center of the towering iconostasis, where only clergy were allowed, careless of the wet trail left by their boots. In the sanctuary by the chapel of prothesis, they huddled together to wait, comforted by the lingering scents of myrrh, incense, and beeswax candles from the vestry. The altar was covered with a cloth, a frozen white drape, anchored by shadowy holy vessels and a seven-tiered candelabra. A boy had been paid to alert them when the vehicles arrived in the churchyard. The Baron dozed under the soft creaking sway of the building, a cocoon of woven timber, until nudged awake by Messonier.

A ghost of movement at the far end of the building. The two men slowly stood up, the Baron's knees stiff and aching from the cold. A thread of light, a thin gray vertical, signaled the opening of the front doors. The light widened and vanished as someone entered and closed the door. Their eyes strained in the dark to find the figure attached to the barely perceptible approaching footsteps. A moving grayness separated itself from the room, followed by colder air as the boy materialized in front of them.

"They're here."

They waited a few minutes, snugging their heavy sheepskin coats tight, before slipping out of the church. The Baron and Messonier ducked behind two wagons drawn up in front of St. Nikolas and watched a group of men, dark silhouettes, gathered in the adjoining cemetery. Soldiers? Corpse carriers?

When it was clear they hadn't been seen, Messonier swung himself into the back of a wagon, landing with a hard jolt. He crawled over to huge metal cisterns upright against the wagon rails, wrapped in heavy quilted cloth and animal hides. The lids were tightly fastened and couldn't be forced open. He shoved the cistern and liquid sloshed inside. The other wagons were loaded with shovels, pickaxes, cords of firewood, stacks of tin buckets, boxes of tools, ropes, and chains. Weapons for dismantling.

"Curse your mother!" a voice shouted. Three men crossed the cemetery in the direction of the church.

Messonier jumped down and, crouching behind the Baron, moved alongside the wagons back into St. Nikolas. Inside the cold hive of the church nave, they gasped, catching their breath, a fog of wreathing white evidence.

The Baron refused to whisper. "Let's wait here. No need to freeze to watch the grave robbers dig."

"There are more men outside than I anticipated. If we're caught, what do we confess?"

"Nothing. Tell them you're a cloistered monk. The church forgives."

"But not the men in the cemetery."

"More likely they'll break into St. Nikolas for the silver candlesticks." The Baron was relieved by Messonier's smile at his weak joke.

"I resent hiding here like a thief."

"Patience, friend. We have the advantage of stealth once the men are busy working." The Baron remembered a window overlooking the cemetery. "Let's go upstairs. For the view."

At the top of a narrow staircase, the window framed a number of fires burning across the cemetery. There were dark circles where snow had melted.

"Now I understand. They must have fire and water," the Baron whispered.

Messonier turned away from the window. "I can't watch." His strained cheer had vanished and he was tense with anticipation. He insisted they couldn't wait, they must risk entering the cemetery immediately.

Outside, snow had leveled the landscape like a stationary flood, hip-deep in places, and the effort to walk around the gravestones strained their hearts and lungs. Breathless, the Baron asked Messonier to stop and rest. He picked up a stone left in the crook of a tree branch, just for luck.

At a slight distance, visible through thick brush, a steaming cauldron hung on a stand over a log fire. Moving as slowly as sleepwalkers, men filled buckets with hot water from the cauldron, then poured them into a partially excavated grave. A fury of steam rose from the hole as the frozen earth bubbled and softened. Vapor wisped from the exposed coffin. A man jumped into the grave, landed on top of the coffin. An ax was placed in his hand and he splintered the rotten wood into an opening large enough to remove the corpse. At the side of the grave, another man waited with ropes to free the frozen body from the coffin.

Messonier clapped his hand over his mouth to stop his cry. They turned away from the grave diggers, their axes and fires, moved deeper into the cemetery.

"What's this?" The Baron noticed a long strip of red cloth tied around a gravestone. Then he understood. The strips marked the graves of plague victims to be disinterred by the men. The Baron kept this discovery to himself.

"Are we closer to her grave?" The Baron avoided using Maria's name so as not to upset Messonier.

His answer was hesitant. "I believe so. Yes."

Messonier turned around to get his bearings, place himself in relation to the gate, two spindly trees, the cross atop a monument. "I remember the church roof was visible from a certain angle near her grave. But this side or the other side? I think it's this direction."

They skirted a small copse of trees. The Baron's nervousness increased, and he stayed close behind Messonier. A spark, a bright point, moved in their direction. Frightened, they waited, and it silently passed by. Or perhaps whoever carried the light was invisible.

Messonier became increasingly disoriented in the unfamiliar landscape. The hood of his coat was loose, and his breathing was strained. The Baron watched his every step, fearing he'd shout or confront the men.

Lost in the forest. The Baron remembered his babushka's folktale of Baba Yaga. The witch lived in a house mounted on the legs of a chicken so she could chase her victims. He grasped Messonier's shoulder. Pull him to earth, pull him back. Messonier stared at the Baron, not seeing him. "If there was sun I'd know the direction." He took five steps forward, then slipped and fell.

The Baron helped him up, his limbs slow and heavy with cold. He urged Messonier to rest for a moment.

"No, no. Am fine." His eyes confused in a pink face surrounded by dark fur. Messonier peered around, mumbling calculations. "I've never walked this way before. Snow buried the usual landmarks. I'm lost." He angled his head as if he'd heard a sound or someone speak.

The Baron stood in front of him, the deep snow holding them both locked in place so there could be no sudden movement. Messonier dodged clumsily around him, staggered a few steps forward, then dropped to his knees and clawed at the ice on a gravestone.

"Help me." Breathing heavily, Messonier stared at the grave marker. "We have nothing. No tools."

"Here. Get back."

The Baron struck the gravestone repeatedly with a stone, gripping it in his clumsy mitten, the dull thwacks of breaking ice echoing around them. Thick ice fell away and they read the inscription. The first letter was wrong. Not *M*. Messonier scrabbled through the snow to the next grave marker, furiously rubbed his arm across it to clear a cushion of snow. The Baron read the names.

Sonya Vasilevna, daughter. Dmitry Vasilevich, father.

The poor girl and her father. So she had died. A lifetime ago. Their gravestone was tied with a cloth, blood red in this light. He tore the red strip from their cross, stuffed it in his pocket.

Messonier was already at the next grave, speaking to himself now. "Maria. Maria Lebedev. She's very near. No one will take my ring from Maria's finger."

Heedless of the risk, the Baron shouted at Messonier, "Calm yourself! Maria waits for you. Let her speak."

Messonier stopped and turned to his friend, a strange expression on his face. "Yes. She tells me what to do. Come."

The two men floundered from grave to grave, their legs punching through snow. They slid and fell, exhilarated, tearing away the red flags, the notices of exhumation. The sky darkened, pressure tightened around them, and a furious snow began to fall. Within an hour, it would conceal all signs of their presence. Messonier halted by a tall grave marker with a distinctive carved wreath. He tenderly brushed away snow, revealing Maria Lebedev's name etched in stone. He untied the strip of red cloth fastened to her gravestone with intimate familiarity, as if adjusting her veil or a scarf.

For Epiphany, the Sungari River was transformed into the Jordan River for the blessing-of-the-waters ceremony. A broad area of ice was shaved and smoothed with metal scrapers to a mirrorlike surface and a red carpet had been unrolled from the bank near the flour mill, spanning a distance across the river. A large temporary building, a white and scarlet temple surmounted with a cross, had been carefully pulled by horses into position over a large hole bored in the ice at the end of the carpet.

The Baron had sworn he'd have nothing to do with the church, but after weeks without public gatherings, he was curious to see who had survived the plague. Li Ju had accompanied him. General Khorvat had given permission for the ceremony, as it was held outdoors in an unconfined space.

A crowd, smaller than previous years, waited near the temple for the procession.

With measured steps, a long line of archimandrites and priests, stiff as candles in gold-threaded vestments, slowly approached. No priest wore a protective face mask. Observing this, many in the crowd also slipped off their masks, as if it were a pious act. Standing in front, a sizable group of Chinese who had converted to the

Russian Orthodox faith bowed and removed their masks simultaneously. Nothing could change the strangeness of this time.

A face without a plague mask was reckless. A loaded weapon. The Baron turned away in anger. His hands trembled, and he prepared to step forward on the bright carpet. To do what? Confront the priests in embroidered robes, warn them of death that waited for their mistake? Li Ju gripped his hand, and clouds of incense from the swinging censer rose around them.

Inside the temple, the priests made a formal circle around the hole in the ice, blessed it, and slowly lowered a gold cross on a long chain into the colorless water.

Messonier arrived with tins of peaches shipped from Paris, a gift for the Baron. When the first tin was opened, they both blinked, surprised by the orange-yellow of the peeled fruit, bright as a paper lantern. "Look. Summer is here."

"Seems a pity to damage the fruit. To spoil it with a spoon." Messonier tenderly transferred the peaches into the blue-and-white porcelain bowls from the Baron's prized collection on the table.

"Our reward. The loveliest peaches between here and Beijing. Possibly the only peaches between here and Beijing." The Baron smiled.

Messonier hesitated, puzzling over his thoughts. "Pleasure seems out of place. I can't quite enjoy the fruit."

"My friend. You're in mourning." The Baron poured tea.

"Why aren't we dead of plague?"

"Why are we blessed with health?" An attempt at a joke to ease the solemnity between them. Since Maria's death, Messonier had isolated himself, refused invitations and everyone's concern. He avoided St. Nikolas Cathedral.

The Baron was tender with his friend, self-conscious, his words carefully considered so as not to upset Messonier. Not to remind him of Maria. Not to mention her name. But did Messonier wish to erase her memory? How to ask him? What was the lesson?

Messonier painted the scene for him. "Everyone who died was expendable. But we foolish doctors rushed in to save lives, bring hope. Earn gratitude. How can I blame Maria for her choice? I was also a believer."

They locked eyes until the Baron's gaze faltered. "What will you do?"

"I don't know. I don't know what happened to my skill. I feel like a witness, not a doctor. I can neither sit nor stand."

"I count to calm myself. It's better than pacing. I count heartbeats. Breaths."

"Counting won't keep anyone alive, if that's your secret purpose. It won't even bring luck." Messonier recognized the pattern of the Baron's thoughts. "Doctors cling to the belief they have a remedy."

"A remedy is a delusion shared with a patient. No one admits the plague has no cure. Everyone at the hospital works a fraud."

Messonier was too dispirited to argue. "There's nothing but uselessness. Not a single life saved. I want to leave Kharbin."

Startled, the Baron looked up from his cup. "No one could fault you for leaving. Your service has been heroic." He struggled for a steady voice. "But perhaps you should rest. Take time away from the hospital."

"I will regret leaving Maria."

"I'll be here to honor her grave. If you leave."

Messonier's eyes were glassy with tears. The Baron wanted to embrace his friend but stayed still, the impulse stopped by habitual fear of contact after months at the hospital. This was the way he'd been damaged. "But how will you leave Kharbin? Not by train. Too risky. Sitting for hours next to strangers who are likely infected."

"Anyone with a handkerchief is suspicious."

"Doctors leaving Kharbin are suspicious."

"Perhaps I can bribe a driver with a wagon to get past soldiers at the barricades."

"Andreev has vanished. He's the only one I'd trust to get you safely away from Kharbin." The Baron built the case that travel was unfeasible.

"Then I'll go by water. A ferryboat."

The Baron shook his head. "If a boat manages to get through to Tsingtao or Chefoo, all passengers are locked in quarantine for seven days before disembarking. If you aren't already infected, you will be after quarantine. Entry to other towns is strictly enforced. Everything that goes in or comes out is sprayed with formalin."

"That rules out my disguise."

The Baron had another strategy. "Stay as our guest for Easter. Li Ju would be pleased. By that time, the churches might open again for the midnight service. We'll break our fast together, although the celebration will be less lavish this year."

"Thank you, but I'm finished. We'll meet again in Beijing."

"Or Paris. In springtime."

In St. Petersburg, the Neva River froze to a pale slate-green color, finely fractured like white moss along its thick stone banks and bridges. The Sungari was wider, wilder, its ice cloudy with yellow clay, streaks of sediment, gritty and opaque.

The Baron and Messonier had hauled the iceboat to the river and it tilted precariously on the frozen water between them, sail wrapped around the tall center pole. The Baron had reluctantly agreed to take him by boat from Kharbin to Hulan across the Sungari. His possessions would be shipped later. This was the most secure route, as there were fewer soldiers. Farther downriver, Tsingtao was ringed with barbed wire, and searchlights were set up on the wharves to catch smugglers and those fleeing quarantine.

"This is a strange farewell to Kharbin. Leaving the city like a smuggler." The Baron squinted at his friend, relieved the harsh sunlight on his face imposed another expression over his sadness.

"I know. Forgive me."

At faint shouting, the Baron turned into the wind, coat whipping around his legs, to peer at a long line of people walking down the snow-covered bank onto the frozen river.

Who are they? Soldiers?

They straightened the boat and prepared to launch it. The sail flapped, filled with wind, and the Baron jogged alongside and jumped in, bending his long legs under the hull. Half-reclining, the two men fit snugly inside the vessel, the canvas sail with its faint oily odor swinging over their heads. Balanced on two narrow silver runners, the boat could easily be overturned by rough ice, rocks, a branch, or a hole. The boat picked up speed, hurtling across the ice, shaking and rattling over the continuous scrape of the metal blades. Their faces were quickly numbed by cold.

In the distance, the crowd slowly fanned out over the river, a strangely measured procession with the formality of a dance as they tentatively tested the ice, maintaining a distance from one another to evenly distribute their weight. Sunlight traveled across the sheet of ice, suspending the dark figures on its suddenly brilliant surface.

The Baron turned his attention back to the boat, pulling the tiller to steer. He caught Messonier's expression as he leaned dangerously far over the side of the boat into the raw wind, watching the unrolling blur of ice as if inviting a crash, the smashing impact of his body against it. He'd float, then submerge, his eyes becoming whitened and blank. Messonier was ready to throw himself away.

Alarmed, the Baron tugged the sail to steer back to land but wind forced another direction. The boat edged near the crowd of walkers on the ice and he noticed many of them wore masks. They were infected and had escaped quarantine. Voices shouted at them as the walkers spotted the boat. Men ran, sliding and falling, directly into their path, risking themselves to stop the boat and avoid being returned to quarantine.

The Baron quickly jerked the tiller, yelling for Messonier to hold the boom as they swerved to avoid one man and a second fell just as their prow cut past him. The Baron angled them toward an open area, racing parallel to the crowd, the sound of their blades changing as they hit rough ice.

The boat caught the edge of a branch protruding from the river, spun wildly in a circle, and skidded, hurling an arc of droplets far over the pursuing men. The impact flung the Baron and Messonier halfway out of the boat and they struggled to balance it. With an effort, the Baron clambered back inside as the boat slid to a stop. In a single wave, the scattered group of men pivoted toward the stranded boat.

There was no time to relaunch the boat, so the Baron and Messonier waited inside, as it offered some protection. The wary Chinese and Russians circled them unsteadily, surrounding the boat like swimmers. Breathing hard, coughing, the gaunt men and women grasped the sides of the boat, facing the two men. The Baron gripped the mast for support and stood up, stripped off his hat and mittens. He extended his hands, palms open, to show his helplessness. No weapons. The two strangers were no threat. Wind whipped the sail. Moments passed. The walkers released the boat and turned away.

But the iceboat was unable to sail, captive in place, as hundreds of ragged people slowly streamed past it across the river. The Baron and Messonier waited, half-dreaming, hypnotized by the endless murmuring procession, the pattern of order.

After a time, they gently pushed the boat through the thinning crowd to a clear space and steadied it between them. Messonier was silent and the Baron spoke first.

"Which direction?"

Messonier pointed over the Baron's shoulder.

The boat entered the slipstream of movement, speeding alongside the ice walkers away from Kharbin.

AUTHOR'S NOTE

The Winter Station was inspired by Baron Rozher Alexandrovich von Budberg's memoir of the plague, *Lungenpest-Epidemien in der Mandschurei,* published in 1923. His book about this lost epidemic was published in Germany, likely because no Russian company dared print the Baron's exposé about his government's controversial conduct fighting the plague. While based on historical figures, the characters in *The Winter Station* are fictional, and some aspects and events of the epidemic are not present in this book. The actual plague epidemic was as complex as warfare; the accounts written by various witnesses and participants, both Russian and Chinese, were frequently entirely contradictory.

In *The Winter Station,* the Baron's calligraphy lessons on pages 45, 96, 160, 248, and 266 were drawn from *Creativity and Taoism* by Chang Chung-yuan. The quoted lines on page 44 are from *Tao of Painting* by Mai-Mai Sze, and the description of brushstrokes on pages 159 and 248 are from *Chinese Calligraphy and Painting,* edited by Laurence Sickman. The Baron's last words to his calligraphy teacher on page 294 and the words about grass-style calligraphy on page 191 are from *A Background to Chinese Painting* by Soame Jenyns. I would also like to acknowledge Hellmut Wilhelm's magisterial *Change: Eight Lectures on the I Ching.* A valuable source of information about Chinese medical practice was

AUTHOR'S NOTE

Shigehisa Kuriyama's superb *The Expressiveness of the Body,* especially for the passages and quotes about *mo* on pages 145 and 190. The poem recited by Chang on page 167 is from *Tea in China* by James A. Benn. For translations, I relied on the expertise of John Major (Chinese) and Mila Nortman and Jesse Browner (Russian).

ACKNOWLEDGMENTS

Thank you to the following for their generous support: Susan Bachelder, Elisabeth Biondi, Kathleen Bishop, Karen Blessen, Lizi Boyd, Anne Carey, Sarah Cohen, Marilyn Cooperman, Simon Costin, Grazia d'Annunzio, Mark Epstein, Giuseppe Gerbino, David Gonzales, Linda Mason, Audrey McGuire, Lee F. Mindel, Catherine Orentreich, Jim Perry, Ann Shakeshaft, Leo Shields, Lori Shields, Valerie Steele, Donna Tartt, Andrea Valeria, Jaime Wolf.

At Little, Brown, my thanks to Reagan Arthur, Betsy Uhrig, Alexandra Hoopes, and Tracy Roe.

Finally, I'd especially like to acknowledge my gratitude to Anne Edelstein and my editor, Judy Clain.

ABOUT THE AUTHOR

Jody Shields is the author of two previous novels, the bestselling *The Fig Eater* and *The Crimson Portrait*. Formerly contributing editor at *Vogue* and design editor of the *New York Times Magazine,* Shields is also a screenwriter and a collected artist. She is a resident of New York City.